What Readers and Reviewers Are Saying
About Trish Perry and *The Guy I'm Not Dating*

"Three cheers for *The Guy I'm Not Dating*! Trish Perry captures the tone, struggles, and joys experienced by today's twentysomething Christian men and women as they search for true partners while holding to their core beliefs. You'll love Kara and Gabe, laugh at Tiffany and Addie, and learn a lot about yourself in the process of reading this book."

—*Melanie Rigney, former* Writer's Digest *editor*

"I never knew reading a story could be this much fun! You'll laugh out loud all the way to the end."

—*Eva Marie Everson, coauthor of* The Potluck Club *and* The Potluck Club: Trouble's Brewing

"Warm and witty, Trish Perry's delightfully humorous romance deftly explores the very real challenges of Christian courtship in this refreshing contemporary story of how (not) to date."

—*Melanie M. Jeschke, author of* Inklings, Expectations, *and* Evasions

"*The Guy I'm Not Dating* is a refreshing, warmhearted read...a book chock-full of romantic, laugh-out-loud fun. This might be Trish Perry's first novel, but it surely won't be her last!"

—*Loree Lough, bestselling author*

"Perry's true-to-life characters sparkle, and the fast-paced conversational thread weaves a story destined to look good on you!"

—*Lt. Colonel Marlene Chase, author and editor in chief, Salvation Army*

"Trish Perry has delivered a warm, engaging, humorous, heartfelt read. You will become Kara's friend and you will cheer her on as she remains true to a heavenly love in the midst of finding an earthly one."

—*Ellie Lofaro, speaker and author of* From Battle Scars to Beauty Marks

"Hey, guys LOVE romance too! Trish's warmth and fabulous sense of humor are seen in each wonderful character she has created. I simply could not put this book down and I am anxiously awaiting the sequel—or the movie."

—*Ray Linder, author of* What Will I Do with My Money?

"Trish Perry brings a fresh, fun voice to the world of hip chick-lit!"

—*Ellen Vaughn, author of* The Strand *and coauthor of* Gideon's Torch *(with Chuck Colson)*

The Guy I'm Not Dating

Trish Perry

HARVEST HOUSE PUBLISHERS

EUGENE, OREGON

152 5034

Cover by Terry Dugan Design, Minneapolis, Minnesota

Published in association with the Hartline Literary Agency, Pittsburgh, Pennsylvania

This is a work of fiction. Names, characters, places, and incidents are products of the author's imagination or are used fictitiously. Any resemblance to actual persons, living or dead, or to events or locales, is entirely coincidental.

THE GUY I'M NOT DATING
Copyright © 2006 by Patricia Perry
Published by Harvest House Publishers
Eugene, Oregon 97402
www.harvesthousepublishers.com

Perry, Trish, 1954-
 The guy I'm not dating / Trish Perry.
 p. cm.
ISBN-13: 978-0-7369-1872-5
ISBN-10: 0-7369-1872-8
I. Title.
PS3616.E7947G89 2006
813'.6—dc22

2006010923

Printed in the United States of America

06 07 08 09 10 11 12 / LB-SK / 10 9 8 7 6 5 4 3 2 1

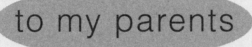

to my parents

Chuck and Lilian Hawley

Married 61 years and counting.

Now *that's* romantic.

acknowledgments

My first novel. I'd love to express appreciation to everyone who brought me to this point. I'll likely forget someone important here, and for that I apologize. That said, I sincerely thank:

Tamela Hancock Murray and **Kim Moore**—two dynamic women with a firm grasp on what works and what doesn't.

Carolyn McCready, Nick Harrison, and the many talented people of **Harvest House Publishers.**

The generous authors who provided endorsements. I hope to return the favor someday, if people ever care what I think.

Writers Betsy Dill, Mike Calkin, Gwen Hancock, and **Vie Herlocker** for reading and advising between lattes and greasy fast food.

My friends at Capital Christian Writers; Cornerstone Chapel in Leesburg, Virginia; and prayer warriors **Betty Shifflett, Cindy Williams, Gerry Stowers,** and **Linda Wallace.**

The Driscolls: Erik (for "pudding"), computer doctor Russ, and Wendy (not enough room to list all the reasons!).

Debbie Rooks, my expert on broken legs.

My parents, my sibs—John, Donna, and Chris Hawley—and the Perrys, Rabideaus, and Johnstons. You make life a fun story to tell.

My daughter, Stevie Burkart; her hubby, **Kevin;** and my unbelievable grandson, **Bronx.** You guys inspire me (and a few of my characters).

My son, Tucker, who has a dazzling imagination and a sense of humor as weird as mine. Thanks for "newsprint," Tuck.

Hubby Hugh, who always supports my writing, even taking over the icky household tasks when deadlines loom. Though even you had your limits ("I don't want to be the lady anymore!").

My late sister, Noreen, and my late friend, **Van Ardan,** both of whom drew me toward Christ. See you soon.

I owe my life to **my precious Lord Jesus,** who placed all of these people in my path. His abundant patience and blessings blow me away. I hope my work honors Him.

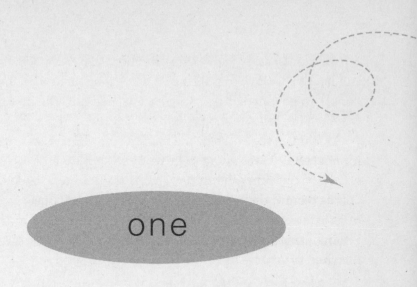

one

"Yowza!"

The word flew out of Kara's mouth before she had time to think.

Yowza? What was she, a comic book character? Quick—she should say something clever. The gorgeous man was turning around...

Kara heard herself sputtering words. Her mind was suddenly like a shooting gallery with rubber walls and thoughts ricocheting out of control. What was the matter with her?

You'd think she'd never seen a good-looking man before.

She touched her hand to her hair. Praise God she had finally taken the time to get it done this morning. She'd been working too hard to visit the salon before today.

Did she have time for these thoughts?

Focus, Kara. Don't say anything else without thinking!

Gorgeous Man looked at her and smiled. Wow.

How had she gotten here? Her mind performed a 30-second review, from salon to swoon...

The cloudy skies had opened moments after she left the salon, and her deliberately tousled blond hair threatened to become a real, honest-to-goodness mess. Kara had dashed into the first shop she came to. This fellow's shop.

As soon as she entered, she realized the place wasn't really open for business. It was going to be a coffee shop or a café; that much was clear. But other than a few chairs, the counters, and two menu boards behind them, nothing was set up. Tinny music filtered out of a distant radio. The smell of latex paint wafted from the walls. Feeling like a trespasser, Kara frowned at the weather outside and prepared to venture back into it.

"Hi! Can I help you?"

Kara turned to face the voice—a nice voice—and saw just the top of a man's head cresting above the counter. Short, dark curls and nothing more.

"Oh!" she said. "Um..."

"I'd get up," he said, "but I'm setting a few electrical wires here. Be with you in a sec."

"No, no, that's okay. I'm sorry. I didn't mean to intrude," Kara said. She pointed toward the window, at the downpour outside, even though it was unlikely the guy would see her. "I'm just trying to keep dry 'til my ride gets here."

"Take your time. Nice to have the company. Been setting up here for the past few days. Way too quiet." He grunted as if he were squeezing himself into an awkward spot back there.

"Is this your place?" Kara asked. "Or are you just working here?"

He chuckled—a nice chuckle. "Both. I just moved up from Miami. My folks have a deli business down there. Twenty-five years now. I was ready for a change. Thought this was a nice place to set up a shop of my own. Was I right?"

She smiled. "Yeah. I think so, anyway. I love Northern Virginia. And this is a good spot. They really need a decent deli out here."

"That's what I like to hear," he said.

She heard pleasure in his voice.

Kara turned away from him and watched out the window for her best friend, Ren. She said under her breath, "I should have asked her to meet me at the salon. Can't really see—"

"Pardon?" he called out.

"Oh, nothing, sorry," she said. "I was just talking to myself. I asked my friend to pick me up in front of the bookstore down the street. I didn't quite make it there before the rain got crazy on me."

"Ah."

Kara felt it would be rude not to talk to him while she stood in his shop, so she kept it up. "My car's near death. It's been in the shop for three days already."

"Hmm," he said, sounding distracted by whatever he was doing back there. "Sorry to hear that. I had to replace my car just after moving up here."

Kara squinted to see through the rain outside. Was that Ren approaching? No. "I hate depending on my friends for rides, you know?"

"I hear ya," he said, his voice slightly strained, as though he was moving something heavy.

"But it's great to have an excuse to spend more time with my best friend." Kara spoke toward the window. "We didn't get to spend all that much time together when she was married. But now... well..." Kara frowned. Would Ren appreciate her telling such personal stuff to a total stranger? But the stranger seemed to pick up on her intentions.

"Yeah, that can be tough," he said, "having your friendships interrupted. I miss my Florida friends already. Say, can I get you something? Soda? A cup of coffee?"

Kara turned around to decline. And that was when it happened, the "Yowza!" He wasn't hidden anymore, and Kara's verbal outburst was her unguarded proclamation that this guy was one of God's finer works of creation.

Stunning. He had climbed a small stepladder, his broad back turned to Kara. He was fastening a lamp to the ceiling behind the counter, and his face—a very nice face—was in profile. A sharp, masculine nose. Full lips. His hair was dark and wavy, his cheekbones prominent, his jawline strong. Though dressed simply, in a white BVD T-shirt and faded jeans, he looked like a *GQ* model. His arms, raised as they were, would be the envy of any of Kara's male clients at the gym. He turned to look at her, his dark eyebrows raised in amused confusion.

What had he asked her? Coffee! Did she want coffee? And her answer? "Yowza!" Terrific.

"I...I mean, no!" she said. "Thanks a lot, but no coffee for me! No, sir! Trying to cut down on the caffeine..." She trailed off in a mumble.

He laughed. "Sounds like that might be a good idea. Didn't mean to alarm you with the offer."

Kara smiled weakly. He had no idea how striking he was. Now that was attractive.

He climbed down from the ladder, wiped his palms against his jeans, and approached her. Goodness, he had long legs. His confident stride and bright smile made her palms sweat. And his eyes! Sultry brown. And prettier than hers! He extended his hand to her. "I'm Gabe Paolino."

She tried not to cringe or apologize about her sweaty palms before taking his hand. She was relieved when he didn't seem to notice. As a matter of fact, she recognized a flicker of attraction in his eyes. Her neck felt suddenly hot. "Kara Richardson," she said.

He nodded and released her hand. "Please, have a seat. I can dust off a chair—"

"No, really, my friend will be here any minute. I'll just stay here at the window and watch you. Her! I'll watch for her."

He laughed, looking her in the eye. "Okay," he said softly and went back to his work.

Kara turned away from him and rolled her eyes about her

behavior. He was so handsome! And she was acting like an adolescent. She'd break out in giggles any minute now.

"You work around here?"

She looked at him. He had his back turned to her again as he connected another lamp to the ceiling. She couldn't help staring at him while she talked. "Work? No, I was just at the body salon a few doors down." She gasped. "Beauty! Beauty salon!" She smacked her forehead with the palm of her hand. *Please, God,* she prayed quickly. *Help me here!*

She shook her head at her word fumble. "Sorry, I guess I was thinking about work, since you asked. I work at American Gym on the other side of town. You know, I...help...people...with their bodies." Even she heard how weak the connection was.

But he just glanced over his shoulder at her and smiled. "That right? So it's a good gym? I've got to find one now that I'm up here. Would you recommend American?"

Ah, a topic she could discuss comfortably, even in her sleep. "You bet. Excellent value for the monthly dues. And you can hire a personal trainer, if you want. That's what I do there. I'm a personal trainer."

Now that string of sentences sounded downright adult. Kara sighed with relief. She saw Ren's silver BMW pull up in front of the bookstore. "Oh, there's my friend. Gotta go." She opened the shop door and looked back over her shoulder at him. "Nice meeting you, Gabe," she said. "And welcome to Virginia."

He stopped working and looked as though he might have been planning to walk her to the door. She'd moved too quickly, though, too nervously. Now it would be awkward to stop and wait at the open door.

"Thanks, Kara," he called, giving her a small wave of the hand as she walked out. "Nice meeting you too. God bless."

Kara stopped outside the door and stood under the shop's awning.

Hmm. "God bless," huh? She wondered if he was a Christian. Not that it mattered, really. She wasn't in the market.

Ren pulled up closer, but the rain continued to hammer down. Kara wanted to keep her expensive haircut from getting drenched, so she'd wait until Ren was right in front of the shop.

Just before running out to the car, Kara treated herself to one more peek over her shoulder. What harm could it do? He'd be hard at work, oblivious to her schoolgirl ogling.

But he wasn't. He was standing right there, at the window, watching her. He smiled and gave her another wave goodbye. He looked genuinely pleased that she had looked for him again.

Kara was duly mortified. She returned a feeble wave, turned, and ran to the car.

"Ooo," Ren said, glancing at the shop window when Kara got in the car. "Who's the cutie-pie?"

Kara dropped her head back against the headrest and sighed. "The most gorgeous man I've ever acted stupid in front of."

"You? Stupid? In front of a man?" Ren drove forward, raising her eyebrows and smiling. "Well, Kara! This has to be a first. But I thought you weren't interested in dating."

Kara snorted. "Who said anything about dating? As goofy as I acted back there, I'd be lucky to get a deli delivery out of the guy, let alone a date."

Ren didn't say anything.

"Besides," Kara said. "You're right. I'm not doing the dating thing anymore. So it doesn't matter, anyway."

But she couldn't help sighing when she glanced in the side mirror and saw the shop get smaller and smaller until it disappeared from her sight.

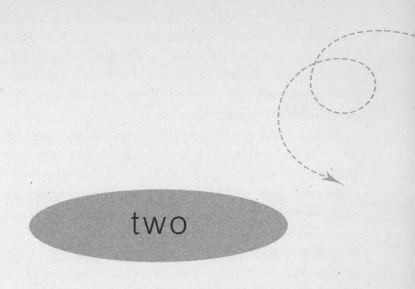

two

Mo Richardson thought about Kara while soaking in the tub. She couldn't help feeling a little sorry for herself. She missed her girl so much!

She lifted her hand from the water and closed the small gap between the shower curtain and the newly tiled wall. Mo sank deeper into the hot bath and glanced up at the fine paint job she and Stan had done. Yes, early retirement was wonderful. Stan had earned it, that's for sure. And their new home was a dream. But why Florida? So stereotypical! And so far away from Kara. She closed her eyes and prayed.

Lord, thank You for helping me accept Stan's desire to move here. Well, I kind of accepted the move. But I miss Kara. If there's any way You'd see fit to have her come visit, I'd be so grateful. I hated not being there for her when Paul broke up with her. Such a helpless feeling, not being able to hug her when she needed it. But Your will, not mine, Lord.

At least, that was the attitude she tried to hang on to. She knew the Lord would honor her obedient spirit, but now and then she struggled with where that obedience landed her. Sugarwood Hills. Median age 65. *Median!* That meant there were just as many people— living people, mind you—over that age as under it. At 55 she was a spring chicken, for goodness' sake.

Shrugging off her self-pity, Mo got out of the tub and grabbed her towel. As soon as she stepped outside the shower curtain, she smelled something nasty. Although her bath oil filled the room with a lovely fragrance, something else invaded the heavenly steam.

Mo wrinkled her nose and thought out loud. "What is that?"

She sniffed her towel. Laundry fresh.

It seemed that the noxious smell was coming up through the air-conditioning vent. She got down on all fours and breathed in. Maybe it was coming from there, but it was hard to be sure. The smell was taking over. Soon she'd lose all sense of where it was coming from. Was it...skunk?

She opened the bathroom window. A strong, salty smell hit her. But because of the fragrance of her bath oil, she wasn't able to detect if that was skunk or something else. She closed the window, dried off quickly, threw on her pajamas, and walked into the bedroom.

Stan was already in bed, but he wasn't snoring yet. The room was dark, and it stunk too. Mo felt her way to the window and quietly cranked it open. There was that same, salty odor. They weren't exactly in the country, but skunks weren't unknown around here.

She sighed and looked at the lump in the bed. "Stan?"

He stirred. "Mmm?"

"I think I smell skunk."

He said groggily, "I thought I smelled that too. Yeah. I was afraid it was me."

"Well, I opened the window to make sure the smell wasn't from something inside."

No comment from Stan.

"Stan."

A quick snort alerted Mo. She was losing him fast. "What should we do?" she asked him.

"Just keep the window closed. It'll go away."

"But the windows are closed. That stink was in the house before I cracked them open to smell outside. They were only open for a second."

Stan said nothing.

"Stan?"

He shifted in the bed again. "Hmm?"

"Honey, wake up. All the windows are closed and the skunk smell is in here. And I think it's getting stronger. Maybe the skunk is in the house."

Stan sat up, his voice only a shade more alert. "No, he couldn't have gotten into the house, Morine. Maybe the dogs tangled with him."

Their dogs, Beebo and Freckles, slept in the garage at the other end of the house. It seemed unlikely to Mo that their smell could reach all the way to the master bedroom. And, despite Stan's certainty that the critter wouldn't be in their house, it was possible. Stan often left the door wide open when he went out to work in the yard. She had just fussed with him about that this afternoon.

"Could you check, Stan, please? Could you check for me? I won't be able to fall asleep if I don't know what's making that smell."

Without a bit of complaint, Stan swung his legs out of bed. Scratching and shuffling, he walked past Mo, gave her a kiss on the cheek, and headed to the garage.

Mo watched him, droopy boxers and all, and smiled. Her knight in shining armor. She'd follow him anywhere. She walked over to her side of the bed, turned on the reading lamp, and heard the door to the garage open and close.

Stan returned within a minute, his eyes watering and his clothes reeking. As he talked, he got fresh boxers and a T-shirt to change into. "It's Beebo. He definitely found a skunk. For cryin' out loud, the smell's so bad you can just about *see* it coming off him. Couldn't get him to leave the garage, and I didn't want to touch him. We'll just have to take him to a vet or car wash or something tomorrow." He rubbed tears from his eyes. "Big stupid mutt."

Mo got air freshener and sprayed Winter Mist everywhere. Now the house smelled like a skunk wearing cheap perfume.

"Ah, well," she said. Sighing, she got into bed since Stan had already settled back in. She switched off the lamp and lay back, feeling restless. She was missing Kara. And smelling skunk. "How can the skunks stand their own smell, I wonder?" She didn't really expect an answer.

"Same way the Castelles do it, I guess."

Mo groaned. "Not again with the Castelles, honey. We've spent enough time being angry with Paul and his family."

"Rich elitists. If Kara had introduced us to them sooner...well, I could have warned her about Paul. Country club rich boy."

"Oh, nonsense. Their wealth had nothing to do with it," Mo said.

"Kara's wealth mattered to them, didn't it?" Stan said. "Her lack of wealth, I guess I should say. So we're not millionaires. Bunch o' snobs."

Mo sighed. They had been a bunch of snobs, Paul's family.

Stan added, "Paul. What a wimp! Kowtowing to his family like a beat pup. He never realized what a girl he had in Kara."

"That was a blessing, honey." She stroked his arm. "The Lord kept Kara safe from what would have been a very hard life with those people. It was a blessing."

"Yeah, well."

"You know you need to let this go, right, Stan?"

He grunted. "I'd like to give 'em all a piece of my mind for how they hurt my little girl. Talk about something stinkin'."

Mo sighed again and patted Stan's hand. "Not tonight, honey." She stared up through the dark for a moment. She hadn't meant to get Stan stirred up with her question about the skunk's jaded sense of smell. She said, "But, you know, that's what's going to happen to us. We're going to end up smelling like that skunk, and everyone else will be able to smell it on us. We'll get used to it, and we won't know we stink."

She heard Stan sniff. "I don't think I'm going to get used to this," he said. He rolled over on his side, mumbling, "I just hope that skunk learned a lesson."

Mo looked at him, but the room was too dark for her to see him. "I think the skunk was the one doing the teaching, hon."

The phone rang and they both jumped. Late night calls set Mo on edge, especially now that they lived so far away from Kara. She grabbed the receiver. "Hello?"

"Mo? Morine?" an old woman said. "Is that you?"

"Yes, this is Morine. Who's calling?"

Stan asked, "Who is it?" just as the caller identified herself.

Mo waved him off and spoke into the phone again. "I'm sorry, who did you say this was?"

"Well, honey, I said it was Addie, and it *is* Addie. Don't you remember me, for corn's sake?"

Addie. Addie. Mo had to think a moment or two before remembering the woman—her Aunt Emily's sister-in-law. They had met a few times in the past at family reunions, but they hadn't spoken for several years. And they'd never shared a phone call before. "Of course I remember you, Addie. Uh...how are you?"

"Who's Addie?" Stan asked.

Mo shushed him gently because Addie was talking again. She seemed to be reciting a litany of ailments. Mo picked up her alarm clock to check the time. Why would this woman call her at 10:30 at night? When she heard a moment's lull in Addie's narration of illnesses, Mo tried to bring order to the conversation. "Yes, well, I'll pray for you on those things, Addie. I will. But...why did you...was there a particular reason for your call?"

"Of course there was a reason, girl. I'm not an idiot, am I?"

Mo raised her eyebrows. She frankly didn't know Addie well enough to answer that one. But the woman's bluntness made her smile.

"I want to come to Florida and visit you," Addie announced. "Soon as possible."

Visit them? They were practically strangers. "Why?" Mo asked, incredulous. Then she realized how rude that sounded. "I...I mean, why, that's a nice thought! When were you thinking of coming?"

"Well, that would be up to you, wouldn't it?" Addie said. "When could you come get me?"

Mo scratched her head. "Oh. You need to be picked up?"

"Yes, honey, I do. Soon as possible."

"But...don't you live...where are you living now, Addie?"

"Still in Smithfield," Addie said. "Right here where I've always been."

"Smithfield...uh...Virginia?" Mo asked. It was like trying to pull information from a five-year-old. And she knew so little about this woman. Or geography.

"Virginia? Mercy, Morine!" Addie said. "North Carolina! Smith-field, North Carolina! Now, when can you come get me?"

Mo stammered. "I...can't...that is..." She looked over at Stan, who had been silenced one too many times. He was on his side, and now he produced a great, gravelly snore in answer to Mo's helplessness.

"Look, Addie," Mo said. "How about I call you in the morning? It's late right now, and I can't make any plans with you unless I talk with Stan first."

Mo heard Addie sigh. "I guess that makes sense. All right, then." She gave Mo her telephone number. "I'll wait 'til tomorrow," Addie said. "You talk with Stan and call me first thing, you hear? I'll be up at the crack of dawn."

"Fine," Mo said. "Bye, then."

"One thing," Addie said.

"Yes?"

"Who's Stan?"

After explaining her marital status to Addie and wondering if she would understand the woman's plans any better tomorrow than she did right now, Mo lay on her back, unable to sleep. Addie had managed to distract her from the skunk for a few minutes, but now Mo felt overwhelmed by stink, confusion, and...what was the other thing? Ah, yes. Missing Kara. She was worried about how long she'd have to go without a visit from her daughter. And now she was worried about smelling like Pepé Le Pew when she went to church in the morning. Not to mention trying to figure out how to transport a strange woman from North Carolina to Florida for a stay of indefinite duration and for no apparent reason.

Mo fluffed her pillow, sighed, and tried to snuggle into her covers.

Somehow she had expected retirement to be a little less complicated.

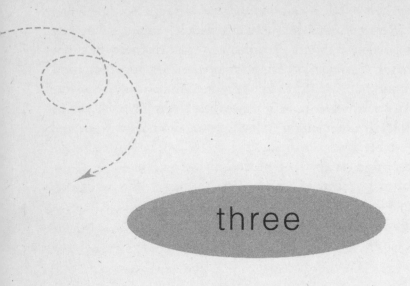

three

Kara grunted through another rep on the Nautilus machine before she noticed him walk into the gym. Gabe.

Despite the early hour, this time she thought quickly enough to avoid spouting off something stupid in reaction to his good looks. But she did catch her breath. Was he here because of her? She stopped trying to lift the weights that were suddenly so heavy.

He hadn't seen her yet. He scanned the gym's lobby. He was wearing khaki pants and a white golf shirt. The contrast against his tanned skin was so striking Kara stared openly at him.

She grabbed her towel and dabbed at her face. She stole a glance at herself in the mirrored wall. Her blond hair was damp and flattened on her head, and what little makeup she had applied this morning had long lost the battle with her sweat glands. Kara wanted to run back to the locker room and freshen up, but just as she turned in that direction, she saw her coworker Tiffany move toward Gabe, her long auburn hair flowing, almost in slow motion.

Tiffany. Ugh. What was she doing here, anyway? Not just today, but ever. Plenty of physically beautiful people worked in the gym industry, but Tiffany was Hollywood material. Right down to the perfect, vacant face ripe for habitation by some fictional character's expressions and emotions. Kara had seen Tiffany's chameleon-like talent in action before. She could become a Southern belle, a savvy city girl, or even a snooty pseudo-intellectual, as the need arose. And the need was usually based upon the man she was addressing.

Kara took hold of her jealous thoughts. She had sworn off dating anyway. Tiffany's behavior was none of her business. Neither was the fact that Tiffany was practically throwing herself at Gabe.

But then he turned his head and locked eyes with Kara. The life that sprang into his expression made her pulse rush. He had come here because of her. She couldn't help it. She had to approach him now, Tiffany or no Tiffany, dating or no dating.

Kara heard Tiffany's breathy voice as she got closer to them and had to fight to keep from rolling her eyes. Tiffany was in her Marilyn Monroe mode.

"And even though the gym has nice, long hours for your convenience," she cooed to Gabe, "the staff is still able to leave early enough each evening to have, you know, a social life, and things like that." She lowered her chin just slightly and looked up at him through her thick lashes, suggestion dripping everywhere.

When Tiffany followed the direction of Gabe's focus and saw Kara approaching, she said, "Oh, Kara, you are here." She shot a quick glance at Gabe and looked back at Kara. "Sorry, hon. I thought you were off today."

Kara gave Tiffany an empty smile. They had both arrived at the same time this morning, and Tiffany had put her belongings in a locker very near where Kara was changing into her workout clothes.

"But, wow," Tiffany said to Kara, her eyes doe-eyed and innocent. "You're all nasty and sweaty, aren't you? And you're not even officially at work yet. I'd be happy to show...Gabe, was it? I can show Gabe around while you go, you know, pretty yourself up."

Kara suddenly felt so unattractive she couldn't help reaching up to run her hand through her damp hair.

"Oh, please," Gabe said. "Don't go." His eyes, which he quickly widened at Kara, said, "Help! Don't leave me alone with this man-eater!" But what he said out loud was, "You look pretty just like you are."

Kara smiled, almost laughing at how quickly he had grasped Tiffany's predatory nature. "Thanks," she said to him. Feeling magnanimous, she shared her smile with Tiffany. "Thanks for your help, Tiffany."

Marilyn Monroe left Tiffany's face, and Tiffany's own disappointment took over. "Sure," she said, nearly pouting. Before leaving them, she fired up the breathiness one more time, fluttering her eyes at Gabe and slowly grazing her long, pressed-on talons along his arm. "So nice to meet you, Gabe. I'd like to see a lot more of you."

Kara actually blushed out of embarrassment for Tiffany. She was amazed that this aggressive, affected method worked so often for her. Then again, Tiffany was usually unhappy about her romantic relationships.

Gabe gave Tiffany a polite smile and turned away to join Kara. Once out of range, he said, "Well. She is certainly...scary."

Kara chuckled. "She's all right. She's actually quite clever and a real asset to the gym."

Gabe turned, a twinkle in his eyes, and looked directly at Kara. "Funny. I got the impression that she rubbed you the wrong way too."

She tried to look back at him innocently. "Really?"

He smiled, his eyes boring into hers.

Kara sighed. "Fine. She's really obnoxious with the phony, sexy thing. I have to pray daily to keep from being rude to her."

He laughed.

Kara shook her head and pointed at him. "Now, that's scary."

"What?"

"I don't even know you, and you knew exactly what I felt. That's not usually a guy kinda thing."

He pulled himself up and tilted his head, considering her statement. Kara found herself distracted by his strong, clean-shaven jawline. After a moment's hesitation, he asked, "But is it a bad thing, you think, my being able to tell what you were feeling?"

She smiled at him. "Not really. I mean, women always like to be a little mysterious." Her eyes flitted involuntarily to his broad shoulders. "But I prefer thickness in a man's build, not his head."

A subtle smiled crossed Gabe's lips. He simply looked at her and nodded once.

Had she just flirted with him? What was she doing? She was still new to the whole dos and don'ts of the no-dating concept, but flirting probably wasn't at the top of the "do" list.

"So," she said, attempting to be more professional, "did you come by to consider joining American Gym?"

He looked away from her and glanced over the gym again. "Yeah. Looks like you've got it all here. Universal, Nautilus, free weights. And you're right on my way to work in the morning or home in the evening. Can you give me some information about membership fees and contracts and stuff?"

Kara nodded, completely at ease now that they were discussing business. "Let's use one of the offices and I'll tell you what your options are." She walked ahead of him toward the nearest cubicle.

"And maybe we could talk about, oh, lunch together sometime?" he said casually.

Kara turned to look at him, her mouth dropping slightly open.

He smiled at her. Then his eyes darted beyond her, and he blurted, "Watch out!"

But it was too late. Kara had misjudged her distance from the cubicle when she looked around at Gabe. She smacked right into the corner, nearly knocking herself down. She shouted out a quick, indecipherable sound and staggered sideways, like a drunk, working to catch her balance.

Gabe jumped forward to steady her, his strong arm wrapping around her side. "Are you okay?"

She brought her hand up to the side of her face, which already felt swollen. She opened her mouth to speak but stopped when she heard a snort of laughter behind her.

Tiffany was just behind them. She threw her hand over her mouth, apparently masking her glee over Kara's clumsiness. "Oops! Sorry!" Tiffany said, shrugging her shoulders forward. Marilyn Monroe was back. "Don't mind me. Just thought of a funny story I heard the other day, that's all." She coquettishly wrinkled her nose at Gabe and turned away, hips swaying like a lead pendulum.

Gabe watched her while he muttered to Kara, "Does she actually do anything around here besides harass you?"

"Shhhh," Kara said, eyeing Tiffany sideways. "I'm praying again."

Gabe looked at her and chuckled, and then he glanced down at his arm, still wrapped around her. He cleared his throat and loosened his grip.

"Oh, good grief," Kara said, stepping away from him. "I'm all sweaty from working out. I'm sorry."

"Not at all," Gabe said. "My pleasure. But you look like you're going to have some swelling there, on your cheek."

Kara gingerly dabbed at the side of her face, grimacing. "Well, I always wanted higher cheekbones."

His deep brown eyes sparkled with appreciation. "You're... really sweet."

Sweet. He said it as though she were his little sister or something. But, strangely, she liked how he said it because of how he looked at her. As though he wanted to protect her. Or be her best friend.

She smiled and walked inside the cubicle, motioning with her head for him to follow her. "Come on. I'll tell you about the different kinds of memberships we have here." She sat at the desk and pulled out a membership form and some sales material.

As Kara reached across the desk for a pen from a mug, Gabe said, "So, what do you think about lunch together?"

Like a spastic monkey, Kara knocked the entire mug of pens over the side of the desk. Half of them landed in Gabe's lap. "Oh, good night! What's wrong with me?"

Gabe overcame a moment of shock and laughed. "You mean, you don't do this with all potential members?"

Kara was so embarrassed she couldn't even laugh back. She reached up and gently touched her cheek again.

Gabe jerked his head over his shoulder, as if danger lurked behind him. "Watch it! I'll bet Tiffany's right outside the door," he whispered conspiratorially.

That made her laugh. Then she sighed. As she and Gabe replaced the pens in the mug, she said, "Okay, here's the thing, Gabe. I'm not dating anyone right now."

He smiled. "Great! So you're free to have lunch with me."

She shook her head. "No. I mean, I'm not *planning* on dating anyone right now."

Gabe just stared at her for a moment. Then he frowned in confusion. "What do you mean? Are you...did you get badly burned by someone or something like that?"

"No. I mean, yes, I did. But that's not why I'm cooling it right now," she said. "Or maybe that does have something to do with it." She sighed. "I don't know."

He sat back in his chair and looked a little surprised. "Huh."

"But we could be friends," Kara said, struggling not to change her mind and say yes to lunch with him. He was wonderful, from what she could tell, but she'd been wrong before.

"Boy," he said, lifting his eyebrows. "Can't say I ever got the let's-just-be-friends talk without even going on a date."

Kara grimaced. "Oh, no. It's not you, Gabe."

He laughed and pretended to ward her off with his hand. "Oh, man! Not the it's-not-you-it's-me thing too? Ouch!"

She laughed, despite her discomfort. "Stop," she said.

He arched an eyebrow at her. "I'm guessing you're the top salesperson here at the gym. Charming 'em by the dozens, am I right?"

"Oh, you're awful!" Kara said, laughing, even as she felt the blush run up her neck.

Gabe smiled and looked at her for a moment. He nodded his head once in a gesture of acceptance. "Okay, then. I'll respect your wishes, how about that? Just friends. Maybe that will make you want to go out with me someday."

She wanted to go out with him right now. But she had made this decision, and she was going to stick with it. Unless it drove her insane. She could already see what it was doing to her equilibrium, and it wasn't pretty.

She smiled at him. "Thanks." She straightened the papers on the desktop. "Do you still want to hear about the different membership options?"

He shook his head. "Nah. That was just a ploy." He started to get up from his chair. "Not much point now." He glanced at her and caught her smiling. His eyes twinkled, and he sat back down. "Okay. Shoot. Whatcha got?"

Kara went over the membership material and helped Gabe choose a plan. She gathered together his membership card and the various brochures he needed while he finished reading and then signing his contract.

Without looking up from his signature, he said, "So. Are you thinking about getting married someday?"

The question jolted her back out of her comfortable, professional frame of mind. "W-What?" she said.

He looked up and smiled. "I just...I don't know if I really under-stand what...the whole no-dating thing...I don't quite get it." He grimaced. "I'm taking for granted that you really aren't going to date anyone for now. I mean, you're not just being kind in how you turn me down, right?"

Kara smiled. How cute that he wasn't too cool to discuss why she turned him down. "No. I'm not being kind. Wouldn't think of it."

He laughed. "Okay. So, do you plan on marrying someday?"

She nodded. "Yeah. If that's God will for me. And I hope it is."

He leaned back in his chair and chewed for a moment on the end of his pen. "But how will you get to the marrying point if you don't date? How exactly does that work?"

"Well, you just...when the right person comes along...at that point..." She frowned.

Gabe watched her, his expression wide open.

Kara sighed. "I don't know just yet, okay?"

Gabe laughed out loud, which made Kara chuckle at herself. He asked, "Is this a pretty new decision, then?"

"Guess that's obvious, huh?" she said. She took the signed contract from him and separated his copy, placing it in his membership packet. "I heard about the idea at church from some of the other singles—"

"Which church?" he asked.

"Hmm? Oh, Christian Chapel of Reston. Not far from here."

"Good church?" he asked. "I need to find a new church too. New gym, new church..."

Kara stopped working with the membership packet. For goodness' sake, he was a Christian! This was going to be more difficult to pass up than she thought.

"Yeah," she said. "Excellent church. You...you should come check it out."

He nodded. "Okay, I will. But I interrupted you. You were saying? About the singles there?"

Kara hesitated. "Yeah. Well, the no-dating thing. It seemed like a good idea, considering a few of my...past experiences."

He nodded, still listening.

"But," she said. "I'm not really clear on the particulars yet. You came along too soon, sort of." She blushed.

"Or too late," he said, sighing. Then he blushed. He quickly stood and smiled at her. "Okay then, Kara." He extended his hand to her. "Friends."

She stood too and shook his hand. It was warm. And strong. And gentle. "Friends," she said.

As she walked him to the front of the gym, he said, "I really am interested in...what did you call it? The particulars? About the no-dating idea."

She smiled. "All right. I'll fill you in as soon as I know what I'm doing."

He nodded. "See you later, then." And he walked out of the gym. Kara sighed.

"Wow, what a hunk." Tiffany's voice intruded from behind, inter-rupting Kara's thoughts.

Kara steeled herself to be casual about Gabe with Tiffany.

"So?" Tiffany asked, her voice oozing anticipation. "Did he join?"

"Yeah," Kara said.

"Oooooo goody," Tiffany said, rubbing her palms together. Then she looked at Kara, as if an annoying thought had just occurred to her. "Hey. You're not dating him, are you?"

It took a quick prayer to keep Kara from changing life strate-gies right then and there. She sighed in resignation. "No. I'm not dating him."

"Hot diggidy!" Tiffany said. "This is going to be fun!"

Kara didn't respond. She quietly walked toward the women's locker room, attempting to act disinterested.

She had made the decision to change her approach to dating after her painful breakup with Paul. She didn't want to keep giving her heart to the wrong men. Still, Gabe seemed terrific. Handsome, kind, enterprising, and, doggone it, he was a good Christian man from the sound of it. He was batting a thousand, as far as she could tell.

And now Tiffany would be on the prowl anytime he came to the gym, like a hyena in heels. Gabe hadn't seemed interested, but Kara had seen Tiffany's skill at breaking down a man's resistance before. This could get ugly.

Kara walked into the locker room and back to the showers. *Please help me to know if this is what You want from me, Lord. Help me to trust You for what's best, even if it wasn't Your plan for me to stop dating.*

Of course, she didn't always feel peace immediately after praying.

And this was one of those times. She looked in the mirror and reached up to touch the bruise already forming on her cheek. She remembered the comfort she felt when Gabe caught her in his arms. She reviewed her dismissal of his offer for lunch.

She had good intentions. But Kara couldn't help wondering if she had made a really bad mistake.

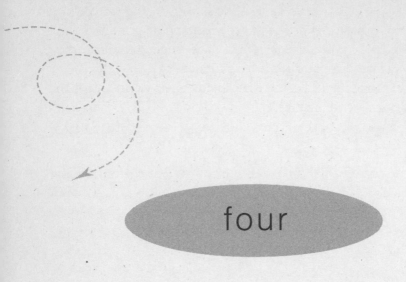

four

"He's finally lost it," Mo muttered to herself. She didn't really believe this, of course. But, as she watched her husband out the kitchen window, she was both amused and intrigued.

She had planned on calling Kara when she woke up that morning. Last night's call from old Addie had contributed to a restless night for her. And when Mo slept poorly, her imagination became morbid. She awoke certain that something life changing was happening to Kara that morning, a concern she mentioned to Stan at breakfast.

"Well, why would you assume something bad happened, Mo?" Stan had said. "Let's say you're right. Women's intuition or something." He passed a cup of coffee to her. "Maybe something terrific just happened to Kara, didja think of that?"

Mo had shrugged in response. He was right, of course. And her so-called intuition was probably just sleepiness. "I'll give her a call once she's had a chance to get up and about," she said.

"There you go," Stan said, giving her shoulder a casual squeeze as he headed for the garage. He stopped and turned when he reached the door. "Now, listen, honey, about this Addie person..."

"Yeah, what should we do? I barely remember her. If she's who I think she is, she was already ancient the last time I saw her, and that was over a decade ago. But I promised I'd call her after talking with you."

Stan leaned against the doorjamb. "She didn't say why she wanted to visit us?"

Mo shook her head. "I think she's just lonely. She's been a widow for a while now. Maybe she's not all that close with Aunt Emily's family. They were always kind of standoffish. And everyone else in that family lives in colder climates. Although, I think she has a sister somewhere in the South."

Stan sipped his coffee and looked thoughtful.

Mo took her last bite of raisin toast and said, "You know, someone directed her to us. How else would she have known to call down here?"

Stan nodded. "Well, she sounds like a real character. Could be fun to meet her. Even have her visit for a while, as long as she's healthy enough to take care of herself. But I'm not sure I want to run up to North Carolina to get her."

"Goodness, no," Mo said. "If we go that far away, I want it to be for a visit to Kara."

"Hmm. Now, there's an idea. Maybe offer to pick her up and bring her down the next time we drive back from visiting Kara."

The thought brightened Mo's mood. "That would be great. I'll call Kara first to see what works for her."

Stan walked back into the kitchen to give Mo a kiss on the cheek. "Settled, then."

A whiff of skunk filtered in when Stan walked outside, but the possibility of visiting Kara kept Mo from letting it bother her.

She glanced at the old clock on the wall, the one that looked like a map of the world. She smiled at the memories it evoked. When Kara was a teen and heading for a night out with girlfriends, Stan would point to the clock.

"Both hands in Europe, sweetie," he'd say, indicating the position of the clock's hands at her midnight curfew.

"Aw, Dad, come on," she'd argue. "At least the Baltics, huh? I'm almost eighteen!"

"Europe!" he'd bellow, with a gruffness Kara knew was pretense but still a demand for compliance.

Mo determined to wait another hour before calling her daughter. In the meantime she could tidy up the breakfast things. The kitchen was the most recently remodeled room in the house. Next to the heavenly Jacuzzi tub in their new bathroom, the sunny, immaculate kitchen was Mo's favorite spot in the house. The dark granite countertops were devoid of the clutter that Mo was used to in kitchens past; she planned to keep them that way. While she cleaned she occasionally stopped at the window over the sink and watched Stan.

She had that thought—that he had lost his mind—after he drove his little Bobcat tractor up to the back end of their old SUV.

"What is he doing?" she said out loud as she rinsed out the coffeepot.

Stan had opened the back cargo door of their SUV and laid a tarp over the carpet. He had crisscrossed cords all over the opening of the tractor's front loader—what Stan called the "bucket" because of its deep, scooping shape.

"Are those bungee cords?" Mo asked, continuing her kitchen sink inquisition.

And that's what they appeared to be. Stan had wrapped a series of bungee cords back and forth over the opening of the bucket. So now it was like a deep trough with a green, spiderweb barrier across the top.

Mo was used to Stan's inventiveness when it came to getting things done around the house. He never threw anything away unless he was certain he would never, ever find a use for it. While some people attributed Stan's pack rat mentality to a tight grip on the wallet, Mo knew otherwise. Her husband got a thrill from effective patchwork and jerry-rigging, so he liked to keep his resources abundant.

The phone rang and took Mo's attention away from Stan for the moment.

"I was afraid you'd forgot about me," Addie announced, as soon as Mo answered.

"Oh. Not at all, Addie. I just didn't want to call too soon. And I wanted to talk with our daughter, Kara, first because—"

"She's shy about having people visit," Addie said.

Mo stopped in her tracks. "Pardon?"

"You were going to tell me Kara's scared of strangers," Addie said.

"Uh...no," Mo said. Where had Addie gotten that impression? She'd never even met Kara. "Actually, I need to find out when Kara would like Stan and me to visit her next. She lives in Virginia, and Stan and I thought we might visit her and pick you up—"

"To go visit her with you," Addie said. "That's nice, Morine, but that's more traveling than I wanted to do."

"No, Addie," Mo said, shaking the confusion from her head. "We thought we might visit Kara in Virginia and then get you on the way back home. You see?"

"Sure I see, Mo. I'm old, but I'm sharper than you think."

"I didn't mean to imply—"

"Mo, don't worry about that. Just tell me when you're picking me up."

Mo was watching Stan out the window while she talked, but she wasn't focusing clearly; the conversation with Addie required too much concentration. "Well, that's just it, Addie, I need to see which dates work for Kara."

At that moment Mo paid closer attention to what Stan was doing. He had donned his heavy canvas overalls and work gloves. He had a scowl on his face, most likely in reaction to the amazing stench all around him. Using dog treats, he coaxed Beebo—their 120-pound Great Pyrenees dog—into the tractor's bucket through an opening in the bungee cord web. Then Stan climbed onto the tractor and raised the bucket so it was level with the cargo section of the SUV.

Mo nodded, understanding the point of the bungee cord barrier.

Without it, Beebo would never have sat still in that bucket once Stan started raising it off the ground.

"Okay," Addie said, interrupting Mo's focus on Stan and Beebo. "You go on and call Kara and get right back to me. I'll be right here waiting."

Clearly Stan hoped to get their smelly dog into the car without actually touching him. He wanted to get Beebo to the vet's office for a de-skunking without needing a de-skunking himself. Stan climbed up and straddled the two vehicles—one foot on the bucket's lip and the other on the SUV's threshold—and removed enough of the bungee cords for Beebo to be able to slip into the SUV. It appeared, however, that once Beebo had settled into the tractor's bucket, he was hesitant to leave. It seemed his fear of heights had kicked in.

"You there, Morine?" Addie asked.

As a feeling of impending chaos seeped into Mo's chest, she was able to hear Stan giving orders to the dog, although his words weren't entirely clear. With both arms he gestured to Beebo, enthusiastically encouraging him to haul his stinky carcass into the car.

"Addie, let me call you—"

Within the span of two seconds, Beebo decided to make a break for freedom. He attempted to jump down to the ground, but Stan's network of bungee cords caused the dog to bounce forcefully back into the tractor's bucket. The jolt of Beebo's weight caused Stan's foot to falter from the lip of the bucket, a circumstance Beebo used to his advantage. He leapt between Stan's legs but managed to take Stan with him as he headed groundward. Stan was thus forced to ride Beebo, bareback and backward, the three feet from tractor to asphalt.

Mo gasped. "Stan!"

Beebo ran off, his tail between his legs, but Stan was a slumped mass of man on the ground.

Without much thought, Mo yelled into the phone. "Call you later, Addie!" She hung up, ran out the door, and was immediately assaulted with the stench. No wonder Stan had been trying not to touch Beebo. Mo hurried over to her husband, who was still on the ground, pushing himself up to rest against his elbows.

"Blast that dog!"

"Oh, honey, are you okay? What can I do?"

Stan grimaced when he tried to move any further. "I think you're going to have to call 9-1-1, Mo."

Mo looked down at the odd positioning of Stan's left ankle and could tell immediately that it was broken. Her stomach clenched, and she tried to hold her breakfast down. She turned back toward the house, saying, "I'll get the phone."

She came back out moments later, barking information into the phone and carrying a pillow and blanket. As soon as she shut off the phone, she placed the pillow under Stan's head, while he grabbed the blanket from her and attempted to cover his legs, groaning with the effort.

"Here, Stan," Mo said, pulling the blanket from him, "let me do that."

"No!" Stan shouted, immediately gasping from the effort. He grabbed the blanket back from her. "You step aside for a minute, you hear me?"

Her feelings hurt, Mo stood and did as he asked. "Why won't you let me help you, honey?"

Now Stan moaned openly. He had quickly covered himself without Mo getting a good look at him. He managed to nod once toward the broken ankle she had seen. "That's the good break," he said.

As Stan fell back against the pillow, Mo glanced toward Stan's right leg. He had covered himself to save her the sight. When she saw the slow spread of blood on the blanket, she understood. He had broken both legs, the right one far more seriously.

All of her concerns of the night before and this morning were suddenly gone. Mo started crying. "God, please be with us here. Oh, Lord, we need You. Take away Stan's pain. Please get that ambulance here quickly."

His eyes closed, Stan still had the presence of mind to pray, "And please forgive me for the words that came out of my mouth when I landed. Really sorry about that, Lord."

They both sighed when the distant whine of a siren pierced the quiet—a swift answer to their prayer.

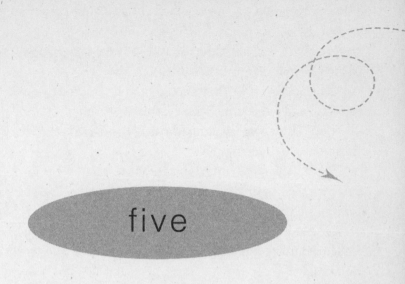

five

Kara placed her hand on her client's shoulder and gave him a big smile. "Look at that, Oscar." She pointed to the stack of weights on the exercise machine. "Would you have guessed four months ago that you'd be pressing eighty-five pounds on the delt machine today? You were only doing forty when we started."

"I feel like I should be running around the track in slow motion, pumping my arms in triumph, with the theme from *Rocky* playing."

"Well, you should. You've been working so hard. I wish all of my clients were this dedicated."

"My wife's pretty happy about it," Oscar said, and then he looked down, suddenly embarrassed.

Kara nodded and smiled. Such a dear, humble man. "I'm sure. You're a whole lot healthier now."

Kara's coworker Mickey Pecora interrupted them. "Hey, Kara. You still need that ride to the car place?" He nodded a greeting at Oscar.

"How ya doing?"

Mickey was a huge, buff version of John Travolta. He'd been involved with bodybuilding for more than a decade, and it was hard to imagine him in any other setting.

"Yeah," Kara said. "They should have it repaired by now." She gestured toward her client. "Mickey, this is Oscar."

"Hey," Oscar said, shaking Mickey's hand. He looked back at Kara. "Listen, we're done, right?"

"Right," she said. "But don't forget to stretch for a while before you hit the showers, okay? See you in two days. I've got you down for four thirty."

As Oscar left them, Mickey looked at Kara. "I'm working late tonight, but I've got a break in about an hour if that works for you. Bud's, right?"

"Yeah. Are you sure you don't mind?"

Mickey shook his head. "Becky asked me to swing home with some Chinese takeout on my dinner break. She and Paula have a Kung Pao craving. I'll order from the restaurant across from the garage."

Kara laughed. "Seven-year-old Paula eats Kung Pao? It's not too spicy for her?"

"That girl's a wild woman, just like her mother." Mickey looked past Kara and smiled. "How ya doing, Rennie?"

Kara turned. Best friend Ren clearly wasn't doing all that well. She taught second grade, which sometimes left her disheveled and tired by late afternoon. But her deep blue eyes expressed a different kind of fatigue today. Her long dark hair was drawn up in a haphazard ponytail and her shoulders drooped. She'd just walked in, but she looked as though she'd already done a taxing workout.

"Hey, Mickey," Ren said. Kara saw her working hard to achieve a smile for him.

"Okay, Mickey," Kara said. "I'll come get you in about an hour. Thanks for your help."

"Am I being dismissed?" Mickey asked. He was playing, oblivious to Ren's true mood.

Kara gave him a gentle shove. "Girl stuff. Go."

He sauntered away and sang along with an old Supremes song playing on the gym's music system. "Stop! in the name of love, before you break my heart, think it over…"

Kara and Ren chuckled. Then Ren shook her head. "Painful words. But Mickey's just too sweet to make me sad."

"So let me guess who did make you sad," Kara said.

Ren sighed and slung her gym bag over one shoulder. "You'd be guessing right, I'm sure."

"What did Greg do now?"

They walked together toward the locker room.

"Nothing, really. Only being an ex-husband, which still sounds so horrible to me. He just wanted to get my okay on selling some of our stock and splitting the proceeds into our two separate accounts. Stuff I was supposed to sign before the divorce became final."

"Was he a jerk about it?"

Ren shrugged. "No. He was…certain. I guess I should be as certain as he is." She looked at Kara with weary eyes. "I can't help hoping he'll change his mind and come back. Try again. Look to the Lord."

Kara put her hand on Ren's shoulder and gave her a gentle squeeze. "You've been such a prayer warrior about him, Rennie." And Greg had been so heartless with her. Kara sighed. "Free will sure does get in the way sometimes."

Ren took a big breath and released it audibly. "Okay. Pity party's over. Time for some healthy distraction." She walked into the locker room. Over her shoulder she said, "I'll be right out. You want to give me some pointers?"

"Sure," Kara said. "Warm up for five minutes. Do your stretching."

As Ren walked out of earshot, Kara muttered, "And avoid Greg as if your sanity depends on it."

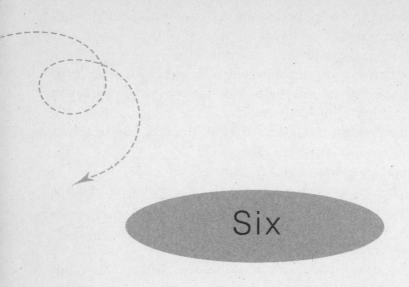

Six

While Mickey picked up his family's dinner at the Lotus Blossom, Kara got the bad news at Bud's Car Repair.

"No way, no how," said Bud. He wiped his hands on his oily jeans. A whiney country song echoed mournfully against the garage walls, adding to Kara's sense of dismay.

"What do you mean?" she said. "I thought it would be fixed by now. You've had it more than a week already."

"Didn't you get my messages? I told you the transmission was shot. I told your answering machine, anyhow."

The loud trill of a lug drill kept Kara from responding for a moment.

"Hang on, Jasper," Bud called. He looked at Kara and waited.

"Well, yeah, I heard your messages," she said, tilting her head sideways and sighing. "But I thought you were just going to go ahead and fix it."

Mickey walked into the garage, bellowing in mock anger. "What's this cheatin' rip-off artist feeding you, little lady? Want me to open up a can o' mechanic whup for ya?"

Bud looked sharply at Mickey, and then he grinned and shook his head. "Pecora, you old pile of muscle. Where you been hiding?" Bud gave Kara a friendlier look than he had before. "You know this troublemaker?"

Kara nodded. "One of my best friends."

"Are you kidding?" Mickey said. "She was one of Becky's whatch-macallits—bride thingies—at our wedding."

"Bridesmaid," Kara said. She was starting to relax a little, now that Mickey had arrived and seemed to be improving Bud's mood. Maybe Mickey would be able to make better progress with her mechanic than she had.

The two men chatted briefly, catching up on whatever it was they had missed over the past few years. When Kara glanced at her watch, she saw Mickey react.

"So, Bud, what's happening with her car? Don't you have it ready yet, man?"

Bud shrugged. "Like I told her, the transmission's shot."

Mickey whistled and rolled his eyes over to Kara. "You're in trouble, girl."

"What trouble?" Kara asked. "That's a big deal, the transmission?"

Bud crossed his arms over his chest. "This car ain't exactly in tip-top shape in other respects, either." Kara saw him shoot a quick glance at Mickey, as if he and Mickey were going to enjoy what happened next. He walked toward Kara's car, waving her to follow him. "Let me ask you something." He reached into the open hood with both hands, and retrieved something that he held forward for her to take.

She took what he offered.

"What are those?" Bud asked, lifting his chin toward her.

Silly man. Kara looked into her palm and had no question in her mind about what they were. "They're safety pins. What did you think they were?"

"Mm-hmm," Bud said. "Pretty good rule of thumb with air filters? See, your average mechanic has another name for the safety pin stage. We call it the you-need-a-new-air-filter stage."

Kara said, "But the guy at the lube place said the filter was pretty clean and really only needed to be changed because it had some rips in these flappy thingies. I thought—"

"And right here," Bud said. He looked into the engine and pointed. "What would you say that is?"

Both Kara and Mickey peered into the engine. Mickey snorted as Kara said, "That's duct tape." She was starting to catch Bud's drift.

Kara had inherited her father's penchant for home repair. In some areas she was quite gifted, but car repair had always been left to her dad. Now that he and Mo had been in Florida for a while, Kara's attempts at taking up the mantle were apparently having an unfortunate effect on her pitiful little old Sunbird.

"What are you saying?" Kara asked Bud, glancing at Mickey for assurance that didn't come. "What's this going to cost me?"

Bud raised his eyebrows and pushed out his lips. "Going to cost you a car, I'm afraid."

"A car?" Kara said. This time, when she looked at Mickey, he had such sympathy in his expression it scared her. "What does he mean, it's going to cost me a car?"

Mickey made a clenched-jaw expression before answering. "Look, you can ride to and from work with me until you can get a replacement, but this old clunker's had it. It'll cost you more to replace the transmission than the car's worth."

Kara gasped at the same time Mickey heaved a big sigh. Then he said, "Girl, you're totaled."

On the way home, the smell of Kung Pao chicken added to the sick feeling in Kara's stomach. She wasn't prone to tears over practical headaches like this, but she left it to Mickey to fill the silence for both of them.

"You've got some savings, right?"

She nodded.

"And I'll bet you can get a car loan with no problem."

Another nod.

Finally she said, "I'm just spoiled by not having a car payment. Maybe that's why this bothers me so much. And I don't know diddly about cars. You may have figured that out."

Mickey chuckled. "Listen, I'll help you shop for another car."

That was when Kara realized that she was most upset by what was missing. Her dad always handled this part of her life. She missed him. And her mom. And she was appalled at her own lack of independence in this area, considering what an independent woman she liked to fancy herself.

For some reason she thought about Gabe. About dating. About how nice it would be to have a man in her life who would handle this stuff for her. She blew out a big breath.

"I am certainly not going to start dating until I can take care of a stupid car by myself, I can tell you that right now."

Mickey looked at her as if she had just yodeled "The Star-Spangled Banner." "Yeah," he said. "That was going to be my next suggestion too."

Kara's phone rang the moment she slumped into her apartment. A glance at her caller ID told her it was her parents calling. She smiled and sighed.

"Ah, good," she said out loud as she reached for the receiver. She could always count on her parents for uplifting news.

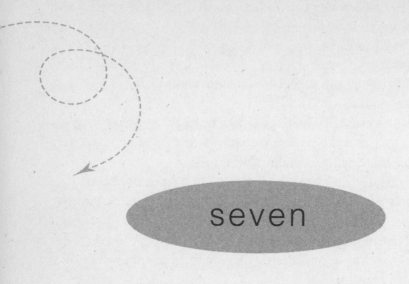

seven

"Kara, honey, don't cry," Mo's voice urged across the phone line. "Dad's going to be fine, really."

Kara walked into her darkened bathroom and yanked several tissues from the box on the counter. She kept swallowing, trying not to sob while she pictured the fall her mother described. "But he must have been...in so much...pain, Mom. Both legs? Were they both compound fractures?"

"No, no," Mo said, almost sounding dismissive. "Just the right one, sweetheart. The left leg was a clean break, all under the skin. They set that one without surgery."

"Poor Dad," Kara said, wiping her eyes and struggling not to choke up again. She walked into the kitchen and leaned forward over the counter, resting her head in her hand. The laminate countertop was cold and sticky against her elbows.

"They had to put him under for the right leg," Mo said, "so they could go in to make sure there was no infection. You know, since the...the bone had...well, honey, you don't need all those details. He's probably going to come home tomorrow. We can call you again then, and you'll hear for yourself how well he is."

Kara sniffed and pressed a tissue against her face. "I can't talk with him before then?"

"They've got him sedated right now. And it's a little late, anyway, to be calling over there. How about we call you as soon as I get to his hospital room tomorrow?"

Kara sighed. "Yeah, all right." She sat down at the kitchen table. "How're you doing, Mom? Are you okay there all by yourself?"

Mo's short, quiet release of breath was full of appreciation. "I'm fine, honey. Just tired. It's been a long couple of days."

"Stupid Beebo," Kara said. But she really loved that lunk of a dog.

Mo chuckled softly. "He's so distraught, poor thing. He knows he's done something wrong. And Freckles won't go near him 'cause he still stinks so bad."

Kara laughed despite her sadness. "You know you stink when you're too stinky for Freckles. She's about the smelliest dog I've ever known."

"Yeah, even more so as she gets older, I'm afraid," Mo said.

Before Kara could speak again, Mo gasped and said, "Oh, my goodness!"

"What is it, Mom?" Kara sat up, new concern filling her.

"Addie!" Mo said. "I completely forgot about her!"

Kara frowned and looked up while she searched her own memory banks. "Addie? Who's that?"

"I promised her I'd call her back. I was on the phone with her when your dad fell."

Kara heard her mother's breathing increase slightly, as if she were exerting energy. "Who is she, Mom?"

"Hang on, honey. I'm going back into the living room to check the answering machine. She's...she's my Aunt Emily's...um...yeah, that's

right, her sister-in-law. Elderly. Distant relative— Oh, for goodness'
sake, there are fifteen of them!"

Kara frowned. "Fifteen relatives?"

Mo sighed with gusto. "Fifteen messages on the answering
machine. I'll bet every one of them is from Addie."

Kara scratched her head. "You guys have some old lady stalking
you? Is she selling something?" She got up and opened her refrigerator, seeking dinner without paying much attention to the chore.

"No, she seems harmless," Mo said, sounding resigned. "But we
kind of told her she could come visit. I think she just wants some
company, poor thing."

"Is she spry enough to help you with getting Dad around?" Kara
asked. She pulled a plastic carryout container from the refrigerator.
"Maybe you should still have her come." She popped the lid open and
sniffed. Curry. Kara's brow furrowed. She didn't remember ordering
curry. She tossed the container into the trash.

"It doesn't really matter anymore. I don't know how agile she is,
but we were going to go pick her up. She lives in North Carolina. We
had talked about coming up to visit you and then getting her on the
way back."

With a quick intake of breath, Kara smiled. "I'd love to have you
guys visit, Mom!" She opened her pantry door and retrieved a can
of tuna.

"Well, that will have to happen later, sweetie. Obviously, Dad
won't be driving for a while with two broken legs. I wouldn't put it
past him to want to make the trip anyway, but there's no way I'm
driving all that way. You know me and driving."

Kara smiled fondly. "Yeah." She pictured Mo driving her to her
various sports events in grade school. Kara and her girlfriends always
got a kick out of watching Mo's transformation from calm, in-control
mother to nervous, insulting crazy woman whenever she got behind
the wheel.

"Although..." Mo stretched the word out over the phone lines,
clearly thinking something through. "Maybe you'd like to take a

little time off and drive down to visit us? And get Addie on the way? Maybe you could take some of that vacation time you've got piling up and do an old lady a favor."

Kara chuckled. "I'd love to do you a favor, Mom, but—"

Mo gasped. "I meant Addie, young lady!"

Now Kara laughed openly. "Sorry!" She had opened the can of tuna, drained it, and was picking at bits to pop directly into her mouth. She picked up the can and sat back down at her table. She sighed. "Mom, I miss you so much, but I can't drive down there. I can't even drive down the street. My car's dead. Totally."

"No, it's not!" Mo said. "Really? I thought Dad had that thing in good condition before we left."

Kara thought about the safety pins and duct tape. "Um, yeah. But I don't seem to have Dad's way with cars. My mechanic says I have to get another one."

"Can he be trusted, honey? Maybe he's just trying to sell you a car."

Kara wrinkled her nose at the can of tuna. This was not doing the trick. "No, the guy doesn't sell cars, Mom. It would be better for him if I paid him to fix the Sunbird, but the repairs would cost more than the car. My friend Mickey promised to help me find a good deal on something else."

"Oh, I'm so sorry, sweetie," Mo said, sighing. "I hate being so far from you. I really do. We've got an extra car here you could be using in the meantime. Listen, we'll have Dad talk with you tomorrow about what to look for, okay? When we call?"

"Right, Mom." The mention of Mickey suddenly made Kara hungry for Chinese food. She opened her junk drawer and began flipping through carryout menus. "I'm working tomorrow afternoon, so call me in the morning if you can."

"Got it," Mo said. "Say a prayer, will you, honey? It's going to be hard for him, not being able to get around like he's used to."

"The second I hang up, Mom. Love you."

But Kara's phone rang again as soon as she hung up, interrupting her intention to pray.

"Please tell me you haven't had dinner yet, love," said the kind British voice on the phone. It was Jeremy, one of her dearest friends.

"I haven't! You?"

A heavy sigh preceded his words. "Got stood up, can you believe that? I can pick 'em, eh?"

Kara shook her head. It was the story of Jeremy's life. As long as Kara had known him—one of Ren's fellow schoolteachers—he had struggled to find the one for him. He was young, funny, and sweet as could be. And he looked a bit like Jude Law with straight hair. Adorable. But as cute as he was, he seemed to have a difficult time in the relationship-longevity department.

"Ah, I'm sorry. It's her loss, Jeremy. You know that, right?"

"Hmm. I suppose. Come out with me, love."

"You're on. My car's dead, though. You'll have to pick me up. How do you feel about Chinese?"

"Chinese it is. Twenty minutes."

Just before she hung up, Kara pulled the phone back to her ear. "Hey, wait! Jeremy?"

"Yeah?"

"Call Rennie. She came by the gym today. Her face was so long she had carpet burns on her chin."

"Pardon?"

"Never mind. Just see if she wants to come too, okay? Greg called her this afternoon. She could use some cheering up."

"Right-o, love. Ta."

Kara ran into her room to change out of her work clothes.

What a trio they were, Jeremy, Ren, and herself. Jeremy had been dumped by this evening's date. Ren had been...well, seriously dumped by her husband. And Kara had been dumped by Paul, had a broken car, and a broken dad.

"Oh! Dad!" she said aloud. She had promised to pray for him. She stopped what she was doing and closed her eyes.

Thanks, Lord, that Dad's outcome wasn't even worse. Please heal him quickly. And I pray You'll bless Mom with patience while she acts as nursemaid to him.

Before she finished, she threw in a quick request for guidance with regard to her car, dating, and this odd little Addie woman. Way back in her mind, she felt as though they were all related in some mysterious God kind of way.

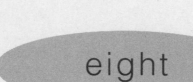

eight

Kara's phone rang again within minutes after she had hung up with Jeremy. She grabbed the receiver and rolled her eyes. Had he already changed his mind?

"You'd better not be canceling our dinner date, mister," she said, instead of "hello." "Not after getting my hopes up."

The lack of response told her she had made a mistake. "Jeremy?"

"Uh, no." The voice was definitely not Jeremy's. "This is Gabe Paolino. From the deli. This is Kara, right? Kara Richardson?"

"Gabe! Hi!"

"Catch you at a bad time?"

"No, not at all." Without knowing why, she checked in her hall mirror to see how she looked. "How...how'd you get my number?"

"Phone book. You are listed, you know."

She smiled. He had remembered her full name, thought of her again, and took the time to try to reach her. But she wasn't going to date him. No. That would be wrong.

"It's so nice that you remembered my last name. I'm flattered."

"Actually, I started at the front and called every Kara in the book until I got to you. I knew I should have started with Kara Ziminski and moved backward. I've been here all night, valiantly searching for you."

She sat on the couch and pulled her legs up, hugging her knees. What a great voice he had. "Well, I appreciate the fact that you didn't find a better Kara before you got to the Richardsons."

"A better Kara? Not a chance. But tell me...how'd this Jeremy guy work his way around the no-dating zone?"

She grimaced. What a stupid choice of words she had used in answering the phone. "He didn't. He's...well, he's just a friend."

"Oh, good. We're just friends too. We shook on it and everything."

She laughed and said, "Yeah, but I'm not attracted to him."

The implication was there before she realized what she said. In the ensuing silence, she smacked her hand to her forehead. That might have constituted flirting...

Gabe sounded more serious when he spoke softly. "Now I'm flattered."

She had nothing. Couldn't think of a single clever thing to say.

Eventually he spoke again. "I guess I don't really need to tell you that I'm attracted to you too, Kara."

She pictured him standing on the stepladder in his shop. She remembered the way he looked at her in the gym, when he caught her in his arms.

Kara pulled her collar away from her neck. "Um..."

She heard the smile in his voice when he said, "I don't want to keep you—"

"No, you're not keeping me. Did you call for a reason? I mean..."

"No reason at all," he said. "Just relaxing after work and thought about you. But I'll see you tomorrow."

"Tomorrow?" she asked.

"If you're working. I'm going to the gym around lunchtime. I'm opening my deli soon. I want to get in all the workouts I can before I have to focus on the lunch crowd."

There was still a caressing tone in his voice despite the practical words he was saying. It was almost as though he were right there with her.

"I'll...I'll be there," she said. "At work, I mean."

"Great. That gives me something to look forward to. Night, Kara."

"Good night. Gabe." It felt good to say his name.

She was still smiling when Jeremy knocked at her door.

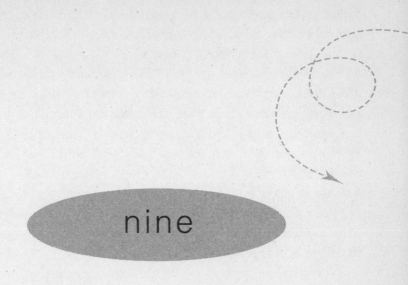

nine

At Cheng's Jeremy questioned Kara as she bit into a spring roll. Chinese mustard shot heat straight to her sinuses.

"So explain to me, love, how this bloke, Gabe, managed to sweep you off your feet so quickly."

Kara's eyes widened. She had to take a long drink of water before she could talk. Once her mouth cooled off, she said, "Did I say he swept me off my feet? I didn't say anything of the sort!"

Jeremy looked sheepish. "Well…" He darted a glance at Ren, who suddenly seemed fascinated by two rice kernels on her plate.

Kara looked at Ren and snorted softly. "You told him, didn't you?"

Ren looked up, her false expression of innocence lasting only seconds before she laughed at herself. "I'm sorry, Kara." She pointed at Jeremy. "He's very persuasive, you know."

He smiled and shrugged. "We have to talk about something during our lunch break at school. Have a heart, love. We talk at a child's level all day long. Your social life is the most adult topic we've had lately. Ren was just...impressed, I'd say, with the effect this fellow seemed to have on you." He exchanged nods with Ren. His excuse seemed to suit them both just fine.

Kara rolled her eyes at them. "Well, he hasn't swept me. Don't get all melodramatic, guys. He's just..." Kara tilted her head back and looked at the ceiling. "He's, you know, beautiful, that's all. Unbelievably beautiful. And funny. And nice. And probably Christian."

Ren's smile deepened with each of Kara's adjectives. "But you're not swept."

Kara shook her head emphatically. "Not swept."

Jeremy sighed, pushing his soft brown hair out of his eyes. "If only I could not sweep a bird off her feet like that. I just don't seem to fancy sweepable women."

With a sudden rush of maternal affection for him, Kara used her chopsticks to place a dumpling on Jeremy's plate before taking one for herself. "This dim sum is awesome. And that woman who stood you up tonight doesn't deserve a guy like you."

"Amen to that," Ren said. "But are you sure she stood you up? Did you have your communication straight with her?"

"There was a note on her door saying she'd changed her mind," Jeremy said. He dipped the dumpling in one of the sauces on his plate. "I think that was rather straight communication, don't you?"

Kara grimaced. "Ouch. You deserve better, Jeremy. Man, there are so many gutless people in the world."

She and Ren exchanged a look that had "Greg and Paul" written all over it.

"Yes, well," Jeremy said, "that's why I'm amazed at your standing firm about not dating, now that this latest fellow has come along. He sounds decent enough."

"I'm telling you, I'm not going to go out with Gabe," Kara said. "I've got to give this idea a try."

He shook his head at her, his hair falling right back over his forehead. "What an insane concept." He looked at Ren and, as if she had just joined them, said, "No dating!"

She said, "Don't look at me. I haven't dated for years, and I can't say I'm eager to start again. Not dating was one of my favorite things about being married to Greg."

Both Kara and Jeremy looked at her in silence for a moment.

She chuckled. "I mean, there was more to it than that, of course. But...ugh, I just loved being done with all of that. All that...you know, newness."

Kara said, "Keep it up, Rennie. You're going to talk me right into dating at this rate."

"Good!" Jeremy said. "You're going to make yourself crazy, you know." He scooped sesame beef onto his plate. "You're my age. Aren't you a bit old to start shrinking, Violet? A little too experienced on the dance floor to start wallflowering?"

"Maybe," Kara said, not at all bothered by Jeremy's comments. She'd thought the same things herself. "But...well, even you could do with a bit of preliminary research, don't you think? Aren't you tired of the emotional roller coaster you're always riding?"

At that precise moment the Chinese muzak featured an instrument that sounded like a woman's painful caterwauling. They all laughed.

"Couldn't have said it better myself," Jeremy muttered. "You're a bit right with the roller coaster idea. I'll give you that." He chased some noodles around his plate with his chopsticks. "But I can't imagine restricting myself like that. If I find a woman attractive or interesting—"

"And, of course, the first quality guarantees the second, in your book," Ren said.

"Granted," Jeremy said. "But I simply don't know how you expect to get to know someone if you don't go out. What are you going to do? Ask this fellow to carry your books to geometry class?"

Kara smiled. "God will honor my attempt to be careful here. And don't give me that look, Jeremy."

Jeremy's face had run the gamut in seconds, from skeptical to offended to innocent. He looked from Ren to Kara. "What? What have I done to deserve such disdain from my dearest friend?"

"Hey," Ren said, "I thought I was your dearest friend."

Before he could speak, Kara continued. "What you've done is let your face go all 'there she goes with the God talk again.' I'm telling you, Jeremy, you need to join us at church and start to get a clue. Life is hard enough with the Holy Spirit's guidance. I'm worried about you out there in the big, bad world."

"Mm-hmm," Ren said, pursing her lips, arching an eyebrow, and nodding at him as though she were the school principal confronting an errant pupil.

Jeremy laughed and passed a plate of shrimp and scallops over to Ren. "I'm going to join you two at church someday."

"Really?" Kara and Ren said simultaneously, their enthusiasm obvious.

Jeremy smiled at both of them with unabashed fondness. "You truly are dear friends, you know? Thank you for caring about me. I'll go with you soon, all right?"

"Just let us know when you're ready," Kara said.

"Right," he said to her, "but you have enough to worry about at the moment, what with your dad, your car, and that odd old bird in North Carolina." He winked at Ren. "Not to mention that right wonderful guy you're not dating."

Kara couldn't think of Gabe without smiling. Right wonderful. Yes. He was that. She wasn't going to date him, but there was no denying it. She was eager to get to work tomorrow. Just around lunchtime.

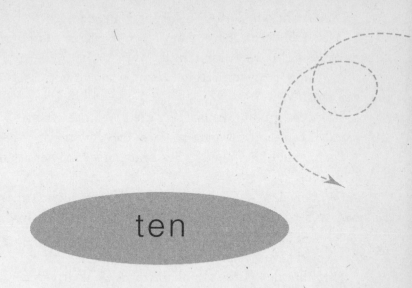

ten

The next morning Kara lifted her head from a deep sleep. Had she heard a man's voice?

"So you give us a call when you can, sweetie."

That was her dad! She jumped out of bed and ran into the living room to catch the phone. It wasn't as if she couldn't call him back, but her last image of him—falling fast and breaking hard—gave his calm voice real drawing power.

"Dad!"

"Well, hey there, honey. We didn't wake you, did we? Your mother said you wanted to hear from us right away."

"No, no problem, Dad. Mom was right." Kara walked into the bathroom and briefly recoiled at the disheveled vision in the mirror, a definite "before" look. "Are you home now?" She finger-combed her short blond hair.

"Not just yet," he said. "We're waiting for the final okay from the surgeon, but I'm dressed and ready to roll."

"You sound wonderful. You're not in any pain?"

"Nah. I think I still have some of their magic juice flowing through my old veins, to tell you the truth."

"So...how are you getting around? You've got casts on both legs, right?"

He made a grunting kind of sigh. "Yep. Well, the left one's only from midcalf down, so I can bend that knee. They gave me a walking cast."

Kara brought her hand to her heart, picturing her active father so injured.

"Whoopee, right?" he said, before a short laugh. "Anyway, that makes a big difference. I can use crutches instead of having to be in a wheelchair. I think a wheelchair would have made me nuts, although they would have given me a motorized one."

Kara chuckled. "I don't think the roads would have been safe with you in a motorized chair, Daddy."

"I can tell you that mutt *Beebo* wouldn't have been. At least this way he has time to get back in my good graces before I'm able to catch him and tan his hide."

In the background Kara heard, "Oh, Stan, like you would do that to your faithful old friend."

"Hey, there's your mother," Stan said. "Let me turn you over to her so I can try to hurry up that doctor. I love you, sweetie."

"You too, Dad. I'll talk with you later."

As Stan handed off the phone, Kara heard him whispering to Mo. Words like, "don't bother her with that" and "not important right now."

A moment later Kara heard her mother's voice. "You see, honey? Didn't I tell you he was bouncing back quickly?"

"He sounds great, Mom. But what aren't you supposed to—"

"Hang on, Kara," Mo said. "Your dad wants me to tell you something. What, Stan?"

It was often like this when Kara talked on the phone with her parents. Her father had more to talk about after Mo had the phone than he did while on it himself.

Mo said. "Your dad wanted me to tell you about our wonderful neighbor next door. He loaded Beebo into his pickup and took him down to the vet and had him de-skunked for us."

"How nice!" Kara said.

"Yeah, and—"

Another interruption from Stan.

"Hold on," Mo said. "Your father says the neighbor was probably sick of the stink, himself."

Kara chuckled. "I'll bet. But still—"

"Wait a second, honey," Mo said. Then, "Stan, why don't you just get back on the phone with her? What? Which surgeon? Oh, all right, you go on and find him, then. But let me talk with her, will you?"

Mo sighed but then laughed with Kara. "He will drive me insane, that man. Anyway, Dad wants to talk with you later about what kind of car you might want to look for."

Kara walked into the kitchen to start her coffee and get a glass of orange juice. "Okay. But what did he tell you not to mention to me, Mom?"

"What? Oh...it's just about Addie."

"Addie? The old stalker lady?"

Mo laughed. "Don't call her that! She's not stalking us. But she is putting in some serious phone time with us."

"What doesn't Dad want me to know?"

Mo sighed. "He just knows me too well. I'm feeling so guilty about her, and he knows I'm going to want to talk with you about it. He doesn't want you feeling guilty too."

"Why would I feel guilty?"

"Because I know you, Kara, and so does your dad. She's...Addie was just so sad that we had to cancel her visit with us. But with your dad's accident and your car problems, there really wasn't anything we could do."

"Why doesn't she just fly down?"

"She's apparently scared to death of flying."

"You mean since 9/11 and all that?"

"I mean since the Wright Brothers. She says she's never flown and never will."

"How about a train? Or a bus?"

"We've been through all of that with her. She's afraid she'll get lost in one of the stations. Apparently she leaned pretty heavily on her husband, Uncle...somebody."

Kara chuckled. "Well, good grief, Mom, she doesn't sound like the closest relative in the world if you don't even know her husband's name. I mean, I feel bad for her, but—"

"I know, honey. I was the same way. But when she mentioned Lurlene and started crying—"

"What's a lurlene?"

"That seems to be her sister's name. As soon as Addie mentioned the name, she started crying, and I had a hard time understanding her after that. She said something about Lurlene's time running out, and I couldn't grasp anything else she said."

"Oh, my."

"She hung up after saying something about calling back later. So now I don't know if I'm supposed to call her again or wait for her to call me. Either way, we can't help her. I just feel so bad about that."

"Yeah," Kara said. "Me too." And she really did. She tried to tell herself it was Addie's fault for being so stubbornly frightened of every available form of transportation, but she also felt insensitive for not empathizing sooner.

"Mom, I'd be down there in a shot if I had a car, really—"

"Now, just stop. Your father will kill me if he knows I went ahead and pulled you into my guilt thing after he asked me not to. We'll say a prayer together, how about that?"

Kara smiled. "Absolutely. I don't know why I don't think of that more often." She closed her eyes and listened for Mo to take the lead.

"Heavenly Father," Mo prayed, "You know our hearts. And we know You're in control of everything. We'd all like to help Addie and...Lurlene. We don't know how they stand with You, Lord. But if there's some way we can reflect Your love by helping them out, we ask that You show us how. Help us to listen for Your guidance in that. We pray in Your holy name."

"Amen."

Kara heard Stan call out an enthusiastic "Amen!"

Mo laughed. "He wasn't even praying with us. I think he finally found that surgeon and got released. I'd better hang up and help him make his way to the car."

On a light intake of breath, Kara said, "Oh, you drove?"

"Never you mind, young lady," Mo said. "I may not be the best driver in the world, but I can at least handle a ten-mile drive to and from the hospital without causing too much damage."

"Um, can we pray again?"

Mo tsked. "Be glad you're too old and too far away for a spanking."

Kara laughed. "Just be careful, okay? And calm."

"Stop worrying. We'll be fine. And we'll call you later so Dad can talk with you about cars."

"I love you, Mom."

Kara was off the phone for a full ten minutes before remembering that Gabe was coming to the gym today. With a grin she checked her watch. Ren would be here in an hour to drive her to work.

Kara had felt guilty hearing about Addie. But feeling guilty wasn't going to fix anything. She and her parents—and Addie, for that matter—would have to wait for God's counsel.

But right now? A good shower, some hair gel, and a dash of mascara were definitely steps in the right direction.

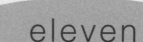

eleven

An hour later, Kara heard Ren pull up and tap on her horn. She ran out and hustled into the BMW. "Thanks. Hi."

Ren pulled away without saying a word.

Kara looked at her and then gasped before bursting into laughter. "What happened to you?"

Ren scowled but started laughing with Kara, despite herself. She grabbed a handful of carryout napkins from the glove compartment and dabbed at her blouse and pants. "You can still see it pretty well, huh?"

"Still see it? What exploded?"

"All I can say is that it's a good thing I got an *iced* latte this morning. Stupid guy didn't put the top on right."

Kara wiped tears away. "That's a latte, huh? Good grief, Rennie, it's everywhere. Do you want to go back and borrow something of mine? Oh, my goodness, it's even in your hair!"

"It is?" Ren stopped at a street corner and lifted the ends of her long brunette hair. She blotted the moisture with some napkins, blowing exasperation through her lips.

"Come on. Let's go back and get you cleaned up," Kara said. "You must be so uncomfortable."

"No. I mean, yeah, I'm uncomfortable. But we're both going to be late—"

"You can't go through the day like that," Kara said. "You look like you've been assaulted by an angry Starbucks mob. Your students are going to be so distracted they won't pay attention to a thing you say."

"Yeah, like that's going to be a big change."

"Oh, now, come on. They love you and you know it."

Ren sighed. "Yeah, I do. I'm just feeling sticky, which isn't my favorite way to start the day." She rubbed the side of her car seat. "At least it didn't spill on the car upholstery. And I've got a change of clothes at school."

"You do?" Kara asked. "Is second grade that messy?"

"Just a habit I got into when Greg and I were still married. Sometimes he'd want me to meet him downtown for dinner or something. It was easier to change at school, rather than driving all the way home."

Kara hesitated to say anything. Ren still seemed so fragile when Greg's name came up. Kara was able to discuss Paul without crumbling, but she and Paul hadn't even talked about marriage.

"Hmm," Ren said. "I can't remember which outfit I brought in last time. It's been...wow, maybe six months. Seven, even."

"Sure you don't want to turn around and change at my place?" Kara asked.

Ren shook her head, glancing at her watch. "I'm sure. Sandy asked me to stop in and see her before school started this morning. I can tidy up and change beforehand in the teachers' restroom. Just as long as we don't hit traffic."

Kara raised her eyebrows. "What's the meeting with Sandy about?"

Ren lifted a shoulder. "Don't know. She left a message on my answering machine. Probably an update on Casey."

That was what Kara suspected too. When Ren and Greg were married, they had begun the process of adopting a darling boy in Ren's class who had been in foster care for several years. Now that Greg had left, no one was sure what would become of Casey. As the school counselor, Sandy had been Ren's contact with Social Services. Eventually Sandy had become a good friend.

"But, to tell you the truth," Ren said, "I've been meeting with Sandy a little bit lately. For me."

"How do you mean?"

Ren's cheeks colored. "You know, for...counseling. For me."

"Oh!" Now Kara flushed, but she wasn't sure why. "Well, of course! Who wouldn't need counseling after what you've been through? And that's what Sandy's there for, isn't it?"

"For the kids, though," Ren said. "I feel a little silly going to her. I didn't plan it. We just got to talking one afternoon, and she's such a good listener." She sighed. "Lately I've felt kind of like Alice."

A question crossed Kara's face.

"You know, in Wonderland," Ren said. "Completely disoriented, chasing down the wrong paths, concerned about who I might meet next. Who I might be next."

"Oh, yeah," Kara said, "I can relate. I got a taste of that when Paul split up with me. Like I had completely misjudged him. Just because a guy is an attractive Christian doesn't mean he's going to be all that great. Paul was like those mean flowers—"

"Which flowers?" Ren asked.

"In *Alice in Wonderland*, remember? The ones hanging out with that stupid smoking caterpillar?"

"You're thinking of the garden of live flowers from *Through the Looking Glass*. The caterpillar was in the first book."

"The point is, those flowers seemed so sweet at first," Kara said. "And pretty. I have to admit, Paul was pretty."

"Long eyelashes," Ren said.

Kara scoffed. "The swine."

"Definite swine. And the flowers?"

"Yeah. Remember how snooty they got with poor Alice? She was really taken by surprise. I think she almost decked one of those lilies."

"You go, Alice," Ren said.

"Right on," Kara said, raising a clenched fist like an activist. "But that's what you meant, isn't it? About feeling like Alice? The creepy thing about Wonderland and the Looking Glass House was that nothing was really what it seemed to be."

Ren nodded. "Yep. That's how I've felt since Greg left. Even...even at church."

"At church?" Kara's eyes widened.

"I just feel that maybe people act normal around me but see me as a failure as a Christian wife."

Kara was surprised when she felt her eyes tear up. "Rennie Young, you listen to me. You did nothing against your marriage vows. You were a good, faithful, loving wife. Even now you talk about how you hope Greg will come back and try again."

"Yeah, but—"

Kara reached over and placed her hand on Ren's shoulder. "Ren, look—eww." She withdrew her hand and wiped her palm with one of Ren's napkins. "Latte on your shoulder, girl. Anyway. You're among friends at church. I'd be amazed if anyone judged you at all, let alone because Greg walked out. None of us is perfect—"

"Well, I sure wasn't the perfect wife."

"When you come across the perfect wife, please make sure to introduce me to her. I know I haven't met her yet."

Ren smiled. "Thanks."

They pulled up in front of the gym. Kara did a last check in the mirror before grabbing her purse and gym bag.

"You know," Ren said, "you look kind of perfect today."

"I do?"

"Uh-huh. Your hair. And makeup," Ren said. "You're looking especially pretty."

"Thank you!" As Kara reached for the door handle, she thought she heard Ren say something.

"What?"

"He's coming to the gym today, isn't he?"

Kara willed herself not to blush. She got out of the car and bent down to glare playfully at Ren. "*Mean* flower."

Ren laughed. "I love you, Kara."

They shared a smile right before Ren drove away.

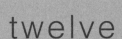

twelve

"Are you expecting someone, Kara?"

Kara glanced at her client Mary, a big redhead with dreams of sweating down to a size 10.

"Sorry, Mary. I'm not giving you much attention, am I?"

Mary lifted two dumbbells and smiled at Kara. "It's just that you've checked your watch about a gazillion times in the last half hour."

Kara sighed. "Just waiting for a friend who was going to come work out about now. No big deal."

"Maybe the adorable guy heading this way?" Mary asked, nodding at someone behind Kara.

Kara brightened and turned.

"Oh. No. That's...hey, Jeremy! What are you doing here?"

"And a cheery hello to you too," he said. He gave Kara a brief kiss on the cheek and smiled at Mary. "Hello."

"Hello!" Mary looked at Kara. "So you're waiting for someone better than *this* to show up today? He's perfect for you! What a cute couple!"

"Just friends, I'm afraid, Miss..."

Kara said, "Jeremy, this is Mary." With a mild frown she said, "Mary, this is Jeremy, who appears to be playing hooky from school. What are you doing here in the middle of a weekday, all decked out in your gym gear?"

"Whom are you waiting for?" Jeremy asked. He broke into a knowing grin.

"I asked first."

"Pardon me, kids," Mary said. "But if I keep lifting these dumbbells, my biceps are gonna be large enough to take over Manhattan."

"Oh, good grief," Kara said. "Let's move you on to the leg press."

Jeremy followed along, humming for a moment with the ballad playing through the sound system. At the leg press machine, he said, "Today's a grading day. No classes. Thought I mentioned that last night."

"Last night, huh?" Mary said.

"Just friends," Kara and Jeremy said at the same time.

He tossed his towel across one shoulder. "I decided to take a workout break just because I can. I think Ren was considering it too, but she had a bit more work to do first."

Kara started Mary on the leg press machine.

"And you?" he asked.

Kara rolled her eyes at him. "All right. I was waiting for Gabe. He said he was coming today at lunchtime to work out. It's one thirty already. I was just wondering—"

A velvety female voice interrupted them. "And just *who* is this hunk of manflesh, Kara?"

Jeremy turned immediately, but Kara closed her eyes and tamed the sneer that threatened to rise before she turned to face Tiffany.

Jeremy extended his hand. "Jeremy Beckett."

Tiffany gasped. "Oh! Listen to that accent! You just get better and better, Mr. Beckett!" She laughed like the hostess of a cocktail party, tipping her head back a little, false pleasure overwhelming her.

Jeremy beamed and looked at Kara, who made huge warning eyes at him, as if he were approaching a pit bull whose chain wasn't as secure as it appeared. He gave her a puzzled look and turned back to Tiffany.

"Please call me Jeremy. I don't think we've ever met before, have we?"

"Well, definitely *not*," Tiffany said. "I just know we would have gone out for drinks by now if we had met before."

Kara was about to groan, but Mary beat her to it, with a loud, disgusted "Ugh." Kara, Tiffany, and Jeremy all turned to look at her. She had stopped doing leg presses to watch Tiffany's performance, a sickened expression on her face. When she saw that she had called attention to herself, she jolted alert. "Wow. Yes, sir. That was an intense series of leg presses there, you betcha."

Kara's eyes twinkled at Mary, who didn't work very hard to suppress her own amusement.

Tiffany regarded Mary with an arched eyebrow.

Mustering a more Christian attitude toward her, Kara said, "Jeremy, this is Tiffany, one of the trainers here."

"He can see that, silly." Tiffany turned to Jeremy, still acting as though she should be wielding a long cigarette holder and maybe a tiny poodle. "I'm in this boring uniform, for goodness' sake. Just hides everything, you know?" She glanced at Kara. "For some of us, that's a drawback."

Jeremy smiled at her. "You look absolutely lovely, Tiffany. Nothing boring about you at all."

Tiffany wrinkled her nose at him. Tickled. Simply tickled.

"But I'll have to excuse myself and get going here," he said, checking his watch. "I've got to get back to work shortly. Nice meeting you, Tiffany." He looked at Mary and gave her a genuine smile. Taking her hand and shaking it, he said, "Mary. Enchanted."

Walking past Kara, he leaned his head forward in a gesture much like a subtle grab and pull. Kara followed him dutifully.

"Be right back, Mary," she said over her shoulder.

When they were beyond Tiffany, Kara said, "Jeremy, I should warn you—"

"No warning necessary, love. She's blasted awful."

Kara's chin dropped. "I thought you were charmed by women like that."

He shrugged. "Suppose I am sometimes, but I didn't like the way she talked to you. Quite a nasty comment about your figure. Which is better than hers, if you'll pardon my noticing. And you weren't silly at all. You were downright polite, even though you can't stand her."

Kara grimaced. "Is it that obvious?"

He tipped his head. "Is to me, but I know you. She doesn't. Maybe she's unaware."

Kara sighed. "I guess I need to be more charitable toward her."

"She is a bit of a pill to swallow, I'll give you that."

Mary called out to Kara, "How about the lat bar, Kara? Should I go ahead?"

"That's good, Mary, right. You poor thing, I'm being a terrible trainer today." When she went to help Mary set the weights, Jeremy followed her back.

"But, listen, love, about Gabe..."

"Oh, yeah." She looked toward the front doors again. No sign of him.

"Tell you what. If you can take a break when I'm done here, and he still hasn't shown up, why don't we stop by the deli? Have a look to see he's okay."

Kara couldn't help breaking into a smile. "You're the best. You don't think that will seem pushy?"

"How can it be pushy, love? You're not after the bloke. You said so yourself. Told me, told him, told all your friends."

"Told *me*, even," Mary grunted out while pulling down the bar.

"I did not," Kara said, chuckling.

Mary looked at Jeremy. "'No big deal,' she told me. Between the fifteenth and sixteenth time she checked her watch."

Jeremy nodded. "Right, then. I'll be less than an hour here. How's that?"

"Perfect. I have two open hours after Mary and I finish." She turned to Mary and put on a stern face. "Now. Let's get back to you, Miss Fifteenth and Sixteenth Time. I think it's time for some harsh and painful leg extensions."

"Aw, shucks," Mary said. "Ya party pooper." She gave Jeremy a wink and a smile before she followed Kara like a shackled convict headed for hard labor.

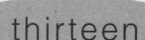

thirteen

Ren parked outside the gym just as Kara and Jeremy were about to leave. They stood next to Jeremy's Mini Cooper and waited for her to emerge from her car.

"Where are you guys going?" Ren asked, reaching for her gym bag.

Before Kara could answer, Jeremy piped in. "That bloke was supposed to come by the gym today—"

Ren looked at Kara with a shrewd expression.

"Not one word," Kara said. She crossed her arms over her chest and tried not to smile.

"But he didn't show," Jeremy said. "We're worried." He looked at Kara. "Aren't we worried, love?"

"Well, a little." She uncrossed her arms and looked as though she didn't know what to do with her hands, as if she were the awkward one at a party.

"So we're going by his deli to check on him," Jeremy said.

"Ooo! Field trip!" Ren said. She tossed her gym bag back into her car. "I'll drive."

"We can't all go," Kara said. "We're going to look stupid."

Ren put her hands on her hips. "Why does my coming suddenly make the group look stupid? I don't look any more stupid than Jeremy."

Jeremy feigned indignation. "Well, I *say*."

Kara tsked. "No, it's just a numbers thing. If...oh, all right, let's all go. Good grief."

Like two eager terriers, Ren and Jeremy jumped into the front seat of Ren's car.

"Wait'll you see him, Jeremy," Ren said. "I only got a glimpse, but he's a knockout."

"My heart's aflutter."

Kara got into the backseat. "Something tells me this might not be such a good idea, guys."

"Not to worry, Kara," Jeremy said. "We'll be the picture of maturity and grace."

"Right," Ren said.

Jeremy turned and smiled at Kara. "Anyway, you're just friends. What have you got to lose?"

The door to the deli was unlocked, but Kara and company saw no one when they entered. Kara glanced around.

Gabe had made great progress since her initial visit. The deli looked nearly ready for business. The colors of the Italian flag—red, white, and green—were repeated throughout the decor, from the walls to the red-checkered tablecloths. The chairs had rich green upholstered seats, and the menu boards listed delicious-sounding sandwich combinations and desserts. The food photos on the walls made Kara's stomach grumble, and she realized she had forgotten to eat lunch.

"Can't imagine Gabe would leave the door unlocked if he was going to be away for long," Kara said.

Just as Jeremy lifted his hand to the side of his mouth to call out a hello, they were startled by Gabe's angry voice, coming from the back room.

"Don't be ridiculous, Rachelle. Of course I missed you."

Ren shot Kara a sideways glance. Without thought Kara took a step or two backward, toward the door.

"But this was wrong, and you know it," Gabe said. "You know it!"

They heard a young woman's voice answer. "I guess I didn't think it through, Gabe. Come on, don't be mad at me."

Jeremy raised his eyebrows and spoke out loud. "She sounds a bit young, wouldn't you say?"

The sudden silence in the back room took Kara aback as much as Gabe's anger had. She widened her eyes and brought her finger in front of her lips to shush Jeremy, but she could already hear foot-steps coming their way.

"Great," she whispered to him. "They heard you!" She found herself heading toward the door as quickly and quietly as possible.

Jeremy whispered back at her, following her lead with Ren close behind. "Well, you were talking when we first walked in. It's not just me, you know."

Gabe's voice bounced against their backs just as they were about to exit. "I'm sorry, may I help you?"

Kara cringed. She turned around. Jeremy and Ren followed suit.

"Kara!" Gabe said, his troubled face relaxing into a smile.

A gorgeous smile, Kara registered, somewhere between her hot red ears.

Gabe approached them and closed the door. "Come on in. I'm so glad you came by."

"She was concerned, you see, since you didn't show up at the gym like you promised," Jeremy said.

Kara whipped her head toward him, horror in her eyes, and Jeremy's face fell.

"Oh. Well," he said, "she was merely worried because she's like that, you see—"

"It's true," Ren said. "She's ultra considerate to her friends. Not boyfriends, just friends—"

"Always the utmost concern, you know," Jeremy said.

Ren said, "Not that she's unkind to her boyfriends, mind you—"

"Not at all," said Jeremy. "And that's certainly not to say she's had a *lot* of boyfriends, don't get us wrong—"

"Jeremy." Kara stated his name, her jaw clenched. One word. It sounded like she had said "shut up." And that's what he and Ren did.

Kara looked at Gabe, who was staring at Jeremy and Ren, his mouth open slightly. But she also saw a sparkle of amusement in his eyes.

Gabe reached out to shake Jeremy's hand. "Nice to meet you, Jeremy. I'm Gabe."

"Yeah," Jeremy said, shaking Gabe's hand. "I'm the idiot friend."

Ren reached out her hand. "And I'm Ren, the other idiot friend."

Gabe chuckled.

Kara looked over his shoulder at three teenagers who had emerged from the back room. Gabe turned and let out an exasperated sigh. "Speaking of idiots," he said.

"Hey!" said the pretty young brunette. But she laughed, clearly relieved that Gabe didn't seem angry anymore.

He said, "Kara, Ren, Jeremy, this little troublemaker is my sister, Rachelle." He walked over to the group and stood behind them. He draped his arms over Rachelle's shoulders and those of the boy standing next to her. "And Ricco here is her twin, her partner in crime, along with this lug, Jake." He nodded toward the third kid.

"Jake's my boyfriend," Rachelle said, looking at Jake with a wistful smile.

"Yeah," Ricco said, "and if her boyfriend had half a mind, none of us would be here taking lip from Gabe."

"No one asked you to come along," Rachelle said.

"Okay, not again," said Gabe. He looked at Kara and crew. "They just finished high school back home in Miami. So the lovebirds here get the idea to come visit me."

"I missed my big brother, is that so bad?" Rachelle said. "And Jake just wanted to make sure I was safe on the bus ride."

Ricco snorted. "And who's supposed to protect you from Jake, I want to know?"

Jake finally spoke. "I told you, Ricco, I haven't touched her. I'm not going to touch her."

"Stop." To Kara, Ren, and Jeremy, Gabe said, "None of this would be so bad, but they left without telling my parents or Jake's." He stepped away from the teens. "Rachelle and Ricco, you're on line one, over there by the register. Jake, you take line two on the phone near the sink. Hop to it. And I want to talk with whomever you reach. Go."

All three teens scattered. Gabe said, "They meant well, but they couldn't have picked a worse time."

"How come?" Kara asked.

"I'm probably going to have to escort them back home, and I was planning on doing the back room this week. Painting, crown molding, everything. I want to have it ready for overflow business, with more tables and chairs. Now I'll have to postpone my opening."

"Why not put them to work?" Jeremy said. "Make them help getting the place tip-top in exchange for transport home."

Kara watched Gabe, who was obviously considering Jeremy's suggestion. He grinned and said, "You know, Jeremy, I like the way you think. If all three of them work back there with me, we'll get it done a lot faster. I could still make the round trip to and from Miami in time for the opening."

"Do you have room for all of them?" Kara asked. "I mean, here in Virginia? At your home?"

"Oh," he said. He blew air through his teeth. "Didn't think of that. I have plenty of room, but I'm not too comfortable having Jake and Rachelle both there overnight."

"She could stay with you, Kara," Jeremy said, sounding pleased with himself. Then his hand shot up to his mouth, as if he had just played the idiot again.

Kara and Ren laughed at him. "You know, that's not a bad idea, Gabe," Kara said. "I've got a guest room she could use."

"You sure?"

She nodded. "Sure. How about a trade? I'm stuck without a car right now. I'll take in Rachelle while she's in town if you guys can give me a ride to and from work each day. Could you manage that?"

"You'd have to stop at Kara's to get Rachelle anyway, yeah?" Jeremy said, obviously enjoying this turn of events.

Kara looked at him. "You're quite the cruise director, aren't you?"

"Just happy to help out a couple of friends," he said.

"Gabe!" Rachelle called out. "Mom wants to talk with you."

"Gotta go," Gabe said. "Okay, then. What a blessing that you three stopped by! I'm feeling a whole lot better than I did just half an hour ago. I'll call you at the gym this afternoon before we leave, then, Kara. Thanks."

"Our pleasure, Gabe," Jeremy said. "See you Friday night, then?"

Everyone regarded him with confusion.

Jeremy looked at Kara. "Dinner party? My place? Ring any bells?"

"Ah! Dinner party," Kara said. "But..."

"You'll come, right, mate?" Jeremy said to Gabe, who watched Kara, apparently trying to gauge her wishes.

"That's a great idea!" Ren said.

"As a *friend*, all right?" Jeremy said to Gabe. "Think about it. Kara has my number."

Gabe nodded. "Okay, thanks."

"Gabe!" Rachelle called, shaking the phone in the air. "Mom!"

"We'll talk later," Jeremy said, leading Kara and Ren out of the shop.

The door closed behind them and Jeremy let out a self-satisfied sigh. "I'm good. I'm really quite good."

"For Pete's sake, Jeremy," Kara said, as they walked to the car.

"You were all over the poor guy with your plans. I think he was a little overwhelmed. Is this how you approach women?"

He stopped dead in his tracks. "You know, I think it might be. Is that bad, do you suppose?"

Kara and Ren looked at his troubled expression and laughed. Kara gave him a brief hug. "I don't know. I'm a little overwhelmed myself. We'll have to think about that."

They got in the car and headed back to the gym.

Jeremy stroked his chin. "Cruise director," he said. "I rather like that."

fourteen

So Gabe made, like, a *huge* big deal about how I shouldn't make trouble for you," Rachelle told Kara. She flipped her long hair behind her shoulders. "Am I trouble for you?"

They walked into Kara's house. Gabe, Ricco, and Jake had dropped them off moments before. Kara was glad she hadn't left the place too disheveled when she went to work this morning.

Kara waved her off. "Not at all. It'll be fun." She picked up her coffee cup from the living room coffee table and dropped her mail there in its place. "Make yourself at home. I have a guest room you can use. I'll show you in a second. We'll both be at work a lot while you're visiting, anyway." She brought her cup into the kitchen and gathered up the morning paper, which was spread over the counter.

Rachelle blew air through her pouting lips and flopped into a big comfy chair in Kara's living room. "Huh. I never thought I'd end up working on my vacation." She kicked off her sneakers.

Kara stayed silent and just smiled. Rachelle was a pretty young female version of Gabe, with the same dark eyes and hair. But she was too much of a teen to have Gabe's strong work ethic. So far, anyway. Kara remembered sporting the same attitude for a short span during her teen years.

She hoped she could identify with Rachelle in other areas, as well. Otherwise this could turn out to be a long evening. A long week.

She got spring water for both of them from the fridge and sat on the couch across from Rachelle. "How do you like being a twin—or are you sick of answering that question?"

Rachelle shrugged. "No. It's pretty cool, I guess. We loved it when we were little. We were awful close. Went everywhere together. Even played on the same sports teams until, you know, they made me switch to girl teams, like softball. Ricco's been getting really bossy lately, though. 'Specially since I started dating."

"Hmm." Kara took a drink from her bottle. "I never had a brother, but my dad certainly acted a lot differently when I started dating. I'll bet Ricco's worried about you. You know, about guys trying to take advantage of you."

"It'd be nice if he trusted me better than that." She crossed her bare feet at the ankles and rested them on the coffee table, only to lift them quickly back off. "Do you mind?"

Kara leaned back on the couch and put her own feet on the table. "Help yourself. It's not a pricey piece of furniture, by any means. But back to your brother, I think...I mean, I don't know Ricco, but in my singles group at church—"

"You a churchy-type?" Rachelle pointed at Kara. "Like Gabe?"

Oh. Well. That raised a few questions.

"Yeah, you could call me churchy, I guess, if you mean I'm a Christian. I think that would probably describe Gabe too."

"Yep."

"But not you?"

Rachelle lifted a shoulder. "I go to church with Mom and Dad once in a while. They'd like me to go more, but they don't pressure me much. They used to just, you know, live regular lives. Go to church for Christmas and funerals and stuff. A few years ago, though, they started getting into it more and talking with us about it. But Gabe's the only one who got all whacked-out into it."

Kara smiled politely.

Rachelle tilted her head and considered Kara. "So that's probably one of the reasons he likes you so much."

Despite herself, Kara smiled genuinely. "We don't know each other very well yet. We're new friends."

Rachelle nodded like an ancient sage and raised a finger. "Trust me on this one. He *likes* you."

Kara felt as though they were passing notes in school, but her heart raced anyway. "How...what gives you that impression?"

Rachelle said nothing, but she watched Kara for a while before smiling. "You like him too, don't you?"

Savvy little stinker. Kara blushed and stood up. "Like I said, we're new friends still. But, yeah, I think he's a nice guy. You want some ice cream?"

"Sure. Thanks. I'll help." Rachelle followed her into the kitchen. "So how come you two haven't gone out yet? Are you seeing someone? Cause I can promise you, he's not. I think that was one of the reasons he moved up here."

Kara looked in the freezer and waited for the rest of that comment, but it didn't come. Now Rachelle backs off? What did that mean? Was he running from someone whose heart he broke? Was his heart broken? Had he moved to Virginia because he couldn't get a date in Miami? Oh, that couldn't be it, considering what Kara'd learned about him so far and how he looked, for goodness' sake.

"Chocolate fudge okay?"

"Yep." Rachelle opened a few cupboard doors and found bowls for them. "So? What's up with you two?"

Kara finally looked Rachelle in the eyes and raised her eyebrows. "You're really persistent, aren't you?"

Rachelle laughed. "Sorry. I just love a good story. And I love my big brother."

Kara sighed and scooped ice cream into the bowls. "Okay, here's the deal. We only met each other last week. And yes, he did ask me out. To lunch. But I'm going through a period right now when I'm trying to avoid dating for a while."

"You got a disease?" Rachelle rested against the counter.

Kara dropped the ice cream scooper, and it clattered to the floor. "Good grief, no!"

Rachelle gasped, abruptly standing straight. "Oh! Oh, no! I didn't mean like a...one of *those* diseases. I just thought maybe you were sick or something." She squatted down to retrieve the scooper. "Oh, man, I'm so sorry. You must think I'm the rudest!" She made a long groan that sounded like pure self-frustration. "Gabe's going to kill me."

Kara started laughing. "Don't tell him about this conversation, Rachelle. Please!" She tore a paper towel free to wipe ice cream from the floor.

Rachelle thrust her hand toward Kara. "Neither one of us, promise?"

They shook hands, partners in secrecy. Rachelle nodded once and took the towel from Kara to do the cleaning herself. Then they carried their bowls back into the living room and resumed their leisurely positions before eating.

"See, I've always been really careful about who I'll go out with," Kara said. "I grew up going to church and studying the Bible and trying to live a good, Christian life."

"Okay," said Rachelle, stirring her ice cream into a creamy soup. She actually had the tip of her tongue sticking out the side of her mouth and a frown over her eyes as she focused on what seemed a daunting task for her.

Kara watched her with a crooked smile. Such a kid. "And the Bible tells Christians not to marry non-Christians."

"No way!" Rachelle looked up in surprise.

She had actually been listening.

Kara nodded. "Yes way. It's hard enough to make marriage work without fighting over spiritual beliefs. Especially if you end up having kids and arguing about which faith they should be raised in."

"Why can't you just bring 'em up in two religions? Or none? Let them choose later?"

Kara shrugged. "I guess you could if neither of you felt very strongly about your faith. But I feel strongly about mine. My kids will have to choose on their own faith, but I want to make sure they're well grounded in Christianity while they're with me."

"You are like Gabe."

"But," Kara said, "even though I only date Christian guys, my past relationships just haven't worked out." She took a big bite of her ice cream.

"So you...what? You gave up? You're not all that old, are you?"

Kara almost spit out her ice cream. She swallowed and choked out a laugh. "I'm still a few years away from the grave, God willing. I didn't give up. I'm just trying a different approach."

"Ohhhhhh, okay. Like hard to get!"

"No!" Kara sat up and put her ice cream bowl on the table. She pressed her fingers to her temples for a moment. "Ooo. Brain freeze." The feeling passed within seconds. "I want to become friends with the guy first. Really get to know him. Have him get to know me. I don't want romance to become part of the relationship unless there's a strong foundation there."

Rachelle sat up and put her bowl on the table too. "Huh. Sort of like what you said about your kids and religion."

"Pardon?"

"You said your kids will have to choose which religion they want. But you want them to be...how did you say it? Grounded?"

"Yeah, grounded in Christianity."

"And you'll choose which person to date—Gabe or some other Christian guy, but you want the romance grounded in friendship."

Kara stared at Rachelle for a moment. "Wow. That's pretty straight thinking."

Rachelle smiled and picked her ice cream back up. "I'm going to go pour this into a glass. You don't mind, do you?"

"Nope." Kara followed her back into the kitchen. "Um, Rachelle, what I was going to say about Ricco? Before we went off on 'churchy' stuff—"

Rachelle chuckled.

"He probably trusts you but feels protective of you because guys are really...driven. They struggle, you know, with sexual temptation a bit more than girls do."

Rachelle nodded. "I can tell. Sort of."

"Ricco's probably nervous because he's a guy and knows what kind of thoughts Jake's probably having."

The telephone rang. Kara said to Rachelle, "Why don't you take your stuff back to the guest room, there at the end of the hall. The room with pink and gray walls. Bathroom's right next to it."

"Okay." Rachelle nodded and left as Kara answered the phone.

Gabe was on the other end of the line. "Has she driven you crazy yet?"

Kara thought about what Rachelle said—"He *likes* you"—and smiled broadly. "What are you talking about? She's terrific."

"Yeah, she's a good kid. Listen, I wanted to make sure you're all right with my going to Jeremy's Friday night. That doesn't mess up your new lifestyle thing, does it?"

Kara laughed. "No. I mean, I'm fine with your going. It'll be fun."

"Okay if I bring a date?" he asked.

"I...um..."

Gabe laughed. "I'm kidding, Kara. As I told you, I am really interested in hearing more about the no-dating idea. So I'll get Jeremy's address from you tomorrow, okay?"

"Sure, okay. Did...did you want to talk with Rachelle?"

"No. Just you. Hadn't heard your voice for about an hour. Good night, Kara."

"Good night." She hung up smiling. Funny how things were working out. She was seeing him almost as much as if they were dating.

I hope that's all Your doing, God, and not my being manipulative without realizing it. You know my heart. I want to do this right. Will You please help me listen to You? And I know there are other things You want me to focus on besides romance. Please help me to recognize those other areas, Lord.

"Hey, Kara," Rachelle called, walking out of the guest room with Kara's spare Bible in her hand. "Show me the part about Christians only dating Christians."

Kara closed her eyes for just a moment. *Got it, Lord.*

fifteen

"Hey, Kara," Ren called out from Jeremy's kitchen. "Can you come help us for a second?"

A clatter of pans was followed by Jeremy voice. "Blast!"

Kara watched a lone dinner roll escape through the kitchen doorway. Dinner rolls—that's what that delicious smell was.

Kara and Sandy were setting Jeremy's table in his small dining room. As the oldest, most mature, and only married member of the group, Sandy had quickly commandeered the dining room details once she arrived.

Sandy was large, loud, and thoroughly loved. Her husband— dubbed the Marvelous Rick due to Sandy's constant, glowing praise—was absent tonight. Friday was bowling night. "Nothing interferes with bowling night, kids," Sandy had announced when she arrived, a big bowl of melon balls in tow. "So you got one for the price of two tonight."

"I'm beginning to think I'll never meet Rick," Jeremy said.

Kara and Sandy were trying to be creative with what little dinnerware Jeremy had on hand. For some reason he didn't have a complete set of dishes, silverware, or glassware. It seemed he had built his entire dining collection from the remains of other people's discarded sets.

"You go on, girl, I've got this," Sandy told Kara. "Hmm. I didn't know they still made these." She held up a Flintstones jelly glass.

Kara laughed. "Only for the finest collections, you know." She picked up the dinner roll and joined the fray in the kitchen.

The oven fan was running at full speed, the refrigerator door was hanging open, and something brown was about to boil over on the stove. Ren held one of Jeremy's hands, palm up, and she studied it like a carnival fortune teller.

"Uh-oh," Kara said. "What happened?" She reached over to turn down the fire under the boiling pot.

"Forgot the bloomin' oven mitt," Jeremy said.

"He's just trying to do too many things at once," Ren said. "He grabbed the tray of rolls out of the oven without thinking. Where's your first aid kit, Jeremy?"

"My what?"

Ren looked at him and shook her head. "You are such a bachelor." She lifted her head and called out. "Hey, Sandy!"

Sandy strolled into the kitchen, a huge serving platter in her hands. "This appears to be your fifth dinner plate, Jer. We expecting Paul Bunyan tonight?"

"No, I've got a fifth in the sink here," Jeremy said. "I just need to wash it."

Kara said to Sandy, "Okay, Mom. You're the only one here who knows about boo-boos. What can we put on Jeremy's burn? Even I know butter is the wrong thing."

Sandy looked at Ren and Jeremy and frowned. "Both of you work all day long with kids. What do you do when one of them gets hurt?"

"Isn't that what the school nurse is for?" Jeremy said. He grabbed a paper napkin and blotted his forehead. "I give them solace until she steps in."

"I have a first aid kit in my classroom," Ren said, raising an eyebrow at Jeremy.

"Well, I suppose I do too," he said. "But it's not doing me much good here, is it?"

"All right, all right," Sandy said. "I'll take care of it." She walked swiftly to Jeremy's knife block and extracted a nine-inch carving knife.

Kara laughed. "I think amputation is a bit over the top, don't you, Sandy?"

"Hang on." Sandy walked out of the kitchen. They heard Jeremy's balcony door sliding open, then shut. Sandy returned with the end of a cactus-like plant in her hand, a gooey substance forming at its wound.

"You've murdered my plant!"

"Aloe," Sandy said. "I saw it when I came in. These things are great." She approached Jeremy and gently rubbed the sloppy liquid on his hand.

Ren sniffed and stepped back. "Kinda stinky, isn't it?"

"I say," Jeremy said. "That's brilliant." He looked at Sandy with admiration. "You're aces, Sandy."

Sandy tilted her head and regarded him. "I'm going to trust that that's a good thing."

In minutes he was back to work. Sandy washed his fifth dinner plate and went back to the dining room.

"Get me the plastic bag from the refrigerator, will you, Kara? The one with the sliced beef in it."

"Mmm," Ren said. "Bag o' meat."

He gave her a supercilious look of disdain. "It's marinating, thank you."

Kara brought the bag over to him. "Why do you have newspaper under it?"

"In case it leaks," he said. "Didn't want to take a chance on making too big a mess." He reached over to turn on his blender, and both Kara and Ren shouted out, "No!"

Jeremy stopped in his tracks and looked at them, surprised.

"Lid's not on," Ren said.

"Right," he said, shooting a quick glance at his ceiling. "Right." He secured the blender lid and whipped ice, fruit, and juice together for a few seconds. "Now everything's on plan. Guess I need the glasses off the table."

The doorbell rang, and all three friends looked at each other.

"That'll be Gabe, right?" Kara asked Jeremy. "You didn't invite anyone else, right?"

He smiled. "Didn't have any more plates." He lowered his voice. "If the Marvelous Rick had come, one of us would have had to use Sandy's Paul Bunyan platter thing."

Ren looked at Kara, who was no longer paying attention to Jeremy. "Just relax. This is the best way to get to know each other without actually going out. And you look like a dream."

"Smashing," Jeremy said. "You're a vision in white. And it would have been totally ruined had I turned on the blender any sooner."

Kara laughed. She felt little beads of perspiration along her upper lip.

"I'm going to make sure not to drop another clanger on him, Kara," Jeremy said. "No embarrassing comments. We'll just have fun."

She gave him a quick kiss on the cheek. "I swear you're the brother I always wanted, Jeremy." She turned to leave. Before walking out of the kitchen, she took a deep breath, released it, tousled her hair, and quickly swiped the mist of perspiration from her face.

The bell rang again. Where was Sandy?

Kara went to the door and opened it. She almost forgot to breathe when she saw him. He was everything she wasn't: dark hair, dark eyes, thoroughly masculine. He was wearing a soft black collared shirt, with the sleeves rolled up on his forearms, and black trousers.

He looked trim, fresh, and hard to resist.

The toilet flushed before either of them had a chance to speak.

"Well, there's a mood setter," Kara said, prompting a laugh from Gabe.

Sandy walked out of the bathroom, took one look at Gabe, and said, "Woo, Zorro! You are fine looking!"

He laughed and glanced at the ground before looking back at Sandy.

"Come on in, Gabe," Kara said, her heart pounding like a rabbit's. "This is..." She completely blanked on Sandy's name.

"Sandy," said Sandy, a smile on her face. "It'll come back to you eventually, Kara. You're a little distracted right now."

Kara gave Sandy a desperate look, and she frowned.

"What's with the black?" Sandy asked.

"Sandy!" Kara said. "What do you mean? He looks great in black." She looked at Gabe. "You look *great*." Good grief, if she told him he looked great one more time she was going to have to start a fan club or something.

Gabe smiled. "Thanks. But—"

"No," Sandy said to Kara. "I meant you. What's that on your face?"

"What?" Kara said. "Who, me?"

Like a hitchhiker, Sandy pointed behind herself with her thumb. "You might want to take a quick trip to the bathroom. I'll bring this dashing caballero in to inspect the rest of the troops."

Suddenly Kara couldn't even meet Gabe's eye. She looked down and brought her hand up to cover her face. She pretended to scratch her eyebrow, stepping away as quickly as possible. "Be right back."

She groaned out loud the moment she turned on the bathroom light. Grime! Under her nose, across her cheeks, even above her eyebrows. She looked like a character out of *Oliver Twist*, ready to steal some fine gentleman's pocket watch. But how...?

She glanced down at her hands. Equally grimy. Newsprint! It had to be. She had barely held that stupid newspaper on which Jeremy set the bag o' meat. How had she managed to get it all over her face? Her palms must have been sweaty from nerves.

And then she remembered, as if she were watching herself on TV, that she stood at the kitchen doorway and wiped her hands across her face just before going to the front door.

So close. Just inches away from making a good impression on Gabe. For once.

Oh, Lord, am I really that full of myself that I need humbling every time I'm around this guy? Is that what I'm supposed to get from this?

She sighed and balled up some toilet paper. She attempted to wipe the grime away, but she knew she'd have to completely wash her face to truly remove it. She struggled with the choice: made-up and slightly grimy or plain and clean?

There was a knock at the bathroom door.

"Kara," Ren said. "Come on out. We're all waiting for you."

Kara cracked the door and peeked out. But where was Ren? Kara whispered, "Ren!"

"Come on out," she repeated, at full voice.

Kara was going to kill her! But she opened the door and nearly started crying.

There they stood: Ren, Sandy, Jeremy, and Gabe. All of them had newsprint smeared all over their faces. They acted as if nothing was amiss, and Jeremy handed Kara a slushy, fruity drink in a Flintstones jelly glass.

"To my mates on National Chimneysweep Night," Jeremy said, raising his own glass. "As Honest Abe Lincoln once said, 'The better part of one's life consists of his friendships.' "

Kara sighed and then grinned at him. "You said it, brother."

By the time Jeremy served dessert—a huge tray of miniature cheesecakes from the local bakery—the friends had all been thoroughly loosened by laughter. When Jeremy described his latest dating fiasco, Gabe laughed to the point of tears. Kara had so much fun she was almost not distracted by how fantastic he looked. Almost.

Then she told them all about her poor old car, held together with duct tape and safety pins. "I mean, I didn't have any intention of leaning on that shoddy stuff forever. But I just never got around to actually doing anything about it until the poor thing died."

"I never thought I'd come across someone harder on cars than I am," Sandy said, still laughing. "But, listen, Kara, you know, don't you, that my absent, but much-loved hubby—"

"The Marvelous Rick," Jeremy said.

"—rents cars," Sandy said. "He could have you set up with a rental tomorrow—"

"No!" Both Kara and Gabe said it at the same time and with the same intensity, bringing all eyes on them.

"I...I'm giving Kara rides this week," Gabe said to the suddenly silent group. "In exchange for her letting my sister stay with her."

"That's right," Ren piped in. "That's a good setup there, and we don't need to complicate it, right?" She reached under the table and squeezed Kara's hand.

Sandy nodded. "All righty, then." She popped a mini cheesecake in her mouth and wiggled her eyebrows at Kara.

"Which reminds me, actually," Gabe said, rising and gathering his dessert plate and water glass. "I've really got to get back home. Rachelle's hanging out at my place with Ricco and Jake, but I need to get her back to Kara's."

Sandy said, "Are you leaving with him, Kara? Since he's going to your place anyway?"

Kara knew that made sense, but she also knew she probably shouldn't be alone with Gabe right now. Grimy face or no, he did look like Zorro, and she had always been a big Zorro fan.

"Nope," Ren said before Kara could reply. "I'm going to stay overnight at Kara's place, so how about we follow you, Gabe? We'll pick up Rachelle and save you the trip."

"That's great. Sure," said Gabe. He looked both confused and disappointed.

As they walked to their cars, Kara whispered to Ren, "Thanks.

You're kind of getting the hang of working this no-dating thing, aren't you?"

"You bet, honey. Guess I'm a natural. But I won't be a liar for you, so I hope you've got a spare toothbrush for me."

Kara nodded. "I had Rachelle grab a few from the store yesterday. She bought kiddie toothbrushes. She thought they were funky. I think she's using the Sesame Street one, so yours will be Wonder Woman."

Ren polished her nails against her chest and made a haughty face. "Very suitable, if I do say so myself."

sixteen

I just figured out the drawback to this idea," Kara said, pointing at her feet.

She, Ren, and Rachelle all sat on the couch in pajamas. They faced the television, feet up on the coffee table, with strips of cotton threaded between their toes. In true girly, slumber party fashion, they had painted their toenails when they arrived home from Jeremy's. Rachelle had thrown together a plate of nachos and melted cheese, although she was the only one with an appetite.

"What's the drawback?" Ren asked. She wiggled her toes and flipped through the on-screen television guide, looking for something fun to watch.

"We can't go to bed now that we've done this," Kara said. "We'll all end up with sheet marks on our otherwise fabulous toenails."

Rachelle shrugged and tried to bring a chip to her mouth without dripping cheese on her lap. "So we stay up for another hour or two. We can handle it."

Ren and Kara smiled at each other.

"I remember having that kind of energy," Ren said. She looked at Rachelle. "There's something about spending the day surrounded by thirty second graders that demands more than four hours of sleep a night."

"Man." Rachelle shook her head. "I couldn't sleep enough hours to do something like that for a living. Crazy."

Ren tilted her head. "It does require a certain amount of insanity, I suppose. But I love the job. I only started teaching a few years ago, but I definitely should have done it from the start."

"What'd you do before?" Rachelle asked.

"Investment banking."

"Hmm," Rachelle said, raising her eyebrows. "That sounds like a lot of money."

"Yeah. But it wasn't right for me."

Rachelle made wide eyes at Ren. "How could a lot of money not be right for you?" She looked at Kara for support.

Kara shook her head. "If you're not doing what you were created to do, no amount of money will be enough."

"You like what you do? Personal training?"

"Love it. Always have. It's like helping caterpillars turn into butterflies. I'm still amazed at how people blossom inside when they get healthier on the outside." Kara dabbed lightly at her big toenail. "Still pretty wet."

"Yeah," Ren said. "I think we're going to have to watch at least the beginning of something."

"Ooo." Rachelle picked up the remote control. "I think Orlando Bloom is supposed to be on Leno tonight. Let's watch that." She turned to the channel but muted the sound.

Kara snorted. "Orlando Bloom. You really think he's cute? Both of your brothers are miles ahead of him, looks-wise."

"Eww," Rachelle said, stretching the word into at least two syllables. "And they're my brothers."

Kara laughed. "Good point. I don't have siblings—sorry. Didn't think that through."

"What do you want to do for a living, Rachelle?" Ren asked.

"Yeah," Kara said. "Are you going to college in the fall?"

Rachelle's shoulders drooped a little, and she lowered the nacho she was about to put in her mouth. "Don't make a big deal about this in front of Gabe, okay? He's going to be mad, I think."

"You're not planning on going to college?" Kara asked.

Rachelle lifted her hands in surrender. "I'm clueless about what I want to do. Maybe I'm just cut out to be a wife."

Kara and Ren exchanged glances.

"There's nothing wrong with being a wife," Kara said, "but you might want to treat that job as more than just something to fall back on."

"Do you and Jake talk about marrying?" Ren asked.

"Not much, no," Rachelle said. She ate another glob of chips and cheese. "But I might be interested if he is."

"You know, Rachelle," Kara said, leaning forward to meet eyes with her. "Marriage is a really big deal."

Rachelle said, "I guess that two-egg thing goes for marriage too, just like it goes for dating?"

Both Kara and Ren frowned in confusion.

"Two-egg thing?" Kara said.

Rachelle waved a chip at her. "That part in the Bible you showed me, about the yolks and stuff."

"Oh!" Kara nearly burst out in laughter. "Yoke, you mean. It's not eggs. It's...well, Paul was giving the Corinthians a word picture to help them understand the reason for the rule he was teaching them."

"They didn't understand eggs?" Rachelle asked, an incredulous look on her face.

Ren snorted.

Kara said, "Of course they understood eggs, if that's really something you need to understand. But Paul was talking to them about farming."

Rachelle said, "I thought it was about dating and marriage and stuff."

Kara sighed. Maybe college wasn't the place for Rachelle. She tried again.

"Okay, listen. Paul was trying to tell the Corinthians that believers—people who accept that Jesus was the risen Son of God—should not intermarry with people of other faiths."

Rachelle pointed at her. "Right. That's what I thought. So where's the farming part?"

"See," Kara said, "oxen are used in farming, and the farmer puts this getup on their shoulders to steer them. That thing is called a yoke."

"Ohhhhh," Rachelle said. "I knew that. I think."

"So if you had two oxen and you put the one yoke on them, you'd need both oxen to go in the same direction, or the farming equipment wouldn't work. Imagine if one ox went to the left and the other demanded they go right."

Rachelle nodded. "So if you're a Christian ox, and you marry or date an ox who doesn't go in your direction..."

"There you go," Kara said. She thought Rachelle had made the full connection. She didn't realize she had been leaning forward on the couch, but now she flopped back in triumph.

"Well," Rachelle said, "what if neither of you is a Christian ox? Then you wouldn't have that problem."

Kara grimaced. "To tell you the truth, Rachelle, I'm hoping to convince you of how wonderful it is to be a Christian ox."

Rachelle looked at her, and her expression was hard to read.

Kara chuckled lightly. "And don't think that two nonbelieving oxen will agree on direction, either. When Paul talked about being unequally yoked, it was a given that the first step of hope for anyone was to become a believer."

"There are so many ways a person needs to grow before getting married," Ren said. "Especially spiritually, but also in things like education, life experience—"

"What do you mean, life experience?" Rachelle asked. She got off the couch and sat on the floor at one side of the coffee table, so she could look at the TV when she wasn't looking at Ren and Kara. She stretched her legs under the table and pulled the plate of nachos closer to herself.

"Um, like the kind of experience you get when you go to college, for one thing," Kara said. "If your parents are able to support you when you go to school, it's kind of a safe way to, you know, get your feet wet out there in the world. Get a feel for living away from home and experience making a lot of your own decisions."

Ren took one of Rachelle's chips. "Because once you finish college, you have the added responsibility of having to earn a living."

"Yeah, see," Rachelle said, "if I get married, I can just get right to all that. I can earn a living right away. I'd rather not put it off by going to more school."

"But that's not a good enough reason to get married, Rachelle," Kara said. "And, you know, it doesn't really matter right now that you don't know what you want to do for a living. You can go to college without knowing. Lots of kids do that."

Ren nodded. "Yeah, look at me. I got a degree to work in the financial industry, but I changed my mind later on."

"So why bother going?" Rachelle said. "It sounds like you wasted time getting your degree."

"No. I couldn't have switched to teaching if I hadn't already gotten my degree." Ren leaned forward and dabbed at her polished toenails. "I had a lot of flexibility to make that change because I already had most of the education I needed to teach."

Rachelle fiddled with a chip, tracing a name into the melted cheese on the plate. "I don't know. I really hate school."

Kara removed her feet from the table and leaned forward just enough to see what Rachelle was writing in the cheese. "If Jake weren't in the picture, do you think you'd be more interested in going away to college?"

Rachelle studied her nachos. Her lips formed a sheepish smile.

Then she turned to Kara, looking helpless. "I just don't want to leave him behind, you know? If I go away, he's not going to be able to come see me. He's got, like, no money. Then what will happen?"

Kara nudged Rachelle's knee under the table. "You've got it kind of bad for Jake, huh?"

Rachelle sighed. "He's awesome." Then she jumped for the remote. "Orlando's on!"

She turned the sound back on the TV just in time to hear the studio audience's enthusiastic welcome for the handsome, waving Orlando.

Kara smiled at Ren, who tilted her head and raised her eyebrows.

Kara already felt a protective concern for Rachelle, maybe because she reminded Kara of herself at that age. At 18 she had experienced similar fears. She had even put off college because she was afraid she'd lose her boyfriend.

And how many boyfriends had she had since then? Too many, in her opinion. That was one area of experience she focused upon heavily when she was Rachelle's age.

And to this day she struggled with focus when it came to men. Here she was, regretting the fact that Gabe would be gone for a while when he took the teens back to Florida. And, not only were they not dating, she barely knew the guy!

She looked at Rachelle, a fond smile spreading. She knew how Rachelle felt. But she also knew what was truly important. If only she had more time with her. She closed her eyes for just a moment.

Lord, I feel such a tug to guide her—to You, to better decisions about college, to a healthier perspective about Jake. If that tug is from You, could You please help me out here? Thanks. I love You. Amen.

When she opened her eyes, she noticed Ren watching her.

In a soundless gesture, Ren pointed to herself and then put her hands together, prayerlike. Kara read her lips clearly when she mouthed, "I'll pray too."

seventeen

I haven't seen that hot guy in here lately," Tiffany said to Kara at the gym the next afternoon. She finished brushing her thick auburn hair upside down and flipped her head up, just as though she were on a shampoo commercial.

They were both changing in the ladies' locker room. Tiffany was leaving work for the day, and Kara was just starting.

Kara finished lacing her shoes. "Which guy?"

Tiffany wiggled her shoulders like a go-go dancer for emphasis. "The one I've got my eye on."

"I'm going to need more specific information than that, Tiffany."

Tiffany put her hand on her hip. "Mee-*ow*."

Kara bit her lip. She really had to change her attitude toward Tiffany. "You're right. I'm sorry."

"Whatever. I meant Tall, Dark, and Ooo-la-la. The one you signed up for membership last week."

Kara wanted to act ignorant and keep Gabe all to herself, even if he wasn't hers to keep. He wouldn't go for Tiffany, would he? He had called her...what was it? Scary. And he seemed way too substantial to fall for this...this...absolutely perfect-looking woman. Kara sighed. "I think you mean Gabe."

Tiffany pointed her hairbrush at Kara. "That's him. Where's he been, do you know? I haven't been taken out to dinner for three whole nights. I'm so overdue for some pampering." She looked at herself in the mirror and pouted like Shirley Temple.

Good attitude, good attitude, good attitude. "I think he planned on coming a few times, but he's been too busy."

Tiffany turned sideways and checked her profile in the mirror. She pulled her tank top straight, accentuating her shapely figure. "He thinks he's busy now. Wait'll I get a hold of him."

That did it. "You know, Tiffany—" Kara stopped herself.

Tiffany looked at Kara. She seemed oblivious to how deeply under Kara's skin she had crawled. "Yeah?"

Kara shook her head. "Nothing. Have a great evening." She walked out to the workout area, and her spirits instantly lifted when she saw Ren on one of the treadmills.

"Oh, sister, pray for me, please," she said to Ren.

Ren looked around the gym before responding. "I thought Tiffany wasn't here today."

Kara laughed. "I love you. She's in the locker room, pondering on ways to draw me over to the dark side."

"Uh-oh," Ren said. "One way is walking through the door right now."

Kara followed Ren's gaze and saw Gabe entering the gym.

Kara sighed. "Mercy, he's something, isn't he?" She glanced over at the doorway to the women's locker room. "Poor thing's a dead duck if Tiffany—"

At that precise moment Tiffany walked out, wearing the revealing tank top, a denim miniskirt, and four-inch heels.

"Ugh," Kara said. "Viper at two o'clock."

Ren started laughing. "The dead duck is on the run." She tipped her head in Gabe's direction.

Kara looked and couldn't help but laugh with Ren. Although Tiffany hadn't noticed Gabe yet, he had obviously noticed her. He dipped his head down and picked up his pace toward the men's locker room as if he were dodging bullets.

"Gotta love him," Ren said. "Look at every other guy in this place."

Kara checked around her. Some men had stopped exercising altogether just to gawk at Tiffany. A fellow on the treadmill next to Ren lost his footing and was nearly launched into the vending machine behind him.

Both Kara and Ren breathed with relief when Tiffany walked out the front door. Kara said, "You know, the world feels just a little safer when she isn't around."

Behind her Kara heard Mickey chastising his client. "All right, Gus, show's over. Back to your crunches."

Ren turned off the treadmill. "I needed that laugh. I was a little down today."

"How come? You seemed fine this morning."

"Yeah, well weekends are always the hardest for me." Ren brought her towel to her face and wiped her forehead. "I'm still not quite adjusted to Greg not being home." She shrugged. "It's just easier when I'm at work and more busy."

"Let's do a movie tonight," Kara said. "Something funny."

"Okay," Ren said. "Want me to pick you up when you finish work?"

"Um..."

Ren gave Kara's shoulder a playful nudge. "I know. You want your ride home, don't you?"

"It's innocent enough," Kara protested. "The kids are with him."

They saw Gabe walk out of the men's locker room. He was dressed in a plain T-shirt and gym shorts but was striking, nonetheless.

Ren blew through her lips. "No need to explain, ma'am."

Gabe saw them and smiled. "Hey, ladies." He approached them

and gave Kara's shoulder a brief squeeze. "Thanks for including me in your group last night. I had a great time."

Kara could smell his soap or cologne or something. A delicious smell. She felt her nostrils flair and quickly scratched at her nose so she wouldn't be so obvious.

Gabe said, "Rachelle told me she kept you both up for a while, asking about 'some religious stuff,' as she called it."

Kara's heartbeat picked up with an excitement that actually had nothing to do with Gabe, for once. She loved the fact that, out of all the things they discussed last night, Rachelle seemed most impressed by the "religious stuff."

"You know, Gabe, I think she might be searching right now. It's very cool."

He shook his head. "I'll tell you, that would be great. I haven't been able to get through to her much myself up 'til now."

Ren stepped off the treadmill. "Hey, you should both join us at church tomorrow. Bring the boys too."

"We have a terrific teen group," Kara told him. "Cool but grounded."

Ren said, "Kara and I are working in the nursery during the early service. We could bring Rachelle and have her help us."

"Yeah," Kara said. "Meet you guys at the second service."

"Taking care of babies, huh?" Gabe said. He cracked a wicked smile. "That's the kind of reality Rachelle should experience right now. I like it."

"Great!" Ren said. "It's a date!"

Kara and Gabe looked at each other and then at Ren.

"I mean, we're on!"

Gabe nodded. "Okay. Later, then." He gave Kara a wink and walked toward the free weights on the other side of the gym.

Both Kara and Ren watched him all the way, much as those men had watched Tiffany.

Finally Kara spoke. "Hmm. Dead duck, my eye."

eighteen

Take him! Take him! Take him!"

Rachelle held an undiapered baby boy toward Ren and Kara, who promptly ducked out of the way. They had to sidestep a couple of crawling baby adventurers underfoot.

Kara grabbed a diaper and gently blocked the little fellow's impromptu fountain as Ren took him from Rachelle.

Kara laughed. "Take him?"

Rachelle shrugged. "I didn't know what to do with him. I've never seen anything like that."

Kara squatted down to give a pacifier back to a whining, curly-topped baby in a bouncy chair. "Haven't you ever babysat before?"

Rachelle shook her head. "Not this young. Only a couple of neighbor kids after school once in a while. They weren't in diapers. Yuck."

"Aw," Ren said to the baby boy, who was fresh and diapered now. "You're not yucky, are you, Jonathan?" She stroked his bald head, and he gurgled at her.

"We're almost done, right?" Rachelle said. She rubbed the fronts of her legs, looking ready to run. "Their parents will be getting them soon?"

Kara smiled. "Almost done. But, come on, Connor needs to be changed too." She picked up a little redhead who was happy just sitting in his own stink and watching the other babies. "I'll show you how to do it without risking assault."

"No, no, that's okay," Rachelle said, holding up her hands.

"Don't be a wimp," Kara said. "You're going to need to know this sooner or later, girl."

"Later," Rachelle said. "Absolutely later."

Ren shook her head. "So says the young woman who's eager to skip college and get married right away."

"Yeah, well, I said marriage, not babies." But Rachelle stood next to Kara while she changed Connor. When Kara looked up at her, she nodded. "Okay. I get it. But I'm only going to have girl babies."

Ren laughed. "It's not like God gives you a gift receipt with them, Rachelle."

"Then I'll just adopt."

Kara glanced at Ren, who looked back at baby Jonathan. She touched his cheek with her fingertips. "Maybe."

By the time they found Gabe, Ricco, and Jake in the fellowship hall, all three of the girls were ready for adult company. The youth leader, guitar slung over his shoulder, welcomed the teens into the youth room for their service, and Gabe, Kara, and Ren joined a large group of singles sitting near the front of the church sanctuary.

Kara sat next to Gabe. "I think Rachelle's first encounter with babies has had the desired effect," she whispered in his ear.

He turned to smile at her before she had fully pulled away, and they brushed cheeks. Their eyes met briefly before they busied themselves with the church bulletin, both of them red-faced but smiling.

The worship leader swiftly corrected their focus the moment he began to play the opening music. Gabe seemed to know every song the worship team played, although he didn't sing out very loudly. Kara sensed that singing might not be his strong suit.

And halfway through the pastor's sermon, Kara laughed at the story he used as an analogy for Doubting Thomas. She felt Gabe's shoulders shake as he laughed too. A warmth spread over her and kept her smiling well beyond the end of the pastor's tale.

"I'm glad Pastor Dan was so sharp today," Kara said to Ren afterward. Gabe had gone to retrieve the teens and bring them to the fellowship hall. "Whenever I bring someone new to church, I hear everything through their ears."

"Yeah," Ren said, "I do that—"

"So, Kara," a tall, burly young man said, interrupting them. "Who's the new guy? Is he just passing through, or should I meet him? I mean, I'd like to meet him either way, but—"

"Hi, Mike," Kara said to the singles pastor. "That's Gabe. I'll introduce you. I hope he'll be coming here again—"

"Kara, please tell me that's your new boyfriend," a young woman said, interrupting them again. She had a number of women with her, all members of the singles group. Two young men joined the group within seconds. The talk quickly moved away from Gabe and on to other issues.

But once Gabe returned with the teens, everyone made of point of introducing themselves to him.

One of the youngest men asked Gabe, "Are you and Kara dating?"

"I—"

Kara said, "We're...I'm...you know the thing that Chip and Jennifer told us about a while back? The no-dating thing? I'm kind of doing that. Gabe's a new friend."

The silence that followed seemed eternal. Kara noticed she had started to perspire. Not only did she feel as though she had just served up Gabe on a platter to all the eligible women in the group, but she felt as though she was the only one there who had embraced the no-dating concept.

"I think it's a fine idea," Ren piped in, prompting a grateful smile from Kara.

"Right," said the singles pastor. "A terrific idea, Kara."

"But, Kara," one of the younger men said. "Aren't you in your late twenties? I thought—"

"Gary, did anyone ever tell you that you had the manners of a potbellied pig?" his girlfriend said.

"But I—"

"Just shush, will you?" she said.

"I just thought that was for when you were too young to consider marriage," he said. "Or too broke or something. Or busy with college. I didn't mean you were old, Kara. Really. I'm sorry."

Kara shook her head, but she felt hot enough to melt right in front of everyone. "No problem, Gary."

"I'd never heard of the idea before I met Kara," Gabe said. Everyone else stopped talking and looked at him. "But now I'm intrigued. It actually makes some sense to me. I'd like to learn more about it."

"Gabe's right," the pastor said. "Your age doesn't really matter. It's always smart to get to know a person well before you even consider dating."

He talked for a moment longer, but Kara didn't hear him. She just locked eyes on Gabe as he listened to the pastor speak. She tried not to run over to him and plant a big kiss right on his face.

Ren sidled up to Kara and whispered, "It's all about getting to know him first, right?"

Kara looked away from Gabe to answer Ren. "Yep."

"Well, I don't know about you, but I really like what I just learned about him."

Kara smiled and looked at him again. "Yeah. Loyal."

"Brave."

"Sensitive."

As if he sensed he was being studied, Gabe suddenly looked over at Kara and Ren and smiled. Then he only looked at Kara and his smile changed just a little. There was something almost serious behind it. And just as the word came to Kara, Ren whispered it in her ear.

"Romantic."

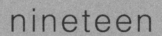

nineteen

A group of the singles from church headed to the local Ruby Tuesday's for brunch after the service.

"You all coming?" Pastor Mike asked Kara and Gabe's group. He had his arm draped over his wife's shoulder. Mike and Helen were a cute couple—he looked like a linebacker and she looked like a little blond gymnast. She was practically lost in his embrace.

"Come with us," she said, her voice all whispery gentle and Southern-sounding.

"I've got the teens with me," Gabe said. He patted his pockets, a slight frown forming.

"Bring 'em along," Mike said. "The bigger the group, the better."

Kara smiled at Gabe. "Can you spare the time?"

"Uh, sure," he said, looking distracted. He stopped to brighten his expression. "Yeah! Definitely." He looked at Kara and Ren. "You're up for going?"

Kara nodded, and Ren said, "I'm starving!"

The teens seconded that comment in garbled unison.

"We'll meet you there," Kara told Mike and Helen as they headed out.

Rachelle sighed. "Gabe, did you lose your keys again?" She put her hands on her hips and looked as though she were his mother.

He blew air through his lips and squinted his eyes, as if he were trying to mentally retrace steps. "No. You know, I think I forgot them in the van. Yeah. I'm sure of it."

"You left your keys in your van?" Kara said. "Isn't that asking for trouble?"

"Yeah. I didn't mean to leave them there, but now that I think of it, I know they're in there. Guess I was too busy thinking about getting in here in time and finding you."

"Excuse me?" An older gentleman walked out of the sanctuary. He dangled a simple key ring from his hands. "Aren't many folks left here, so I thought these might belong to one of you."

Rachelle groaned. "See? You did lose 'em again, Gabe. One of these days we're going to get *so* stuck."

"I didn't lose them," Gabe said, fixing his grin on Rachelle. "See? There they are."

He walked over to the old man and thanked him, shaking his hand.

"What?" Kara said to Rachelle. "He loses his keys a lot?"

Ricco said, "His keys, his movie ticket, his wallet..."

"I don't know what it is with him," Rachelle said. "I think he needs one of those man bags for his stuff."

Kara grimaced but laughed too. "I suppose it must get rough for a guy to carry everything around. But a man bag?" She grabbed Rachelle's arm in pretend desperation. "Please don't suggest that to him!"

She and Rachelle both laughed.

"That's like a purse for a guy, right?" Ren asked.

"Hey," Gabe called out, as he headed back toward them. "I heard that man bag talk, ladies. Not gonna happen." He laughed.

Kara pretended to fan herself. "Good to know."

Kara, Gabe, and Rachelle drove to the restaurant in Gabe's van while the boys rode with Ren.

"Wanna ride in the Beamer," Ricco had said, his voice full of appreciation. Jake was equally eager.

Before they left the church, Rachelle muttered to Kara, "Guess you can't afford a car like that without going to college, huh?"

Kara looked at the car and at the smile on Jake's face. She shrugged. "It helps, that's for sure. Of course, there are more important reasons to go to college." She smiled at Rachelle. "But if that will motivate you to go, I sure won't discourage you."

The group of singles who went to Ruby Tuesday's was huge and took up an entire room. They were just getting seated when Kara's team walked in.

"Man," Rachelle said, "it's almost like a party. And I smell fried onions. Yummy!" She corralled Jake and Ricco to sit on either side of her, and Kara, Gabe, and Ren sat with them at the same long table.

In fact, the decibel level was almost as high as a party's, dropping to silence for only a moment when Pastor Mike prayed over the food. While they ate, Kara and Ren talked with Gabe about some of the subjects they covered with Rachelle the night before. They avoided mentioning her aversion to college, as she had requested.

Before Kara was aware of it, though, Ren had casually involved herself in the conversation on her other side.

Kara and Gabe spoke as quietly as they could and still hear each other over the crowd.

"I agree that Rachelle's a little too focused on Jake right now, but that's normal for girls at her age," Kara said as she sliced a strawberry in half.

"I know. And sometimes for guys too. I remember being Jake's age and thinking I was in love with the perfect woman."

"There are two of us?"

Gabe laughed. He wagged his finger and looked at her as though she were sneaky. "You *seem* perfect, Kara Richardson, but even you must have something quirky about you."

"Like I can't walk a straight line without tripping over a dust particle or running into the only corner in an entire room?"

He smiled. "All part of your charm." He sat back and finished a glass of orange juice.

She returned his smile. "So what happened to the perfect love from your teen years?"

He shrugged. "She ran off to Vegas with a much older man."

Kara frowned. "Wow."

"I think he was at least twenty."

She slapped his forearm. "Oh, stop. Really?"

He nodded. "They got married. I was devastated. Got a little bitter; you know how people do."

"Mm-hmm."

"I took out my resentment on a few girlfriends after that. I'm not proud of how I acted the next few years."

"Well, I was never all mean and nasty like you were," Kara said with a straight face, "but I just didn't give enough thought to my relationships until...really, until the last year or so. I think I was more focused on having fun than anything else."

He nodded and cut into his omelet. "When you told me about the no-dating thing, you hinted at being hurt not too long ago." He glanced around. "That wasn't by anyone here, was it?"

"Oh, good grief, no," Kara said. "I really don't know what I would have done if Paul had kept going to this church."

"So you met him at Christian Chapel?"

"Yeah. In the singles group. He was new to the area. I thought we hit it off really well. It was the first time, as an adult, that I seriously thought about marriage and the future, and all that. I think we were on the verge of discussing it."

"But?"

Kara shook her head and looked down. "This still embarrasses me a little." She looked up at him. "His parents disapproved of me."

He frowned. "What could they have possibly disliked?"

"They were wealthy. Very wealthy. And they thought I was below... their station."

Gabe set his fork down and looked at her as if she had just spoken backward. "What?"

She shrugged. "They wanted Paul to marry a girl who had grown up the way he had."

"Man! And what way was that? Born and bred to look down on everyone?"

Kara chuckled. "You sound just like my dad. He'd like you."

"Would he? Well, then, I like him already!"

They just smiled at each other for a moment and then looked around themselves, as if they might get caught enjoying each other's company too much.

"What about you?" Kara asked. "You said you got all mean and nasty—"

"Excuse me," he said, holding up a finger to stop her. "I don't believe I said I was mean and nasty. Bitter, yes. But mean and nasty—"

"Okay, that was me," Kara said. "But you seem to have overcome your cruel and vicious tendencies." She tilted her head and acted as though she had a microphone to hold up to him. In a fake, perky voice she said, "Tell us, Gabe, how you did that."

He just looked at her, smiling, for a moment. Then he leaned forward, as if he were talking into Kara's pretend microphone and spoke in a DJ-type voice. "Well, Kara, I got my heart stomped on like a tumbleweed in a prairie stampede."

She cracked up, but her face filled with sympathy at the same time. "Oh, Gabe. That's awful."

"Hey, it was the best corny voice I could come up with."

"No, I mean that your heart got smushed. I'm so sorry."

"Yeah. I might actually have a worse dumping story than you do."

She just looked at him and waited.

"I started seeing a young woman who was a regular customer at one of our delis in Miami."

"One of your delis?"

"Yeah. Mom and Dad have three of them down there. But Maggie was a regular customer at the one I managed. And like you said about Paul, we hit it off. But...well, we weren't...I mean, our relationship was pure."

Kara frowned. "And that was a problem?"

He chuckled. "No. At least, not as far as I was concerned."

"Ah. So that must have caused plenty of tension between you."

He snorted. "Yeah. Especially when she got pregnant."

Kara's eyes popped open. "Pregnant!"

She didn't realize how loudly she said the word, but despite all the chatter in the room, Ren and a few other people turned their heads.

Kara weakly raised a hand at everyone. "Sorry." She looked sheepishly at Gabe. "*Really* sorry."

He smiled and shook his head at her. "No problem."

"But, how? I mean, who?"

"One of the deli employees. Ex-employees, I should say. I didn't realize Maggie was coming to visit both of us."

"Wow. And that didn't make you mean and nasty?"

Gabe shook his head. "No. It's funny how God can use awful experiences like that to teach you stuff you already know but don't really want to know. I mean, I had outgrown the callous attitude, especially after becoming a believer. But...well, even though Maggie wasn't a Christian, she was pretty and had a good sense of humor. So I got involved with her anyway. Our values were totally different."

"It's the two-egg thing."

"The what?"

Kara smiled and shook her head. She tilted her head toward the teens and lowered her voice. "Does Rachelle know the details of your breakup with Maggie?"

Gabe shrugged. "I think so."

"Did you ever tell her that part of the problem was your differences of faith?"

He stuck out his lower lip when he thought about that. "Nope. I don't think I've ever told her about that, since she's not a believer yet."

Kara nodded. "Yeah, but she might be ready to hear that part of the story now, anyway. You ought to tell her what you just told me. About how God used that experience to make you stronger. How He can do that. You know, tout the whole guidance thing to her."

He smiled and put out his hand. "It's a deal."

She shook his hand.

Ren glanced over at them. "You two look like partners in crime."

"Partners in something," Gabe said before leaning over to talk to Ricco.

Kara blushed, even though it was her best friend who looked at her as if she knew every thought going on in Kara's head.

twenty

I can't believe how dazzling you looked in that dress," Ren said to Kara as they left the Femme Fit-All Boutique loaded down with shopping bags. "I'd love to be able to wear that shade of green. You looked like a snappy little poster child for spring."

The sun bore down on them, and Kara stopped to put on her sunglasses. "For that price, I'd better look like the poster child for spring and summer. And I'm sorry, but that was just cruel, displaying those shoes right next to the dress." She made a Tiffany-like pout at Ren. "Who can resist fashion coordination like that?"

Ren returned the look, adding a prissy, limp-wristed hand gesture. "You said it, girlfriend. It was to die for, simply to die for!"

Kara laughed. "Stop it. We're attracting attention." She nodded toward the bookshop a few doors down. "Want coffee?"

"You bet. And a big fat chocolate chip cookie."

A tiny bell jingled on the door when they walked in, and Kara closed her eyes to savor the rich smell of coffee and pastry. She removed her sunglasses with a flourish. "Mmm. Make that two big fat cookies."

They placed their order and grabbed a spot in a quiet corner somewhat removed from the steamy thunder of the latte machine. They settled into plush, upholstered chairs. Ren pulled a pale pink blouse from one of her bags and then frowned. "Uh-oh."

"What?" Kara asked.

"Don't I already own a pink blouse like this? Oh, man, I do! I just spent two days' salary on something I already own."

Kara shook her head. "No, you're thinking of your peach-colored blouse."

"Aren't they the same?" Ren said.

Kara gasped. "And you call yourself an art teacher."

"No, I don't."

"Well, you call yourself a teacher. And you teach artsy stuff sometimes, don't you? Anyway, you can't possibly wear peach with the same stuff you'd wear pink with. This was a necessary purchase if I ever saw one."

Ren stared at her for a moment. Then she nodded. "I'll go with that." She smiled and put the blouse back in her bag just as a young man brought them their coffee and treats. Ren glanced around and sighed, contented. "You know, I really backed off of the clothes shopping thing. I think it was about the time I found the Lord. Shopping just doesn't hold the same allure it used to. But every once in a while, there's nothing like new clothes, coffee, sweets, and books. Really caps off the day nicely."

"That reminds me. I hope they have this book I wanted to get. It's by one of those no-dating experts."

"You need to read a book to know how not to date?" Ren asked. She carefully sipped from her steaming cup. "I seem to be pretty good at it, and I haven't read anything."

"You're understandably gun-shy right now."

Ren sighed. "And hopeful, I guess. Greg might change his mind, you know. The Lord might have a miracle waiting for me."

"True," Kara said. She dipped her cookie in her coffee. "Well, from what I understand, this guy's book isn't just about not dating. It's also about how to decide whom to date and when to date. And about your attitude once you start dating."

"Attitude? You coppin' a 'tude after you finally say yes to Gabe?"

"You know, I'd give you a good shove if you weren't face first in a hot drink. There's no guarantee that Gabe and I are ever going to date, although I have to admit that thought makes me a little sad."

Ren's eyes softened. "You honestly think there's a chance you two won't eventually get together?"

Kara shrugged. "I'm the one taking the stance, not him. I mean, he's definitely intrigued with the idea, but there's no reason to expect him to sit around forever, ignoring all the women throwing themselves at his feet."

"But at church yesterday, after the service, he told everyone—"

"Yeah, but I think he was trying to help me out in the crowd since I was taking heat for being the old maid trying not to date."

Ren grinned. "Maybe."

"He has been burned before—"

"Really?" Ren lifted her eyebrows. "By whom?"

Kara shook her head. "I didn't get his permission to tell, so we'd better just leave it at that right now. But, despite having his heart broken, if some terrific young babe comes along, why wouldn't he—"

"Some terrific young babe has come along. Maybe he thinks you're worth waiting for."

Kara chuckled. "He hardly even knows me. That's a lot to expect of a guy."

Ren tipped her head and shrugged.

"Anyway," Kara said, "what I meant about dating attitudes was just how both people approach the relationship once they start seeing each other romantically. Like...their goals."

Ren set her cup down and popped the last of her cookie in her mouth. "Okay. Makes sense. Goals are good. Let's go see if they have the book. And maybe something for me. I'm all caffeined up and raring to shop a little more. You ready?"

After they searched the shelves for a short time, the shop owner approached them. In her floppy, peasant skirt and blouse, she looked like an old hippie from the '60s. A hair clasp, adorned with a small eagle feather, pulled her long gray hair loosely up on her head. She smelled faintly of patchouli and wore a name tag that read *Peace. I'm Lorna.* "Can I help you ladies find something?"

"Yeah," Kara said. "I'm looking for a book by...I think his name is Harris. It's about not dating."

Lorna raised her hand up to her hip and looked at Kara as if she had just answered the riddle of the ages. "You're not serious?"

"Hey, it's not all that weird," Ren said. "There's kind of a new movement—"

"No, no, that's not what I meant," Lorna said. She walked behind the information desk and started tapping keys on the computer. "And the author's name is Harris."

"You've heard of it, then?" Kara asked.

"Not 'til this morning." Then she belted out a one-note laugh. A big, loud "Ha!"

Both Kara and Ren started.

"Isn't that a hoot?" Lorna said. "Weirdest idea I've ever heard of, and you're the second one to ask me today."

"You don't have it in stock, I take it," Kara said.

"Nope, I don't. But I will in two days. I ordered a few copies this morning. One's for a fellow who works down the street, but I'll have extras if you want to give me your name and number."

Kara stopped to think. Gabe's deli wasn't too far away. She looked at Ren. "You don't suppose—"

Ren lightly elbowed her in the ribs and addressed Lorna. "So it was a guy asking, huh? Kinda nerdy looking, was he?"

Kara looked at her and frowned.

"Not at all," Lorna said. "I'd say if this guy is trying not to date, he's going to need a baseball bat. A real man. He must have women chasing him like bears after honey."

"Hmm," Ren said. "You have to wonder why a guy like that would be interested in stepping away from the dating scene."

"Isn't that the truth?" Lorna said. "I asked him about it. I'm old enough I can get away with stuff like that." She winked at them. "You know what he said?"

"What?" Kara blurted. She looked at Ren, who smiled affectionately back at her.

"Yeah, what did he say?" Ren asked Lorna.

"Some woman," Lorna said. "I mean, that's how he referred to her, said she was *some* woman, like they used to say in old movies, you know, when they appreciated a woman?"

"Got it," Ren said, glancing at Kara. "*Some* woman."

Lorna nodded and chuckled. "Apparently he met this woman at his shop—he owns the new deli that's going in down the street. He thinks she's amazing, but she's into this new thing about not dating and just being friends."

Kara tried to keep the insecurity out of her voice. "I guess he thought that was odd, huh?"

"No, I thought that was odd," Lorna said. "But he said he had a lot of respect for this gal. Said it had to be hard for her to say no. Apparently she's quite a looker herself."

Kara and Ren shared a smile.

Lorna pushed a pen and a piece of paper toward Kara. "So you want me to call you when it comes in?"

"Yes, thanks," Kara said. She wrote her information down before she and Ren left the bookstore.

"That was cool," Ren said. They walked toward the parking lot while she dug in her purse for her car keys.

"Very," Kara said, donning her sunglasses again. She grinned freely now that Lorna wouldn't see. It was all she could do to keep from skipping down the sidewalk.

"One thing I wonder about, though."

"What's that?"

"Well, it sounds like you've got Gabe interested in the idea of just being friends."

"Sounds like it."

"And you're each planning on reading that book, so you'll both get good and disciplined about not dating."

"Hopefully."

"So what happens if you get to the point where you think Gabe's the one? And you're ready to take the friendship to a new level?"

"What do you mean?"

"What if he's totally sold on the no-dating idea right about the time you're all set to give dating a shot?"

Kara looked at Ren for a moment. "Hmm."

They reached the car without speaking.

Kara said, "I guess I'll just have to lean on the Lord. On His timing. And on the fact that He might have different people in mind for each of us."

That sounded right to her. And she knew she needed to lean on the Lord no matter what. But Ren's question brought a strange image to mind, and the feeling was unsettling.

Kara remembered a sweater she bought last winter. It was a lovely sky blue angora-wool blend. The first time she wore it, she noticed a loose thread at the bottom. Without much thought she gave the thread a quick pull, trying to break it off. Instead she lengthened it by half. Before she knew what she was doing, she had pulled a small wad of wool away, actually ruining the sweater.

Now she reflected on that feeling—that sense that she had interfered with something nearly perfect, only to watch it swiftly ravel away.

twenty-one

Kara smiled at Gabe when she answered his knock at the door. "You know, you don't have to come to the door for us each morning. We can meet you out front. Your van is pretty easy to spot from the kitchen."

"It's my pleasure," Gabe said. He called past Kara. "Rachelle, let's get going. Don't make Kara late." He sniffed. "Mmm. Coffee smells good."

"Want some?" Kara stepped back to welcome him inside.

He shook his head. "I'll grab some near the shop, thanks."

Rachelle jogged out of the guest room, her sandals in her hand. "Sorry, Kara. Didn't mean to make you late." She ran into the kitchen and emerged with a banana in her other hand. "Okay if I eat this?"

"Absolutely," Kara said, "and I'm not late." She looked at Gabe. "Really. My first client isn't due for an hour."

Rachelle ran ahead of Gabe and Kara, releasing a tiny squeal of delight when she saw Jake in the van.

Gabe snorted softly. "You rescued me, taking her in this week, Kara. I don't think I would have slept a minute with those two in the same house overnight."

"She's a good kid," Kara said. "She's smitten, but I think they're trying not to get too serious."

"Yeah, I get the same impression from Jake, to tell you the truth," Gabe said. "But I'm still relieved she's with you at night."

Just before they reached the van they heard all three teenagers laughing together. Kara smiled and looked at the van. "I'm going to miss this."

"So am I," Gabe said. When Kara looked at him, he wasn't looking at the van. He was looking at her as he held the door open for her.

Her stomach flipped. She was both thankful and disappointed when he looked away and got into the van.

They hadn't driven far before Gabe glanced at Kara and said, "Rachelle told me you've got a problem with your parents?"

"My parents?" Kara looked back at Rachelle, her eyebrows raised.

"You know," Rachelle said, "that great-great-great-aunt lady who wanted—"

"Oh!" Kara said. "Yeah, my Aunt Addie. Or someone's Aunt Addie. She's a distant relative on my mom's side, apparently. She wanted to visit my parents in Florida but she doesn't fly. Or drive. Or take trains, buses, or donkey carts."

"I suppose a Harley would be out of the question," Gabe said.

" 'Fraid so," Kara said. "So she asked my parents to pick her up in North Carolina."

"But Kara's dad had that accident—" Rachelle said.

"The skunky-dog accident?" Gabe asked. "That's the one you told us about at Jeremy's dinner."

"Right," Kara said. "So they asked if I could pick her up and go down to visit them. Which I'd love to do, but—"

"No car," Gabe said.

"No car."

"What was the skunky-dog accident?" Ricco asked, leaning forward and crowding Rachelle back.

"Yeah, I missed that one," Jake said. He, too, jostled forward. The three of them were like puppies in a pet shop back there.

Rachelle said, "I'll tell you later." She brought her finger to her lips, signaling them to keep quiet. She looked at Gabe, anticipation in her eyes.

"Does anyone have a seat belt on back there?" he asked. He frowned in the rearview mirror. The teens all sat back and clicked themselves in.

Gabe tilted his head and said, "Okay, Kara, so here's what I was thinking—or what Rachelle got me thinking. We're planning on heading to Miami on Saturday. We should have the deli ready by then, and I need to get this band of pirates back home."

They had reached a red light, and Gabe looked at her. "What do you think about coming with us? We could take the scenic route through North Carolina. Pick up your aunt. I'd be happy to take you both to your folks' house."

"Awesome idea!" Rachelle said. She leaned forward as far as her seat belt would allow. "Come with us, Kara!"

Kara turned and smiled at her. The idea sounded so fun she couldn't help but feel it was wrong, in the no-dating scheme of things. "I don't know..."

"This many people in the van might be a problem for your aunt, of course," Gabe said. "But she might like the company."

Rachelle stage-whispered, "Built-in chaperones, Kara."

Kara wasn't sure why, but that sales pitch made her blush, especially after Ricco and Jake chuckled. Rachelle did have a point, though.

Then again, three teenagers and a dotty old aunt might not be deterrent enough if close quarters led to too much familiarity between Gabe and her.

"Just give it some thought," he said. "You can decide right up to the last minute."

Kara nodded. "I'll call my parents and see what they think. That's really a nice offer, Gabe. Thanks."

. They moved on to other subjects, but Kara's pulse never quite slowed back down to normal. When they pulled up to the gym, the teens were in the middle of a lively discussion about last night's reality-TV show. They didn't notice when Gabe leaned over to speak quietly to Kara.

"The trip would give us a chance to get to know each other better, don't you think?"

The frankness of his statement and the warmth in his eyes completely startled her. She attempted to keep her cool, nod in agreement, grab her gym bag and purse, and open the car door, all at once. Of course, she failed miserably.

In hindsight she saw God's protective hand in the circumstances. When she misjudged the distance to the sidewalk and fell sideways out of the van, she was blessed by the fact that her gym bag broke her fall.

twenty-two

Mo's whoop of joy on the phone that afternoon told Kara everything she needed to know.

"She's coming to visit!" her mother shouted. "Stan! Kara's coming this weekend!"

"So...so...Mom!" Kara called into her cell phone. "Mom?"

"I'm sorry, honey. Didn't mean to scream in your ear." Mo let out a big sigh of satisfaction. "I am so happy."

Kara smiled. "I am too. But...do you think the trip's a good idea?" She sat down gingerly on a bench outside the gym. She was sporting a new bruise, thanks to her graceful flight from Gabe's van this morning.

"Well, sure it's a good idea. That friend of yours is a gem, honey. You make sure and tell him what a blessing he is."

"Uh...yeah."

Mo laughed. "What am I saying? I'll tell him myself! You think he

126

and the teens will need to stay here overnight? I'll have to figure out where to put everyone—"

"No, Mom, probably not. I...we haven't really discussed anything specific yet."

There was a moment's silence before Mo said, "All right, Kara. Tell me what's wrong."

"Wrong?" Kara echoed. She shook her head. Why didn't she just say it?

"Have you told me everything about this trip?" Mo asked. "Are these people really as kind as you said? I don't want you feeling pressured to—"

"No, no, I don't feel pressured. And yeah, they're all terrific people." She tilted her head. "Well, I can't speak for Aunt Addie."

Mo laughed. "You're horrible. She's a dear old lady, I'm sure."

Kara laughed too. "No doubt."

"So why do you sound so strange about this?"

Kara sighed. "Okay, here's the thing. Gabe, my friend? He's..." She looked around to make sure no one was near. "I'm really attracted to him."

More silence. Then, "You'd rather travel with an ugly fellow, is that it?"

"Mom!"

Mo laughed. "I'm sorry, Kara. I just don't see the problem. Is he already involved with someone?"

"No, not yet. But, well, I'm trying to take it easy on the dating thing."

Kara heard Mo's sorrowful sigh. "Paul really hurt you, didn't he?"

Kara shrugged. "Yeah. But, you know, I've probably hurt people in the past too. I just don't want to...experiment like that anymore."

"Oh, my goodness," Mo said. "I'm never going to be a grandmother, am I?"

Kara rolled her eyes. "Don't be ridiculous, Mom. I didn't say I never wanted to get married. But there's this...movement, I guess you could call it. It's all about taking a more old-fashioned approach to relationships. You get to know each other really well as friends before you even consider dating."

"Well. That does sound like a good idea. I suppose."

"I think it's a very good idea."

"So you're concerned that you'll be tempted if you spend all that time with Gabe traveling down here?"

"Exactly."

"Well, good grief, honey, you're not going to be in the most romantic of settings, are you? A deli van full of people? I mean, it sounds like the ideal situation to get to know him without attacking him or anything."

Kara laughed out loud. "Yes, Mom, that's me, Kara the Vamp. I'll have to make sure they seat belt me in real good."

"Well, you're the one who's worried about self-control. Hey, I know! Ask Rennie to go with you!"

Kara almost argued without thinking. Then she thought.

"Hmm. You know, that's not a bad idea. But..." She quickly counted on her hands to make sure there would be enough seats for everyone. "Yeah. There'd be room for her. And her counselor has been telling her she needs to take some time off and relax."

"Her counselor?"

Kara grimaced. Ren might not have wanted that shared. "Don't say anything to her about it, okay?"

"Of course not. Anyway, there's nothing wrong with getting counseling once in a while. I've done it."

"You?" Kara couldn't believe it. Her mother had always been such a rock.

"When we first came down here. To tell you the truth, honey, I just didn't want to be here. Away from home. Away from you."

Kara bit her lip.

Mo sighed, resigned. "But I'm fine now. A real happy-go-lucky gal. That hooting and hollering I did when you said you were coming down to visit?"

"Yeah?" Kara said, a lump of guilt forming in her stomach. She should call more often.

"I do that all the time, now. Beans on sale at the grocery store. Reruns of *Gilligan's Island*. Your daddy putting the seat down. You know, it's just one big party."

"Is it really that bad, Mom? You sound so lonely."

"No, honey, I'm exaggerating. Actually, I just met up with a great group of women through one of our neighbors. A book club. I think that's going to be lots of fun, really. And your dad and I get out and do things. And we're talking about traveling some, after Dad gets his casts off and finishes his physical therapy."

Kara smiled. "Okay, good. Dad's doing all right, then?"

"He's in ecstasy! Now that he has to stay off his feet, he's fixed every doggoned broken thing he didn't have time for before. I dropped the coffeemaker yesterday and it kind of fell apart. He looked at me with a love I don't think I've seen since our honeymoon."

Kara was laughing.

"But, Kara, I am excited about your coming down. And do ask Ren. I'd love to see her too. You know how much your dad loves her."

"Yeah. I'm getting together with Jeremy and her tonight. I'll ask her then. Jeremy will encourage her to come with me."

"How is Jeremy?" Mo asked, and Kara could hear genuine fondness in her mother's voice. "Has he found a girlfriend yet?"

"This week?" Kara asked. She looked at her watch, even though the gesture was lost on Mo. "Let's give him a few more hours."

Mo laughed. "One of these days, some girl's going to be blessed to find him."

"They find him just fine. They just don't seem to appreciate what they've found for very long."

"Maybe he should try your no-dating thing."

"Yeah. Right after I win the Nobel Prize in Astrophysics."

"Well, I'm praying for that boy," Mo said. "Love him dearly."

"Me too," Kara said. She saw her next client walking toward the gym. They waved to each other, and Kara stood up from the bench. "Gotta go, Mom."

"Okay," Mo said. "I'm going to call Addie and let her know what's going on. I'll have her call you so you can fill her in on the details."

"Tell her not to call me until tomorrow. I need to talk with Ren and Gabe before I know exactly what the plan is."

"Honey, she's going to call you five seconds after she hangs up with me. I'll wait 'til tomorrow before I call her."

Kara smiled. A woman that hyper wasn't going to miss a thing. She'd make a perfect chaperone and would keep Kara and Gabe in line. Kara actually liked that thought.

Then she realized she was already thinking "Kara and Gabe." Like a couple.

She said goodbye, closed her phone, and walked into the gym, certain of one thing.

That little old lady was going to have her work cut out for her.

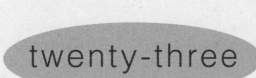

twenty-three

"Of course you're going," Jeremy said to Ren the moment Kara mentioned the trip. He put down the sparerib he was eating and grabbed his napkin, as if he were suddenly too excited to eat.

"Oh, am I?" Ren said, laughing. She sipped her iced tea and winked at Kara.

"You'll come back a whole new you, love."

Kara nodded. "I'm with Jeremy on this one." She pushed her half-empty plate away, hoping to save room for the double hot fudge brownie cake.

Ren set her glass down. "And what's wrong with the old me?"

Jeremy reached over and gently squeezed Ren's hand, leaving a trace of barbeque sauce behind. "Oops, sorry." He used a clean napkin to wipe the sauce away. "The old you is enchanting, Rennie, but you've had a bit of a rough go these past few months. You deserve some fun."

Ren opened her mouth to argue.

Kara said, "But more than anything, Ren, I really want you to go. I need you with me. We'll have fun. And even if we don't, we'll have each other."

Ren smiled at her. "You're probably right. We haven't taken a trip together since—"

"Ever! Think about it. The longest trips we ever took together were one or two women's Bible conferences. Quick little overnight trips. We've never done anything like this before."

"Well, Greg always expected...when we were still married..."

Kara nodded and tried to tread more lightly. "I know. But—"

A big family—happy husband, adoring wife, and gaggle of kids—jostled loudly past their table. Kara glanced at Ren, who looked away from the group and quietly placed her knife and fork together on her plate.

Kara said, "But, Ren, right now seems like the perfect time for us to go." She ticked the points off on her fingers. "It won't cost us a fortune to get there. No one will be too put out if we head to Florida Saturday—that ought to be enough notice. I can reschedule my clients easily—"

"And we have plenty of subs to fill in for you," Jeremy said to Ren.

"I haven't taken a vacation for a long time," Kara said.

"Neither have you, Rennie," Jeremy said.

Ren laughed. "We're teachers, Jeremy. We get two months off every summer."

Kara was reminded of how Ren spent her last summer, shocked and constantly tearful over Greg's leaving.

"And Sandy's all but ordered you to take a break," Jeremy said. He picked up another sparerib. "I don't relish the alternative, love. Walking into your classroom, finding the kids swinging from the chandeliers. And you babbling and drooling because you've tried to work steadfastly through the stress of..."

He trailed off and they all seemed to mentally fill in the blanks with words like "loss," "abandonment," and "divorce."

Ren sighed. "That would never happen. I don't have chandeliers in my classroom."

Kara gave her a fond smile before looking at Jeremy. "And she hasn't drooled in weeks." When Ren laughed, Kara said, "Check with your principal, Ren, will you? See if she'll give you the time off?"

Ren nodded. "I'm pretty sure she will. But have you asked Gabe about my coming?"

"Yep. Asked him when he picked me up from work today. He said the more the merrier. And Rachelle was thrilled. She really enjoyed that evening you stayed at my place."

Ren looked at Jeremy, who had finally finished eating. "Jeremy, maybe you should come too." She gave him a sly grin and glanced at Kara. "We could tag team Kara—make sure she stays on her side of the van."

Jeremy shook his head. "Can't oblige you there, ladies." He wiped his hands clean and looked for the waiter. "There's a charming young sub working at the school this week and next. She might need some assistance. Someone to show her the way we do things."

Both women rolled their eyes.

He opened his hands and shrugged. "What can I say? I live to serve. Just give, give, give, that's me."

"Yeah, okay, you noble man, you," Kara said. "Give me the dessert menu." She cocked her head toward the kitchen. "Somewhere back there is a piece of double hot fudge brownie cake with my name on it."

"Mmm," Ren said. "And it's sitting right next to mine."

Kara smiled at her. "See? Two chocoholics hitting every coffee house from here to Miami. How can this trip fail?"

twenty-four

Kara took advantage of a two-hour break between clients and worked out on the elliptical machine. She usually timed her pace to the music in the gym, but at the moment a dirge-like drumbeat droned out from the speakers. She felt as though she were wearing moon boots.

"Yo, Kara." Her coworker Mickey approached. "Just wanted to let you know I haven't forgotten about the car hunt. I've got some friends in used cars looking for something good for you. Something reliable. And a new car might even be affordable for you. We'll look into that too."

"Thanks, Mickey. I've been kind of lazy about that since Gabe and the kids have been so helpful with rides."

Mickey gave her a knowing smile. "So I noticed."

Kara chose not to acknowledge his ribbing. She glanced at the control panel on the elliptical. "Man, I hate working out on this thing." She picked up her towel and wiped her forehead dry.

Mickey gave her a nod. "Yeah, Becky says the same thing." He adopted an exaggerated New York palooka accent. "But my wife, I tell ya. She's some wo-man!"

Kara laughed. "Yes, she is. I hope I can get my figure back after childbirth the way she did."

Mickey raised his eyebrows. "You got a husband on the horizon?"

With a snort Kara said, "I don't even have a date on the horizon. It'll be some time before I seriously consider husbands and babies."

At that moment she looked up to see Gabe walk in with all three teens. They were early to pick her up. Watching Gabe, Kara felt a quick shiver run through her, although she was far from cold. She saw him scan the club until they locked eyes. He smiled and walked over to her, the teens following like goslings.

She knew she was a sweaty mess, but she figured she needed to be the real Kara if she was going to be honest in this friendship thing with Gabe. She smiled back and turned off the elliptical machine. "Hey, you guys are early! I still have another client in about fifteen minutes."

"Not a problem," Gabe said. "Hey, Mickey, how ya doing?" He and Mickey shook hands. Gabe introduced his siblings and Jake to Mickey before turning to Kara again. "I figured I'd use my free-visit coupons for the teens. Let them work off what little energy they have left today. We won't be ready to leave until you are. That okay?"

"Perfect," Kara said. "Rachelle, come on back with me, and I'll show you around the locker room. I need to go shower off before my client gets here." She looked at Gabe. "Let's touch base in an hour or so."

When Kara reentered the workout area, all freshened up, the first thing she saw was Tiffany hovering around Gabe like a fly around a picnic. Her heart sank. But in Gabe's expression she saw the look one gets when a store clerk has become pushy enough to make you want to just put down the Prada shoes and leave the store.

Then she saw Ricco step between Tiffany and Gabe to ask for Tiffany's advice on the abdominal press machine.

Kara smiled. God would do what He willed with the situation. She let it go and went up front to meet her client.

An hour later Kara walked her client to the door. Gabe had hit the showers. The teens, who quit exercising before Gabe finished, waited near the front desk.

Again, Ricco demanded Tiffany's attention. When Kara sized up the situation more closely, she realized Ricco was enthralled with Tiffany. And Kara wasn't sure what Tiffany was up to, but, boy, was she working it. Even though the front desk separated them, she and Ricco might as well have been slow dancing.

"So y'all are from Miami?" Tiffany asked, opening her eyes as wide as an African bush baby's.

Y'all? When was the last time Tiffany had done an Elly May Clampett impression? But, judging from Ricco's flushed face, the character choice was an effective one.

Kara stood before the sports drink vending machine and acted as though she were trying to decide which to buy. But she was actually trying to eavesdrop. And sneak a peek every now and then.

"Yeah, Miami," Ricco said, "but we've been meaning—or at least I've been meaning—to come up and check out Northern Virginia."

"Oh, as if," Rachelle said, resting against the desk. She looked at Tiffany. "The only reason he came up here was because Jake and I wanted to come visit Gabe."

Ricco tugged his pants up a bit. "Well, that too." He looked at Tiffany and tipped his head toward Rachelle. "You know, a guy's got to look out for his sister. I didn't know if Jake's intentions were honorable."

Even though Rachelle and Jake both shook their heads about him, Tiffany acted impressed. "Well, that's just gallant, isn't it? I'll bet you learned that gentlemanly behavior from your big brother. He seems like a real gent to me."

Ah, there it was. The motive, at last. Kara suddenly noticed her teeth were clenched, and she breathed deeply to relax.

Ricco shrugged. "I guess. But he wasn't too gentlemanly when we got here. He was pretty mad we came up without...well, he seems to think our folks were worried about us, even though we're, you know, practically old enough to vote and all."

Jake said, "Yeah. Gabe's driving us all back to Miami on Saturday."

Kara's stomach suddenly tightened, as if something bad were about to happen. She looked at the group and tried to interrupt the flow of the conversation. "Guys, maybe we should wait outside for—"

"Yeah," Rachelle said. "Kara's coming on the trip too, aren't you, Kara?"

There you go. That was the bad thing.

Tiffany turned on Kara and shot her a look of extreme indignation. "Why, I had no idea you were so close."

The woman was a dead ringer for the evil queen Malificent.

Kara wondered why she felt as though she had done something inappropriate. She found herself stumbling for words. "Well, it's not like—"

Tiffany gasped and looked at Ricco. "I just got the craziest idea!"

Ricco gave her his rapt attention.

"Why don't I go too!"

"What?" Rachelle said, standing more upright. "Why would you want to go?"

Kara loved that girl.

"You'd go with us?" Ricco asked Tiffany. As if he were five and she were Spiderman. "Oh, yeah!" he said. "You should so go with us! Awesome idea, right, Kara?"

They all turned to look at her. She hoped her expression didn't say *How about we bring a swarm of killer bees instead?*

"But, why—"

Tiffany interrupted and spoke to the teens rather than Kara. "See, my folks live in South Carolina, where I'm from," Tiffany said. "And

I've been planning on visiting them, only I just despise traveling alone. I do so love people, you know!"

Rachelle said, "But we're going all the way to Miami. You aren't planning on going all the way down, are you?"

"Oh, no," Tiffany said. "I'm just going as far as my folks' place in Florence."

Kara stood in shock, hearing just two words: "I'm going." Tiffany had actually invited herself along. Kara blurted, "But Ren and my Aunt Addie are coming. There won't be room for you."

"Sure there will!" Ricco said to Kara. "Gabe's van seats eight!" He counted off names on his fingers. "That's you, Gabe, Ren, Aunt Addie, Rachelle and Jake, and Tiffany and me!" He looked at Tiffany and said, "Perfect!"

"What's perfect?" Gabe asked.

They all turned as he joined them, his dark, wavy hair still damp from his shower. Kara looked at him helplessly and felt she should warn him, but she didn't know how.

Tiffany switched from Elly May Clampett to Marilyn Monroe, her persona of choice for Gabe. Her voice was suddenly whispery light. "Your charming young brother invited me to join you on your trip this weekend!"

Kara almost stomped her foot on the ground. Ricco had done no such thing! Tiffany had bamboozled her way into this.

"But..." Gabe said. He scratched his head. "I mean, that's a nice idea, but I don't think we'll have room since we're picking up Kara's aunt on the way down."

Tiffany simply looked at Ricco, who dutifully piped up with his annoying finger counting again.

When Ricco finished, Gabe looked at him for just a moment as if he wanted to throttle him.

"Now, you understand," Tiffany said to Gabe, "that I'll only be able to be with you as far as Florence. In South Carolina. But my folks will be delighted. I just can't tell you how grateful I am, Gabe."

Gabe's smile looked pasted on. "Well, sure. My pleasure."

Kara doubted he was pleased, but she still hated hearing him say that to Tiffany.

As Kara and Gabe followed the teens out of the gym, she heard Tiffany whisper to Gabe the very thing he had said to Kara the other day.

"We'll finally have a chance to get to know each other better, won't we?"

twenty-five

Well, that does it," Ren said to Kara, late the next day. "I'm definitely going on the trip now." She paid the girl at the snack bar and handed bags of movie popcorn to Kara, Jeremy, and Sandy. "It's going to take both of us to keep Gabe safe if Tiffany goes."

Kara just grimaced and nodded.

"Too right, love," Jeremy said. He handed the movie tickets to the young man as the women filed past him. "She's a huge bother and all that, but Gabe's resistance might take a hit with that kind of proximity."

The women stopped abruptly, as one unit, and looked at him.

Sandy took her hand out of her popcorn and pointed a buttery finger at Jeremy. "That's not the most helpful comment, Jeremy. From what I saw of Gabe at your dinner party last week, the man's a pillar of virtue. Someone as obvious as that Tiffany chick isn't going to crack his armor." She glanced at Kara. "Don't let Jeremy worry you, hon. You take that trip and have a great time."

"Yeah, take Sandy's advice," Ren said. She smiled at Sandy. "I know I am. She's a good counselor."

Jeremy shrugged and led the way to their seats. "Yes, you're a crackerjack counselor, Sandy," he said over his shoulder, "but I've got all of you beat in the being-a-man department. I'm simply telling you that you'd best make sure Tiffany doesn't get a chance to spend too much time alone with Gabe on this trip."

Kara snorted. "I think Ricco will see to that. Poor kid's obsessed."

They took the best seats in the sparsely populated theater. They were early and didn't expect a large crowd at the weekday matinee. A Muzak version of "Light My Fire" played, and the lights hadn't yet dimmed.

"Anyway," Ren said. "The trip is going to be chaperoned to the max. Tiffany doesn't stand a chance. The whole point of Kara's going was for an ultra-chaperoned chance to get to know Gabe better."

Kara said, "Well, that's not really the whole point—"

"Yeah, I know," Ren said, "you're picking up Aunt Addie too—"

Kara gasped. "Oh, man! I just remembered! I was supposed to talk with her after I knew more about the trip. She's probably freaking out if she tried to call me at home. She left Mom a gazillion messages the last time she couldn't reach her."

A cheesy ad for a carpet store suddenly blasted from the screen and they all fell silent. When it ended, a more soothing real estate ad began.

Jeremy leaned forward to talk with Kara. "Isn't Gabe's sister at your place? She'll catch Addie's phone call, won't she?"

Kara shook her head, glancing at her watch. "No. They're probably all still working at the deli. Not everyone works teachers' hours or has the flexibility of my schedule."

"Shame on you!" Ren said. "Teachers' hours! I'll be grading papers and doing lesson plans the whole time I'm eating dinner tonight."

Jeremy held up his popcorn. "This is dinner for me. Book reports. Blimey."

Sandy spoke over the ad for candy and popcorn. "I guess we could have picked a better afternoon for a movie. I didn't realize how busy you two were. It's just not often that Michael's after-school events go on long enough for me to fit a movie in like this."

Jeremy waved her off. "Surely you jest, love. I know I'm pleased with this plan. Even cancelled a racquetball game for this. An afternoon movie with three ravishing women?" He raised a rakish eyebrow. "I'd have to be daft to miss—" but then he broke into a harsh squawk, like a large bird. He quickly grabbed his soda and drank before having to cough several times, hard, and drink again. He lifted his bag of popcorn by way of explanation.

Heads turned.

"Are you okay, Jeremy?" Kara asked. Clearly he had choked on a sizable popcorn kernel. But they could all tell he was fine, and none of them could help laughing at his awkward struggle. He even hammed it up a bit, once he was more comfortable.

Sandy said, "You are way too suave for me, dude."

"See, if Gabe had been here," Kara said, "I would have been the one making a fool of myself over popcorn."

"I say," Jeremy said. "I don't know if I like being called a fool." But he followed his complaint with several more inane-sounding hacks, obviously appreciating the women's laughter.

"That's not all that unusual, you know, Kara," Sandy said. "The awkwardness in front of someone you're attracted to."

"I swear I've never been all that clumsy before. I mean, I'm actually a pretty athletic woman, but I can't seem to relax around Gabe. It's like I'm always going to trip over my own toes or get spinach between my teeth when he's around."

"It's just because you care too much about how you'll come across to him," Sandy said. "Old issue, believe me. And too many people misread that concern for love. Years ago, this French guy, de la Bruyere, said something like 'We judge when love begins and ends by our embarrassment when we're alone with each other.' Something like that."

Kara chuckled. "Well, there's certainly been plenty of embarrassment."

Sandy sipped her soda and wagged her finger. "But that's not love. That's infatuation. Lasting love happens when you get beyond that stage with a person—survive the embarrassing times—and still want to be together."

Sandy nudged Kara's shoulder with her own. "Give it time. You'll stop being thrown by his gorgeous looks. The fabulous, funny Kara we all love will take over again."

Ren nodded. "Well, then. I guess it makes sense for you two to get to know each other really well before going out together. By the time you guys date, you'll be all comfy and bored and sick of looking at each other's faces."

Kara started laughing.

Jeremy said, "Maybe you should wait for him to get bald or fat or something before you date. Think that might help?"

"We might not date, remember?" Kara said. She was still smiling when she said, "Anyway. I kind of like bald men." She looked at Ren and Sandy. "Captain Jean Luc Picard on *Star Trek*, how about him?"

Ren and Sandy gave a collective sigh of appreciation.

"Ah, well, yes," Jeremy said. "He's a Brit, of course. He's got that going for him as well."

Sandy added, "And, Jeremy, if you ever get a chance to meet my man—"

Like a Greek chorus, the others said, "The Marvelous Rick."

"You'll see that bald and portly can be devastatingly attractive." She patted Kara on the knee. "You just give it time. You'll get used to being around Gabe. The trip to Florida will be good for that."

The lights dimmed and the movie previews started, so they all stopped talking. But Kara didn't notice the first few minutes. She still had the Florida trip in mind, and she suddenly pictured a justice scale as it balanced the trip's participants. On one side she pictured her parents, Ren, the teens, and Gabe (who was the most adorable, fat, bald man ever). On the other side was Tiffany, voluptuous as always, causing the scales to tip heavily in her favor. Kara wasn't sure yet where Aunt Addie belonged, but she knew she was going to need a whole lot of something to keep the scales from being overwhelmed by Tiffany.

Kara looked at Ren, who was looking at her. Ren smiled and whispered, "Don't worry. The trip's going to be great. When I pray about it, I get the feeling everything's going to work out."

Kara returned her smile. The trip needed a whole lot of something. Prayer just might fit the bill.

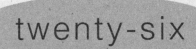

twenty-six

"Wow," Kara said aloud when she arrived home and saw her answering machine messages. "Only two."

She kicked off her shoes, turned on the machine, and started for the refrigerator to get a bottle of water. She stopped when she heard Gabe's voice instead of Addie's. A smile formed on her lips.

"Hey, Kara, it's Gabe. Give me a call when you're home from the movie. I don't want to bring Rachelle over too early. Love ya. Bye."

Kara's smile dropped, along with her jaw, as she spun to face the answering machine. Had she just heard what she thought she heard? The next message interrupted her thoughts.

"Carol?" the withered voice asked. "Is that you, Carol? Morine's girl? This is Addie—"

Kara stopped the machine and backed up to Gabe's message again. Hit play. Yep, there it was. "Love ya. Bye." "Love ya." She played it five times, as if it might change. Every time: "Love ya."

Kara grabbed her phone and hit her speed dial to Ren's cell phone.

"Mercy, girl, I'm barely out of your neighborhood—"

"Listen to this!" Kara said. She held the phone near the answering machine and played Gabe's message again before bringing the phone back to her ear. "Did you hear that?"

"Did he say 'love ya'?" Ren asked.

"What do you make of that?" Kara asked. She pulled her blouse away from her body, suddenly aware she was perspiring.

"I wonder if he even knows he said that. Did he call back afterward?"

"No. The only other message is Addie calling Carol."

"Who's Carol?"

"I think she's me. Addie's got my name wrong. I'm starting to think she might end up on Tiffany's side of the scale."

"Tiffany's side of what?"

"Nothing." Kara flopped down onto the couch. "Just a weird picture I've got in my head when I worry about this trip."

Ren sighed. "I told you not to worry about it. Pray about it when you start to worry. And Addie's probably going to be fun. You're such a pessimist, Carol!"

Kara laughed. "Okay. But what do you think about Gabe's 'love ya'?"

Another sigh from Ren. "As much as I'd like to say he's madly in love with you and just waiting for you to come to your senses and marry him—or even go on a date with him—I think it shows he's feeling really comfortable with you. Like he would be with a...um..."

"If you say 'sister,' I'm going to have to hurt you."

Ren chuckled. "I was going to say 'friend.' But this is what you want, right? I mean, not the sister part, but you want to get beyond infatuation and into reality, don't you?"

Kara thought a moment. "Yeah. You're right. If that's how he's starting to feel, I should welcome it." She sighed. "Rennie, I can't believe how hard it is to change attitudes like this. After years of looking forward to that special tingle, and then to suddenly strive for something so platonic."

"Hey, there's nothing that says you have to give one up for the other. You're really just slowing the process down a little bit. I'll bet that tingle is especially terrific when it happens between best friends."

Kara's smile returned. "I like that idea. And I guess that is what Gabe's 'love ya' sounded like—something you'd say to a close friend. Maybe I'll stop klutzing all over the place when he's around if I can get used to the idea. Stop being thrown by his gorgeousness, like Sandy said."

"There ya go."

Kara got up, walked into her kitchen, and got a bottle of water. "Okay, well, let me give my friend Gabe a call to tell him to bring Rachelle over."

When Kara called the deli, Rachelle answered. "Oh, hey, Kara. We're just about finished here. You back from the movie?"

"Yep. Come on home anytime."

Rachelle giggled softly. "That's sweet, your calling it home. To me, I mean."

Kara smiled. "I love having the company. You're always welcome here."

Kara heard a muffled sound and then Rachelle's lowered voice. "I heard what he said to you."

"You...pardon?"

"I heard Gabe say 'love you' on the phone."

Kara raised her eyebrows. "Oh. Well. 'Love *ya*,' actually. I think he was just being friendly, Rachelle. Comfortable, you know? As if he were talking with you, for instance."

Rachelle made a little singsongy sound that suggested deeper knowledge than Kara had. "I never heard him say it before." She said it "be-foh-or," and it sounded as though she was saying, "I don't *think* so."

"Kara, he doesn't talk like that to me."

Kara couldn't help it. She felt a tingle. Then she heard Gabe call out something to Rachelle.

"It's Kara," Rachelle called back to him. "Let's go." Then she spoke into the phone again. "We're heading over, okay? Gabe says we'll bring dinner, so don't cook anything."

Kara sat for a moment after she hung up the phone. Who was right about Gabe? Ren or Rachelle? And if Rachelle was right, what did that mean? Wasn't it awfully soon for Gabe to have developed feelings of love? Yes. Too soon. He must have meant it as a friend.

Either way, Kara felt certain she was doomed to walk into furniture and shoot soda out of her nose around this man until she chilled out about him. If only he would get a pimple on the end of his nose or something.

She shook her head and picked up the phone. Addie would get her mind off of Gabe's apparent perfection.

"Why, Carol, I was afraid I'd miss your call," Addie said immediately, even though Kara had only managed to say, "Hi, Addie—"

"I was out," Addie said, "shopping for some sensible shoes for the trip."

Kara chuckled to herself. Addie had to be in her eighties. How wild and wacky could her everyday shoes be? "I'm glad I caught you at home, Addie. But it's Kara."

"What is?"

"My name isn't Carol. It's Kara."

A moment's silence. Then, "You'd think Morine would know that, wouldn't you? Her being your mother."

Kara's eyebrow arched. "So, Addie, we'll be coming to pick you up, probably late afternoon on Saturday. There are actually going to be quite a few of us. I hope that's all right with you. There'll be seven—"

"Yes, yes, I know, seven more hours to drive from my place to Morine's."

Kara stopped and frowned for a second. "No, I was going to say— Well, actually, there might be another seven hours to Mom and Dad's. But I meant people."

"Well, of course you meant people," Addie said. "Your parents aren't monkeys, are they?"

"No, I mean there will be seven people in the van."

"What van?" Addie asked.

"The one we'll be traveling in. We're driving to Florida in a van, okay?"

"Oh. Okay. Like a moving van."

"Um, not exactly. This will be more comfortable than that. And smaller. It's a deli van."

"A what?"

"A deli van." Kara tried to sigh without breathing into the phone. "You know, from a place where you get deli food."

"Uh-huh. And that's what, from some other country, that deli food? Is this like one of those foreign jalopies that's going to fall to pieces as soon as we cross the American border?"

Kara pulled the phone away from her ear and looked at it, as if the phone itself were insane.

"Addie. We're not going to be crossing the American border. We're only going to Florida. We can get there without leaving the country. And I think the van is made by General Motors. American." Kara stopped to ponder. Did she dare try to explain deli food to Addie?

"Got it," Addie said, in an apparent moment of clarity. "I'll be ready for you. Seven of you. In a deli van."

"Yes!" Kara said, a smile of relief spreading.

"Will there be pudding?"

Kara's smile faded. What in the world was this woman going to be like in person? Kara glanced at her watch. Gabe and the kids would be here soon. Both Kara and her home needed a little tidying up. She was a firm believer in good communication, but she saw no other recourse.

"Yes, Addie. There will be pudding."

twenty-seven

Gabe and the teens arrived shortly after Kara hung up with Addie. They brought dinner from Bacchus, a little Greek restaurant in Leesburg. They brought enough for Alexander the Great's troops.

"Oh, my goodness," Kara said when they spread all the dishes out on her dining room table. "It's a good thing I don't have anything in my fridge. I think we're going to need the room unless you boys are willing to take the leftovers home with you."

Gabe laughed. "What makes you think there'll be leftovers? You've never seen teenaged boys eat before?"

"Don't worry," Jake said. "Ricco and I can eat plenty."

"Yeah," Rachelle said, "you should see how much Jake eats. I can't believe he's still *so* not fat."

"Well, it sure smells great," Kara said. "I think we'll all reek of garlic for the next week or so. Let me get some plates and stuff."

Gabe followed her into the kitchen. "You okay with us barging in with dinner?"

"Are you kidding?" She looked over her shoulder at him. "I'm a pushover for a ready-made dinner. I've never been much of a cook myself."

"That's fine with me," Gabe said. He took plates from her as she removed them from her cupboard. "I'm big on cooking."

He walked out of the kitchen, and Kara caught herself grinning into the silverware drawer. That was a we-could-be-a-couple comment if she'd ever heard one.

She had to snap out of this. They were not a couple. Just a couple of friends.

She counted out forks and knives and tried to will the giddy expression from her face.

Gabe walked back in as she turned around. He returned her grin. "What are you so happy about?" he asked, clearly eager to feel as happy. He picked up one of the chairs from her breakfast table. "Okay to take this out there?"

She nodded. "I think I'm starting to look forward to the trip."

She saw relief cross his face. "Oh, good. I was a little concerned that I had cornered you into coming along with us. I didn't mean to. It just seemed to fit. You know, the circumstances."

"That's exactly how I feel."

They walked out of the kitchen and saw Rachelle and Jake flipping through the CDs in the living room.

"Wow, Kara," Jake said. "You have a lot of cool-looking groups I've never even heard of."

Kara chuckled. "Most of those are Christian groups."

"Oh," Jake said. The drop in his excitement level was palpable.

She walked over to him. "Don't be so quick to write 'em off, mister. I think you'll really like some of them. After dinner I'll play a few for you. We could play them now, but some of them are a little too rowdy for dinner music."

Jake looked at her. "You mean you want us to be able to talk at dinner?"

Kara laughed. "You make that sound like such a bad thing."

Gabe spoke in a low, dull tone. "Talk good. Make learn speak like people civilized. In shoes. And pants."

Rachelle laughed. "Talking's cool. We can do that, Jake. I talked all night with Kara and Ren last week." She glanced at her bare feet. "And got some totally hot nails out of it too." She smiled at Kara. "But I think I need to freshen 'em up before Saturday."

Kara pointed at her. "Tomorrow. First thing."

"What're you looking at over there, Ricco?" Gabe asked. "Why don't you come help me get water for everyone?"

Ricco was sitting on the carpet with one of Kara's coffee table books. "Yeah, okay." He put the book back on the table and stood.

"You like Winslow Homer?" Kara asked Ricco.

He nodded and followed Gabe toward the kitchen. He stopped at the doorway and faced her. "Specially the seascapes. Even the calm ones are kinda emotional."

"Passionate," Kara said.

"Yeah," he said, bobbing his head like a surfer dude.

Rachelle went to the dining table and tried to make some order of all the food, plates, and silverware. "There's not much art that Ricco doesn't like."

Jake went to help Rachelle. "Yeah. He's going to college for art, ya know. In the fall."

"No, I didn't know that," Kara said. She was about to call into the kitchen to ask Ricco about it when Rachelle suddenly waved her hands at her, silently. Kara looked at her, confused.

"Don't start talking about college," Rachelle whispered. "Not while Gabe's here."

As Gabe and Ricco walked back in with glasses of water, Jake looked at Rachelle but didn't comment.

"I think that's everything, right?" Gabe asked.

Kara laughed and looked at the packed table. "And we do mean everything!"

They sat, and Kara saw all eyes turn to Gabe. She smiled at him; he had obviously become the prayer spokesman of his group in the short time the teens had been visiting. They all bowed their heads.

"Gracious Father, we thank You for this food. We thank You for our family and friends. We thank You, especially, for the gift of salvation. We ask for Your protection on our trip this Saturday, Lord, and we pray for those friends who are not here tonight but will join us then: Ren, Aunt Addie, and...and Tiffany. Amen."

The boys had barely "amened" before reaching for containers of food. Kara was awed by their speed and efficiency in transferring kabobs, pilaf, and grilled zucchini to their plates.

Gabe put his hand out to Kara. "Would you like me to serve you, Kara? I've been exposed to these Miami piranhas before. I know how to maneuver amongst them without incurring too many injuries."

"Oh," Ricco said. He put down the container he held in his hand. "Sorry, Kara."

"Yeah," Jake said. "Didn't mean to be rude."

She laughed and shook her head. "Not a problem." Kara looked at Rachelle, who was unfazed by the flurry of activity. "I think I missed a lot in not having brothers."

Rachelle snorted. "And I've missed a lot of meals in having brothers."

"You have not," Ricco said. But he slowed his pace and even passed a couple of containers to Kara before taking anything else for his own plate.

Gabe gave Ricco a nod of appreciation before looking at Kara again. "Have you talked with your aunt yet? Is she expecting us on Saturday?"

"Yes. At least, when I hung up with her she was expecting us. But she's also expecting pudding, so I'm not sure how on the ball old Addie is. We might need to give her another call or two to remind her as we get closer."

"Did you say pudding?" Jake asked, no inflection whatsoever in his speech.

"I did."

"Okay," Jake said, digging into his food.

Gabe and Kara both looked from him to each other, amusement in their eyes.

"So I take it she's a little eccentric?" Gabe asked.

"Maybe," Kara said. "Or just confused. Or forgetful."

"Is she at least nice?" Rachelle asked.

"She seems very nice."

"As long as she's nice and not a mean old lady like Mrs. Flint back home," Rachelle said. She pushed her veggies to one side on her plate. "You remember Mrs. Flint, Gabe?"

"Yes, I do," he said. "I think she had some pretty hard knocks in life, poor thing." He looked at Kara. "She blamed God for them. And other people. Made her pretty harsh."

Ricco looked up from his meal long enough to ask, "Who should she have blamed?"

Gabe shrugged. "I think it's human nature to look for someone to blame. Kind of helps us feel more in control if we can point at someone and say, 'This wouldn't have happened to me if you had blah blah blah.' "

Kara nodded. "Blame really doesn't help, though. I still feel awful after blaming someone for something."

"Me too," Gabe said. "In my few mature moments I try to reflect long enough to see if there's anything I could have done differently, and then I try to move on and make better choices or avoid whatever caused my problem. That kind of thing."

"So you don't think Mrs. Flint did that?" Rachelle asked. "She didn't reflect?"

"I don't know, Rachelle," Gabe said. He lifted a shoulder. "Maybe she did but still didn't find any answers."

"Hmm," Kara said. "We don't always get to know why bad things happen."

"But we don't always know why good things happen, either," Gabe said. "You don't hear many people asking 'why' about the good stuff, do you?"

Rachelle thought about that for a while before smiling. "I guess we usually think the good stuff is because of something we did, right?"

Ricco laughed. "That's human nature too, huh?"

"I think so," Gabe said.

"That makes us seem so selfish," Jake said. "Or self-centered."

Kara liked that Jake didn't sound defensive when he said that. He sounded humbled.

When they had almost finished dinner, Kara went into the kitchen. "Who wants coffee?" she hollered out to the dining room.

She wasn't aware that Gabe was right behind her until he answered her at the same decibel level. "I'd love some, thanks!"

Kara jumped and turned. Then she looked at him with exasperation.

Gabe had carried some empty containers in to throw them away. Now he stood there and chuckled. "Sorry."

She gave him a dirty look, but she didn't really mean it. "Really. You're sorry."

He pointed at her coffeemaker. "Hey, I thought you were trying to cut back on the caffeine."

"Since when?"

He studied her as he spoke, the slightest hint of skepticism in his voice. "Since you told me the first day I met you. At the deli. Remember? When I offered you coffee?"

She almost gasped. The babbling she did after gushing about how gorgeous he was. Somewhere in there she had said something about coffee.

She studied him right back. "Oh. Of course I remember." They had started talking to each other like two spies in a bad movie. "I changed my mind," she said, her eyes haughty.

"Did you?" He mirrored her silly, suspicious look.

"I did. And I thought you were only bringing dinner over tonight."

He feigned a cornered look. "Yeah. So?"

"So," she walked dramatically over to a separate bag from the Greek restaurant. "What do you call this?" She thrust the bag toward him.

He squinted his eyes, villain fashion, and grabbed the bag from her. "Ha! That's baklava!"

"Ha!" Kara answered back. "I know!"

Melodrama dripping from his face, he asked, "But, but, how?"

She gave him as shifty a look as possible and hissed, "I peeked!"

"Man, you guys are so weird," Jake said.

Kara and Gabe turned abruptly and chuckled at the face Jake was making about them. He had a stack of dirty dishes in his hands.

Kara stepped forward and took them. "Thanks, Jake," she said. "I really appreciate it."

She sounded as though she were talking about his help with the dishes, but to some extent she was talking about his interruption of her game with Gabe. She was having way too much fun. And for that last line of hers she had been somewhat in his face, for effect. But now that they had stopped joking, she realized how warm she had become playing the game.

They had pretended they were in a poorly written scene. But now Kara felt as though the scene might just have ended with a kiss.

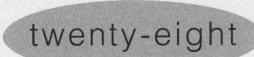

twenty-eight

If she knew how to, Kara would have whistled a happy tune when she got home from work the next day. Tomorrow's trip was just around the corner, she had rescheduled all of her client appointments without a snag, and the only thing left to accomplish this evening was her packing.

"Give me a call tonight," Ren said as she dropped Kara off, "if you think of anything you need." Ren had driven Kara home so that Gabe and the teens could put the final touches on the deli decor.

"Yeah, and you too," Kara said. She gave Ren a big grin. "This is going to be so much fun! I'm suddenly really excited."

"Hey, does Gabe's van have a CD player?" Ren asked. "I'll bring a bunch of music."

"Yeah. Bring stuff the teens might like. Something cool but about Christ, okay? I played a bit of what I have for them last night, and they seemed pleasantly surprised. I'd like to use this trip to convince them—especially Rachelle—that Christianity doesn't have to be rigid and dull."

Kara was a woman of purpose when she walked through her front door. After emptying the contents of her gym bag into the laundry basket, she began pulling together outfits that would travel well.

When she opened her storage closet to retrieve her suitcase, her eyes alighted on a box that had been on her closet shelf since the day Ren gave it to her. "Wax Warmer," it said. Ren had given her the leg waxing kit as a little gift shortly after the two of them had spent time complaining about their least favorite beauty regimens.

"I hate shaving," Kara had said, "but I feel like I have to do it regularly because of how often I'm undressed around clients."

"Oh, really?" Ren had said.

"You know, in the locker room. Female clients, of course, but still."

So, the next time they got together, Ren gave the Wax Warmer kit to Kara. "This way you won't have to go to the salons for waxing, but you'll hardly ever have to worry about shaving again."

Although the idea had merit, Kara simply hadn't gotten around to using the kit. She glanced at her watch and then at the nearly complete pile of clothes she had chosen to pack before looking at the waxing kit again.

Why not? She had pulled out several pairs of shorts for the trip. If she waxed now she wouldn't even have to think about nubs while she was traveling.

She unpacked the kit and scanned the list of dos and don'ts. Very simple. An idiot could do this. She chuckled to herself, remembering the movie scene when Mel Gibson attempted leg waxing. Of course, his experience was a disaster, but that was just because it made for good comedy. All Kara expected was pain. But *brief* pain.

While the wax warmed, she went into the living room and turned on her CD player. "What's good waxing-slash-packing music?" she said aloud. She chose a Motown compilation CD and doo-wopped her way back to her bedroom.

She changed into an outfit she wouldn't miss should she destroy it with dripped wax. An old black-and-yellow-striped tank top that made her look like a bee. And the only pair of shorts she'd ever bought through a catalog. Hot pink, they had looked adorable on the six-foot Swedish supermodel. On Kara they pooched out like loaded diapers.

She finished packing. By the time she had everything but her toiletries in her suitcase, the wax was ready.

"It's go time!" Kara said to the mirror, laughing at her outfit. She opened the package of muslin strips and laid them out in a neat, organized row. She removed two of the Popsicle sticks from the box, in case she needed more than one to spread the wax. "Mel Gibson, eat your heart out," she said, proud of her feminine forethought.

She peeled back the lid and was surprised by the wax's apparent thickness. She had expected something more like melted candle wax, but this looked like her grandma's molasses.

A dense glob of wax was still stuck to the lid. Even though Kara held it aloft over the can of wax, the glob seemed to be cooling. "Oh, no you don't." Kara grabbed one of her Popsicle sticks and tried to scrape the glob back into the melting pot. But the wax was thicker than expected, and the lid almost flipped out of Kara's hand. With catlike reflexes, she grabbed the lid before it hit the wall or bathroom counter.

But now it was in her palm, sticky side down.

"Ick." Kara used her clean hand to pull the lid away and set it down messy side up. She gingerly set the waxy Popsicle stick on top of the lid.

Kara had spilled drops of candle wax on her fingers in the past, so now she did the same thing she did then. She rubbed her hands together to roll the wax away.

But the wax didn't roll away. It spread. It spread like honey and stuck like tree sap.

"Does it smell like sap?" Kara said, still talking out loud. Not yet panicking. She brought her hand to her nose and promptly placed a healthy dollop of wax on her nose.

"Oh, for goodness' sake." She grabbed a tissue and tried to wipe the wax off of her nose. The wax spread and grabbed at little pieces of tissue, so now Kara's nose looked as though it had been tarred and feathered by a village of very tiny people.

And the remainder of the tissue was stuck to Kara's right hand.

"Forget it!" Kara said. Waxing wasn't worth the hassle. Shaving was a breeze compared to this. She took the hand towel off the rack—it wasn't one of her favorite towels, anyway—and tried to wipe the entire mess off of her hands.

The hand towel was a deep forest green.

And now so were Kara's hands.

She rubbed her hands together, again hoping to dislodge the ever-growing mass of matter adhering to her palms, but the stuff just kept moving around.

Now Kara felt the slightest bit of panic. She was trying not to swear or even think of a swear word. As always, she stopped to pray at that moment.

Lord, I know You're way too busy and I shouldn't really bother You over this stupid thing, but could You maybe help me out here? And please help me to be patient. Amen.

She thought of Ren and went to the phone. She used a pencil to touch the speed dial buttons.

"Ren, you've got to help me here," she said, the second her friend answered. "I'm coated with wax and tissues and towel fur. And...Oh! Good grief, I've got a pencil stuck to my right hand and the phone is glued to my left."

There was a dead silence coming from Ren's side of the phone before Ren finally said, "Is that you, Aunt Addie?"

"Ren! This isn't funny! How do you get this horrible wax stuff off? The leg waxing stuff. I've got it all over the palms of my hands. I can't get it off."

"Kara, you're supposed to put it on your *legs*. Even Big Foot doesn't have hair on his palms."

"I never got that far. I spilled, sort of."

"Wasn't there a bottle of wax remover in that kit?" Ren asked.

Kara shook her head as she walked back to the bathroom to check. "No. I don't think so. Just the warmer, the wax, the muslin, and the sticks. Hang on a second."

She attempted to nudge the box on its side, using the backs of her wrists. She wanted to read the contents list, just in case they had stiffed her on the wax remover. The box tilted at a readable angle, but in the process Kara's hands picked up two strips of muslin and the wax warmer's one-year warranty card.

"Oh!" she huffed. She brought the phone hand back to her ear, shaking the strips of muslin away from the earpiece. "I'm growing, Ren. It's getting worse. I'm like Edward Scissorhands."

Ren sighed. "All right. I'll be right over. Just don't touch anything else unless you want it stuck to you."

Kara looked at her hands and then she looked at her nose in the mirror. "I've figured that out, yes."

Ren said, "What's that playing on your stereo?"

"Motown."

"I can tell it's Motown. Is it Martha Reeves or the Supremes?"

"Will you please get in your car and get over here?"

"Okay! I'm coming," Ren said. "Grouch."

Kara heaved a great sigh. She returned to the living room and tried to hang up the phone, but it came right back up with her hand, the strips of muslin dangling like wilted streamers. She knew she could peel it all away if she really tried, especially if she incorporated her feet or her knees in the effort. But considering the mess she'd already made, she feared she'd end up stuck to the curtains or the carpet by the time Ren arrived if she didn't just wait patiently for that wax remover.

While she stood there she began to see the humor in her situation. Why worry? Ren was on the way over. Relax.

And she did just that. She faced the stereo speakers and began to dance to the music—Gladys Knight and the Pips were singing about the grapevine now. She even pretended the phone was a mike, and she started belting the song right out there with Gladys.

If the song of the moment had been a ballad, something soft and mellow, she might have heard when Rachelle rang the doorbell. Or when Rachelle let herself in with the key Kara gave her. Or when Gabe called her name the first time.

But it was on a particularly well-executed spin and dip that Kara faced Gabe and the teens, all of whom stood in her foyer, holding yet another night's carryout dinner and staring with varying degrees of amusement on their faces.

After her initial yelp of surprise, Kara imagined what they were looking at—her fuzzy nose and furry green hands, adorned with an assortment of accoutrements. Plus, she was dressed like a circus clown, and her legs needed shaving.

When she finally reacted, Kara considered how proud Sandy would be of her. Instead of making matters worse by trying to fake any semblance of dignity, Kara looked right into Gabe's smiling eyes. And laughed.

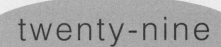

twenty-nine

Kara," Tiffany snapped the following morning, "I certainly could have used a little more warning about space limitations for this trip."

Tiffany's perfectly glossed lips were pursed with disapproval as she checked out the back of Gabe's van. Gabe had parked in the gym's lot, where everyone agreed to meet.

"You knew we were going to be a good-sized group, Tiffany," Kara said. She took a bite of one of the bagels Gabe brought that morning. Otherwise she might have pursed her lips right back at Tiffany. It was all she could do to keep from suggesting that Tiffany undo the invitation she had wrangled out of Gabe and just stay home. The perfume Tiffany had poured on this morning almost needed a seat of its own, as it was. "We all have to scale back on what we're bringing."

Tiffany sighed and looked at Kara with pity. "That's easy enough for some of us, I'm sure. But there are a lot of people looking forward to spending time with me back home. I can't very well entertain in..." she gave Kara's jeans and T-shirt the once-over "farm wear."

Rachelle stuck her head out the van window. "You know, Tiffany, they had lots of storage space on the Greyhound bus the guys and I took to get up here. I hear the same about Delta and United."

Tiffany looked up at Rachelle, ice in her eyes.

Gabe closed the van's hood. "Oil's fine, water's fine, gas is fine. Everyone ready to roll?"

Kara pointed behind him at Ren, who had just pulled up. "Almost."

Gabe looked around at Ren as she got out of her car. "I almost forgot about you, Ren!"

"Well, thank you very much!"

Gabe went to take her small travel bag and they chuckled together. "You ladies are going to have to make sure I don't drive away from a rest stop and leave anyone stranded."

Behind the van, Tiffany threw her bag to the ground. "This is impossible! Somebody had better help me here."

Gabe headed in her direction.

Ren said to Kara, "Yeah. We wouldn't want Gabe to leave anyone stranded, now would we?"

Kara handed Ren a bagel. "I find these are quite effective in keeping your mouth too busy to say anything you're itching like crazy to say."

In moments Tiffany's voice floated gently in their direction, having undergone an amazing transformation from petulant to flirtatious. "Why, Gabe, I should have asked you in the first place. You're a genius."

"Oh, brother," Ren said. "Doesn't she realize he heard her stomping around like a two-year-old just a second ago?" She looked at Kara, who pointedly took a big bite out of her bagel.

"I'm riding shotgun," Ricco called out. He and Jake had just walked over from the grocery store with two shopping bags of snacks and water.

Kara smiled. Ricco had obviously taken extra care with his grooming this morning. When he was scheduled to work at the deli, he was scruffy and uncombed. Today his hair was perfect, and his face was as smooth as polished granite. Kara hoped he didn't get terribly hurt when Tiffany finally let him down.

"I'll help you navigate, Gabe," he said.

Gabe nodded as he closed the back of the van. "All aboard, then!"

Rachelle and Jake piled into the back seat and Ren and Kara into the middle. Tiffany looked at the empty seat next to each couple as if choosing between endless torture and a swift death. Clearly there was only one seat she considered acceptable, and Ricco had beat her to it. She gave Ren and Kara a pained smile and sat next to them, pulling the door closed.

As they drove away and Tiffany buckled up, Kara lifted the bag in her lap and said, "Bagel, Tiffany?" She was determined to be gracious while Tiffany was with them. Only yesterday she told Ren, "I swear, I'm going to put my best foot forward and turn the other cheek whenever necessary."

But she felt nothing but tension in her feet and cheeks when Tiffany curled her lip and said, "Ugh. Who needs those empty calories? You trying to fatten up your behind, Kara?"

Kara couldn't help it. She had to watch the girl squirm. She smiled at Tiffany and said, "Gabe brought them for us."

Kara had to give Tiffany credit—she was a world-class quick-change artist. The curled lip softened, the eyes and eyebrows lifted, and sweetness and light emanated from her as though the sun itself was her backdrop.

"And what a *dear* gesture that was, Gabe," she said. "But, my goodness, only a big, active man like yourself can afford to eat like that and keep such a marvelous shape. I simply can't indulge and hope to look like I do for long."

"Well, help yourself if you change your mind," he said.

Ricco turned in his seat and said, "You look perfect, Tiffany. Really." For Ricco she giggled. "Oh, go on."

Kara and Ren just stared at her for a moment. It was as if Tiffany switched personalities every other second, regardless of who heard the difference. She was Beast Woman with Kara and a coquette with Gabe and Ricco, and the contrast was to be ignored.

Kara started to doubt her own powers of perception. Could it be that Gabe hadn't heard any of Tiffany's spoiled or snide comments and had only heard the ones Tiffany meant him to hear?

As Kara settled back in her seat, she got her answer. In the rearview mirror, Gabe caught her eye. The amusement in his was clear. Without speaking a word, he communicated that he was absolutely aware of Tiffany's falseness. Kara smiled back just before he looked straight ahead and focused on the road.

They had driven for about an hour when Tiffany startled them all by shouting out an emphatic expletive. Gabe glanced quickly over his shoulder at her before looking back to the road. All other eyes—wide with shock—focused immediately on her. She was rummaging through her purse and seemed to have lost all concern over image, especially when she repeated the word several times in a kind of vulgar panic.

Rachelle whispered to Jake. "Whoa!"

"Uh, Tiffany," Gabe said. "I should set some rules right now about language while we're traveling—"

"Oh! I-I know," she said. She seemed to be struggling to get breathy for Gabe's sake, but she couldn't quite pull it off. "I'm sorry. But...oh, I hate to ask you to do this, but we have to go back."

"What?" both Rachelle and Jake said from the backseat.

Tiffany's color heightened. "I forgot something. We have to go back to my place."

"Is it something Kara or I might be able to share with you?" Ren asked.

Tiffany's jaw went tight. "No. It's...something personal."

Kara leaned forward and opened her purse enough for Tiffany to see inside. "I have—"

"No!" Tiffany said. "It's not..." she lowered her voice. "It's not a girl thing." She sighed heavily. "Look, Gabe, I just need you to take me back. Please."

Gabe glanced at her again and nodded before looking for a place to turn around. "Okay."

"Good grief," Rachelle said.

Ricco said, "Give it a rest, Rachelle."

The ride back was quiet in comparison to the first hour's travel, but that was mainly because Tiffany seemed so uncomfortable. When they got closer to town and Tiffany had to give Gabe directions to her apartment, she gave them in a subdued voice. Not an ounce of flirtation or self-confidence.

Kara and Ren exchanged glances, and Kara shrugged gently.

"That's my place right there, number 511," Tiffany said. "I'll be right back down."

She jogged toward her building but stopped midway and ran back to the car to retrieve her purse. "Sorry. Be right back."

The moment she entered her building, Ricco got the talk going.

"Wow, she's so...mysterious!" The awe in his voice made Rachelle laugh.

"Mysteriously weird, maybe."

"Be nice, Rachelle," Gabe said.

"But, dude," Jake said, "the girl's kinda strange, you gotta admit."

Kara sighed. She had never envisioned a role as Tiffany's defender, but she spoke, nonetheless. "Well, who isn't strange once in a while? The only reason this seems strange is because we don't know what it's about."

"Yeah," Ren said. "There's probably a rational explanation for why we had to drive all the way back here instead of stopping at a Piggy Wiggly on the way down to replace whatever she forgot." She looked toward Tiffany's building. "Even Tiffany wouldn't want this kind of attention."

Rachelle said, "I swear, if it's a tube of her favorite lipstick or something—"

"Aw, man, don't even say that," Jake said. "I will go freaky on her over that, for sure."

Kara knew he'd have to stand in line, if that's what this detour was about.

Gabe said, "Hey, Kara, maybe we should call Addie and let her know we'll be late getting there."

"Good idea," she said. When she was unable to get a clear signal on her cell phone, Kara stepped out of the car. The signal seemed better, but she thought maybe she should go ask Tiffany if she could call from her home phone.

She knew, though, that part of the reason she wanted to go that route was in the hope that she'd be able to determine why Tiffany brought them all the way back home.

Just as Kara was about to give in to temptation, Addie's answering machine kicked on, and the signal was fine.

"Hello?" Addie's voice rang out. "Hello?"

It was as if Addie recorded the message thinking someone was supposed to answer back. "This is Addie. Stepped into the twentieth century and got me an answering machine."

Kara smiled. Twentieth century.

"So tell me—" At which point the machine produced the beep that signaled its readiness to record.

Momentarily confused, Kara hesitated before speaking, but she finally filled Addie in on the fact that they'd be late. "Don't worry about a thing, Addie. We'll be an hour or two late, but we'll be there."

Kara closed her phone and looked toward Tiffany's building just as Tiffany stepped out. She was still stuffing in her purse whatever she had retrieved from her apartment.

It was definitely too big to be a lipstick. But Kara couldn't tell what it was. As Tiffany approached, Kara looked at her with eyebrows raised, as if she were willing to hear anything Tiffany wanted to share. But Tiffany simply gave her a curt nod as she passed her and got into the van, leaving a trail of heady perfume in her wake.

Kara returned just behind her, and they started their trip for the second time.

No one said anything for a number of miles, but Kara could feel a dense fog of curiosity in the van that lingered even after the group's astonishment at Tiffany's next words.

A slight frown forming, Tiffany asked, "So how far out of our way do we have to drive to get this Addie woman?"

thirty

Kara leaned forward in the middle car seat and pointed her finger straight ahead, between Gabe and Ricco. "There. That lime-greenish house at the end of the street. Middle of the cul-de-sac. That's the one Addie said."

"Whoa," Rachelle said. "That is one nasty color of green. For a house, I mean. It wouldn't look so bad on..." She paused and then shook her head. "No, that color wouldn't look good on anything."

Ren laughed. "Well, it's sure easy to spot, isn't it?"

Gabe pulled into the driveway, and they all piled out. Gabe walked next to Kara as she approached the front door. "I'm glad we stopped for that late lunch," he said. "I'm starting to get hungry for dinner already."

Kara rang the doorbell. "So am I. That backtracking really dug into our progress." She checked her watch.

Gabe said, "I was actually figuring we'd need to break the trip into two days, anyway. Maybe we should go ahead and see if there's a decent hotel here and make a fresh start tomorrow."

She nodded. "I'll give Mom and Dad a call and let them know not to expect us."

Gabe gave the doorbell a try too. "Yeah, I'll call my—"

The front door swung open and an elderly man stood there wearing nothing but a T-shirt, boxers, and a frown. He aimed a fried chicken leg at them like a tiny sword of justice. And he had no teeth.

"This had better be important!" he said, his voice rather high and nasal. "You made me miss the final round of *Jeopardy!* Now I'll never know the winning answer." He jabbed the chicken leg toward them for emphasis.

"You mean the winning question, right?" said Ricco, who had walked up behind Gabe and Kara. They turned around and frowned at him.

"What?" asked the old man.

"If you're watching *Jeopardy!* they've already given the answers. The contestants are supposed to—"

"Ricco," Gabe said, "I don't think that's important right now." He looked back at the man. "We're sorry to disturb you, sir."

"We were told Addie lived here," Kara said.

The man had apparently grown hungry. He started gnawing on his chicken leg while he stood there, but he stopped at the mention of Addie's name. "Who? Annie?"

"No," Kara said, but then she and everyone else turned at the sound of Addie's voice from the front step of a house two doors away.

"Yoo-hoo, Carol!"

At a glance Addie looked much younger than Kara expected. Her hair was cut in a cute gray bob, and she was wearing black pants and a bright red swing jacket.

"Her?" the old man said to Kara. "She's the one who sent you here?" He stood on his tiptoes, as if his voice would thus carry farther. "Annie Rogers, how many times have I told you to stop sending people to my house?"

She called back, "It's *Addie*. Addie Rogers. Oh, for goodness' sake, Elmo, put some pants on!" She waved Kara and company over. "Come on, kids. Thanks, Elmo. I'll take it from here."

The old man shouted, "It's *Elmer*, doggone it—" but then he abruptly stopped. He held up his hands in an attempt to keep everyone quiet. The chicken leg was much worse for the wear. A lively theme song filtered out from his house.

Elmer's eyes widened and he announced with excitement to no one in particular, "*Wheel of Fortune!*" He turned swiftly and slammed the door behind him.

While Gabe, Kara, and Ricco stared at the closed door, Ricco said, "Hey, man, let's not get chicken for dinner tonight, okay?"

"Come on, Carol," Ren called from the driveway. "Let's go over to Annie's. Leave poor Elmo alone."

"Yeah," Rachelle said. "And Big Bird too."

Kara shook her head at Gabe. "Everyone's a comedian."

Gabe smiled. "Why don't you go try to make some progress with Addie. I'll move the van out of Elmer's driveway."

Tiffany was just ahead of Kara in reaching Addie's front step.

"So!" Addie said. "Are you Carol?"

Tiffany snorted. "You mean Kara? No, I'm Tiffany."

Kara and Ren reached Addie together. Kara extended her hand to the diminutive woman in wire-rimmed glasses. "I'm Kara, Aunt Addie. I'm so glad to meet you."

Addie pulled her close and gave her a warm hug. Kara hugged her back and felt how very small she was under that jacket. And she smelled like baby powder.

Kara finished introducing everyone else just as Gabe walked up.

Addie looked at Gabe and said to Kara, "Is this splendid man your husband, then?"

Before Kara could answer, Tiffany laughed out loud. "Hardly!"

Gabe took Addie's hand and said, "I'm Gabe. Kara and I are very good friends."

Rachelle looked at Tiffany and then at Addie, and said, "*Very* good friends."

Kara asked, "So why did you send us to Elmer's house, Addie? We could have come straight here."

Addie waved her off. "Nonsense. Look at this house. Beige. Boring. It's much easier to find that tacky green house. It's like a lighthouse. A beacon in the night. Then I call 'em on over here."

"Ah," Kara said, as if that were a perfectly good reason for inconveniencing poor Elmer.

"Besides," Addie said, "he likes the visitors."

"You sure about that?" Gabe asked.

Addie nodded. "Yep. Told me so himself." Then she looked off in the distance for a moment. "I think he told me so." She shook her head as if too much information was floating around at once. "Anyway."

She stepped back into her house. "Come on in, all of you. Let's figure out where you're going to sleep tonight."

Ren stopped midstep and looked at Gabe. "Oh, are we done driving for the day, then?"

Gabe gave her a quick nod before addressing Addie. "You can't possibly put us all up here," he said. "We can stay at a hotel and come get you in the morning."

With a sigh, Tiffany said, "I vote for that idea. I need a good night's sleep tonight. And hot running water."

Addie looked at Tiffany for what seemed like a long time. "Got three full bathrooms here, honey."

Tiffany said, "That may be, but—"

"And four bedrooms."

"But—"

"And a rollaway bed."

Rachelle said, "Awesome! Slumber party!"

Addie turned a brilliant smile on Rachelle. "With popcorn, you think?"

Rachelle smiled right back. "Rock on, Aunt Addie!"

"Do what?" Addie asked, her smile fading a little.

"All right, then," Gabe said. "We'll bring the bags in so everyone can unpack enough to get through the night. And then I'm taking everyone out to dinner. Okay with you, Addie?"

"I love going out to dinner!" Addie said.

Kara gave Ren a smile. Addie was turning out to be delightful.

As Gabe, Ricco, and Jake went to retrieve the bags from the van, Kara asked, "Do you have any favorite restaurants, Addie?"

"Too bad you folks weren't here a month ago. You just missed the Ham and Yam Festival. Big to-do here in Smithfield, I'll tell you what."

Tiffany rolled her eyes. "Pity."

For the second time, Addie studied Tiffany openly. Then she said, "You know, don't you, that attitudes are contagious?"

Tiffany arched an eyebrow at Addie. "Is that right?"

"You bet," Addie said. "And you don't want me to be catching your attitude. It looks bad enough on a pretty young thing like yourself."

Tiffany looked indignant. "Well, I—"

"I know, I know," Addie interrupted. "You're sorry and will try harder to be pleasant. That's a given, honey. You're a grown-up, after all."

And with that she turned her back on Tiffany and said to Kara, "There's a reasonable family restaurant just five miles away. They'll have something for everyone there."

She regarded Kara's expression, which was similar to Ren's at the moment. "Why you two look so pleased you could laugh. Good for you!"

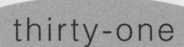

thirty-one

Kara snickered as Rachelle and Addie walked into the living room carrying a large bowl of buttery smelling popcorn and a stack of smaller bowls. "I cannot believe you two are going to eat more after that huge dinner."

"You wait and see," Addie said. "You'll all be nibbling at it in no time."

"I'm with Addie," Gabe said. He helped her set everything down on the coffee table and popped a couple of kernels in his mouth, giving Kara a quick wink in the process.

At Kara's side, Ren gave a tiny sigh of appreciation for Gabe. Kara looked at her and smiled, even while raising her eyebrows.

Ren chuckled and muttered to Kara, "Oops. Did I do that out loud?"

Ricco and Gabe talked loudly enough together so that only Ren heard Kara's response. "You did. But I can't say I blame you. You'd better sit in my seat in the van tomorrow. I'm having a hard time not staring at his eyes in the rearview mirror."

Ren said, "Speaking of eyes, I need to get my contacts out. I don't suppose you packed a pair of tweezers, did you?"

"You use tweezers to remove your contacts?"

"No," Ren said, laughing. "But I get these stupid eyelashes that hang down sometimes and get all stuck in my bottom lashes. They bother my eyes like crazy, especially when I have my contacts in. The only thing I can do is pluck 'em out. I didn't think to pack my tweezers."

Kara shrugged. "I just grabbed my cosmetics bag when I was packing. We can go see if my tweezers are in there."

Before they left the room, they heard Addie arguing with Jake and Ricco, who were looking through her small collection of videotapes.

"No, let's watch *It's a Wonderful Life*," Addie said. "I've got that one in there."

"Isn't that a Christmas movie?" Jake asked.

"With sappy stuff?" Ricco asked.

"Yep. It's the perfect movie for the Christmas season."

Jake scratched his head. "But it's June."

Addie frowned and looked upward in thought. "June?"

"Yeah," Ricco said. "It's summer."

"Oh," Addie said, obviously still processing. "Yeah, that's right. Summer."

Ricco pulled a movie out of the cabinet. "How about *The Great Escape*? This looks like it might be good."

Addie shook her head. "No. That was one of Willard's. My husband's. I feel like seeing snow. It's too hot for any of those other movies."

"We're watching *Wonderful Life*," Rachelle said. "This is Addie's house, and she wants to watch it. You guys can go in another room and talk about football or blowing things up if you want."

Gabe said, "Oz has spoken, boys." He reclined in a big sofa chair. He already had his own bowl of popcorn in hand and looked completely relaxed.

Kara and Ren headed for the largest guest bedroom, where Gabe and the boys had placed all of the girls' luggage. Neither Kara nor Ren thought much about the fact that the door was closed before they walked in.

"Oh, my goodness!" Ren said.

Tiffany jumped and uttered a quick yelp before anger filled her eyes. "Did it occur to either of you to knock?"

Both Kara and Ren were dumbstruck by the fact that Tiffany held a full syringe in her hand.

With an angry sigh, she returned to the position she was in when they entered. She stood on one leg, facing the bed, and propped her other leg on the bed.

"Stop staring at me," Tiffany said. "And close the door!"

"But, Tiffany..." Kara said.

Ren turned and closed the door on all the lively voices outside. She would have locked it, but there wasn't a lock on the knob.

"It's diabetes, okay?" Tiffany said. She spoke with the defensive voice of someone guilty of a crime.

"I'm sorry, Tiffany," Kara said. "I didn't know."

Tiffany shot the insulin into her leg, which made both Kara and Ren wince.

"Yeah, well, I don't want anyone else to know, all right?" She wrapped the syringe and threw it away before putting her kit back in her purse.

"That's what you forgot this morning?" Ren asked.

Tiffany nodded and sat on the end of the bed. "I had just picked up a refill from the pharmacy and forgot it on the kitchen counter."

Kara sat down on the bed. "I hope we weren't too hard on you about that. Sorry."

Tiffany looked uncomfortable with the compassion. She spoke to the carpet. "It's why I sometimes don't teach my aerobics class. The exercise is good for me, but my levels are just off sometimes." She looked up at Ren and Kara.

They just nodded, which Tiffany seemed to misunderstand.

"Yeah, so I'm not quite as perfect as everyone thinks I am," Tiffany said. "So what?"

Kara shrugged. "Yeah. So what? There's nothing shameful about it. And these days diabetes is really manageable, right?"

"Well, if you tell Gabe or anyone else—"

"Gabe?" Ren asked. She shot a quick glance at Kara before looking back to Tiffany. "What does he have to do with this?"

Tiffany's expression went smug. She finally seemed herself again. "I happen to have it on very good authority that he's interested in me."

A knock on the door startled all of them. Rachelle's voice came through the slowly widening crack in the door. "You guys coming out or not? The movie's going."

Kara loved this movie. Especially the scene she had always considered ultra romantic, when Jimmy Stewart and Donna Reed share a phone together and realize how attracted they are to each other. How in love.

Kara frowned. There was no way Ricco would have told Tiffany that Gabe was interested in her. Neither would Rachelle. And Jake was usually oblivious to just about everything around him. Had Gabe said something? Had he and Tiffany had some romantic phone-sharing-type epiphany Kara didn't know about?

Ren put her hand on Kara's arm and made a face that said, "Don't believe it." She gave her head a barely perceptible shake before opening the door. "We're coming right now," she told Rachelle. She and Kara found tweezers in Kara's luggage and then followed Tiffany back into the living room.

But Addie didn't last much longer after the women joined everyone in front of the TV. Her clear blue eyes struggled to stay open. "I need my beauty rest," she said. She pushed herself up from the couch. "You kids go ahead and watch the rest of the movie."

"First, let's figure out who's sleeping where before Addie goes to bed, gang," Gabe said. "I don't want us making noise moving suitcases around later." He stood while Rachelle paused the movie.

Addie said, "There are twin beds in two of the bedrooms and a queen in the other. The rollaway's in the laundry room, and you can just set it up here in the living room."

"Twin or rollaway for me," Ricco said.

"Ditto," said Jake.

"I'll sleep on the rollaway," Gabe said. "You two guys sleep in one of the twin rooms. Let's go move your bags there." He looked at the women as he walked out. "Okay, ladies? Could you work out the rest of the logistics between yourselves? We'll move your bags for you."

"Sure," said Kara. She naturally assumed she and Ren would share a room, just because they were old friends. But then she realized who that left for the last available room. Rachelle and Tiffany. Like putting two Fighting Beta fish in the same bowl. Actually, Kara couldn't think of anyone who would be thrilled to share a room with Tiffany.

"Um, Tiffany—"

"I'll sleep on the couch," she said.

Kara thought she might have made that suggestion because she'd been rude to every woman in the group. But there was also the chance that Tiffany wanted to sleep in the living room because that's where Gabe would be.

"Listen," Kara said to Ren, "why don't you and Rachelle share the queen bed and Tiffany and I can share the twin bedroom."

"Works for me," Rachelle said.

"I said I'd sleep on the couch!" Tiffany snapped.

Kara was shocked. Tiffany *was* trying to sleep near Gabe.

As if on cue, Addie walked back into the living room. She was wearing pink pajamas and slippers. It looked like there might be bunnies on her pj's. And she wore a hairnet, light as a spider's web, to protect her hairdo.

Addie looked right at Tiffany. "Aren't you a dear to offer to sleep on the couch? But there's a much more comfortable twin bed available for you. That's where you should sleep."

"But I—"

"Yes, dear," Addie said. "You want to make sure that everyone is comfortable. But that good-looking young Gabe will be sleeping in here. It would be inappropriate for me to expect you to sleep on the couch. I'd only expect that of a complete floozy."

Gabe and the boys walked in. "Okay," Gabe said, "just tell us where to move the suitcases."

Tiffany and Addie were still looking at each other. Tiffany tried to look fierce. Addie yawned.

Tiffany looked away and exhaled her frustration. "Kara and I are in the other twin room."

Ricco said, "Okay, let's hurry up and move their stuff to their rooms. I want to see what happens next in the movie."

"Ha!" Rachelle said. "And you thought it would be sappy."

"Hey, I got into the guy," Ricco said. He shrugged. "Sometimes people surprise you. You know, they got more going for them than you thought they did."

Kara watched Addie shuffle out of the room and nodded. "Indeed."

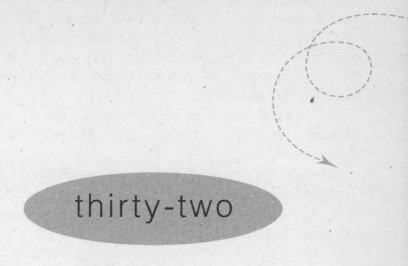

thirty-two

Kara awoke suddenly, as if a bugler had belted reveille directly into her ear. One second later she heard a gargantuan snore coming from Tiffany's bed.

Kara sat up and rubbed her eyes. She pulled back her covers, stretched out her foot, and gently jiggled Tiffany's bed. Tiffany turned onto her side while making a choppy sound not unlike the snort of a full-grown pig at chow time. Then she fell silent.

Kara flopped back down but hadn't even pulled her covers up before the snoring started back up again. Blowing air through her lips, Kara got out of bed. She picked up her Timex from the nightstand and pushed the little light-up button. Five o'clock.

She was dying for something to drink. Last night she had succumbed to the buttery popcorn, and all the salt had taken its toll while she slept. She remembered seeing orange juice in Addie's fridge. She slipped her jogging pants on under her T-shirt and tiptoed out of the room.

The living room was dark, but she knew where Gabe had set up the rollaway, so she took care in choosing her route.

Addie's kitchen had a full-length swinging door, much like those used in restaurants. Kara noticed a pale light coming from beneath the door just before she entered. And the moment she walked in, she smelled freshly brewed coffee.

Gabe sat at the small kitchen table, pouring cream into his cup. Only the light over the kitchen sink was on. He smiled at Kara when she walked in.

"Morning," he whispered. "You couldn't sleep either?"

She stared at him for a moment before she realized she was doing it. His lids were sleep heavy, and he had stubble across his chin. His hair was tousled from bed. The BVD T-shirt he wore with his pajama pants was a reminder of their first meeting, at his deli. Kara had seen ads for cologne that attempted to capture the very look Gabe achieved without effort at that moment.

She shook her head. "No, couldn't sleep." She decided to take the high road and keep Tiffany's cacophonous snoring to herself. She poured herself a glass of orange juice and sat opposite Gabe at the table. She didn't even have to think about propriety when choosing where to sit. Without having brushed her teeth, there was no way she was going to sit any closer to him than she had to.

"If you want some help with the driving today, just let me know," she said. "You know, if you start to feel drowsy."

"Thanks." Now he appeared to be studying her. He looked pleased but also amused by what he saw.

"Do I look awful?" Kara asked. Why hadn't she thought to tidy up a bit before coming in here? She started to rise. She wanted to see what he saw.

He put his hand on hers to stop her. "No, don't go." He immediately took his hand back. "You look great. And this is the closest thing to a date I'll ever have with you."

She sat back down and laughed softly. "Ever?" Then she remembered Tiffany's claim that Gabe was interested in her. Had he really started looking in that direction?

He smiled and shrugged. "Well, maybe that's a bit extreme. There's still a chance, I guess."

Kara returned his smile and drank her juice.

"I read a book about your no-dating idea," he said. "It made a lot of sense to me."

She remembered the hippie lady at the bookstore and her disclosure about Gabe's ordering the same book Kara had. "I'm glad. That's good."

"Yeah," he said. "I mean, the author opened my eyes a lot about how much I take women for granted. I take dating for granted. But it seems smart to use more discernment. As a Christian, I feel I should put more store in how I treat women."

"How long have you been a Christian?" Kara asked. She finished her orange juice and took her glass to the sink.

Gabe got up after her and took a coffee cup out of the cabinet. "Coffee?"

She nodded. "Thanks."

"I accepted Christ just three years ago," he said as he filled her cup. "You?"

"I was raised Christian, but I really only started to understand my relationship with God when I was about thirteen. So I've been a Christian about fifteen years, I guess you'd say."

"Wow," Gabe said, handing her the cup of coffee and looking her in the eye. "That's a little intimidating."

She looked back at him and noticed her hand shake a bit when she took the coffee. How could a conversation about one's day of salvation suddenly feel so intimate? But from the look in his eyes, he seemed to notice the same thing.

"Go," he said, gently turning her by the shoulders until she faced the table. "Sit there." He loped, almost monkey-like, back to his seat. "Tarzan sit here."

She cracked up and had to put her hand over her mouth.

His eyes no longer looked sleepy but flashed with humor.

Kara sipped her coffee. "Mmm. Good job with the coffee." She glanced over her shoulder. No one seemed to be up yet. "So, Gabe.

I love hearing people's conversion stories." She raised her eyebrows at him.

He tilted his head in consideration. "It's a pretty tame one. My parents have always been good people. Strong morals. Kind." He looked back at Kara. "But while I was away at college, they started going to this church with the neighbors. They ended up hearing what they needed to hear."

Gabe took his napkin and wiped a coffee ring off the table. "When I came home from school, they both talked to me about it. Said they hadn't even realized what was missing. That neither of them had a true relationship with God. Both of them had become believers. Christians."

"So they talked you into it?" Kara asked.

He shrugged. "I think the timing was just so right for all three of us. I had just broken up with a girlfriend at college—a harsh breakup on both sides. And I was confused about whether I had made the right decision, degree-wise."

"Which was?"

"Culinary management. What Mom and Dad told me carried a lot of weight. I've always had so much respect for both of my parents. They're really fine people."

Kara smiled. "Mine too. We're both blessed, huh?"

"Mmm. Anyway, I went with them to church the first Sunday after I came home from school, and I liked the pastor a lot, but I still wasn't sure about the whole salvation thing. I talked with my dad about it that evening. I asked him, 'What about the people who don't ask Him to be their Savior?' and he said, 'You let the Lord worry about that. What about you?'

"I said, 'But, Dad, I don't get it. Why would Jesus have to die for my sins?' and he said, 'Because death is the penalty for sins. And we all sin.' So I said, 'But why would He do that for me?' And my dad opened his arms."

Gabe opened his arms like Christ's arms on the cross.

"And Dad said, 'Because He loves you. This much.'" Gabe brought his arms down and looked at his coffee cup. "I've seen that image since then. You know, on T-shirts and stuff, but at that point I hadn't heard that before. And hearing it from my dad..."

"Powerful, isn't it?" Kara said, her voice barely a whisper.

"Even today, when I think of it," Gabe said, "it makes me..." He stopped and swallowed. Kara saw the hint of tears in his eyes.

"Now I just need to get Ricco and Rachelle thinking straight."

"They both seem like good kids, Gabe. And you're setting a good example for them. Rachelle certainly knows about your faith. She thinks that's why you—"

She halted midsentence. She almost said 'that's why you like me,' but she caught herself.

"Why I what?"

Kara sighed with relief when Addie walked in.

She was fully clothed and ready to go. But she had forgotten to remove her hairnet. "Ah, the happy newlyweds!" she said.

Despite a sudden blush, Kara laughed. "No, Addie," she said, rising and gently removing Addie's hairnet. "We're good friends."

Addie nodded and winked at Gabe, as if the two of them shared a secret. "Sure you are, honey." Then she did a double take at Kara. She pointed at Kara's hair. "This is a new look."

"What is?" Kara asked. She reached up to touch her hair.

"Kinda roosterlike, isn't it?"

Kara looked at Gabe, horror in her eyes. He looked at her as if she were the cutest rooster in the world.

"Why didn't you say something?" she asked him. She turned and ran out of the kitchen in search of a mirror, a comb, or a high mountain from which she could throw herself.

"You're adorable!" Gabe called after her. He was loud enough to wake the rest of the house, but only Rachelle seemed to actually stir. She opened the bedroom door, scratching her head.

"Who's adorable?" she asked Kara.

Kara rushed past her and into the bathroom attached to the room Rachelle and Ren shared. She saw her lopsided Mohawk in the mirror and groaned.

"Ohhhhh," Rachelle said, grinning. "Gabe said that to you." She tilted her head and looked over Kara's shoulder into the mirror. "That's actually a good look for you, Kara. Kinda punk."

Kara looked at Rachelle in the mirror and frowned.

"But you can't pull off that look making a weenie face like that. You gotta *own* the punk look." Rachelle lifted her upper lip, Elvislike. "Like this."

Despite herself, Kara laughed. "I love you, Rachelle," she said. "Now let me use your shower."

"Yeah, okay," Rachelle said as Kara shut the door. Two seconds later Kara heard Rachelle gently knocking. Kara opened the door a crack.

Rachelle was grinning again. "Told you he liked you."

Kara said, "Go away now," and closed the door again. Even though the door was closed she could hear Rachelle's parting shot.

"Love ya. Bye!"

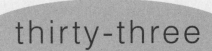

thirty-three

I still don't know why you wouldn't let me cook you all breakfast," Addie protested from the middle seat in the van later that morning.

Ren put her hand on Addie's. "You've done enough for us, Addie. Let's just relax and have a nice breakfast in town, like we discussed."

"Well...but I wanted waffles," Addie said.

"You hear that, Gabe?" Kara called from the back of the van. She had given Addie her place in the middle since it was roomier. She also thought she'd have an easier time focusing on more than Gabe's dark-lashed eyes now that she couldn't see them.

Gabe saluted as he drove. "Waffles! Aye, aye, Cap'n! Hey, Addie, are you sure you don't want to sit up here where there's more leg room?"

Addie waved a wrinkled hand in the air and laughed. "Leg room for what? I think I'm the shortest one here!"

Jake groaned from the backseat. "Man, how can you guys be so chipper this early in the morning?"

Kara laughed. "It's almost ten o'clock, Jake. You were getting up earlier than this to work at Gabe's deli, weren't you?"

"Well, yeah, but I was a slug about it. You guys are like the Brady Bunch or something."

"I'm just excited about getting home," Tiffany said. "We're really only about two hours away, aren't we, Gabe honey?"

Silence hit the van like a stink bomb.

Rachelle finally added her two cents to the conversation. "Gabe *honey?*"

Tiffany turned in her seat to look at Rachelle. "What? Did I say that?" With a shallow giggle, she said, "Oh, my. That just slipped right out, didn't it? Just ignore me, y'all."

"Workin' on it," Jake muttered.

Kara looked up at Gabe, who turned his head for a second, with a subtle shake. Even from the backseat, she could tell he was beet red. What in the world did Tiffany think she was doing? Kara was 95 percent certain that nothing was developing between Gabe and Tiffany, but the woman had a way of throwing suspicion into a situation as if she worked for the *National Enquirer.* She was hard to ignore.

"I think that's an IHOP up ahead," Gabe said. "How's that, Addie? You like IHOP?"

"Love IHOP," Addie said.

Tiffany sighed. "IHOP. How quaint. And how typically thoughtful of Gabe." She looked at Ren. "Isn't he just the *most* thoughtful?"

Ren frowned and opened her mouth, but she didn't appear to have anything to add.

Tiffany said, "Gabe, when we get back home—"

"Excuse me, dear," Addie interrupted. "Are we still supposed to ignore you?"

Rachelle snorted for one and all.

Tiffany crossed her arms and pouted. "Fine. I'll just stop talking altogether."

Addie patted Tiffany on the knee. "There you go, honey."

After parking the car, Gabe opened the side of the van where Addie sat and helped her out. Kara then saw him offer his arm to escort Addie.

"Well, I think you just scored points with both of us," Kara said. "Don't you agree, Addie?"

"He's a keeper."

Gabe smiled, but Kara saw pleading in his eyes when he said quietly, "Will you two please sit on either side of me at the table?"

Kara couldn't help but laugh. "Poor Gabe," she whispered. "You look like a fox surrounded by horses and hounds."

"Just a little uncomfortable right now."

His discomfort gave Kara confidence. "Hang in there. Just a few more hours 'til we have more room in the van. Maybe you'll feel more comfortable then."

Breakfast was a success, other than the mutual pouting that went on between Tiffany and Ricco. They sat next to each other, but Tiffany hardly noticed Ricco, and he was finally facing reality about his chances with her.

Addie got her waffles and amazed everyone by finishing them all and asking for a double side of bacon to go.

Kara laughed. "You're getting bacon to go?"

"People get bacon to go all the time when they get those bacon burgers, don't they?"

Gabe chuckled. "She's got a point."

"Yeah," Jake said, flashing an uncharacteristic grin, "but people get mayo on their burgers too. You wouldn't order mayo to go, would you, Addie?"

"Sure I would, son," she said. "Why do you think they have mayo in those little packets at fast-food places? Mayo, ketchup, relish, all kinds of stuff."

"Oh, pu-lease," Tiffany said, finally breaking her sulky silence. "Why are we arguing about condiments and greasy pork products? Can we just get going?"

The silly mood of the moment froze. Everyone seemed to be

biting their tongues. Clearly, the ever-thinning patience for Tiffany's barbs threatened to spawn some nasty comebacks.

As it was, they were all taken aback with Addie's next comment.

Her face as sweet as could be, she said to Tiffany, "It's a good thing we're dropping you off soon, dear."

Kara drew her mouth down and sucked her breath in.

Tiffany's eyes narrowed to slits when she looked at Addie. "What did you say?"

Addie wasn't the slightest bit intimidated. "I said it's good we're bringing you to your folks' place today. Otherwise, we wouldn't have a seat in Gabe's van for my sister Lurlene." She smiled and looked at Kara. "I can see you all didn't think about that, did you?"

Tiffany cooled slightly when it became obvious that Addie meant no harm.

But Kara looked at Gabe, her eyes a bit wide.

"Did you say Lurlene?" Gabe asked Addie.

Addie dipped her finger in the syrup on her plate. "Yes, sir. That's her name. I told you that, didn't I?"

"But, Addie," Ren said, "did you tell any of us that we were supposed to be picking up Lurlene?"

"Where does Lurlene live?" Gabe asked. He stroked his jawline with his open hand.

Kara heard Jake whisper to Rachelle. "If she says Virginia, he's gonna freak."

"She's in Melbourne."

"Isn't that in Australia?" Ricco said, an incredulous smile on his face.

Addie looked at Ricco, and they both started laughing.

" 'Course not," Addie said. "Melbourne's in Florida." She looked around at everyone. "That's where we're heading, isn't it?"

A collective sigh of relief went around the table.

Gabe said, "Melbourne is on our way to Miami. That's good to know." He smiled at Addie. "So we'll have another one of you wild ladies with us, eh?"

Tiffany glanced at Addie right before looking for something in her purse. She quietly said, "Then that makes two of us who are relieved I'm getting dropped off soon."

Rachelle looked at Kara and quietly held up three fingers, pointing at herself.

Kara struggled not to laugh out loud. Instead she took a deep breath and nudged her chair away from the table. "Actually, why don't we go get the van, Tiffany? That all right with everyone else?"

Tiffany looked reluctant about leaving with Kara, but she had already complained about wanting to go. With a frown she pushed her chair back too. "Fine." She walked past Kara. "I'm going to stop at the ladies' room on the way out."

Gabe stood and handed Kara his keys. He raised his eyebrows, the slightest smile on his face. "You going to be okay with that monster?"

Kara's jaw dropped. She spoke softly. "What monster?"

He cocked his head in the direction of the parking lot. "The van, of course. It's pretty big."

Kara blushed at her initial interpretation of Gabe's comment. "Oh. Yeah. Of course."

Gabe lowered his voice and asked, "Why? What did you think I was talking about, Kara?"

She narrowed her eyes and tried not to smile. "What you meant me to think, I'm sure." She pointed at him before walking away. "Don't make trouble, mister."

He chuckled and returned to the table. "We'll be out in a minute, soon as Addie's bacon arrives."

Kara met up with Tiffany as she walked out of the ladies' room. Tiffany had freshened her lipstick and her hair was perfect, but she looked unhappy. Kara couldn't help wondering what it must feel like to be at odds with nearly everyone around you.

"So," Kara said as they walked out to the parking lot, "you must be eager to see your folks and hometown friends."

Tiffany shrugged. "I suppose." She flipped her hair over her shoulder. "I wasn't really able to give them much notice since I didn't get invited along 'til a few days ago."

Kara decided this was a good time to keep quiet.

"Just don't expect a big welcoming party for me when we get there or anything," Tiffany said. "Because I'm usually very popular back home, but, you know, no one really knows I'm coming."

Kara thought Tiffany seemed tense. With a gentle nod, she said, "Sure. Okay."

As they neared the van, Kara asked, "What brought you to Northern Virginia, Tiffany? The job?"

"Of course not," Tiffany said. "I could teach aerobics anywhere." She turned her head away from Kara before speaking again. "I followed a guy up there. Big mistake."

They reached the van and got in. For a moment Kara was distracted. It made sense for Tiffany to sit in the front passenger seat while they drove to the restaurant entrance, but Kara wondered if she'd relinquish it to Ricco when everyone boarded again.

"It didn't work out with the guy, I take it."

"Obviously." Tiffany pulled down the visor and studied herself in the mirror. "He acted like he wanted me to follow them up there, and then he got all weird when I showed up."

"Them?" Kara asked.

"Hmm?" Tiffany looked away from the mirror. "Oh. He and his wife."

Kara had to fight to keep her expression neutral. She concentrated instead on driving up to where everyone waited.

Tiffany didn't move from her seat. "Trust me, don't ever get involved with a married man."

As van doors opened, Kara stared at Tiffany. "No. I won't."

Gabe and Ricco opened both front doors. "Thank you, ladies," Gabe said. Kara turned and accepted Gabe's hand as she climbed down.

"Are you okay?" he asked quietly. "You look a little upset."

She shook her head. "I'm fine. Just struggling with something. Sometimes I'm…" She glanced over her shoulder at Tiffany, who was finally climbing out of the front seat. "Sometimes I'm not sure if I should confront as a Christian or keep quiet so I don't sound judgmental."

Gabe glanced across the van at Tiffany and then back at Kara. "Want to talk later?"

"Maybe."

Everyone returned to their prior places. Kara worked at rejoining their jovial mood. "So, Addie," she said, "got your bacon?"

"Six pieces!" she proclaimed proudly, holding up a baggie containing a greasy paper towel. "And look what I got for you, Jack!"

"Jake, you mean," Rachelle said.

"Jake, right," Addie said. She handed a small container to Jake. "There's your mayo."

Jake laughed out loud and was suddenly adorable. "I didn't want mayo, Addie. I was just making a point."

"Well, so am I. That waitress hardly batted an eye when I asked for it. I'll bet people ask for bacon and mayo to go every day."

As they left the parking lot, Addie turned in her seat to look at Kara. She brought Kara's smile back when she tucked the bag of bacon into her purse and announced, once again, "Love IHOP."

thirty-four

Kara could tell the moment Tiffany's mother spoke that the cigarette she pinched between her lips had been preceded by thousands of others. The woman had a voice like gravel. And how she spoke around that cigarette was a mystery.

"Hey, sugar baby," the woman growled to Tiffany, a lazy smile on her lips. Her hair was auburn, like her daughter's, but hers had that overall brassiness that comes from too many dye jobs. And it was piled high on her head.

She stepped back from the doorway to let everyone in. The house was small, old, and full of clutter, with a faint odor of dog wafting about. A Yorkshire terrier bolted into the house through a doggie door in the kitchen and yapped incessantly at everyone while Tiffany's mother yelled, "Shut *up*, Boomer! Pipe *down!*" She finally picked the dog up, one-handed, and tossed it back outside. She pushed a chair up against the doggie door as if it were part of her daily routine.

Within seconds they heard several "thunks" against the doggie door before Boomer gave up and sought prey elsewhere.

The teens, in particular, enjoyed Boomer's performance.

Tiffany's mother removed the cigarette from her lips just long enough to kiss Tiffany on the cheek. "Welcome home, baby." She stepped back and studied her daughter. "You putting on weight?"

Tiffany didn't address the question. "Mama, let me introduce you to my dear friends."

Before she knew what she was doing, Kara looked over her shoulder to see who Tiffany might be talking about.

"This is Kara, Ren, Gabe, Ricco, Rachelle, Annie, and Jack."

Rachelle said, "*Addie* and *Jake*."

"Right," Tiffany said, waving her hand as though she were dismissing the servants. "This is my mama, Sheila LeBoeuf."

Before anyone could exchange niceties, Tiffany asked her mother, "Where's Daddy?"

"He's working at Melfest this year."

Tiffany gasped. "Melfest is going on now?"

"Today's the last day," Mrs. LeBoeuf said. "Daddy wanted to take you with him, but you got here too late."

Between gritted teeth, Tiffany said, "IHOP."

Ricco asked, "What's Melfest, Tiffany?"

Tiffany looked at him and gasped again, clapping her hands together. "I know! Let's all go!"

Ricco started to ask again. "But, what's—"

"Bluegrass, baby," Mrs. LeBoeuf told him. She took the cigarette between her fingers again. "Annual blue grass festival. Out at White Lake." She blew smoke out of the side of her mouth and then picked a piece of tobacco off of her tongue.

"There's all kinds of stuff out there," Tiffany said. "A really clean beach, boating, rides, and putt-putt golf. And lots of bands."

Kara had never seen Tiffany so animated. Surely this event couldn't be much more cosmopolitan than Addie's Ham and Yam Festival.

"If any of my friends are in town, they'll be at Melfest," Tiffany said.

Gabe said, "But we hadn't planned on stopping over here, other than dropping you off. How far away is this place?"

Mrs. LeBoeuf said, "It's about an hour away."

"See?" Tiffany said. "It will be like driving into DC from Ashburn. You do that all the time, right?"

Gabe glanced at his watch, a slight frown forming. "Hmm." He looked at Kara. "If we go to this thing, we'll end up having to stay another night before leaving again."

"There's a real nice hotel in town," Mrs. LeBoeuf said, and Kara noticed her giving Gabe the once over.

"Actually," Ren said, "I think it sounds kind of fun. Would it be so bad if we got to Florida one day later?"

Kara remembered her mother saying that Addie had cried on the phone about her sister Lurlene. And something about time running out. Now that she knew Lurlene was waiting on them, she was concerned.

"Addie, how about you?" Kara asked. "You needed to get to Lurlene—"

"Lurlene? She'll be fine if we get there one day behind schedule. Probably won't even notice."

Mrs. LeBoeuf rested her elbow against her hip and held her cigarette as if it were in a holder. She looked like Bette Davis in one of her tough gal roles. She said, "Addie. Listen, sugar, if you'd like to stay here while the kids go—"

"Not on your life!" Addie said. "My late husband, Willard, God rest him, played a mean banjo before he got sick. I'd love to go soak up some of that music. Plus I'm allergic to..." she pointed in the direction of Boomer, outside.

"Dogs?" Mrs. LeBoeuf asked.

"Yappy ones, yes," Addie said.

Gabe looked at the teens. "You three all right with going to the festival?"

Jake shrugged. "Bluegrass is cool."

Rachelle and Ricco nodded.

Kara said to Gabe, "Guess we could check in again with our parents. Mine are probably all right with waiting another day."

Gabe nodded. "At this point mine have probably closed up shop and gone on a second honeymoon."

Two hours later they were all tearing around a go-cart track, laughing and trying not to crash into each other or the hay bales bordering the track. All but Addie, of course. Kara waved at her during a slow turn around one corner.

Addie waved back. She sat on a park bench outside the track. She wanted to watch the racing, she said, while listening to the music. Kara saw Addie smile with satisfaction as she watched the breeze spin through the pinwheel given her by a "flirtatious young man" of 65 or so at the cotton candy stand.

Afterward, the teens wanted to spend time in the arcade.

"Give us some money, bro?" Ricco asked Gabe.

Gabe looked at him doubtfully. "Me?"

"Aw, come on, Gabe," Rachelle said. "We did all that work for you at the deli."

"That was supposed to pay for your transport back to Florida," he said. But he had already reached back for his wallet.

"Isn't this part of the transport back to Florida?" Jake asked and then gave Gabe a humble smile.

"Hmm," Gabe said. He patted both hands against his backside, and then he checked the pocket on the front of his shirt.

Rachelle sighed and opened the small purse she carried. She pulled out Gabe's wallet. "You forgot it in the van."

Gabe grimaced as he took it. "Thanks, baby sister."

Kara chuckled. "You weren't kidding when you said you might drive away and forget one of us, were you?"

He smiled at her. "Nah. I'd never forget an entire person."

No sooner had Gabe sent the teens off with money than Tiffany squealed with glee over a group of women who approached.

"Oh! Let me introduce you!" she said, once she brought the two groups together. She counted the women off as she introduced them. "Cindy, Macy, Buffy, Coco, and Nan, this is Gabe." And then, as if she had just remembered, she said, "Oh, and Kara, Ren, and Addie."

They all exchanged hellos before one of the new women told Tiffany, "Misty's here too. She's pregnant."

"No!" Tiffany said.

"Big as a house!" another one said.

Their group reaction sounded like a gaggle of turkeys, and Kara and Ren exchanged deadpan glances.

"I have to go see!" Tiffany said. "Do you mind? I'll meet up with you later."

She only looked at Gabe as she spoke. The suggestion was that they were an item, and Gabe quickly looked at Kara, Ren, and Addie. "Okay with you ladies?"

None of them bothered to pretend anything other than eagerness for Tiffany to go.

The group of women left, giggling like adolescents.

Addie was the only one who didn't breathe out a hefty sigh in their absence.

Kara said, "How about a walk along the beach?"

"That sounds great," Gabe said. "Let me go tell the kids where we'll be. You ladies go on ahead."

"You all right with a walk, Addie?" Ren asked.

Addie nodded and put her arm through Ren's. "I take a walk every day. Keeps me young."

Gabe jogged off toward the arcade as the women headed toward the beach.

"He's a fine father to those kids," Addie said, cocking her head in Gabe's direction.

"He's not their father," Kara said. "He's their brother. Well, he's not Jake's brother."

"He's Jake's father, then?" Addie asked. She was distracted by her pinwheel, which had started to spin again in the breeze.

"Um," Kara said, but then Ren caught her eye. Ren shrugged and shook her head. Kara said, "You like the beach, Addie?"

"Well, I can't tell you that until we get there," she said. Then she looked at Kara again. "Oh! You mean in general, do I like the beach?"

"Yes," Kara said, smiling.

"Oh, girls, let me tell you about the beach house Willard and I used to own. Romantic? Honey!"

She was still reminiscing when Gabe rejoined the group, flashing a smile at Kara.

With Tiffany away, Addie telling romantic tales, and good friends Ren and Gabe by her side, Kara smiled and breathed in the fresh air off the water. A lovely bluegrass song wound its way to the foursome as they walked. Kara eventually recognized the old hymn "I'll Fly Away."

At that moment she was so content, she almost felt as though she could.

thirty-five

What were you talking about this morning?" Gabe asked Kara. They both carried their sandals in their hands so they could wade through the water.

"Hmm? When?" She bent to pick up a smooth, amber-colored rock. The sun seemed stronger here near the shore, but the breeze off the water kept them cool.

"This morning at the IHOP. When you drove the van up for us."

"Ah," Kara said. She glanced over her shoulder. Ren and Addie walked a short distance behind them, deep in conversation. Ren looked up and gave Kara an encouraging grin.

"You said something about being judgmental," he said. "With Tiffany."

"Yeah. Um, I'm not sure how to say this. I don't want to sound like I'm gossiping."

Gabe said nothing and waited on her.

Kara tossed the rock back into the water. "Let's say you knew someone—not a close friend. Perhaps a coworker, like Tiffany and me."

"Okay."

"And let's say he casually mentioned that he had stolen something from someone. Something that couldn't be given back, for whatever reason."

"Got it."

"See, there's a verse in Romans that talks about people doing things that are morally wrong," Kara said. "And it says not only is doing the thing wrong, approving of the immoral action is just as wrong."

Gabe nodded. "So she confessed something to you that—"

"No, it wasn't even a confession. She just mentioned it casually, like it was no big deal."

"But you were wondering if you should have confronted her about it?"

"Yeah, maybe. So she doesn't think I approve of it. As a Christian, you know? But I also don't want to come across as judgmental. I mean, the opportunity has pretty much passed, anyway, but that's what was going on this morning."

He looked at the dock in the distance. "She probably already knows it was wrong, don't you think?"

She raised her eyebrows. "You'd think so. But some people are oblivious about what's right and wrong, even on the big scale."

Gabe looked at Kara for a moment. "I can tell you what worked for me three years ago."

"What?" She was distracted by the sun in his eyes. Their brown color lightened to a shade like warm coffee.

He smiled at her, and she stopped staring. He said, "My parents didn't try to convince me of what I was doing wrong in my life. They just tried to sell me on Jesus."

Kara looked away and thought about that. "Hmm. I can't say I've ever done that with Tiffany. Tried to sell her on Christ, I mean."

Gabe sighed. "Yeah. She's certainly a challenge, isn't she? But so was I when my parents led me to Christ."

Kara nodded.

"Of course," he said, "after I believed, God convicted me on the things I was doing wrong. One by one, like shooting ducks at an arcade."

Kara chuckled. "You make me feel so much better. I'm glad I didn't say anything about it, then. She probably would have just thought I didn't approve of her."

He pointed at her and his voice became more animated. "Yeah! That's right. I remember thinking Christians were so high and mighty. That they looked down on nonbelievers."

Kara frowned. "Wow. I hope I don't come across like that to people."

"Well, I can tell you don't come across to Rachelle like that. I think she's right on the edge of believing."

"Honestly?" Kara said, smiling. "We've only talked about faith in brief little snippets."

"I think it's more how you live that's got her going. She really admires you."

"Huh," Kara said. "I haven't even told her about the four steps to salvation yet."

Gabe laughed. "I think the subtle approach is best for Rachelle. You mention organized steps with her, and she'll think, *School! Run!*"

Kara laughed too. "Ah, so you already knew she hated school. She asked me not to mention it. I guess you know she's not headed for college in the fall?"

He shook his head. "Well, it's not in the game plan so far. But my folks will only give her one year before she has to go. They'll let her work for a year, and then she gets kicked out of the nest." He looked down at the sand. "I think part of her hesitation about college is the idea of leaving Jake. I don't think she's ready to give him up."

"I haven't heard anything along those lines, either."

"That's another way I think you're a good example for her. I mean, with your cautious approach to dating." He skipped a beat and then said, "You know, your eyes are an amazing color of green when the sunlight hits them like this."

Kara was dumbstruck by his throwing that last line in there. "Thanks." She looked away and was suddenly self-conscious again. She grimaced. "I'm bound to do something really clumsy any minute now," she said, more to herself than to Gabe.

But she made him laugh, anyway. He glanced behind them, and then he did a double take and turned around. "Hmm."

Kara followed his gaze and turned too.

Ren and Addie had stopped a little way back and were facing each other, holding hands, their heads bowed. Kara and Gabe looked at each other, and then they quietly approached in time to hear the end of their prayer.

"Thank You for Your free gift of salvation, Jesus," Ren prayed. Addie repeated what she said.

"I put my life in Your hands," Ren said, and Addie prayed the same.

"Amen," Ren said, followed by Addie, Gabe, and Kara.

Addie and Ren looked up in surprise.

"How long have you two been standing here?" Addie asked.

Kara put her hand on Addie's shoulder. "I'm sorry. I didn't realize you weren't already a Christian. I guess I just took it for granted."

"Me too!" Addie said. They all laughed.

Ren said, "We were talking about when Willard died."

"My husband," Addie said. "The nurse told me that just before he died, she led him to Jesus. I didn't know—" She stopped abruptly and choked up. Tears came to her eyes when she said, "I didn't know 'til now what she meant."

Kara ran her hand along Addie's shoulder and pulled her close. She and Ren smiled at each other.

"Poor Willard," Addie said. "He must be so worried about me now."

"No, Addie, he won't be worried," Gabe said. "There's none of that in heaven."

Addie looked at him. "You think he might know I just gave my life to Jesus?"

"Are you kidding?" Kara said. "I doubt he'd be able to ignore all the rejoicing going on in heaven right now! That happens, you know. Says so in the Bible."

Addie grinned and breathed a sigh of contentment.

"Are you two ready to head back?" Ren asked.

Kara opened her mouth to speak just as a Frisbee smacked into her nose.

"Ow!" She was so startled she stepped backward and tripped over her own feet. Then she fell on her backside into the water.

She was remotely aware of a mother chastising her child and apologizing to Kara's group. But she was more focused on her nose and her own embarrassment.

"I had nothing to do with that one!" she said to Gabe as he helped her up.

He was clearly trying not to laugh, but her comment sent him over the edge. "I'm so sorry, Kara."

She punched him in the arm. "Stop laughing at me." But she couldn't keep from smiling about it. "Just do me a favor and don't flirt with me. Something bad always seems to happen to me when you do."

"Me? Flirt?" he said. He pretended offense and looked to Ren and Addie for support. "Do I flirt, ladies?"

Addie said, "Son, you're about the best-looking fella I've ever seen. You flirt just by walking into a room."

"I rest my case," Kara said, pressing her fingers against her nose. "Am I bleeding?"

"You're fine," Ren said. "But you might have a little bruise later."

Kara gave Gabe a dirty look. "I just got rid of the bruise I got from you at the gym."

Addie looked at Gabe with a frown.

He shrugged and put his hands up, gesturing his innocence. "She walked into a wall!"

"Never mind," Kara said. She didn't want to rehash that incident. "Maybe I should go back to the car and get some dry clothes."

Addie put her hand on Kara's arm. "Dear, could we...could we pray about one other thing first, you think?"

"Of course, Addie. What's on your mind?"

Without explanation, Addie just dropped her head and kicked right into prayer. "Me again, Jesus. Addie Rogers. I was the one who just talked with You."

Kara couldn't help but smile at Addie's innocent ease.

"We might as well throw in a prayer or two for the rest of the crew, Jesus," Addie said. "Rachelle, Ricco, Jake, and especially that snippety one, Tiffany. Get 'em, Jesus. You go on and get 'em."

Kara grinned. Nothing could have spoiled the moment for her. Not the Frisbee. Not the sand in her shorts. Not even the snippety one herself, who came running up to them and announced, "There you are. Come on. I'm ready to go home now."

thirty-six

Kara tried to focus on the nicer memories of the day. Still, she rolled her eyes after they pulled up to Tiffany's home.

"That was just the *most* fun," Tiffany said. To Gabe. She had managed to wrangle her way into the front seat for the drive home, and she spent the entire trip finding reasons to put her hand on Gabe's arm or shoulder.

Kara was afraid she might scream if Tiffany tried to kiss him goodbye. She took some comfort in the thought that he would probably scream too.

Ousted from his seat up front, Ricco made a point of sitting in the center of the middle seat. He kept leaning forward to change CDs or adjust the air conditioning. He was obviously trying to interfere with Tiffany's efforts at closeness with Gabe.

After Gabe pulled into the driveway, Tiffany's father—who had made it home from the bluegrass festival ahead of her—came out to the van. He opened Tiffany's door for her and waited for her to get out. Over his abundant stomach, he still wore the Volunteer Fire Department T-shirt he had on at the festival. The smell of barbeque wafted off of him.

"I want to thank you people for bringing my little girl down here. And for coming to the festival. Y'all have a good time?"

A chorus of accolades poured out of the van, broadening his smile. "You drive safe now, hear?" He closed the door, patted the van a couple of times, and waved.

Tiffany looked disappointed at the change in the situation. She had approached Gabe's side of the van after she got out. Now her father was dismissing the van, and Gabe took full advantage of his prompting. He waved in Tiffany's general direction as he backed into the street.

Kara and several others called, "Goodbye, Tiffany," out the windows.

"Go, man, go," Jake urged in a whisper, triggering giggles from Rachelle and the women.

The van took off down the road.

"We're terrible," Kara said, forcing herself to look more serious.

Ren stopped laughing and sighed. "Yes, we are. I just get so uncomfortable when she's on the prowl. Embarrassed, I mean. It's almost frightening to be around."

"Tell me about it," Gabe said, provoking a few more laughs.

Ricco remained silent. Addie, who sat next to him, seemed oblivious to his angst. "So, Ricco," she said, "what's it like being a twin? You and Rachelle, you're twins, right?"

He nodded glumly. "Yes, ma'am."

"I'll bet you look out for your sister, huh?"

He shrugged. "I guess."

"He guesses," Rachelle said. And just as she did earlier with Tiffany, she told Addie, "The reason he's on this trip is because he followed me and Jake up to Virginia when we went to visit Gabe. He wanted to protect me."

Before Ricco could react, Addie looked at him, respect in her eyes. She said, "Well, aren't you a wonderful person?"

Ricco decided not to argue against that point.

Kara said, "I'm impressed by that too, Ricco. If I were you, I'd let Rachelle tease me about that whenever she wanted to. Especially if other girls are around."

He looked at her. "Why?"

Kara shrugged. "It just shows that you have good character."

"Girls of substance really dig guys with good character," Ren said.

Ricco snorted in disdain. "Tiffany didn't seem to dig me."

Rachelle said, "She said girls of substance, Ricco."

"Excuse me," Gabe said. "I'm going to check us in at this hotel up ahead. Then we can have dinner at the steak house next door, if that's all right with everyone. And maybe we shouldn't talk about Tiffany anymore, since she's not here to defend herself."

"What?" Ricco said. "You like her now or something?"

"Don't be stupid, Ricco," Rachelle said. "He likes Kara."

In the silence that followed, Kara felt each person in the van watching her and Gabe for a reaction. Both of them stared straight ahead. They had all gotten a little sunburned, so Kara hoped her red face looked no different than anyone else's.

Gabe pulled into the hotel parking lot. Still staring straight ahead, he said, "I guess there's no point in denying that, Rachelle." He sighed and got out of the van. He looked back in at everyone through his open window. "But we're just friends."

Within an hour they had tidied up in the two rooms Gabe rented. One for the women; one for the men.

The subject of dating was obviously still fresh in Rachelle's mind as she and Kara stood before the vanity mirror in their room.

"Isn't there a chance you could get so used to being friends with someone that you would stop finding them, you know, hot?"

"Hot?" Addie asked, behind them.

Ren smiled as she strapped on her sandals. "Attractive, she means."

Addie nodded. "Hot." She looked off in the distance, as though she was entering the word into her brain's data bank.

Kara shrugged. "I guess there's a chance of that. But if you're going to stop considering someone hot, it's eventually going to happen whether you're dating them or not. Better to not date them in the first place, if you're only attracted to their hotness."

"Is that a new word too?" Addie asked. "Hotness?"

Ren laughed. "Not a very good one. Oh, um, Addie, you can't wear your slippers to the restaurant."

Kara finished messing with her hair and looked at Rachelle. "I just think friendship is more durable than physical attraction. So it should be there before you even consider someone romantically. Usually the friendship is what makes the person attractive."

"You think Jake and I are doomed?"

"Oh, goodness, Rachelle," Kara said, putting her hand on the girl's shoulder. "I wouldn't know something like that. I sure don't have all the answers. Why do you think I'm not dating anymore?"

The atmosphere at dinner that night was far more relaxed than any of their previous meals on the trip, thanks to Tiffany's absence. Still, Kara kept wandering off in thought, replaying her conversation with Rachelle. Now that Gabe had told her how much Rachelle respected her, she felt more responsibility for what she said to her.

She also kept thinking about Rachelle's first question, especially in relation to Gabe. Wasn't there a chance that she and Gabe were destroying their mutual attraction by getting to know each other so well?

If it happens, it happens.

But, as the group walked back to the hotel and went to their respective rooms, she took a quick look at Gabe, considering what a fine friend he was becoming.

Then he turned and gave her a simple smile and a wave. "Night," he said softly.

She returned the wave and walked into her room. She noticed that her heart was racing just a little. When Ren turned on the light at the vanity, Kara glanced in the mirror and saw that her face looked flushed.

Were she and Gabe destroying the hotness? She smiled. Not a chance.

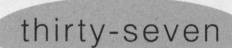

thirty-seven

In the van the next morning, Kara closed her cell phone and looked over at Gabe. "Okay, I've worked it all out with Mom and Dad. They're fine with our going by your parents' place first."

Since Ricco wanted to sit with Rachelle and Jake on this leg of the trip, he designated Kara as his replacement in riding shotgun. She kept the map at the ready and made a point of not acting touchy-feely with Gabe the way Tiffany had. Still, she empathized with Tiffany, especially when she'd sneak a glance at Gabe's forearms or his utterly fantastic profile.

Kara turned and looked at Addie. "Are you sure your sister will be okay going to Gabe's parents' before we get to Mom and Dad's?"

Addie waved the thought away. "Honey, we don't even need to tell Lurlene. She won't know which parents are yours and which ones are Gabe's. I probably wouldn't know if you didn't tell me. Haven't seen Morine since she was...well, I don't remember ever seeing her before. But I must have, or she wouldn't have invited me down."

Kara and Ren smiled together.

At the Denny's restaurant that morning, Kara and Ren had picked up a brochure about Savannah. Now Kara studied it to pass the time.

Gabe glanced over at her. "You want to go?"

She held the brochure up. "To Savannah? I've never been. Is it out of our way?"

Gabe shrugged. "Not really. We'll have to stop for lunch anyway. Maybe we could have a picnic or something."

"That sounds great," Ren said from the middle seat. "I vote yes."

"Ooo, there's a lighthouse on this island here," Kara said, pointing to the brochure. "Tybee Island." She looked at Gabe. "How about that?"

"Lighthouses are awesome," Jake called from the backseat. "I'm in."

"Picnic at the lighthouse!" Gabe called out. "Okay with everyone?"

He was answered by a resounding, positive chorus.

When they arrived in Savannah three hours later, they went to the River Street Market Place to buy everything for the picnic.

"Oh, my goodness, I love Savannah!" Kara said, looking all around them. "The architecture, the gardens, the shopping—and look, they have a dinner cruise! I could spend days just visiting River Street!"

"Yeah, we should remember this place," Gabe said.

Kara looked at him and raised her eyebrows.

He lifted a shoulder. "I mean, you know, just in case—"

"Kara, look at those little pies!" Rachelle said, pulling Kara away from Gabe. "Can we get a couple for dessert?"

"Um, yeah. Sure," Kara said, allowing Rachelle to lead her to the vendor. But she glanced over her shoulder at Gabe, who had already found other things to keep himself busy.

Less than an hour later, they arrived at Tybee Island. Ricco and Jake took off immediately on a race to see who could climb the lighthouse stairs first. Kara and Gabe wanted to make the climb too, but the others preferred to set up the picnic.

"You guys go ahead," Ren said. "We'll get lunch laid out over there. in the grassy area under those shade trees."

"I can't promise anything about these pies being here when you get back," Rachelle called as Gabe and Kara walked off.

The climb was a long one, but the exercise felt good to Kara after spending so much time in the van the last couple of days. Jake and Ricco had already headed back down by the time Kara and Gabe reached the windows near the top. They stood side by side and appreciated the view.

"Interesting," he said, looking out over the water. "You build a tower like this for safety. To avoid problems, shipwrecks. But you can still only see just so far ahead, you know? You can't know what's beyond the horizon until it comes." He looked at Kara for a moment, and then he looked back out the windows. "You can only be just so safe from conflict."

Kara studied him, but he didn't look back at her for a while. When he did, she said, "True. I read about this lighthouse in the brochure. It was washed away by storms a few times, but they finally built it with good, solid brick. Even after that, it was hammered by the Civil War, but the foundation survived. They had an easier time rebuilding on the solid foundation." Now she looked out the windows. "If you build a strong enough foundation, you can weather conflicts."

When Kara finally looked at him again, he was watching her.

He broke into a rueful smile. "Are we having an argument?"

She smiled right back and crossed her arms. "Oh, I'm sure we can do better than this."

He laughed and put his hand on her back. "Come on. Let's go have a picnic instead."

When they reached the others, everyone looked relaxed and satisfied. They lazed under the lush trees. Ren and Addie sat on a park bench just behind the sheet on which they had laid all the scrumptious-looking food. They were drinking bottled tea and finishing crab cake sandwiches wrapped in white paper. The teens lounged on the sheet, picking at various food containers. Ren held up two wrapped sandwiches to Gabe and Kara, who joined the teens on the ground.

Jake and Ricco were having a lively conversation. "The only reason I even mention it, dude, is so you'll stop worrying about me and Rachelle," Jake told Ricco.

Ren said, "I think I've heard of Straight Edge before."

"What are you talking about?" Kara asked.

Ricco said, "Jake's into a punk cult."

"I'm telling you, it's not a cult, man," Jake said. "And I don't belong anymore."

"Yeah, Ricco," Rachelle said. "He already said that. Anyway, he got all the good stuff out of it. I'm glad he thinks the way he does."

"What's Straight Edge, Jake?" Gabe asked.

"Well, it's kinda old," Jake said. "From the eighties."

Addie snorted. "Old, he says."

"It was a youth movement," Jake said. "Clean living. No drinking, no drugs, no smoking—"

Kara pointed at him. "Oh, yeah. I remember seeing some news thing about that movement before. Sounded like every parent's dream. But there was something controversial about it."

Jake shrugged. "My older brother was into it, and so I got into it too. But they got a little...what's the word? Zealous? At least the group I was into did."

Kara nodded. "I think that was what I saw. A bit over the top. Almost militant."

"I don't know if I'd say militant," Jake said. "But listen. The only reason I mentioned it is because I still honor those choices, man. I don't drink, smoke, do drugs, and I will never disrespect Rachelle. No sex."

"Oh, my," Addie said.

Jake looked up at her. "Sorry, Addie."

"Well, Jake, I have to say I'm happy to hear that," Gabe said. "If I had known that about you from the start—"

"You would have asked him to just go on ahead and become a Christian," Addie said.

Everyone looked at her at once.

Kara smiled. She hadn't heard Addie end anyone's sentences since Tiffany left.

Gabe said, "Actually, I was going to say I would have felt more relaxed about Rachelle and him. But sure, Jake, if you ever want to know anything about Christianity—"

"Yeah, I know," Jake said. "Rachelle told me about your faith thing. I'll think about it."

"Oh, look," Rachelle said, pointing beyond their little group. "That little girl with the squirrels."

A family was strolling together, the parents holding hands and their daughter trailing behind them. The girl, about five, was tossing bits of bread out to the eager squirrels.

"Wow," Kara said. "They're pretty tame if they're not running from her. The squirrels back home are way more jumpy than that."

Ricco chuckled. "Look at that one with his back turned. He doesn't even know she's coming."

Suddenly Gabe gasped. He whispered "No" under his breath and was quickly on his feet. He ran toward the girl just as she grabbed the squirrel from behind.

"Don't pick him up!" Gabe called out to the girl, but it was too late.

In a matter of moments, the little girl screamed and tossed the squirrel over her head. It landed on Gabe, who instinctively grabbed at it. But the squirrel was the most frightened of the three. He ran the equivalent of a 10K around Gabe's head and shoulders, while Gabe flailed his arms around, trying to catch the critter. Gabe even did a lively dance at the same time, as if that would help in his efforts.

Ricco and Jake were rolling on the ground, laughing. The women started to laugh too, but then Kara looked at the little girl and her parents. The girl was crying as her parents examined her hands.

Kara looked back at Gabe. The squirrel had dashed away. Gabe touched his ear and then looked at his hand. She ran over to him. He had a small amount of blood on his fingers. "Are you all right?" she asked him.

"Yeah. He bit my earlobe." He looked over at the girl and her parents, and then he approached them. "I'm sorry," he said. "I tried to stop her, and then I tried to catch the squirrel."

"Oh, you've been bitten too!" the mother said.

Gabe nodded. "It's not a bad bite." He squatted down to eye level with the little girl.

She was dark-haired, chubby, and adorable, her damp lashes all stuck together. She reached up to hold her father's hand.

"I'm Gabe. I got a boo-boo too. What's your name?"

The child looked at her mother, who nodded encouragement.

"Chelsea," she said, swaying side to side, her cheeks damp with tears.

"My boo-boo is on my ear. Is yours on your hand? May I see? I promise I won't touch it."

She looked at her parents.

"You can show him, Chelsea," her father said.

Chelsea opened her free hand in front of Gabe.

He looked at it and told her, "Oh, good, that's not a very bad one. You'll be better real soon, Chelsea."

But when he stood up, his expression became more grim. He glanced at Kara and then said to the parents, "Unfortunately, I wasn't able to catch the squirrel. Now we can't be sure it didn't have rabies."

The girl's mother teared up, and the father said, "You're right. He's right, Chandra."

Gabe said, "I think we'd better check in the Visitors' Center and find out where the nearest emergency room is. This isn't something either of us should ignore."

The woman in the Visitors' Center insisted on applying first aid to both Gabe and Chelsea. "You'll need to go to St. Joseph's Hospital, on Mercy Boulevard," she said. "It's not far." She pulled out a local street map and used a highlighter to mark the way for them. "I'd call you an ambulance, but you could honestly get there a lot faster if you just drove there right now."

Gabe nodded. "Yeah, that's fine." He arranged to have the other family follow them, and then everyone headed back to the van.

Ricco said, "Dude, what were you thinking, going after that thing?"

Gabe shrugged. "Just instinct. I really only planned to stop her from grabbing it. The rest was—"

"Awesome!" Jake said. "I never saw anyone move so fast in my life."

Gabe smiled at him. "You talking about me or the squirrel?"

Kara gave him a sympathetic smile and couldn't help but pat him on the back.

Before they got in the van, he muttered to her, "At least when you've done something goofy, it hasn't involved a trip to the emergency room."

Kara smiled. "You were way overdue. Had to do it up big, I guess."

He glanced at the other family, who was buckling their daughter into their car. "I just hope for Chelsea's sake it doesn't get much bigger than this before the day is out."

thirty-eight

Take this next right," Kara said, following the map from the Visitor's Center. "You think you and that little girl will have to get all those awful shots you hear about?"

Gabe shook his head. "I don't know, but I'm not feeling very good about it. Especially for Chelsea."

Their wait in the crowded emergency room threatened to be characteristically long and grueling. The strong smell of rubbing alcohol made Kara feel a little sick to her stomach.

"Why don't you guys go tour Savannah while I'm here?" Gabe said to the group. "I'll just give you a call when I'm done."

"I want to stay," Kara said to him. For all she knew they were going to knock him out or admit him or something. She looked at Ren. "Would you mind going with everyone to see a few sites?"

"I'll drive if you want, Ren," Ricco said.

Ren looked at Addie and the teens. "All right with you?"

Addie nodded, but she stepped up to Gabe and put her hand on his cheek. "You take care of yourself, son. You're a good man, trying to help that little girl."

After they left, Chelsea brought a worn box of Legos over by Gabe and Kara. She sat down on the carpet in front of them.

"You don't mind?" her mother asked.

"Not at all," Kara said. She looked at Gabe and whispered, "I think you've got a fan here."

The child's father, a well-dressed, quiet man, smiled. "She likes you."

Chelsea kept looking up at Gabe as she randomly stuck bricks together. She slightly favored the finger that had been bitten, but she didn't seem to be suffering any real pain.

Finally Gabe asked her, "May I play too?"

She nodded.

Kara watched him transform from a big, muscular man to a big, awkward kid as he hunkered down on the floor with the little girl. He dug in the box and pulled out two green blocks. Then he looked at Chelsea.

"Which one should I use next, do you think?"

She put her finger to her mouth while she considered this, clearly a gesture she had seen an adult do. Kara wanted to give her a hug, but she wasn't really a part of the moment, so she just observed.

Chelsea chose a red block, no different from all the other red blocks, and handed it to Gabe as if it were the Hope Diamond. "This is it."

"It is. You're right!" Gabe said. He added the brick and spoke with awe. "Wow."

Chelsea beamed at him. "Who's your name again?"

"Gabe."

She nodded. "Gave."

They had built a sizable, pointless clump of bricks by the time the nurse called Chelsea. She immediately looked frightened. She looked at her parents as they stood and then at Gabe. "Can Gave come?"

"I don't think so, baby," her mother said.

But just then another nurse called Gabe's name.

"Oh, good," he said, "we can go in together, Chelsea."

"Actually," the nurse said, "we are going to set you up nearby, Mr. Paolino, in case Chelsea's doctor has questions about what happened."

Gabe looked at Kara. "You don't mind waiting?"

Kara shook her head. Now she wanted to give Gabe a hug, but she hesitated.

He smiled at her, stepped toward her, and quickly hugged her. "Thanks," he said.

She barely got her arms around him before he turned to leave. He looked over his shoulder and winked at her. She didn't know why, but her eyes teared up.

Kara flipped through every magazine in the waiting room, and then she resorted to actually reading articles about childhood diseases, garden wall designs, and India's legume industry. Once she started nodding off, she decided to go on a caffeine hunt. But as she stood she heard Gabe's laugh.

He was preceded by Chelsea's parents, who looked relieved. He carried Chelsea. She had her arms around his neck, and both of them had lollipops in their mouths. Chelsea had obviously been crying at some point, but now she giggled about something Gabe said as they walked into the waiting area.

He handed her to her parents when Kara approached. "I'm so sorry you had to wait so long," he said to Kara. He put his hand on her shoulder and reached into his shirt pocket. "But I brought you a lollipop! Were you bored out of your mind?"

She stared at him, zombielike, and spoke in a robotic monotone. "Not-at-all. There-are-fourteen-different-kinds-of-lentil. There-is-no-cure-for-foot-and-mouth-disease."

He frowned at her, even while laughing. "We should have stopped and got you a book before coming."

She smiled. "No, I'm kidding. You get a stitch or two?" She pointed to his earlobe, which just had a small piece of surgical tape on it.

Before he could answer, Chelsea ran back to him and gave him a hug around the leg. "Bye-bye, Gave."

He squatted down and said, "Now remember. Your mom and dad will call me in two days at the number I gave them if you want them to. We both have to go to our doctors again, and we can pretend we're going together, okay?"

Her lip trembled at the thought.

"It wasn't too bad, though, was it?" Gabe asked. "And we got lollipops!"

She nodded and put hers back in her mouth.

Gabe stood and shook hands with Chelsea's parents. "Nice meeting you, Jay. Chandra."

Chandra smiled at Kara. "I'm sorry we didn't get a chance to speak more. But your boyfriend has been a godsend."

Kara opened her mouth to explain that she and Gabe weren't a couple. He caught her eye and gave a dismissive shrug and shake of the head, as if it really wasn't important to set this stranger straight.

So Kara smiled back and said, "I'm so glad."

As Gabe and Kara walked out of the hospital, Kara asked, "Was it really not too terrible?"

Gabe opened his cell phone. "Well, not for a twenty-nine-year-old man, no. But for that poor little thing? Heartbreaking." He sighed. "She's an amazing kid. Didn't seem to have much fear of needles. But she might by the time this is all through. She's going to have to go back four more times before she's done."

"You too?"

He nodded. "I'll have to see Mom and Dad's doctor in two days for the next round."

"In the stomach?" Kara grimaced.

"No, at least they don't do that anymore. They shot me once at the site." He touched the base of his ear.

"Ouch," Kara said.

"And once in the arm." He put his hand on her back to guide her toward a bench outside the hospital. "Let's sit down and get everyone back here." He punched the number on his phone to reach Ren.

Kara glanced at her watch. "Wow, Gabe. It's seven o'clock. What do you think we should do?"

He held his finger up to ask her to wait. "Hey, Ren," he said into the phone. "We're ready for you guys...No, not too bad....Right... Okay, we'll be waiting outside."

He closed the phone and turned toward Kara. "You mean, do I think we should just stay here tonight and head out again tomorrow?" His lips curled up slightly at that.

Kara chuckled. "We're not exactly making good time on this trip, are we?"

Gabe faced forward, stretched out his long legs, and put his hands behind his head. "I don't know. I'm having a pretty good time."

Kara pretended to be suspicious. "Why, Gabe Paolino. Did you do the Macarena with that rabid squirrel just to spend more time with little ol' me?"

He sat up, also acting offended. "Absolutely not!" He waited a beat. "That was the cha-cha."

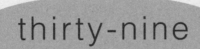

thirty-nine

The next day, as they neared Lurlene's house, Addie kept giving advice to the group.

"Whatever you do, don't say anything about her hair. She's mighty touchy about that."

Rachelle asked, "Why? What's wrong with it?"

Addie touched her own hair as if suddenly concerned with her looks. "She let some kid work on it. Has a pinkish color to it."

"Pink?" Kara asked. "What color were they trying to make it?" She had heard of little old blue-haired ladies, but pink didn't sound likely to happen, even by accident.

"Red, I think," Addie said. "Like Rita Hayworth."

All three of the teens said, "Who?"

"Movie actress," Addie said. She looked at them, surprise on her face. "Mercy, you kids don't watch much TV, do you?"

Gabe snorted. "I wish, Addie. They watch way more than they should. Just not old movies."

"So, Addie," Ren said. "How, um, young is Lurlene to be getting her hair dyed red?"

"Eighty next month. She's my little sister. 'Course, she might not have the pink hair still. That was the last time I visited her, just after Willard passed."

Kara asked, "When was that?"

Addie looked out the window, apparently digging around for the memory. "Been a long time. That white-haired fella was the president."

"Thomas Jefferson?" Jake asked quietly.

Rachelle tapped him on the back of the head. "Shush."

"Clinton?" Kara asked.

Addie pointed at her. "Bingo. That's the one."

Ren smiled. "Yeah, it's been quite a while, Addie. Maybe the pink's grown out by now."

Kara said, "Wow, you must really miss her."

"That's a fact, honey."

Kara was still curious about Addie's initial concern in reaching Lurlene quickly, followed by her apparent ease in taking extra time on the trip down. "Um, Addie. My mom had said something about your hurry to reach Lurlene before it was 'too late.' Do you remember that?"

Addie stared at Kara but squinted as though she were rewinding mentally. "You know, now that you mention it..." She looked past Kara, out the van window. Then her eyes widened. "That's it!"

"What?" Kara asked, sitting up straight. "What's it?"

Ren put her hand on Addie's. "What's the matter, Addie? Did you remember why we needed to hurry?"

Addie shook her head. "No! I mean that's it!" She pointed toward the back of the van. "Back there. That's her house."

Gabe looked in the rearview mirror. "You sure, Addie? This isn't the street you had written down."

"Oh, never mind what I wrote down. Half the time I'm just making it up, anyway."

Gabe laughed. "But Addie, the map says there is a Cascade Drive up ahead. That's what you wrote."

She waved her hand as if smoke were clouded around her face. "That's probably just where the market is or something. I probably remembered it from something like that. I'm telling you I have a good memory for pictures, and that was her house back there."

Ricco said, "Awesome. That's how I remember stuff too. Gabe, let's go see if she's right."

Addie looked at him and frowned. "Of course I'm right, ya little whippersnapper."

"Okay, Addie," Gabe said. He turned the van around. "We'll go back, and you tell me which house to check out."

Sure enough, when they pulled into the driveway of the aqua-colored house, out ran a woman who looked distinctly like Addie, but taller and with a good 40 pounds more weight on her. Lurlene looked older than Addie. She wore glasses, the way Addie did, and she had a more traditional, short hairdo, rather than the cute little gray bob Addie wore. All hints of pink were gone; Lurlene had plain old gray hair, with maybe a hint of blue. She waved her arms as if she were afraid the van might leave. Her upper arms continued to wave a second or two longer than the rest of her.

"Lurlene!" Addie called out the open windows. She gave Kara a tap on the leg. "Come on, honey, let me out so I can go hug my baby sister."

They took short, quick steps, swiftly shuffling toward each other, and embraced like toddlers, nearly knocking themselves down. They both started crying.

Gabe got out of the van and stood next to Kara. "You think you'll be that lovable when you're that age?" he whispered to her.

Kara had a tear in her eye when she looked at him. "Hey. I'm that lovable now."

He reached up and caught the tear. "I believe that's true."

Then he seemed as embarrassed as Kara felt, and they looked away from each other.

Gabe approached Lurlene. She saw him and grabbed Addie by the arm, as if she had to steady herself.

"Sweet mother of pearl, Addie, who's this creature from heaven?" She had a bigger voice than Addie.

Addie looked at Gabe as if he were her own son. "Isn't he the most magnificent thing ever? Love him dearly. Lurlene, this is Gabe, Kara's husband. And that's Kara over there."

Kara chuckled and didn't bother to correct Addie again. She reached her hand out to Lurlene. "I'm sorry we took so long getting here, Lurlene. We've had such a lovely time with your sister. Thank you for sharing her with us."

"Isn't she a pip?" Lurlene asked, shaking Kara's hand.

Addie said, "See, Gabe got attacked by a vicious, rabid badger." She pulled her hands up like claws for dramatic effect.

Lurlene gasped.

Gabe laughed. "Oh, no, Addie. It was just a squirrel."

Frowning, Lurlene said, "Where were you people, to get attacked by rabid squirrels?"

"Actually," Gabe said, "it was only one squirrel, and I doubt it was rabid. It just got scared and bit me on the ear."

Addie said, "And Kara got smacked in the nose!"

"By the squirrel?" Lurlene asked.

Kara laughed out loud. "No, a Frisbee. Just a little accident. Nothing serious."

Ren and the teens got out of the van and Addie eagerly gathered them near her and introduced them all to Lurlene. She got every name right and was perfectly lucid in every detail about them. Except she kept calling the teens "the triplets."

Gabe said, "If you're ready, Lurlene, the boys and I will get whatever bags you have and we can get back on the road. Is that all right with you?"

"I've been ready for two days!" Lurlene said. "Follow me. Only have the one bag, though."

"I'll get it," Ricco said, jogging ahead of Lurlene and holding her front door open for her.

Gabe rubbed his hands together and looked at Kara and Ren. "All right. It only took us three days to accomplish the first, what? Twelve hours of driving? We're about three hours from Miami. So I'd say we'll reach my folks by next week, and yours, Kara, just in time for Christmas."

Both women laughed. Kara said, "You think there's any chance of getting to both your parents' place and mine today?"

Gabe tilted his head. "I'm willing to give it a try. We can grab drive-through lunch and refuse to let my mother talk us into staying for dinner."

Kara frowned. "That's not going to make a very nice impression on her, is it?"

He smiled at her. "You couldn't make a bad impression on her if you tried. She's going to love you." He glanced at Ren. "And you too, Ren."

Ren grinned. "Mm-hmm. I can see it now. 'Mom, I'd like you to meet my good friends, Kara Richardson and Chopped Liver.'"

"Let's rock and roll, Gabe," Ricco called. He carried Lurlene's bag to the back of the van.

"I want to sit with Addie and Lurlene!" Rachelle said, prompting a smile between Kara and Ren.

"Looks like it's me and the boys," Ren said, lifting her chin toward the back of the van.

Gabe placed one hand on Kara's back and the other on Ren's. He guided them to the van and opened both passenger doors. With a flourish, he presented their seats to them. He gestured toward the front seat. "Ms. Richardson."

He motioned toward the backseat and looked at Ren. "Ms. Liver."

As she got in the van, Ren demurely nodded her appreciation. "Badger Boy."

forty

"And after my dear husband, Edgar, died," Lurlene said, "I went up to live with Addie and Willard for some time."

Addie, who sat next to Lurlene in the middle seat, put one hand on Lurlene's and took hold of Rachelle's hand on her other side. "I loved having my baby sister living with me for a while," she told Rachelle.

Kara, watching from the front seat, smiled. "I always wanted a sister."

Rachelle glanced in the back seat at Ricco. "Me too."

Jake snorted at that.

"But lands, who can take that cold up there in North Carolina? It does get cold there!" Lurlene said. "I had to move back down south and give my poor old bones some heat!"

Gabe looked at her in the rearview mirror. "Well, you certainly get that down here, don't you? My folks really like it too. They've lived in Miami almost the entire time they've been married."

"So you never lived anywhere but Miami?" Kara asked him.

He shook his head. "Nope. Well, I went to college in Fort Lauderdale."

"A regular world traveler, bro," Ricco called from the backseat. He pulled some chips from one of the grocery bags.

Gabe laughed. "Yeah. That's one of the reasons I moved to Northern Virginia. I wanted to stay on the East Coast, but I needed a change."

Rachelle asked, "Have you been happy with the change so far, Gabe?" She gave a little kick to the back of Kara's seat.

Gabe kept his eyes on the road. "It definitely has its advantages."

Ricco held the snack bag up. "Anyone want something?"

Lurlene turned and reached for the bag. "Let me see what you've got there, young man."

"Yes, well, I like the changes of season," Addie said. She and Lurlene simultaneously rooted around in the snack bag. Kara could just imagine them as little girls, peering into the cookie jar together. "And Willard's job was always up in North Carolina," Addie said, "so we never considered moving. But—"

"But you're starting to like the warm months better," Lurlene said. She pulled out a bag of pretzels. "We'll share," she told Addie.

Addie nodded. "Right you are."

Kara looked back at them without comment. Did Lurlene just finish Addie's sentence the way Addie did with everyone? Ren caught Kara's eye from the backseat, and they shared a smile.

Lurlene and Addie each pulled pretzels from the bag and passed it to Rachelle.

Ren asked, "What did Willard do, Addie? What was his job in Smithfield?"

"Newspaper man." Addie broke off a piece of pretzel with her hands, rather than biting it, and popped the piece into her mouth.

"Delivering?" Jake asked.

Addie chuckled around her pretzel. "Writing. That man could write a good story."

Lurlene said, "And a love poem or two, if I remember rightly." She pointed her pretzel at Addie and smiled as if they shared a secret.

Rachelle leaned forward to look at both sisters. "Really? He wrote you love poems, Addie?"

"He did," Addie said. She looked at Rachelle and scrunched her shoulders up, a girlish smile on her face.

Kara was touched to see that Addie was still charmed by what Willard did for her so many years ago. What woman wouldn't love a gesture as memorable as that? Kara sighed and then noticed Lurlene watching her.

"You much of a writer, Gabe?" Lurlene asked. She winked at Kara, and Kara suddenly felt obligated, yet again, to define her relationship with Gabe. But before she could give that much thought, he spoke.

"Wish I were, Lurlene. I'm afraid I'm a little weak in that department. I have a hard time expressing myself on paper."

Addie said, "Oh, but, Lurlene, you should see this man with children! There's a gift. He had that little girl, the one who got attacked by the weasel? Had her—"

"I thought it was a badger," Lurlene said.

"Squirrel," Ricco said, laughing.

Addie waved her hand at them. "Yes, yes, all right, a squirrel. But that little girl, before we even left Gabe there at the hospital, she was in love with him. Couldn't take her little round eyes off him."

Kara said, "You should have seen them together after you guys left. Building with Legos, eating lollipops. He even carried her out of the emergency room, not her mom or dad."

"See, there, Gabe?" Addie said. "A man who's a natural with kids. You can't beat that."

"That's how my Edgar was," Lurlene said. "And Addie's right, Gabe. He had the kindest heart."

"He did, Lurlene."

Rachelle was riveted by the two elderly sisters. "How'd you meet Edgar?" she asked Lurlene.

Both Lurlene and Addie smiled. Lurlene said, "at the skating rink.

Riverside Roller Rink in Ohio. Addie and I went pretty near every Friday night. Didn't we, Addie?"

Addie had just put a piece of pretzel in her mouth that was so big it poked the side of her cheek outward. She reached up to hold the pretzel still so she could bite it, but she managed to nod in answer to Lurlene's question, nonetheless.

Lurlene said, "I was around your age, Rachelle. You're about nineteen, right?"

"Eighteen next month," Rachelle said. She smiled, clearly pleased at passing for a 19-year-old.

Lurlene looked up, figuring. "That was...oh, just after the war."

"Which war?" Jake asked.

"Second World War," Lurlene said.

Addie had eaten enough to speak. "That's right, Lurlene, because both Edgar and Willard had been back home for a short spell."

"Yes, and that Edgar just came right up to us and asked Addie to skate couples with him," Lurlene said.

Rachelle gasped. "Addie? He asked Addie to skate?"

Addie laughed. "That boy was scared to death of Lurlene. I think it was love at first sight. He was so afraid she'd turn him down he couldn't ask her. All he'd been through in the war, and here he was afraid she'd say no."

Gabe chuckled. "I don't think it's any easier today for us guys. No one likes getting turned down."

Kara watched his face. She hoped he didn't view her no-dating policy as rejection.

Ricco's voice sounded deflated for a moment. "You got that right, Gabe."

Rachelle sighed and turned to look at her twin. "Really, Ricco, did you honestly think Tiffany was interested? She was just playing you. One of the many reasons I didn't like her."

"Who's Tiffany?" Lurlene asked.

Addie said, "Yeah. Who's she?"

Everyone other than Lurlene looked at Addie. Even Gabe looked at her in his rearview mirror.

"Yo, Addie," Jake said behind her. "Remember the girl—well, woman, I guess. The one with the long, really thick reddish-brown hair and sparkly blue eyes and big...uh, nasty attitude?"

Rachelle slowly turned to look at Jake, squinting at him, as if she needed to see him very clearly.

He looked at her as if he had been caught picking her pockets. "What?"

Rachelle said nothing. Just gave him a subtle nod and turned back around.

Kara watched Ricco, who obviously got a kick out of Jake's temporary discomfort. "Later for you, dude," Ricco muttered through a cynical smile.

"Oh, that one," Addie said, realization finally clicking in. "Tiffany. Yep, I remember her." She tried to look at Ricco in the backseat, but apparently she felt too stiff to turn that far. "Now, son, why would you get your heart in a bind over her? She's not only too old for you, she doesn't seem to have an innocent bone in her body."

Kara was shocked that Addie had forgotten Tiffany yet seemed to have read her fairly well.

Rachelle snorted. "That's probably why he was attracted to her."

"Okay," Gabe said, "let's get off that subject, all right? I don't like where this conversation is going."

After a moment of silence, Lurlene leaned forward and squeezed Gabe's shoulder. "I like you, Gabe."

"Me too," Addie said.

Kara felt another kick from Rachelle. Kara chuckled and said, "I like you too, Gabe."

Ren called up from the back seat. "I like Gabe."

Jake spoke in a fawning falsetto. "Oh, Gabe!"

Rachelle started to chant. "Gabe—Gabe—Gabe—Gabe—"

Ricco gave in to the moment and joined Rachelle, followed by the rest of the crew.

Gabe laughed over the noise and announced loudly, "Now this conversation I like!"

Kara smiled broadly at him and loved how she felt just then. She identified for a second with Lurlene, with her reason for moving back to Florida. This moment gave her bones some heat.

forty-one

The group's arrival at the Paolinos' spacious home was a mix of warm welcome, relief, and more than one parental eyebrow arched at the teens.

And Kara came very close to making an all-around good impression on Gabe's parents, who were obviously affluent but relaxed and down to earth.

Mrs. Paolino gave in to Gabe's insistence that she not prepare dinner for them.

"We've taken days longer than we expected to, Ma," he said. "And Kara's parents are as eager to see her as you were to see Rachelle and Ricco."

Mrs. Paolino put her hand on her hip and eyed her twins scornfully. "Probably a bit more eager, I'd say."

"Come on, Mom," Rachelle said. "I know you were mad, but you're happy to see us, aren't you?"

Mr. Paolino said, "We're overjoyed to see you!" He hugged Rachelle and gave her head a noogie.

Rachelle pushed him away, laughing.

He said, "And we've got all kinds of fun activities for the two of you to do. We don't want you getting bored and running off to Virginia unannounced again."

Rachelle stopped laughing and looked at Ricco with a grimace.

"Ricco," Mr. Paolino said, "you and I can take a little trip out to the garage in a minute. I'll show you what needs to be taken care of over the next week or so. Jake, I know your dad has something special planned for you too. I'll drive you over after Gabe and the ladies head back out."

"And I've developed quite an interest in spring cleaning," Mrs. Paolino said to Rachelle. "Won't that be fun to do together?" She gave her daughter a smile that would have been scary if it weren't so funny.

Ricco groaned. "You guys aren't really that mad, are you? I'll bet you barely even noticed we were missing before we called from Gabe's."

Gabe smiled. "Well, they're good workers, I can tell you that. My deli looks even better than yours now, Dad. I should be able to open shortly after driving back home."

Ren looked at Kara. "Where are Lurlene and Addie?"

Mrs. Paolino said, "I sent them into the living room. You girls go on and join them. I'm putting out a little something for you to nibble on before you get back on the road."

Gabe sighed. "Mom—"

"Just a snack, honey," she said, smiling. She suddenly grabbed him and gave him a big kiss on the cheek. "Oh, I'm so glad to see you. You look wonderful."

Mr. Paolino nodded. "Yes, you do, son." He glanced at Kara and Ren. "Something must be agreeing with you these days."

Ren automatically looked at Kara, and Mr. Paolino's eyes fell more specifically on her. He smiled knowingly at her, bringing a blush to her cheeks.

"Um, where did you say the living room was, Mrs. Paolino?" Kara asked.

"Please, call me Theresa," she said. She pointed out the direction for the girls. "You go on in. Gabe and I will bring the other stuff in."

As Gabe and Theresa left the room, he repeated, "Other stuff? Mom, I told you, we can't—"

"Oh, stop. When was the last time you ate? I'm not sending you off—"

The kitchen door blocked the rest of their conversation.

Mr. Paolino looked at Rachelle. "You go on and help your mother now." He hugged her again. "I'm glad you're okay, pumpkin."

Then he put his arms around the two boys. "Gents, let's step into the garage and let the ladies relax."

Ricco and Jake looked at each other helplessly and headed off with him.

"Nice meeting you, Mr. Paolino," Kara said as she and Ren headed for the living room."

"Ed," he called over his shoulder. "Call me Ed. And we'll talk again before you all leave."

Kara chuckled when she saw Addie and Lurlene in the elegant living room. They hadn't seemed hungry in the van, but they were both camped out on the plush mauve sofa, near the platter of fresh fruit that Theresa had put out. Lurlene's plate held twice as much as Addie's. Addie had a strawberry in her hand and a concerned look on her face. She was eyeballing Lurlene's plate.

When Lurlene struck up a conversation with Ren, Addie stood and tugged on Kara's shirt. She drew her over by the windows for privacy.

"She's allergic to pineapple," she whispered to Kara.

"Hmm?"

"Lurlene. She'll break out in the worst kinda hives if she eats that pineapple on her plate. I tried to take all of it myself so she wouldn't get any, but she got those three pieces anyway."

Kara said, "Why don't we just remind her of her allergy, Addie?"

"She denies it. And the hives are worse every time. I got a call from her neighbor last year. Or maybe the year before, I don't know. Lurlene ended up in the hospital that time."

Kara pictured herself calling her mother and father with yet another delay. "Oh, my goodness, not another day at the hospital. Okay, Addie. If you're sure about this, we'll do something."

" 'Course I'm sure. It's Lurlene who has the memory problems."

Kara simply cleared her throat. She looked over and saw Lurlene holding her plate and talking with Ren. She was about to put one of those pieces of pineapple in her mouth. Kara called out, "Lurlene!"

Lurlene jumped in her seat and replaced the pineapple on her plate. "Gracious, child! What is it?"

Ren looked at Kara, a question in her eyes. "Are you all right, Kara?"

Kara sat next to Lurlene and said, "Oh, sure, I'm fine. It's...it's you I'm worried about, Ren." She looked at Lurlene, who still held her plate aloft. "Don't you think Ren's eyes look awfully...um, swollen?"

Lurlene looked at Ren for a moment and then back at Kara. "Why, no, dear. She looks very pretty to me. You look a little flushed, though. It is a tad warm in here. Maybe we should ask Mrs. Paolino—"

"But look at her, Lurlene. Look more closely. I swear you don't seem well, Ren."

The moment Lurlene squinted and leaned forward to study Ren more closely, Kara quickly but gingerly picked the pieces of pineapple off of her plate. When Lurlene started turning her head back toward her, Kara impulsively stuffed all three pieces into her own mouth.

Kara could barely close her lips around the fruit, so she stood quickly and put her hand to her mouth, acting as though she needed to cough.

As she stepped away from the couch, she saw Gabe and his mother standing in the entrance to the living room. Each held a plate of hors d'oeuvres. And each stared at Kara in shock, having just witnessed her stealing food from the plate of an unsuspecting little old lady.

There was so much pineapple in Kara's mouth, she couldn't even chew. And since she couldn't chew, she couldn't explain anything to either Gabe or Theresa.

As soon as Gabe's smile started to spread she knew he would simply chalk the incident up as another of her goofy accidents. But his mother frowned, and her lip hinted at a curl of disgust.

Worse, Kara could tell that she was about to drool, and there was nothing she could do about it. She had to put her hand to her mouth and slurp, even while trying to delicately ease her way past Gabe and his mother in search of the bathroom.

Two closets later, Kara found the bathroom, spit the pineapple into the toilet, and tried to regroup. Hearing Ren call her name, she opened the door.

"What in the world are you up to now, crazy woman? Do my eyes really look swollen?" Ren sniffed. "And how come you smell like pineapple?"

Kara sighed and explained as she walked out of the bathroom and they headed back to the living room.

Ren chuckled. "I was so busy letting Lurlene study my eyes, I didn't even notice. You're a regular stealth spy, aren't you?"

Gabe waited for them at the living room entrance, leaning against the doorjamb with his arms crossed at his chest. His mother sat with Lurlene and Addie on the couch.

"Okay," he said. "I know there's a good story here. You couldn't have been that hungry, Kara. I've seen you hungry, and you've always managed to pace yourself better than that."

"Go easy on our girl," Ren said. "Lurlene's got a hospital-worthy pineapple allergy."

"And she's in deep denial about it," Kara said. "So I had to steal and stuff it."

Gabe looked in at Lurlene and then back at Kara. He gave her a genuine smile. "Man. You saved us from another trip to the hospital?" He gave her an appreciative hug. "You're my hero." He pulled back and looked at her. "Really."

Kara warmed up all over. But then she saw Gabe's mother looking askance at them.

"You might want to explain it to your mom," Kara said. She heaved a sorry sigh. "I seem to have figured out a way to make a bad impression after all."

forty-two

Within the hour they were on the road again.

"I swear to you, Kara," Gabe said, "Mom thinks you're great. So does Dad. I only hope I can make the same impression on your parents."

Ren leaned forward and whispered, "Maybe you could let them catch you rifling through Lurlene's purse while she's not looking."

Kara turned around and gasped at Ren before laughing. She glanced back at Addie and Lurlene. They were both still napping in the backseat of the van. Nevertheless, Kara talked in a hushed tone.

"Did you explain to your mother about Lurlene's pineapple allergy?" Kara asked Gabe.

He nodded. "Yep."

"And did Addie back you up?"

He chuckled softly. "Addie didn't know what I was talking about."

Kara smacked her palm against her forehead.

Gabe patted Kara's other hand. "Mom thought it was sweet of you to handle it the way you did. Really. So did I." He smiled at her.

"Inventive." He put both hands back on the wheel and looked ahead at the highway signs.

Ren made eye contact with Kara and wiggled her eyebrows. Kara just wiggled hers back. She faced front again and turned up the air-conditioning just a notch.

"There it is," Gabe said. "Homosassa."

"Gesundheit," Ren said.

Kara laughed. She looked at the sign. "Yeah, that's it. That's where Sugarwood Hills is."

When they finally pulled into her parents' driveway, the summer sun had set. Landscape lights cast a welcoming, warm glow upon Morine and Stan's home.

Kara was thrilled. Not only did she love the look of her parents' new home, but Beebo and Freckles stood at the fence, tails wagging in unison. They both looked as though they were smiling.

"Killer watchdogs, are they?" Gabe asked.

Kara laughed as she opened the door of the van. She took a deep, appreciative breath, enjoying the fragrance of Mo's lavender sky vine that weaved in and out of the fence. "I know. The dogs are useless, but they're my babies!" The last two words were said for the dogs' benefit in a high, happy voice.

In the back of the van, Addie and Lurlene stirred.

"What?" Addie mumbled. "Whose baby?"

"We've arrived, ladies," Gabe told them, as he, Kara, and Ren got out of the van. "You go on," he said to Kara and Ren. "I'll wait for Addie and Lurlene."

The dogs finally started barking, obviously excited at the possible attention Kara and Ren represented. The women had no sooner walked past the fence than Kara heard a screen door slam shut. Her mother called her from the side of the house.

"Where is she? Where is she?" Morine said. She came around the corner of the house just as Kara reached it. "Oh, honey!" She threw her arms around her daughter and hugged her as though she had no plans to let her go. "I missed you *so* much, baby."

"Me too, Mom," Kara said, her voice as shaky as her mother's. They were both on the verge of crying when they were interrupted by Beebo, who needed to be part of the moment. He jumped up and nearly knocked Kara down.

"Bad dog, Beebo," Mo said. "Down!" She released Kara and grabbed Beebo by the collar.

Kara wrapped her arms around Beebo's big furry neck, getting white hair all over her clothes. "It's okay, Mom, I've got him. Yes, I missed you too, Beebo, yes."

Freckles, the smaller of the two dogs, simply ran back and forth, wagging and waiting for instructions, occasionally venturing between Kara and Beebo to attempt some contact.

Mo gasped and put her arms out to Ren. "Look at you, Rennie! You look beautiful."

Kara looked up and smiled when she saw them embrace. Ren's mother had never been the most affectionate woman, and Kara always saw a bit of sadness in Ren's expression when Morine treated her as a second daughter.

Morine pulled back and said to Ren, "Are you doing all right? Are you holding up okay?"

Ren nodded. "Yeah." She shrugged. "You know. Some days are easier than others. I'm still not quite used to living alone."

Beebo took off and Kara gave a little attention to Freckles while talking. "This trip has been fun. A good distraction, don't you think, Ren?"

"Distraction from what?" Ren asked, and all three women chuckled.

They heard a weak cry of despair from the driveway. "Mercy!"

"Oh!" Kara said. "That's Addie!"

"Oh, my goodness, the fence is open!" Morine said.

Kara looked down. Freckles must have run off the moment Kara stopped petting her. "I hope Gabe's protecting those poor ladies from the dogs!"

"Beebo!" Morine yelled, even though they couldn't see him. "Down!"

They ran to the front of the house and found Gabe squatting down, trying to control both dogs. He devoted the bulk of his effort to Beebo. Freckles was ecstatic to be able to lick Gabe in the face since he couldn't effectively hold both dogs down at once. Kara tried not to laugh at his grimace as he tried to turn his face out of Freckles' reach and still hold Beebo steady.

Suddenly the front door swung open. Kara's father, Stan, stood in the doorway, holding himself up with one leg and a set of crutches. "Beebo!" he yelled, in a voice that reminded Kara of one of Gandalf's more imposing moments in the Lord of the Rings movies. "Freckles!"

Both dogs looked at Stan and immediately lay flat on the ground. They struggled to behave, even though they were still full of enthusiasm.

Morine quickly ran to the fenced area of the yard. "Come on, both of you. Come!"

Gabe wiped his face with his sleeve and looked at Kara. "She's talking to the dogs, right?"

Kara and Ren laughed.

The dogs ran to Morine, and she closed them in. When she walked away, Kara watched Beebo take in the change in his situation. In moments, he flopped down in the grass with a depressed sigh.

Freckles still hadn't figured anything out. She stood at the fence waiting for awareness to come along.

Kara ran to Stan as he worked his way toward the group. He stopped and held both of his crutches on one side so he had a free arm with which to hug her.

"How's my baby?" he whispered, squeezing her tight and wobbling slightly.

"Oh, Dad, I missed you guys so much." She buried her head into the crook of his shoulder, smelling the fresh soapy scent she had associated with him since she was a child. Now she did cry, although she was able to keep from outright sobbing. She was always a bit more vulnerable around her dad. And seeing him with the casts and crutches was a bit rough.

When Kara turned around, she saw that Morine had turned her attention to the rest of the group. Ren had introduced everyone to her.

Kara and Gabe met each other's gazes. She waved him over. "Dad, this is Gabe. He's a good friend of mine. We all got down here thanks to him."

She glanced over Gabe's shoulder and saw Morine waiting to make eye contact with her.

Morine tilted her head toward Gabe, mouthed "Wow," and waved her hand like something was hot.

Kara laughed and Gabe looked at her, confused.

Stan put his hand out and said, "I can't tell you how grateful I am, son. You helped out a lot of people, making this trip."

Gabe smiled at him. "I've loved every minute of it, sir. I'm...I'm very fond of your daughter."

Kara looked at him, surprised. Not because she hadn't realized Gabe might be fond of her. But he sounded as though he wanted to focus attention on his feelings immediately upon meeting her father. There was something old-fashioned about the moment.

She liked it.

"You and me both, Gabe," Stan said, smiling at Kara.

Morine, Ren, Addie, and Lurlene all joined them.

Stan said, "Oh, to be surrounded by so many lovely women and only have the one arm to hug with!"

Ren laughed and gave him a big hug.

"Kara, honey," Stan said, looking at Ren. "You didn't tell us you were bringing a movie star with you!"

"Don't be silly, Stan," Addie piped up. "I'm just your wife's Aunt Addie."

Morine, who stood behind Addie and Lurlene, brought her hand to her mouth, her eyes crinkling. Then she gently patted Addie's shoulder. "It's too dark for any of us to see each other out here. In we go!"

"I'll get the luggage," Gabe said.

"I'm sorry I can't help you there," Stan said.

"Not a problem, sir."

"Stan."

Gabe nodded and gave Stan a warm smile before walking back to the van.

"I'll help you," Kara said.

Ren put her hand on Kara's arm and asked softly, "Do you want me to help, or would you rather have a little one-on-one time?"

Kara smiled. "One-on-one sounds nice, thanks." She started to walk away, but then turned back. "Ren."

"Hmm?"

"If we don't walk back in soon...I mean, I still want to avoid..."

"I'll send Beebo after you," Ren said.

Kara laughed.

"And remember," Ren said, "there isn't an inch of that handsome face that hasn't been covered in dog spit."

"Eww," Kara said. She pointed at Ren. "You're good."

Ren lifted her eyebrows and her chin. "I try."

forty-three

Gabe smiled at Kara when she joined him to pull bags from the van. "Your parents are so friendly," he said. "Warm."

Kara sighed. "I've missed them so much. I didn't even realize how much until I saw them again."

He nodded. "Mmm. Same with my folks. But I haven't really been living in Virginia all that long, so we've only been separated for a short time. Your parents moved down here a while ago now, yeah?"

"Mm-hmm. Almost a year. They moved down here...well..." She hesitated, surprised by her own train of thought.

He stopped and gave her more attention. "What? When?"

"They moved just before Paul...right before we broke up. I especially missed my mom during that time."

He looked at her for a moment and then nodded. "Was Paul the breakup that put you off dating?"

"Yeah. Well, that was one of my reasons, anyway." She reached into the van and pulled out another bag.

Neither of them spoke for a minute. Then Gabe said, "Kara, why don't you go on inside? You should be with your parents." He put the strap of one bag over his shoulder. "I'll bring these things in."

"I want to help." She looked at him. "You've already done so much, Gabe."

He just smiled and said nothing. He looked tired.

She worried suddenly about having mentioned Paul, even in passing. "Was that insensitive of me? To bring that up, I mean?"

"You mean Paul?"

She nodded.

He took the bag off of his shoulder and turned around to lean on the van's bumper. He patted the area beside him.

Kara copied his stance and waited.

"You were right," he said.

"I was? About being insensitive?"

He chuckled. "No. You were right about not dating. I'm especially...I don't know...aware of how smart your decision was."

She scratched her head. "Why now?"

He shrugged. "Because your mentioning an old boyfriend didn't bother me at all. But if we had jumped into dating when we met each other, I'm pretty sure it would have. Just a different dynamic, I guess."

"Oh. I'm...glad?"

He laughed. "Think about it, Kara. It's probably pretty much the same for you. I mean, there's no denying the initial attraction. Mutual, I think, right?"

She hesitated and then gave him the tiniest nod.

He said, "I especially came on strong, asking you out to lunch before we'd even had a full conversation. It was just what I was used to. Especially after you said something—can't remember what it was—but I figured you for a Christian."

She smiled.

He said, "Seemed single, Christian, and there was no doubt you were one of the most attractive women I'd ever met. I think I was afraid to pass you up, even for a short time."

Kara said nothing, but she remembered thinking all the same things when she met him.

"But you know I told you I read that book about not dating?"

"Mm-hmm."

"I finally realized I was just looking for everything for me. If I end up marrying a woman just for what she can be for me...I mean, what if I end up not being what she needs? Eventually, we'd both feel that we made a mistake."

Despite Kara's effort to remain unemotional, a shiver of excitement ran through her when he mentioned marriage. "I...I think that's right. And I guess you can only really discover what people need by getting to know them as well as possible. But..."

She was glad it was dark and the van light wasn't terribly effective. She could tell she was blushing. "I have to admit I'm glad you're not just thinking about dating. You know, that you're thinking long-term."

"You mean, thinking marriage?"

She laughed. "You just spill it right out there, don't you, Gabe?"

He laughed back and gave her a gentle nudge on the shoulder before he stood up. "That's all you, Kara. You kind of stripped a lot of the mystery away for me. No point in beating around the bush anymore." He lifted the bags again and nodded his head once toward her. "That's one of the things I like about you."

Kara lifted her bags again too and walked beside him toward the house. She wasn't sure she liked the idea of being completely devoid of mystery. "Gabe?"

He looked at her, and she was again struck by how handsome he was. She sighed. "Do you think you could eventually get so comfortable with a woman that you would lose that initial attraction you mentioned?"

He nodded without hesitation, and her whole body drooped for a moment. "Sure," he said. "That's probably not all that uncommon."

He held the front door open for her. As she walked past him, he lowered his voice. "But if you're asking if I'll lose that initial attraction for you?"

She glanced over her shoulder at him.

With a wink he said, "Not on your life."

forty-four

Kara laughed the moment she and Ren entered Morine's kitchen. The decor itself was gorgeous—cherry cabinets, granite countertops, and ceramic tile floors. A pleasant, cinnamon-like smell suggested a homey atmosphere. But everywhere Kara looked was another electronic appliance that had undergone some kind of transformation at Stan's hands.

"Good grief, Mom, the place looks like a medieval torture chamber. Doesn't Dad have a workbench or something?"

Morine shook her head. "Honey, these are the repaired pieces."

Ren chuckled and approached a blender-type appliance. "This is kind of cool-looking."

"Do you use any of these things?" Kara asked.

Morine smiled. "Actually, I do. Some of them are— Oh, Ren, sweetie, you're going to put an eye out if you turn that thing on."

Ren yanked her hand away, and all three of them started laughing.

"Only you, Mom," Kara said. "You're the only woman I know who has to wear safety goggles when she makes dinner."

"Now, it's not that bad," Morine said. "You know, you always liked fiddling with gizmos when you were a little girl. You might have inherited some of Daddy's mechanical genius."

"Me? It takes me half an hour just to untangle my bras from each other when I sort the laundry. I'm very easily confused by mechanics. And logistics. And spatial stuff too, now that I—"

"Mo?" Stan called from the other room. He and Gabe entered the kitchen together. "Honey, how did you want to set up the various sleeping arrangements? Gabe and I aren't sure where to put everyone."

Gabe looked around the kitchen with the same amazement Kara and Ren had when they entered.

Kara waited for his eyes to reach her. They smiled together.

"I thought we'd put Addie and Lurlene in the bedroom across from ours," Mo said, "and the girls in the room beyond the den."

"And Gabe?" Stan asked.

Mo shot a glance at Gabe. "I've put Beebo and Freckles out in the yard, so the garage is free and clear."

Gabe laughed. "Maybe the couch?"

"Absolutely not, Gabe," Kara said. "You had to use the rollaway at Addie's. I'll sleep on the couch this time."

Stan frowned at Kara. "So you're proposing that Gabe and Ren use the room beyond the den?"

Kara's hand flew to her mouth, and she started laughing. "I'm sorry, Ren. Gabe." She looked at Mo. "You see what I mean, Mom? Logistics are not my thing."

Mo said, "Honey, the couch folds out into a queen bed. If you girls are all right sleeping on it, Gabe can use the back bedroom."

"No, really," Gabe said. "I'm just here tonight. I'll be completely comfortable on the foldaway, Kara, and then you and Ren won't have to move a second time tomorrow."

"Right, then," Stan said, resting on his crutches and rubbing his hands together. "Gabe, you know which bags belong to which people. Let me show you the rooms."

Kara said, "Dad, why don't Ren and I help Gabe? You should get off those crutches."

Stan shook his head. "I've been sitting for hours, baby. This is the highlight of my day."

After they walked out, Kara heard Stan say, "Addie? Lurlene? You ladies can freshen up if you want. We'll bring your bags to your room first."

"Stan, you're going to grill the burgers soon, right?" Mo called after him. "It's getting a little late."

"Soon as we drop off the bags, hon."

"Want me to start the grill, Mom?" Kara asked. She walked toward the back deck.

"Nothing doing," Mo said. "I've been trying to get your father to replace that old grill forever. He just keeps fiddling with it, and it's still messed up. The gas jets are all corroded. I'm boycotting that thing, and I don't want you around it, either."

Ren and Kara looked at the harmless-looking grill outside.

"Thing has just two heat settings," Mo said, "*Off* and *The Molten Flames of Doom*. Just stay away from it."

An hour later they all lounged, satiated, on the deck.

"Perfect dinner; perfect night," Stan said. He looked up at the clear, starry sky.

"You said it, Stan," Lurlene said. "Thank you so much for inviting Addie and me to visit. This is just wonderful." She looked at her sister. "You know, Addie, we might want to consider this place."

"For what?" Morine asked.

Addie patted her sister on the arm. "Lurlene and I have decided it's time we moved in together. That last spell between visits was horribly long. It's too hard for either of us to travel to the other to visit, and we get along great."

"Yes, sir," Lurlene said, "no more fights, now that we don't wear the same size anymore."

Gabe chuckled. "What does that have to do with it?"

"Lurlene used to take my clothes all the time," Addie said.

"Used to drive her crazy," Lurlene said, laughing. "But now her stuff is too small for me, so we get along just fine. We're looking for a place to buy. We already put both our houses up for sale."

Kara set her iced tea down and leaned forward in her chair. "So, does that have anything to do with why you needed to get together quickly? Or did you, really? I thought there was a rush, but at other times there didn't seem to be."

"A rush?" Lurlene asked. She looked at Addie. "What rush?"

Addie frowned for a moment, but then she raised her eyebrows and looked at Kara. "Oh, you mean the coupon?"

Mo and Kara exchanged smiles. Mo said, "What coupon would that be, Addie?"

"Lurlene's coupon," Addie said. She wagged her finger in Lurlene's direction. "You know, Lurlene, your discount coupon. It was going to expire."

Lurlene sat up. "Oh! For the cruise! We told you about the cruise, right?"

In the ensuing silence, everyone surveyed the group, but no one seemed to have an answer for Lurlene.

"Oh, goodness, Addie," Lurlene said, "you didn't tell any of these good people why we wanted to get down here in the first place?"

Addie shrugged and took a sip of soda. "Looks like I might have forgotten."

Lurlene tilted her head and nodded. "Well, we were a little busy trying to work things out. First we tried Emily—" She pointed at Mo. "You know Emily?"

Addie said, "My Willard's sister."

Mo said, "Yes, I remember Aunt Emily."

Lurlene said, "When we called her and asked for help in getting

Addie down here, she told us about you and Stan. She thought it made more sense for you to get Addie than for her to."

Mo smiled wryly. "Yes. That sounds like Aunt Emily."

Gabe said, "Well, I'm glad it worked out the way it did."

Kara and Ren added to his comment in a simultaneous chorus.

Lurlene looked at Gabe. "Well, that's mighty kind of you, Gabe. But, if none of you knew why Addie needed to get down here, why did you drive us?"

Gabe smiled at her. "I was coming down anyway to bring the kids back home. Figured I could do Kara a favor and get to know her better at the same time."

Lurlene returned his smile. "Aw, now that's just sweet." She looked at Kara. "Isn't he sweet?"

Before Kara could answer, Lurlene asked her, "And why did you think you were bringing us here?"

Kara shrugged. "To do Dad and Mom a favor."

Lurlene looked at Morine, her next question unasked.

Morine said, "Well, Addie sounded so desperate about getting down here before it was too late."

"For the coupon," Addie said. "Too late for the coupon. Saved us five thousand dollars."

"Five hundred dollars, Addie," Lurlene said.

"Oh. Well, still."

Stan shrugged. "Five hundred dollars is nothing to sneeze at, Addie, you're right." He sighed, sounding contented. "I'm happy you brought this trip about, whatever the reason."

Gabe nodded. "It was a God thing." He smiled at Kara.

"Yes, it was a God thing," Addie said. She looked at Lurlene. "Which reminds me. I want to talk with you about something." She looked at Ren and smiled, as if they had a secret together.

Kara thought about Addie's conversion on the beach and knew Lurlene didn't stand a chance, just as long as Addie could remember what she wanted to talk with Lurlene about in the first place.

Kara said, "So, when's your cruise, anyway?"

Lurlene looked up at the stars, calculating. "We leave from Tampa International Airport on the tenth of June."

Mo sat up. "But that's this Saturday. Four days from now."

Addie pointed at her. "Yep, that's what I remember. It was going to be on a Saturday."

Gabe grimaced and Stan rubbed his chin.

"So we haven't got much time," Lurlene said to Morine. "You think we might go shopping for cruise wear tomorrow?"

forty-five

The envelope lay on the kitchen table when Kara walked in for coffee the next morning. She saw her name written across its face in unfamiliar handwriting. She picked it up and sat at the table.

Morine walked in, coffee cup in hand. "Morning, honey." She walked over and kissed Kara on the head before pointing to the envelope. "That's from Gabe. He asked me for an envelope before he left."

Kara frowned at her mother. "He's gone already?"

"It's ten o'clock, sleepyhead. He said last night that he planned on leaving around six, remember?"

Kara ran her hand through her hair. She had even taken the time to comb it this morning before going public, making sure she didn't have rooster head again. All for nothing. "I feel so bad that I didn't say goodbye. I was sure I'd be up when he left today."

She glanced down at the envelope. Hmm. It must be something

private, or he wouldn't have covered it up. She felt a secret thrill, and her lips curled up at the corners.

"Like him a little, don't you?"

Kara looked up at her mother and blushed. "We're just friends, Mom." She got up and poured herself a cup of coffee.

Mo rested against the counter. "I know that, honey. And I understand what you two are trying to do. I have a lot of respect for both of you."

She raised her eyebrows and leaned in to whisper to Kara. "And now that I've seen Gabe, I can imagine how difficult this is for you."

Kara's eyes widened. "Mom! That's almost gross."

Mo laughed. She touched Kara's cheek and sighed. "Oh, honey. That reminds me of when you were in high school." She turned to the refrigerator and took out the milk. "You'd tell me I was weird if I so much as hinted at having a clue about the male-female drama."

Kara couldn't help but smile. "Did I really?" She sighed. "Ugh. 'Drama' is right." She held the envelope out, as if it were a symbol of her relationship with Gabe. "This is difficult, Mom. I mean, when I made the decision for purity—way back when—that seemed hard enough. Now, trying to keep even the suggestion of romance out of the picture...well, I don't think we've completely succeeded there."

"No, not completely. But I see more comfort between you and Gabe than I've seen between you and any other man before. That's got to be a good thing, no?"

"Really? You can see that?"

"Yep."

Kara thought about her repeatedly klutzy behavior around Gabe and Sandy's counseling that she would feel less awkward as they got to know each other. "Whaddya know."

She sat back down at the table, looked at the envelope, and smiled. She couldn't believe she hadn't torn it open the moment she realized it was from Gabe. Maybe her mother was right. Maybe this whole approach was right.

"Good morning." Ren walked in wearing a sleeveless top and linen slacks. She looked ready for a full day's activity. "Ooo, I thought I smelled coffee!" She headed straight for the coffeemaker.

Mo said, "Morning, Ren."

"How'd you get all purdied up so fast?" Kara asked.

Ren poured her coffee and joined Kara at the table. "I was hard at work scraping and spackling while you snored away the morning hours."

"Did you see Gabe before he left?" Kara asked.

"He left already? No, I didn't see him. You?"

Kara shook her head and held up the envelope. "He left me a note, though."

"And she still hasn't opened it," Mo said.

Ren arched an eyebrow. "Aren't you curious?"

Kara waved the envelope as if it were a hanky. She gave Ren a haughty look and spoke with a voice to match. "I'm very comfortable with our relationship, thank you." She gestured toward Mo. "Even Muh-*mah* has noticed, haven't you, Muh-*mah*?"

Morine sat at the table and mimicked Kara's tone. "Quite." She dabbed at the corners of her mouth with the paper towel she held.

Ren said nothing for a moment. Then she repeated, "Aren't you curious?"

Kara looked at her. "Okay, yeah." She broke the seal on the envelope and looked at Gabe's note.

> *Hey, Kara.*
> *Sorry I missed you. Had to get going.*
> *Call me on my cell.*
> *Gabe*

She read it out loud and then looked at Ren and Morine.

"Hmm," Ren said.

Kara looked at it again, as if something more might be hidden between the lines. "Not exactly a Shakespearean sonnet, is it?"

Mo tilted her head. "Well. It sounds like a note you'd write to a friend, I guess."

"Or your accountant," Ren said.

Addie and Lurlene walked into the kitchen, gabbing away.

"All I'm saying," Addie said, "is that as soon as I woke up this morning—"

"You wanted waffles," Lurlene said. "And you remembered—"

"Those waffles Willard always made when you lived with us," Addie said.

"Yes," Lurlene said.

The younger women stared at them as if they were watching a stand-up comedy performance.

Kara said, "Oh, my goodness, you do both do it!"

"Do what?" Addie asked.

"The sentence thing," Ren said. "You finish each other's sentences. And you get it right!"

Addie and Lurlene looked at them and then at each other, clearly unaware of what the younger women were talking about. Then they both shrugged, and Addie said, "Morine, do you happen to have a waffle iron?"

Mo laughed right out loud and looked pointedly around her kitchen counters. "Do I have a waffle iron? Honey, I have three. You want American, Belgian, or miniature?"

"American, I guess," Addie said. She looked at Kara. "What kind was that I had on the trip down here?"

Kara said, "Those were regular American waffles, I think. I'm not sure, though. Gabe ordered for you."

Addie looked over her shoulder toward the living room. "Where is he? Where's your hubby?"

Lurlene said, "He's not her hubby." She looked at Kara. "He's not, right?"

"Right. And he's gone," Kara said. "He left earlier this morning."

Addie brought her hand to her chest. "Ah, dear, I am so sorry!"

"No, Addie—"

"All for the best, then," Lurlene said. She sat down and sighed. "Men."

Kara said, "But—"

"You said it, Lurlene," Addie said. "Oh, my stars, I'm telling you. I loved my Willard, I swear I did. But there were times—"

"And with my Edgar too," Lurlene said, shaking her head.

"I do love the Lord," Addie said. "I was just telling Lurlene about Him last night, wasn't I, Lurlene? But—"

"She was," Lurlene said. "Told me I needed the good Lord in my life."

"But sometimes you got to wonder what He was thinking when He created men. They can be the most fustratin' people."

Mo was at the kitchen counter, moving appliances around in an apparent search for a waffle iron. "Frustrating! I have to agree. I know Eve was the one who ate the apple. But I'll just bet Adam did something to drive her crazy and chocolate hadn't been invented yet."

She unearthed the waffle iron and heaved a big sigh before turning to see all of the other women staring at her.

At that instant Stan hobbled into the kitchen, crutches pulling his bathrobe all crooked and his hair completely askew. He looked at Morine and said, "Waffles!"

To his confusion, every woman in the room started laughing.

Kara stood up and gave him a hug and a kiss. "Good morning, Dad. I'm going to go call Gabe."

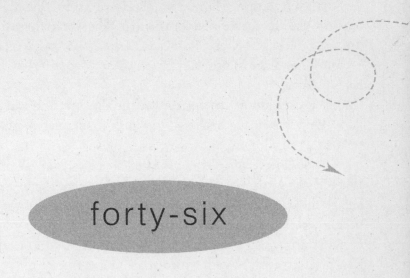

forty-six

By the time Kara reached the room she and Ren were sharing and fished her cell phone out of her purse, she could hear her father joking with the rest of the women. Laughter drifted out from the kitchen, adding to her contented mood. She keyed in Gabe's name on her phone's directory and flopped down on the bed, waiting for him to pick up.

When he did, Kara didn't get a chance to say a word before he spoke.

"I swear, Tiffany!" he said, clearly annoyed. "I said I'd call you later. I'm going to have a car accident if you don't stop. Please."

Kara's mouth dropped and she bolted upright. She pulled the phone away from her ear and looked at the display on her phone. Without another moment's thought, she ended the call.

That had definitely been his voice. That had undoubtedly been his number. And her phone display didn't lie. "Gabe cell," was how it read.

Still, she couldn't believe what she'd just heard. She opened the phone to call him again. Then she closed it. If he was having a hard time driving while on the phone, Kara didn't want to add to his problems.

But if he was involved with Tiffany, Kara was going to be one of his problems.

She looked up at the mirror on the dresser. She was flushed and angry. The image bothered her almost as much as the phone call had.

Her shoulders slumped and she looked away from her reflection. What in the world was the matter with her? Had she been fooling herself all this time? If she truly wanted to be Gabe's friend, what business was it of hers if he was involved with Tiffany?

But Tiffany was a nightmare! Wouldn't Kara feel upset if Ren were getting involved with a nightmare of a person?

Tears came to her eyes when she considered her answer to that question. Of course she'd want to protect her best friend. But this was a different feeling altogether. A bunch of them. Jealousy. Suspicion. Loss.

She looked in the mirror again. She quietly said, "It's all about me."

She was doing exactly what Gabe had talked about last night, out by the van. She was only focusing on what she wanted.

He promised Tiffany he'd call her later. That hadn't made Kara worry for Gabe. She'd immediately worried for herself—she had instantly worried that Tiffany might get something Kara wanted.

Even awareness of her selfish thoughts didn't stop her from reviewing past conversations. Gabe had made it clear several times that he was attracted to her. That he thought Tiffany was scary. He had rolled his eyes over Tiffany's theatrics and shared smiles when Tiffany had acted like a human chameleon with a multiple personality disorder.

But he had promised to call Tiffany. To say what?

"Whoa," Ren said from the bedroom doorway. She looked at Kara with concern. "What happened?"

Kara looked at her before flopping back down against the pillows, one arm over her face. "I'm the world's biggest phony, that's all. I even fooled myself."

"That's not true," Ren said. "I can think of at least one person who could out-phony you with one hand tied behind her back."

Kara groaned. She took her arm away from her face. "Gabe thought I was Tiffany when I called just now."

"What?" Ren's body suddenly looked tense. "Why would he confuse you with Tiffany? You sound completely different from each other."

"Well...I didn't exactly speak."

"What'd you do? Breathe heavily?"

Kara sighed, frustrated. "He just started talking, as soon as he answered the phone. It sounded like she had been calling him a lot. I mean, just now, while he's trying to drive. Sounded like he found her really irritating."

"Oh," Ren said. "Well, that's good. Shows he's a rational thinker."

"But he said he would call her back."

Ren tsked. "Now, Kara, do you honestly think he's going to call back and whisper sweet nothings to her? Sounds like he was just trying to get her to leave him alone."

Kara said nothing.

"Remember," Ren added. "He asked you to call him. In writing, even."

Kara picked Gabe's note up from the bed. She looked at it for a moment—such a normal, boring little set of words. From a guy who appeared to have his head on perfectly straight.

She sighed. "Rennie, I'm not doing this right."

"Doing what right?"

"The friendship thing." Kara felt a tiny sting in her eyes. "I like him."

Ren smiled. "Well, it's all right to like him, Kara. He's a terrific guy."

"But I don't like him like you do. I like him like Tiffany does."

Ren tilted her head and looked at Kara fondly. "Not possible. I don't think there's a whole lot of anything you do like Tiffany does. Trust me. I couldn't hang out with you if that were the case. Even the way she flosses her teeth gives me the creeps."

"Okay, but you know what I mean, Ren. I was attracted to Gabe as soon as I saw him, and that hasn't changed a bit. No matter how much time I spend with him, he's still a total knockout to me."

"So?" Ren chuckled. "Was that the goal? To stop thinking he was good looking?"

"But it's distracting! I'm letting it affect how I see the rest of him."

Ren looked down at the carpet, and Kara appreciated that she didn't just argue that point without thought. Ren looked back at Kara for a moment.

"Are you sure? You really think you're overlooking stuff because you're busy looking at his eyes? Or his...other stuff?"

Kara couldn't help but smile at that last comment, even while she brought her hands to her face in embarrassment. "Yeah, maybe."

"So, tell me one thing he's done during this trip that you thought was, oh, say, really kind."

Kara took her hands away from her face. She looked at Ren. "Um, I thought it was kind that he always took the worst place to sleep when someone had to do that. And he wanted to carry all the bags in here so I could spend a few extra minutes with Mom and Dad. And—"

"I only asked for one," Ren said, putting up her hand and smiling. "Now, how about something that he did that made you respect him more."

Kara nodded. "He told everyone we needed to watch what we said about Tiffany, since she—"

"Wasn't around to defend herself. Yeah, that was cool. Okay, how about funny? What's one thing he did that made you think he had a good sense of humor?"

"All right," Kara said, "I get it. He made me laugh all the time, and he laughs easily."

"So, are you saying that you wouldn't have appreciated those things in an unattractive person?"

"No, but—"

"And more importantly," Ren said, counting points off on her fingers, "let's say Gabe insisted on the best place to sleep, and left us to carry our bags in, and was the worst of us in ragging on Tiffany. Do you honestly think you would have overlooked those things and fluttered your pretty little eyelashes and said, "Oh, but he's so cute! I *like* him!"

Kara snorted. "No. Well, maybe the ragging on Tiffany thing, yeah."

Ren laughed and gave Kara's leg a little smack. "You wouldn't have liked that, either."

Kara shook her head. "No, you're right."

"Look, Kara, you're doing the best you can. You're both trying to get to know each other without clouding your judgment with all the romantic stuff. I think the Lord's honoring that effort. He knows you're human."

Kara looked at Gabe's note again. "Yeah."

"Hey, want to pray about it?" Ren asked. She didn't wait for an answer but put her hands out for Kara to take. They both bent their heads, and Ren said, "Dearest Lord God, we thank You for being with us always. We need Your constant wisdom and guidance, Lord. You know that, of course, but we forget sometimes. Please fill us daily with the discernment of the Holy Spirit and help us to honor our commitments to You. In Jesus' name we pray. Amen."

"Amen," Kara said.

She would have said more, but just then her cell phone rang. She picked it up and read the screen. As before, it didn't lie: "Gabe cell."

forty-seven

Hello?" Kara said.

"Hey, Kara! Morning," Gabe said. "I just got to Mom and Dad's. Made pretty good time."

He sounded so much more cheerful than when she had called him.

Ren waved at her and left the bedroom.

"Kara?"

She realized she was just sitting there, mute. "Yeah, hi."

"I didn't wake you, did I?"

"No, I've been up for a while. You...you sound so upbeat."

Kara could hear that he was exerting himself and then she heard his van door shut. So he had called her the moment he parked the van. That made her smile.

"You know me. I'm usually elated to be at the end of a long drive."

You know me. She liked that too. Of course, she wasn't absolutely certain how well she knew him, but there was time for more of that.

Kara said, "I'm sorry I wasn't awake to say goodbye this morning. I should have set the alarm."

"Not a problem—" and then he sounded like he had been tackled, head on.

Kara heard laughter—his and a girl's, and then muffled talking. Finally she heard him tell the person, "It's Kara."

"Kara! Come rescue me!" the female voice called out.

Gabe laughed and finally got the phone back to his ear. "Rachelle misses you terribly, Kara."

Amid more muffled sounds Kara heard Rachelle saying, "Let me—let me talk to her," before she finally spoke into the phone. "Hey, Kara, really. You should have come back with Gabe."

Kara laughed. "Yeah, and then he could come back with me to my parents' again."

"I need you to keep my mom from freaking out on me with the punishment thing," Rachelle said. "She's gone way overboard. You wouldn't believe it. It's like I ran away to China or something!"

Kara heard Gabe and his mother in the background, and then Gabe got closer to the phone again.

"Okay," Rachelle said to her, "Gabe wants the phone back. I miss you, and hey—I'll give it back to you, Gabe, in just a second—but hey, Kara, thanks for letting me stay with you in Virginia. I don't think I said thanks." She giggled. "Thanks!"

Gabe said, "Hi, sorry about that—" and Rachelle yelled in the background, "You're awesome, Kara!"

"Tell her I said bye," Kara said.

Gabe spoke away from the mouthpiece. "Kara says goodbye and get lost now so she and I can finish a sentence or two."

"Gabe!" Kara said, laughing. "Tell her I didn't say that."

"Kara says she thinks I'm terrific except for my crazy little sister—" and there was that head-on tackle sound again, followed by Rachelle and Gabe's laughter.

Then Kara either heard Rachelle leaving or Gabe walking away from Rachelle. But Kara was still able to hear Rachelle taunt Gabe with one final, "Love ya, Kara!"

Kara grimaced. Gabe said nothing for a moment.

Finally he said, "Why does she keep saying that to me?"

"Um, what do you mean?" She pulled at a loose thread in the bedspread.

"She said that to me a few times at the deli, when we'd be joking around."

"Hmm."

"Especially if I teased her about Jake in some way."

Kara uttered a rather hollow laugh. "You know kids." She saw her false expression in the mirror and rolled her eyes at herself.

"Yeah." He was quiet, but Kara waited him out. "Anyway," he said, "when do you and Ren fly back home?"

"Sunday morning."

"That doesn't give you much time with your parents. I'm really sorry about that."

Kara smiled, "Don't be sorry at all. I loved the trip. And none of our delays were your fault, they just happened."

"The squirrel bite might have been my fault," he said.

"Oh!" Kara said. "What about the other shots?"

"I go for the next one today. I'll be seeing my old family doctor."

"Have you heard from Chelsea at all?" Kara asked.

"Nope, but it's still early. Poor kid."

"Yeah. Poor you too."

"Thank you for your pity."

"You like pity?" She stood and walked to the dresser, where she had placed most of her clothing.

"If it will endear me to you, sure."

She laughed and pulled out a bright red T-shirt to wear. "My mother is impressed with my ability to, um, resist your charms."

"That makes two of us! I'm using some of my best stuff here."

Kara cracked up just as Morine came into the bedroom.

"Hang on, Gabe," Kara said.

"Sorry," Mo said. "Ren and I were going to take Addie and Lurlene shopping. You want to come, too, don't you?"

"Yeah. I need to shower, though, Mom. Can you wait just a little bit?"

"Sure." As Mo walked down the hallway, she called out, "Hi, Gabe."

"Tell her I said hi," he said.

Kara scurried into the bathroom, turned away from the phone, and said, "Mom, Gabe says hi and get lost now so he and I can finish a sentence or two."

Gabe actually gasped loud enough for Kara to hear him. "You did not say that to your mother."

"No, I did not," Kara said, "because I'm a very nice person and wouldn't want to embarrass you." She considered starting the hot water running, but thought better of it. She didn't want to rush this conversation any more than she had to.

Gabe exhaled his relief into the phone. "Yes. You're a wonderful person. I admire you immensely."

She walked back into the bedroom and pulled some jeans out of the closet. "You admire me?"

"If it will endear me to you, sure."

Kara laughed again. She heard voices in the hall. "I have to go. When are you driving back to Virginia?"

"I'll either leave Saturday night and break up the drive or Sunday and drive straight through. You working Monday?"

"Yep." She frowned at the idea of her vacation ending.

"Okay, so I'll probably come by the gym and work out if I can get the time. Going to open the deli the following Saturday."

His mention of the gym brought Tiffany to Kara's mind. She wondered if she should mention the earlier phone call mistake.

"So I'll see you at the gym?" he asked.

"Oh, um, yeah. See you there. Bye."

"Okay. Love ya, bye." And he hung up.

Kara was still distracted by thoughts of Tiffany, so she held the phone for a second before Gabe's last comment registered. Then her mind caught up to what he had said, and she stared at the phone and widened her eyes.

"He did it again!"

Her phone rang, and she nearly dropped it. She juggled it for a moment before she got a good hold on it and opened it. "Hello?"

"I said that, didn't I?" Gabe said.

"Um..."

"What Rachelle teased me about. I said that."

"I...yeah. You did," Kara said. Heat ran completely up and around her neck.

"I must have done it before then," he said. "Did I?"

Kara grimaced and rubbed her forehead. "Um...maybe."

"And you told Rachelle about it?"

"Oh, good night, no!" Kara said. "She heard you. You called from the deli."

"Wow," he said. "That's probably really against the rules."

"The rules?" Kara asked. "You mean the no-dating rules?"

"Yeah."

She couldn't help but laugh. He sounded so shocked by his own behavior. "It's not that big a deal. You were distracted."

"Well, yeah. But I want you to know I don't usually just throw that word around, okay? I'm sorry. And I'm sure you're the only person I've done that with."

"No problem. Really. It was actually very sweet."

"Okay," he said. "Well, I'll see you Monday." Then he carefully said, "Goodbye, Kara."

"Bye."

She smiled. He was sure she was the only person he'd done that with. But now that she thought of it, he didn't sound sure at all. Maybe he was so shocked because he could have said it to one of his deli suppliers. Or his family doctor.

Or Tiffany.

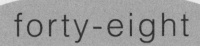

forty-eight

Two days later Stan took all of the women out to dinner. Kara itched with eagerness to get back to Morine and Stan's home. And she wasn't even sure why.

Stan clearly had a great time at dinner. In an effort to keep him from feeling overwhelmed by the abundance of women surrounding him, they had all secretly agreed to dote on him throughout the evening. He had been treated like a sultan, his every word cherished like a pearl of wisdom.

"Ladies," he announced, as Kara pulled the car into the driveway, "this has been an evening I won't soon forget. You've all been absolutely charming to this old codger."

"Watch how you throw that word 'old' around, Stan," Lurlene said. "If you're old, what does that say about me and my sis here?"

Addie patted the underside of her hair, much like Mae West. "That's right, Stan. You just speak for yourself."

Kara, who tried to shake off the compelling anxiety about getting home, laughed along with everyone else. She unlocked the front door, stepped into the house, and stopped to listen. Far off in the distance she heard the faint tinkling of "Clair de Lune," her cell phone tune. She knew immediately that this was why she felt strange during the drive home. She was used to having her cell phone with her, but she had forgotten it tonight.

Good grief. Had she become that attached to the stupid thing?

She shrugged off her earlier discomfort but still ran for the phone. She flipped on the guest room light, and saw the phone sitting right in the middle of the bed, still ringing. A quick glance at the display merely revealed "three missed calls."

Kara flipped the phone open. "Hello?"

"Ah, Kara! Finally!"

It was Gabe.

"Gabe?" Kara said. "I'm so sorry. Have you been trying to call me all night? My cell phone says I missed three calls."

"Well, they're all me, but I just started calling you...let me see... about fifteen minutes ago."

He started either laughing or crying; Kara couldn't tell which. He sounded so emotional.

"Gabe," Kara said, "what's...are you okay?"

"Kara, it's happened!" He was practically whispering, but with an intensity that Kara now heard as joyful.

"What's happened?" Kara said, smiling purely out of relief that he was calling with good news, rather than bad.

"Rachelle," he said. "She's...she just asked Christ to..."

Kara gasped.

"To be her Savior," Gabe said.

Kara stifled a little shriek of joy. "Gabe, how wonderful!"

She heard him sniff. The idea of his crying over this brought tears to her eyes. "I'm so happy for her, Gabe. For you."

"It's because of you, Kara," he said. "I wish you were here."

With a rush of emotion, she sat abruptly on the bed. She almost whispered when she spoke. "I do too."

"She was reading that Bible you gave her—"

"The one from my guest room."

"Yeah. And apparently that unequally yoked thing really made an impression on her."

Kara chuckled. "But, why?"

"I don't know. Earlier she did say that if she became a Christian, she'd have to convince Jake to do the same thing. And that she wasn't sure she'd be able to do that."

Kara scooted back to rest against the headboard. She pulled her knees up to her chest. "She might not be able to."

"I guess that's why she kept going back to that part," Gabe said. "But she said she started reading other parts of that same page, and she read a part about Christians being Christ's ambassadors."

"That sounds familiar."

"Kara, she told me that section made her think of you. She studied diplomacy in school this past year. She said you talked to her with respect—like diplomats do—when you talked about God. And she read a verse to me about God making His appeal through His ambassadors."

Goose bumps erupted along Kara's arms.

"She started..." he sniffed again. "She started crying, Kara. She put her arms around me and cried into my shoulder. She said she had to accept Him because now she knew He had appealed to her, personally, through you. That He used you to...to talk to her. She said she couldn't bring herself to turn her back on Him once she realized that. Even if Jake wouldn't come with her."

"She said that?" Kara asked, wiping a tear off of her cheek.

"Yeah. So right now she's talking with my mother about the church they go to. I told her it was really important that she make contact with other teens who are believers. Told her it would give her strength to stay turned toward Christ."

"Oh, Gabe, I'm so glad you told me. My whole night has just turned right around, thanks to your call."

"Why?" he asked. "Has it been a rough night?"

She shook her head. "Not at all—"

Ren appeared at the doorway, question in her eyes.

"But I just felt this worry on the drive home, and I think it was about your trying to reach me. Now I feel so blessed."

Ren put her hands up and frowned, her expression begging for details.

"Hang on, Gabe," Kara said. She told Ren, "Rachelle just accepted Christ."

Ren's face lit up, and then she began a silent but ridiculous-looking victory dance in the doorway, making Kara laugh.

"Ren's very happy too."

"Tell her I said thanks for the example she set for Rachelle."

"Gabe says stop dancing around like a crazy woman and act your age, for goodness' sake."

"Stop that!" Gabe said. But he started laughing at the same time Ren and Kara did.

Kara said, "Ren, actually, Gabe said he really appreciates the example you set for Rachelle."

"My pleasure, Gabe!" Ren called out. She came over and sat on the bed with Kara.

"Anyway," Gabe said, "She's awfully excited about this. But she's not sure yet about what to say to Jake."

"We'll have to pray about that."

"Yeah," Gabe said. He chuckled. "Do you realize this makes Ricco the only one left in my immediate family? I think Rachelle's going to hammer him pretty hard."

Kara laughed. "Just remind her of the diplomacy thing."

"Will do."

Kara heard a happy sigh from him.

"Well," he said, "it's late. I'll let you go. But say hi to your folks for me, okay?"

"Okay."

"And Addie and Lurlene," he said.

"All right."

"And Beebo and Freckles."

She laughed again. "Okay!"

"Kara?"

"Yes?"

"Thanks." He said it softly, like a gently exhaled breath.

And Kara felt like she breathed it in. Like she could almost taste it. It was so sweet she nearly asked him to say it again.

Instead she thought about Gabe taking up residence in her heart. That's what she pictured when she told him, "You're welcome."

forty-nine

Oh, for goodness' sake, Addie," Lurlene called from the car. "We're going to miss our flight if you don't come along."

"Yes, yes, all right," Addie called back, although she hesitated on the front step of Morine and Stan's house.

Mo ushered her toward the car. Kara sat at the wheel, watching.

Addie looked so nervous. She turned away from Mo for a moment and went back to give Stan one last hug at the door.

Lurlene muttered to Kara and Ren, "I swear, this isn't at all about saying goodbye to Stan. She's just trying to miss this flight. I was afraid she'd do this."

"I completely forgot about her fear of flying," Kara said. "Poor thing. That was the whole reason she didn't fly down here in the first place, isn't it?"

"Well," Lurlene said, "I knew she had that fear, but I was hoping the excitement of the cruise would help her get over it."

"Maybe it will," Kara said. "Let's just try to be encouraging and nonchalant about the whole thing."

As Mo and Addie got nearer the car, they heard Mo trying to soothe her. "You're going to have such a fantastic time, Addie. I wish I were going with you two."

"Uh-huh," Addie said, but she didn't look the slightest bit convinced.

Lurlene moved over in the backseat and patted the area next to her. "Come on, Addie. Everything's going to be just fine."

Addie and Mo got in the car, and then Kara pulled out of the driveway. "You smell wonderful, Addie. What's that fragrance?"

"They call it, um, Safari, I think," Addie said. "I probably shouldn't have put it on. It's making me feel a little sick to my stomach."

Kara suddenly felt moved to pull the car over, even though they had barely left the house. She stopped by the curb and turned to look at Addie. "You know, Addie. I don't think it's your perfume that's making you feel funny. I think it might be fear."

Lurlene actually did the "cut" signal at her throat, widening her eyes at Kara.

Kara shook her head. "Hear me out here, Lurlene. And don't worry." She glanced at her watch. "We'll get there in time." She looked at Addie. "I've felt debilitating fear before too, Addie. When I was a kid, at youth camp, the ropes course—it was way up in the trees—just made me freeze with fear. And when that happened, I found the best solution was to pray for peace about what was causing my fear. Would you like to do that with me?"

"With all of us?" Ren added.

Addie looked no less frightened, but she nodded. "All right."

Mo, Ren, and Addie lowered their heads. Kara encouraged Lurlene with a smile and a lift of her chin. Lurlene lowered her head as well.

Kara closed her eyes and said, "Lord, we love You and we need You. We know You spoke through the prophet Isaiah when You said that we are not to fear because You are with us. That You are our God and You will strengthen us. Lord, today we ask for Your help for our dear sister, Addie, who's afraid of flying. We ask that You would bless her with the constant assurance that her life—every moment of it—is already ordained and in Your hands. We ask for Your peace to fill her heart on this trip, Lord. We pray in the name of Jesus."

"Amen," Mo, Ren, and Addie said, followed by a hesitant Lurlene.

Addie kept her head down for a moment longer. Then she looked up and took a deep breath in and out, a gentle smile curling her lips. "Yes," she said, in a soft voice. "That surely did it, Kara. I thank you."

Lurlene looked at Addie with measured awe. "Really?"

Addie nodded with confidence. "Yep."

"But," Lurlene said, "you've had this fear all your life, Addie. You sure you're okay with it now?"

Addie smiled and took Lurlene's hand. " 'Course I'm not sure—I'm only human, aren't I? I wouldn't be surprised if I take that fear right back again." She smiled at Kara, who started driving again. "But our girl here reminded me of a few things that I can remind my own self of, if I get scared again. I'll be fine."

Lurlene sat back, looking flabbergasted. "Well, I'll be."

Addie chuckled. "Told you, didn't I, Lurlene?"

Lurlene chuckled right back at Addie. "You did, sister."

When they got to the airport, Kara parked the car so that she, Ren, and Mo could help Lurlene and Addie get as far as possible until airport security measures required them to leave the ladies on their own.

Addie looped her arm through Kara's while they made their way to the proper check-in lines. Her pale gray bob looked newly washed, and she wore the same red swing jacket Kara first saw her in. "You've been such a blessing to me, Kara. Both you and Ren. Imagine if I had flown down here and hadn't met either of you. I wouldn't know the Lord now, would I?"

Kara smiled. "You know, Addie, the Lord used us, especially Ren, to lead you to Him, but He was calling you anyway. You were meant to meet Him the day you did. Nothing any of us did or didn't do would have gotten in the way of that."

Addie squeezed Kara's arm. "I believe that, dear." She glanced over her shoulder at Lurlene, who walked behind with Mo and Ren. "And I think He's got a day in mind for my little sister. Any day now."

"I hope so," Kara said.

They checked Addie and Lurlene's bags and then walked with them as far as the security checkpoint, where they stopped to say their goodbyes.

Mo said, "You both have your tickets and IDs ready?"

They both lifted their papers in their hands. "All set," Lurlene said.

Lurlene gave a hug to each of the women before turning to join the line at the security scanners. She gave them a last wave. "Thanks for everything, girls. You were all just wonderful."

Addie gave Mo a hug and a quick kiss on the cheek. She hugged Ren with as much strength as she seemed able to muster. "Thank you, dear, for that day on the beach. You changed my life, you know."

Ren smiled. "I'm so happy I got to be a part of that, Addie. And I loved getting to know you on this trip. You took my mind off of a lot of other things, and I needed that."

Addie patted Ren's cheek and turned to Kara.

Kara was surprised to see tears form in Addie's eyes. The sight caused tears to immediately spring to her own eyes. "What is it, Addie? Are you all right?"

Addie smiled and took hold of Kara's arms, squeezing affectionately. "I'm just wonderful, honey. I have to tell you something, just in case we don't...cross paths again. Here on earth, I mean."

She glanced over her shoulder and made eye contact with Lurlene, who was starting to look worried. Addie raised her hand, gesturing for one minute, before looking back to Kara.

"You, dear, remind me so much of myself when I was your age."

"I do?"

Addie nodded. "I'm not sure why, but, yes, you do. And I didn't get a chance to tell you the other day—when we talked about Lurlene and Edgar meeting at the skating rink—how Willard and I met." She frowned for a moment. "We didn't talk about that, did we?"

This sounded like it might stretch out too long, but Kara was intrigued. "No, we didn't, Addie."

"Well, we knew each other since we were children, honey. And we were friends for...well, forever, before we became at all interested in each other romantically."

"Oh, Addie," Kara said, feeling a tear rolling down her cheek. "We should have talked about this before. I wish I had heard your story."

Addie shook her head. "You don't need my story, honey. We each have our own stories. For Willard and me it was a long process, and we stayed together forever. For Lurlene and Edgar, it was love at first sight. And they stayed together forever too."

Kara nodded.

"But now that I know the Lord, I know for sure that you need to lean on Him for what's best for you." She shook her head. "I can't believe how He blessed both Lurlene and me, even though neither of us was listening to Him."

"Yes, He does that sometimes, doesn't He?" Kara said, smiling through her tears.

"But you be sure and listen to Him, honey," Addie said. "That Gabe is a remarkable fellow. And I have a really good feeling about him. And about you. I think you're both trying real hard to obey God. I'll bet He rewards you for that. Just keep listening. Will you promise me you'll do that, Kara?"

Kara honestly wasn't sure if Addie thought that Gabe was her husband, friend, fiancé, or even runaway husband. But she knew the advice was not only heartfelt but applicable, regardless.

She nodded. "I promise, Addie."

"Addie!" Lurlene called, just before she had to walk through the scanner.

Kara bent down and kissed Addie on the cheek. "You've got to go, Addie. I love you."

"And I love you, dear." She reached around Kara and gave her a hug that felt like two frail bird wings enveloping her with all their might. "Goodbye."

"Bye."

Addie turned and gave a tiny wave to Ren and Mo as she got in line.

Kara watched her approach the first security guard, a stern-looking woman who put her hand out and spoke before she even looked at Addie. Kara saw Addie say something that caused the woman to look at her, frowning at first. Then the woman broke into a smile, despite herself. She answered Addie with more gentleness in her expression.

"What do you think Addie said?" Ren asked when she and Mo stood next to Kara.

Kara shook her head. "You know Addie. She might have asked if there'll be pudding."

Mo and Ren looked at Kara with questioning eyes. Then Ren said, "Might have asked about bacon to go."

Mo nodded and looked at Addie, who was now making some comment to the man on the other side of the security screening archway. "Or about coupons."

"About my husband, Gabe," Kara said.

Ren said, "Her neighbor, Elmo."

They all chuckled and enthusiastically returned Addie's last big wave before she was out of sight.

Ren said, "I'm going to miss her."

Kara put her arm across Ren's shoulders and sighed. "I already do."

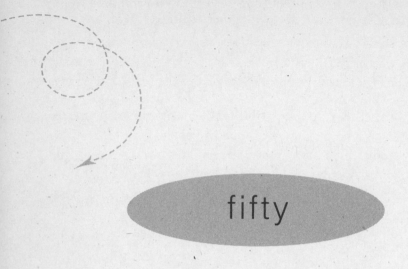

fifty

Kara and Ren were back at the airport the following day.

"Are you sure you don't mind the middle seat, Kara?" Ren asked. They had arrived in plenty of time before the flight, and there was no one yet in the aisle seat on their row.

"Not a problem. Really. Park it by the window, girl," Kara said. She pointed to the aisle seat. "Maybe this person won't show up, and we can spread out."

Ren sat down and stored her bag on the floor. She pulled out her *Contemporary Christian Music* magazine to read. "I think they said at the gate that the flight's totally full."

"No matter," Kara said. She removed her book about not dating from her carry-on bag before she settled into the middle seat.

Ren sighed and looked out the window. "Bye, Florida." She turned to Kara. "Are you eager to get back home?"

Kara shrugged. "I always like the idea of getting back to my own bed and my regular routines, but I feel like this vacation time went so quickly." .

"Mmm, so do I. I can't wait to see my kids—my class—tomorrow. But I loved all the company on this trip. Being with a group like that, you know, and then with your parents. Personally, I'm dreading my empty house a little."

Kara looked at her and nodded. "Do you ever think about moving? Maybe into something smaller, like a condo?"

"I've thought of it," Ren said. "But..." She sighed. "You probably think I'm nuts."

"Why?" Kara asked. "I mean, yes, I often think you're nuts, but why now?"

Ren chuckled, and then she took a big breath and released it. "Well, even though Greg has been pretty clear that he's gone for good—I mean, you can't get much more clear than divorcing someone—I just can't bring myself to give up completely." She leaned her head back and looked over at Kara. "It's not beyond God to change his heart still."

"No," Kara said, giving Ren a sad smile. "It's never beyond Him."

"Sometimes, when I pray for Greg, I feel that, if he'd just accept Christ, maybe he'd eventually realize what we could have had. And, if he did that, and came back, we might be able to go through with Casey's adoption. If all that happened, I'd still want to have our roomy house. The house we put together with a family in mind." She smiled at Kara. "See? Nuts, right?"

Kara shook her head. "Just hopeful." She reached over and gave Ren a gentle squeeze on the arm. "You're about the most faithful woman I know, Rennie. Honestly."

An attractive middle-aged woman stopped at their row and studied her boarding pass. Mild confusion clouded her expression.

Kara saw her check the seat numbers above them. "Did one of us take your seat?"

The woman smiled at her. "No—"

Do you need help, ma'am?" A young male flight attendant

approached and glanced at the logjam of people forming behind the woman. He crooked his neck to study her boarding pass. "Ah, I see the problem." He turned to a teenaged girl sitting in the window seat across the aisle. "Miss, may I see your boarding pass, please?"

Despite wearing earphones, the girl responded. "Sure." She pulled the earphones away and began digging through the book bag at her feet. "I know it's in here somewhere."

The attendant looked at the crowded aisle and then at the woman. He motioned toward the empty seat next to Kara. "Why don't you sit here until we—"

"Found it!" The teen waved her boarding pass in the air, her face red from either embarrassment or from hanging down too long over the book bag.

The attendant gave the pass a quick look. "Miss, you're in the wrong seat," he told the girl.

The woman touched his arm. "Oh, please don't bother. If no one minds, I'll be fine right here." She sank into the aisle seat.

"Problem solved!" Kara said.

"Yes, indeed," said the woman. She sighed as she settled in. "Next to two nice, trim women too." She extended her hand to Kara. "Leslie Verner."

Kara and Ren each shook hands with her and introduced themselves. She lowered her voice. "On my flight down here I sat next to a terribly big man. He couldn't help that he was big, of course, but there were other things. He had been drinking—a lot—and he fell asleep and kept resting his head against me."

"Goodness," Kara said, trying not to smile at the image.

Leslie scrunched her face all together. "Slobbered." She pointed to her shoulder.

"Eww," Kara said, making a face similar to Leslie's.

Beside her, Ren laughed into her hand.

"So!" Leslie said. "This is marvelous." She moved her shoulders back and forth. "We even have wiggle room!"

"I sometimes doze off when I read," Kara said, giving Leslie a wink. "So you just give me a good whack on the side of the head if I invade your space."

Leslie laughed and then waved toward Kara's book. "You just enjoy. I don't want to bother you when you're reading. I have some magazines to keep me busy."

But about 20 minutes after takeoff, Kara sensed Leslie looking at the book too. Kara glanced at Leslie, who eventually noticed and started, embarrassed.

"I'm sorry. That's so rude of me, isn't it?"

"Don't worry about it," Kara said.

Leslie pointed at the book. "That's a fascinating idea, isn't it? It caught my eye."

Kara nodded.

Leslie said, "So, he's suggesting you hold off on dating, is that it? That you concentrate on friendships?"

"Yeah. And on God, primarily. What God wants for you and for people you meet—*men* you meet, in our case."

Leslie laughed, "In your case, maybe, but not mine. I'm all done with that."

Kara smiled. "What? You never meet men anymore?"

"Oh, certainly, I come across men," Leslie said. "But they're all friends for me, at most. Never possible suitors."

Kara lowered her voice. "Leslie, do you mind if I ask how old you are?"

"Not at all. I'm fifty-six."

"But you're still young," Kara said. "Why do you write off the idea of romance?"

Leslie looked at her for a moment. "You mentioned God a moment ago."

"Yes. I'm a Christian."

Leslie nodded. "Me too." She patted Kara's hand. "And I'm very comfortable in my singleness, in the focus it gives me. It's where God wants me now."

Ren laid her magazine on her lap and leaned forward to listen.

Leslie glanced around before speaking again. "I was a teenager during the sixties. I thought of myself as a free spirit. A real liberated woman." She quickly closed her eyes, lifted her eyebrows, and shook her head. "I was a mess."

Kara and Ren both laughed softly.

"I experimented with everything—drugs, religions, men. I got in lots of trouble, got married, got divorced. Finally, I got a clue. But not till I was thirty or so."

"Got a clue? How?" Ren asked.

Leslie shrugged. "The timing was just right. The Lord turned my life around. It was that simple. Eventually I got married again." She sighed. "And George was all the husband I ever needed."

"Was?" Kara asked.

Leslie nodded. "He died five years ago."

"I'm sorry," Kara said. "I mean, I'm sorry for your loss."

"Thank you." Leslie smiled. "I must say, those were twenty of the most pleasurable years of my life."

Kara raised an eyebrow and hesitated before asking, "Pleasurable?"

Leslie leaned her head against the back of the seat. "Oh, he was absolutely beautiful." She looked at the women and laughed. "Beautiful! I had never met a man who was better looking."

Kara and Ren smiled at her enthusiasm.

"I wanted to be a sensible woman and not the wild child of my youth. I was certain that my interest in George had to be tainted somehow, just because I was so attracted to him. I was afraid I was just being..."

"Lustful?" Kara asked.

"That's it!" Leslie said, pointing at her.

Kara looked at Ren, who was grinning at her.

"So I did something very similar to what that book says," Leslie said. She pointed at Kara's book.

"You didn't date him?"

"Not for a month or so," Leslie said. "I know that doesn't sound like much time, but compared to my usual timetable, a month was a long wait. And we were both very active in our community, so we came across each other often before we dated. We were soon comfortable with each other." She leaned in toward the two women. "And don't think that wasn't a God-ordained situation, either. If He wants you to get to know someone quickly, He'll arrange things, believe me."

Ren gave Kara a gentle nudge with her knee.

Kara considered her dash in the rain that first day. To the first shop available. Gabe's shop.

She thought about her car choosing that point in time to surrender to her "mechanical genius," as Morine called it, rendering her helpless for transportation.

And Addie and Lurlene, with their desperate, time-sensitive need to get to Florida right away.

The twins and Jake, showing up when they did, necessitating that drive back to their parents.

And yes, Florida was a big state and a very common site for retirees like her parents, but what were the chances that both sets of parents...

Of course, there was the Tiffany factor. But Tiffany was, hopefully, a glitch. A tiny, removable thorn in the side.

Leslie pulled Kara's attention back by gently placing her hand on Kara's arm.

"Naturally, we dated for quite a while before finally getting married," Leslie said. "But it was with a...with an understanding." She smiled at Kara. "You know what I mean, dear?"

Kara nodded. "Like an old-fashioned courtship, sort of."

"Yes! Exactly. We were all but engaged. Definitely both thinking in that direction. It was much different than how I dated before."

Leslie straightened out the magazines on her lap. "Anyway, I've taken up too much of your reading time already."

"No, I appreciate your input—"

Leslie unlocked her seatbelt. "I'm going to make a little trip back to the restroom."

"Wow," Ren said. "That was pretty amazing, don't you think?"

"Really," Kara said. She shook her head. "But I don't want to see something that isn't there in this. I mean, I love it when God gives you guidance—"

"Which we prayed for the other day, if you'll remember," Ren said, eyebrow arched.

"Yeah, I know. But I always want to be sure I'm not reading my own will and fooling myself that it's God's."

Ren smiled. "I hear you. Been there."

Kara said, "Would I see His hand here if Leslie's story were different? Some lady who held off dating for a couple years could have sat here."

"But she didn't," Ren said. She lifted her chin toward the girl in the earphones. "And neither did she."

With the tiniest lift of her eyebrows, Ren said, "Leslie did."

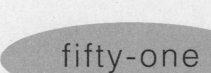

fifty-one

Kara and Ren stood at the luggage carousel watching the same duct-taped duffel bag go around for the third time.

"Is Jeremy parking his car and coming in?" Kara asked Ren.

"No, I told him to wait until our arrival time to drive over. By the time he gets to the Arrivals loop outside, we'll have our bags and can flag him down. He'll have to loop around once, at the most."

Kara nodded. A quiet but active commotion caught her eye beyond the luggage area. "Hmm. I wonder what's going on over there?"

Ren turned to look. "Man, I hope there's nothing wrong security-wise."

Other travelers turned to look.

"Oh, there's a news camera," Kara said. Then she glanced back at the carousel. "Here comes some stuff. Is this from our flight?"

Ren was still looking at the crowd beyond them. "Looks like they're interviewing someone."

"Probably a politician." Kara had seen her share of politicians at Dulles Airport; it was only natural because of its proximity to DC. She imagined the headache of having to be ready for the cameras every time you left the house. She had just thrown on her most comfortable pair of lightweight cargo pants and a simple T-shirt this morning.

"This is our luggage," Ren said, nodding toward the jumbled pile of suitcases and packs coming toward them. "That family over there was on our flight, and they just got their bags."

"Where's Leslie?" Kara asked. "Have you seen her since we got off the plane?

Ren surveyed the crowd before shaking her head. "She must have just had a carry-on."

They both watched unfamiliar baggage go by.

"She was cool," Ren said.

Kara nodded. "Completely. Oh, here comes mine."

Her suitcase was intertwined with the same duct-taped duffel bag, and both were partially covered by a large, black, very-serious looking piece of luggage.

"Oh, and there's mine," Ren said.

Kara tried to get to her bag, but the big black piece was too awkward. She managed to push it farther away from her bag, but she would have had to run into the people standing to her left in order to keep working at it. She sighed and released it for the next go-around.

"I'm going to go over to where they first come out," she told Ren, who had successfully pulled her bag from the carousel. "I wasn't able to pull mine off yet."

Ren nodded, looking back at the camera. "Yeah, okay," she said, distracted by the crowd. She looked at Kara. "I'm just going to take a peek and see who that is over there."

"Right," Kara said, and they went their separate ways.

Just as Kara got to the other side, the trio of bags—which included hers—popped back into view. She had to scurry to get to them before they reached the thickest part of the crowd.

This time she managed to get the black case completely free—

where was the owner? But the strap from the duffel bag had become wrapped around her suitcase in the process. The duffel bag's strap appeared to be jammed in the works of the metal conveyor. Kara was unable to get her bag before she came up against people again.

She hurried to run around the densest part of the crowd and reach an open spot, back where she and Ren had originally stood. "'Scuse me," she said, "Excuse me, please." She worked her way back in, just in time to grab her bag.

But now the strap of her bag was jammed into the conveyor as well. Who designed this contraption, anyway? Acting on instinct and a combination of panic and determination, Kara pulled tightly on her bag. She actually pressed her foot against the machine, hoping leverage would force her luggage out.

It took only a second, however, to realize that a drawstring on the low-slung pocket of her cargo pants had now become wedged in that same junction of the carousel.

Kara had become one with the conveyor belt, attached by that stray drawstring.

She was suddenly forced to forego all sense of decorum. With one foot on the conveyor belt and one on the floor, she ran like Long John Silver along the side of the carousel, desperately trying to keep from losing her pants. "'Scuse me! she said. "Watch...watch out!"

People parted for her like the Red Sea.

And on she ran.

It dawned on her that she might have to actually mount and ride the conveyor to wherever it went when it disappeared beyond the flapping plastic curtains against the wall. Like lightning, she pictured her options: arriving on all fours at the loading dock outside or standing here in the crowd without any pants on. At the last minute she realized she could even be in some kind of machine-chomping danger.

"Somebody help!" she called out, just as the conveyor stopped.

Kara was so flooded with relief that she almost started crying. Instead, she reached down and dislodged her drawstring from the mechanism. She straightened her pants and looked up at the gawking crowd, which had already started to disperse, their luggage and dignity in tow.

Then she saw Ren standing on the edge of the carousel, upon which she had climbed in order to push the big blue emergency-stop button placed just out of reach of normal-sized citizens.

Kara grabbed her bag as she passed it and met Ren halfway.

"I'm so sorry," Ren said. "I didn't know you were having problems, or I would have run back and helped you sooner."

Kara shook her head and put her hand on Ren's shoulder. "You're my hero. I owe you my dignity."

Ren started laughing. "I think you're going to have to save up for a while before you can pay that back."

Kara tugged at her pants and couldn't help laughing too. "You are so mean."

"Sorry, Hop-a-Long." Ren jerked her thumb behind her. "Hey! The camera was for that guy who leaked the story about the insider trading scheme at that techie company, Robert What's-his-name."

Kara shook her head. "I have no idea. They all run together for me."

"Yeah, me too," Ren said. "He just got to Washington to testify or something. That's what a lady in the crowd told me."

"Okay, whatever. Let's go find Jeremy before anything else happens. This place is just a little too action packed for me."

Ren nodded. "It is hoppin'."

Kara narrowed her eyes and looked at her. "So mean."

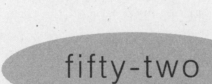

fifty-two

Kara laughed out loud. Her client, Mary—the tart-tongued, hefty redhead—was filling her in on what was missing from the gym while Kara was away.

"I'm telling you, Kara, I think you have a following. A good-looking following." Mary wiped her forehead with her towel.

"And I'm telling you that no one follows me anywhere!"

Mary raised dumbbells straight out in front of her body and lowered them. As she lifted them again, she said, "One week I see all these hot numbers coming through while you're beating me up here. Then you take off for...where?"

"Florida."

"Right, and I see nothing in here but a bunch of guys shaped just like me."

Kara laughed. "Hey, shaped like you is not bad. Look at these delts! You're getting some definition."

Mary snorted. "Yeah, definition." She announced formally, "The definition of squishy: Mary's delts. The definition of hopeless—"

"Nah-ah! I won't have that!" Kara said. "You're making progress. I think we should measure today, just to show you."

"Yeah, yeah. You need to show me a reason to drag my sorry behind in here. Like that cute guy from England. What happened to him?"

Kara smiled. "Jeremy. I just saw him last night."

"Again, the last-night thing with him? You still claiming he's just your friend?"

"Yep." Kara nodded. "He drove me and my other friend, Ren, home from the airport."

"Doesn't he come in here anymore? So cute. A regular Hottie McLicious."

Kara laughed. "You're bad, girl. Jeremy teaches during the day. Elementary school. He usually works out at night. He was off work the day you met him."

Mary's face suddenly froze as she looked over Kara's shoulder.

Kara felt a tap on her shoulder and turned to see Gabe smiling a big white grin.

"Gabe!" She almost threw her arms around him, but she stopped herself halfway. As a result she did a jerky little movement like a puppet whose strings had just broken. She ran her hand through her hair to try to cover up the awkwardness. "When did you get back?"

"Late last night. I decided to do the whole drive in one day."

"You work out here?" Mary asked.

"Oh, Mary, I'm sorry," Kara said. "Gabe, this is Mary. Mary, this is Gabe—"

"Don't tell me," Mary said. "Your friend."

Gabe nodded. "That's right." He shook hands with Mary. "Nice to meet you, Mary." He looked at Kara. "Listen, I lost my membership card. Is that a problem?"

Kara pursed her lips and rested a hand on her hip. "I'm beginning to think so."

He gave her a playful punch on the arm. "I mean, will it keep me from being able to use the gym?"

"No," she said, chuckling. "Not at all. I'll run off another one for you."

He looked down, sheepish. "I have a good excuse this time."

"Uh-huh," Kara said, a dubious look in her eyes.

He looked at Mary for support. "You tell me, Mary, if this doesn't sound reasonable." He looked at Kara. "I had to go to the emergency room before leaving for Virginia yesterday morning. You know, for my next rabies shot."

"Rabies?" Mary said. She scratched her head. "My, my. You are a wild child, aren't you?"

Gabe smiled. "Not really." He touched his ear. "Squirrel bite."

Mary looked at Kara, who said, "I'll tell you later. He's not as crazy as he seems."

Gabe tipped his head at Kara. "I thank you for that." He looked at Mary and put his palms up. "I had to dig out my insurance card for the hospital people, and a bunch of my cards fell out of my wallet. I'm sure that's when I lost the gym card." He looked back at Kara.

She put her hand on his shoulder. "You get extra points for not losing your wallet."

"Thanks." He nodded. "Okay, I'm going to run back to change. I'll see you later."

Mary and Kara watched him leave. He glanced back over his shoulder and gave them both a stunning smile.

Mary said, "I have got to take some lessons from you on making friends."

Kara smiled. "Let's have you work with the ab press for a while."

As they walked to the machine, Mary said, "By the way, Gabe was also not here while you were gone. You see what I mean?"

"Well, that's because he was with me."

Mary stopped midstride and looked at Kara.

"I mean, with me and lots of other friends." Kara knew Mary was most likely picturing her reclining on a lounge, surrounded by gorgeous, strapping young men with palm-frond fans and clusters of grapes overflowing from their hands.

Tiffany's voice rang out from the treadmill area. "Hey, that's Kara!"

Both Mary and Kara turned in her direction. Tiffany stood behind the treadmills, which all faced the televisions. She held a clipboard in one hand and pointed at the TVs with the other. She started laughing, and she was quickly joined by everyone walking or jogging in front of her.

Kara hurried over to the screens with Mary following. When she saw the news, she gasped so hard she almost started choking.

The whistle-blower from the airport was front and center, being interviewed. But the clip was apparently being shown to end the newscast that morning. This was the show's entertaining "One Last Look" segment, which often featured a nighttime comedian's political joke or a blooper of some kind. The cameraman had apparently noticed movement in the background while filming the interview at the airport. He had used up some footage focusing on Kara as she fought the good fight against the luggage carousel.

There she was, hopping along like a crippled grasshopper and then grabbing at her pants as they threatened to desert her.

Just before the clip ended, Gabe approached.

"Oh, Gabe!" Tiffany said, jumping up and down. She giggled. "Hurry! Come see poor Kara!"

Kara looked sideways at Tiffany. Poor Kara, indeed.

Gabe just smiled at Kara. "I saw Kara when I got here, right?"

Tiffany whined, "No, but—oh, you missed it." She walked over to them.

Mary groaned and spoke under her breath to Kara. She jerked her head slightly in Tiffany's direction. "This one is too much for me. I'm going to hit the showers, okay?" She patted Kara on the shoulder and walked away.

"Sure, Mary." Kara didn't look around much. She just wanted to climb behind the front desk and hide from everyone.

"Well, Gabe, you're certainly a sight for sore eyes," Tiffany cooed. "I'd hoped you'd get back in town sooner."

He gave her a polite smile. "We had a few more delays on the rest of the trip." He glanced at Kara and gave his healing earlobe a gentle tug. "But it was fun, right?" he said, and she nodded.

Mickey then walked up and gave Gabe a friendly smack on the back. "Yo, Gabe! How's it going?"

Gabe shook his hand. "Great, Mickey. Good to see you."

Mickey looked at Kara. "Hey! I found the perfect car for you while you were gone. You got a minute to talk?"

Kara was reluctant to walk away and leave Tiffany preying upon Gabe, but there was nothing she could do about it. "Sure." She looked at Gabe and Tiffany. "Excuse me."

Tiffany barely acknowledged her but placed her hand on Gabe's forearm as Kara walked away. "Listen, Gabe, let me ask you something."

Mickey told Kara, "So this car is almost brand new. One-year-old Toyota Camry. White. My buddy will give you an awesome deal as a favor to me. I've even taken it to a mechanic and had it checked out. Terrific shape." He put his hand on Kara's shoulder. "You listening? You okay?"

She nodded. "Yeah. I'm sorry, Mickey. That sounds great."

"But I can't go with you today." He suddenly turned and scanned the gym before he faced the free weight area. "Hey, Gabe, you got time to go with our girl to check on this car today?"

Kara smiled, despite still feeling like the village idiot. "Our girl" from Mickey's lips sounded so much more genuine than "poor Kara" from Little Miss Clipboard.

Plus, she was happy to see that Gabe had swiftly escaped Tiffany's evil clutches.

Gabe just gave them a thumbs-up and smiled at Kara. For some reason she thought about Leslie's talk on the plane, about God working circumstances to suit His will. And for some other reason, that thought made her happy that Gabe was there in the gym, being his regular, comfortable self.

But as Kara passed Tiffany, she noticed Tiffany looking at her as if she were a tedious annoyance. The expression caused Kara to do a double take at her.

"Just don't keep him busy too long at the car dealer," Tiffany said to Kara under her breath. "I have plans for him tonight, and I don't want you wearing him out with stupid finance details and stuff like that."

Kara was so shocked by the implications of what Tiffany said that she didn't even respond. She walked past Tiffany, wondering if Gabe knew about her plans. And she wondered why Tiffany was so certain that finance details were all that would happen while Gabe was with Kara.

Tiffany seemed confident that Gabe and Kara were friends. Nothing but friends.

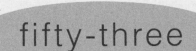

fifty-three

Ah," Kara said, when she sat down in the van's comfortable front passenger seat. "Feels like being home again." She casually breathed in. The van smelled like Gabe.

He smiled at her. "Yeah, this felt like one big, empty vehicle driving home. That's one of the reasons I did the drive home in one day."

"I really appreciate your coming with me today," Kara said. "I know nothing about cars."

Gabe raised his eyebrows. "Well, I have to warn you that I might have ulterior motives at work here. Maybe I don't want you to buy the car, even if it is a good deal."

Kara said nothing. He was teasing about their spending drive time together, which was bound to come to an end now that Rachelle was back home in Florida and Kara had to grow up and be a big girl again with her very own car.

She wanted to say a quick prayer, but she felt as though there wasn't time, so she just plowed into what she wanted to say next.

"Something cool happened on our flight from Florida."

"Yeah?"

"Yeah. And—"

"Does this have anything to do with the luggage conveyor belt thing?"

She whipped her head around to look at him. "You saw that?"

His smile was a closed one, but it was huge, nonetheless. "Never saw anything so cute before in my life. You were like your very own episode of *Laverne and Shirley* or something." He looked at her briefly. "My friend is a celebrity!"

Kara broke out into a sweat. "Oh, my goodness."

"What?" Gabe asked. "It was adorable."

"Why did you act like that at the gym?

"Like what?" he asked.

"Like you didn't know what Tiffany was trying to show you on the TV."

He shrugged. "I don't know. She was being malicious."

Kara sighed. He was too wonderful.

She wanted to date him. No, not date him. To pursue a future with him.

There. She'd arrived at a decision. *Thank you, Leslie.*

"Gabe?"

"Mm-hmm? Hey, which one of these dealers are we going to?"

"That one, Shecky's." She pointed to the right.

He cracked up. "Shecky's?"

She smiled. "I know. Doesn't exactly sound like one of those designer, preowned car dealers, does it?"

He pulled into the parking lot.

"So, anyway. Gabe." She started again.

"Yeah?"

"On the plane. This lady—Leslie—sat with Ren and me."

He turned off the van and looked at her.

"And we got talking about the no-dating thing."

He nodded. "Okay."

"Um, she...I got this feeling after talking with her."

He just waited, looking at her.

She sighed. "She...you know, her second husband—"

"Second husband?"

"Yeah," she said. "She was this wild, druggie, hippie woman the first time around. But then she got all straightened out before she met George."

"The second husband."

"Yeah. They got to know each other really quickly because of... well, circumstances." She swallowed. "It kind of made me think of our situation."

She looked at him, but he gave her nothing but his undivided attention.

She sighed again. "She said they decided to date after about a month of knowing each other—"

"Huh," he said. "Only a month."

"Yeah. Why? Does that sound like a short time to you?"

He shrugged. "Well, not in the regular dating world, no. But you said you and this lady were talking about the no-dating thing."

"Right," Kara said. "We were."

Gabe nodded. "So, yeah, a month sounds kind of short. That's like...well, how long you and I have known each other."

Her heart sank. It was exactly like the two of them. But she had found Leslie's situation encouraging, whereas he seemed to find it...inappropriate.

"So," he said. "What happened?"

She didn't want to talk about this anymore. She felt embarrassed. She felt rejected, even. Or at least that rejection was right around the corner from her next comment.

"Never mind," she said. "Let's go look at the car."

He put his hand on her arm. "Uh-oh. Wait. What did I just do? I did something that bothered you, didn't I?"

She looked at him and then shook her head. "No. You're being honest. You're...you're right. You didn't do anything wrong at all."

But she still felt like smacking him for some reason.

Kara started to open the van door.

"Wait," Gabe said. Now he sounded calm but a little irritated with her. "Kara, I said something wrong. Please tell me what I did."

She sighed. She was an idiot. "Nothing! You didn't do or say anything wrong, Gabe. You never do, okay? You are in total control of your every sense, and I'm being an overemotional, overly romantic moron."

She got out of the van. A little voice in her head told her to calm down. She told the little voice to buzz off.

She walked quickly across the parking lot, her pace matching her heart rate.

Gabe easily met her stride with his long legs. "I don't know how you can say mean words about yourself and complimentary words about me," he said heatedly, "and still manage to sound like you're cutting me down."

She stopped in her tracks and he overshot her a few steps before he stopped and turned to face her. Neither spoke for a moment.

Then Gabe took a deep breath in and out. "I get the feeling you're mad at me because of the no-dating thing. Like you don't think it's enough of a struggle for me."

Kara didn't like the sound of that. Was that what she wanted? For him to pine away for her?

"But believe me, Kara, it's a struggle. It's difficult enough for a Christian guy to live a pure lifestyle. But to give up dating altogether? To treat every woman you meet as nothing but a friend?"

Kara's quick, sharp intake of breath made him stop talking. Every woman? Hey, he wasn't just talking about Kara. He was talking about every woman.

The little voice attempted to grab Kara's runaway thoughts but was trampled like a short clerk at a shoe sale.

"Did I ask you to adopt my no-dating plan?" Kara asked.

"Well, no, but—"

"You can run around and date every woman under the sun, Gabe. I never told you otherwise."

"I know that—"

"And heaven knows I don't want to stand in your way when they're throwing themselves at you like groupies at a U2 concert."

"I never said you were—"

"I mean, even Tiffany has plans for you, from what I understand. Right?"

Gabe's mouth dropped. "What? Tiffany?"

"She asked you to get together with her tonight, didn't she?"

He looked genuinely confused, but then he said, "Well, yeah. But...she does that every time I come into the gym. She's certainly not hard to read. Or to resist."

Kara said nothing. She pulled her shirt away from her body, perspiration soaking through the fabric.

Gabe said, "I thought you knew that about her."

He looked down and swallowed before looking back up. He didn't meet eyes with Kara. "I thought you knew me. Better than that, anyway."

In the silence that followed, Kara knew she needed to step in and say something kind. She felt immense relief, really, in what Gabe had just said about Tiffany. But she couldn't seem to get her thoughts together. She glanced at the glassed-in offices of the dealership, the very last place she felt like going in the next few minutes.

She looked back at Gabe. "I do know you better than that. I'm sorry."

Gabe looked at her then. She had tears in her eyes when she asked him, "Are we still friends?"

He looked so hurt that she turned her eyes away for a moment. He smiled politely and opened the door to the dealer. "Yeah. Still friends."

For the next half hour they kept their polite faces intact. Gabe asked practical questions about the car on Kara's behalf and told her he thought Mickey had found her a winner. The dealer had expected

Kara and was able to pull everything together for her so that she could drive the car away today.

When she sat down to sign the appropriate papers, Gabe gently put his hand on her shoulder.

"I've got to get back to work, okay? I'll talk with you later."

Kara wanted to put her hand on top of his. To bring something remotely intimate back into their relationship. But she knew her eyes would tear up right there while she sat in front of the dealer if she did. So she just returned Gabe's kind smile and said, "Okay. Thanks a lot."

Gabe shook hands with the dealer and then walked out.

"Nice guy," the dealer said. "Mickey too."

Kara nodded and signed another page of her contract. She rubbed her arms, suddenly aware of being cold.

"You really gotta appreciate having people like that for friends," he said.

"Yes, you do. Good friends." And nothing more.

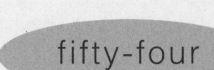

fifty-four

After Kara pulled up in Ren's driveway, Ren came running out of the house, happy as a cheerleader.

"I love it, Kara!" she said, looking at the immaculate white car. "Mickey found this for you? It's fantastic! It looks like you drove it right out of the factory!"

Kara smiled the best she could.

When Ren finally gave her a good look, she stopped short. "Oh," she said. "Ooo, something's wrong." She glanced at the car. "Is it a lemon?"

Kara shook her head. She tried to keep a tough exterior, but she didn't last long. She pointed to herself. "I'm..." She started to cry. "I'm the lemon."

"Oh, Kara," Ren said. She bridged the short gap between them and grabbed Kara up in a big, protective hug. "What happened?" She pulled away and turned both of them toward the house. "Come on in. I'll make us coffee. You want some coffee?"

Kara drew immediate comfort from Ren, who almost sounded like Morine with her maternal concern. Kara nodded.

"What's this about?" Ren asked. "Is this about Gabe?"

Kara sniffed. "Yeah. I just messed that whole thing up."

They walked straight back to the kitchen, and Kara slumped into a chair at the breakfast nook near the window. "I must be the world's worst communicator. Biggest hothead. Lousiest—"

"Hold on there, girl," Ren said. She had her back to Kara while she fixed the coffee. "First, you need to lighten up on yourself."

Kara's responding grunt sounded like an agreement.

"And those titles have to be held by men," Ren said. "Now, if you're talking Biggest Nag? Worst Whiner? Those might be women. But Worst Communicator and Biggest Hothead? Those have got to be men."

Kara looked up and frowned. Her voice was taking on a stuffed-nose sound. "That's not very politically correct of you."

Ren snorted and turned back to her coffee. "Yeah. PC. Try being married for a while. Eventually PC stands for predictable characteristics. In both of you."

"Well, I won't be able to test that theory for a long time." Kara tried to smooth the tension away from her forehead. "If ever. And there's no denying that I'm at fault here."

Ren joined her at the table while the coffee brewed. "Okay. We won't deny it. But tell me what happened."

Kara heaved a sigh. She rubbed at something on the table, although there was nothing there. "Gabe and I drove to the car dealer together. I decided to tell him I thought we should consider dating, but he wasn't into it."

Ren grimaced. "He flat out said no?"

"No," Kara said. "Not exactly. I didn't actually get around to asking him about it."

Ren sat back in her chair. "Then...how could he have told you he wasn't into it?"

"I started telling him about Leslie, the woman from the plane?

And when I mentioned that she and her husband started dating after knowing each other one month, he said, 'Well, that seems like a short time.' Like us, he said—how long we've known each other."

"He said like you two?"

"He did."

"And then he said he didn't want to consider dating yet?" Ren went to the counter and poured their coffee.

"Um, no." Kara said. "Then I got mad."

Ren carried mugs to the table. "But, why? What else did he say?"

Kara took her mug and sipped from it carefully, trying not to burn her lip. "Nothing else."

"So you got mad at Gabe because he thought that Leslie and her husband didn't wait very long before they started dating?"

"Well, that isn't how it seemed at the time." Kara took another sip of coffee. "But, yeah, I guess that's when I got mad."

Ren poured milk into her cup. "But, didn't you think they dated too soon at first?"

Kara looked at her. "Oh. Yeah."

"I think you might be right," Ren said with a nod.

"About what?"

Ren's smile was full of fondness. "I think you might be in the running for Biggest Hothead."

Kara tilted her head back and groaned. "It wasn't really so much that I was mad, Rennie. I just...well, here I thought I was going to get him all caught up where I was with the idea of dating. And then I could see I was wrong about what he was ready for, but I had already started talking about it."

"And so you got mad at him because you were afraid he was going to say no."

Kara snorted. "Ren, it was pretty obvious he was going to say no."

Ren looked at Kara for a moment before taking the milk pitcher and ceremoniously placing it in front of her. "I hereby grant you the Worst Communicator award."

"Ugh. I know! That's what I mean." She looked out the window. "I might as well go home and use that waxing kit of yours on my entire head and join a monastery."

Ren laughed. "You mean a nunnery, I think. A monastery is full of men. Monks."

Kara put her head in her hands. "Yeah, and we both know how successful I am with them."

"Monks?"

"Men!" She looked up. "I totally destroyed any chance I might have had with Gabe."

Ren chuckled and put her hand on Kara's. "Oh, no, you didn't. I'm sorry, I shouldn't tease you with the award stuff. I'm just trying to keep you from getting too maudlin. Look, I got to know Gabe on the Florida trip too. Believe me, you didn't destroy your chances. Gabe's made of better stuff than that."

"But he seemed so...uncomfortable with me when he left the dealership."

"I'm sure he was! Haven't you and I been uncomfortable with each other after arguments?"

They looked at each other for a moment.

"Yeah," Kara said.

Ren smiled.

With a deadpan face, Kara said, "But those arguments were all your fault."

Ren laughed.

"What do you think I should do?"

"Did you apologize yet?"

"Yes, I apologized," Kara said. She paused a moment. "Well, actually, I guess my apology wasn't about losing my temper. It was more about Tiffany."

Ren said nothing.

Kara looked up from her coffee and met Ren's anxious expression. "I forgot to tell you about that. I brought Tiffany into the argument."

Ren raised a hand to her mouth, as if she might start biting her thumbnail. "You mean, like you were jealous? Or did you accuse him of something?"

"Um..." Kara looked as if she were in pain. "Maybe a combination of those, yeah."

"Oh," Ren said. "Well."

Kara felt the sting of tears in her eyes. "See, I really did a number on him, didn't I?"

"Okay, wait. You made some mistakes, but you weren't vicious or cruel. I know you, Kara. You weren't vicious or cruel."

Kara dabbed at her eyes with a napkin.

"What we need to do is pray first. Then I think you need to...well, I think you might need to do some more specific apologizing."

Kara nodded.

"I mean, I know you were attracted to Gabe right from the start. But his friendship is valuable to you too, right? Even if you never date each other, you do still want to be friends, right?"

Kara heard the chance of loss in Ren's words, and her tears came more freely. "Yeah, I still want to be his friend."

"Okay, then." Ren took her hands. "The next time you and Gabe talk, you need to be up front with him about what was going on in your mind today. You've been pretty honest with him up until now. The last thing you want to do is start expecting him to read your mind. Or thinking you can read his."

Kara just shook her head about her behavior.

"So let's pray for guidance, and then we'll both wait for it, okay? And we'll pray that God will help us accept His will, whatever it might be."

Kara looked up at Ren and nodded. "Yeah. His will." She lowered her head and actually started praying silently before Ren prayed out loud.

When Ren mentioned accepting God's guidance and His will, a bell went off in Kara's head.

She had even considered prayer right before she lost her temper with Gabe. But she had ignored the idea. Kara suddenly realized who deserved her first apology, and she made it the moment she finally approached Him in prayer.

fifty-five

"Hey, new car owner!" Mickey said to Kara when he arrived at the gym the next day. "You liked it, I see."

Kara smiled at him. She stood at the front desk, scanning her appointment book. She was determined to go on with life as usual, despite her concerns about Gabe. Despite wanting to call him at that very moment instead of talking about her car.

But yesterday, after she prayed for guidance, she felt strongly that the Lord wanted her to give him some space.

"Thanks so much, Mickey," she said. "You did a great job in finding that car. I owe you big time."

He stepped behind the counter and retrieved a clean towel for himself. "Ah, don't mention it. My wife's birthday's coming up. You help me figure out what to get her and we'll be even." He smiled and walked away.

Kara looked down at her appointment book again and muttered

under her breath. "Right. I can't even figure out what I want, and I'm going to help pick out what Becky wants."

Mickey popped his head back around the corner. "Sorry. Say what?"

Kara started. "Oh!" She shook her head. "Ignore me, Mickey. I'm just mumbling to my sorry self."

"But I heard you mention Becky. She's not giving you a hard time about anything, is she?"

Kara looked at him in surprise. "Becky? She's terrific. Why would you think she's giving me a hard time?"

Mickey shrugged. "Beats me. Just thought I'd ask. You women confuse me to no end."

"Yeah, like men are easy."

Mickey looked over his shoulder before walking back and facing Kara across the desk. "Do I hear some oppressed anger there? Hmm?"

She looked up at him, surprised again.

"Hey, I watch the talk shows."

Kara laughed. "I think you mean repressed anger, Mickey. But you're probably right. Only I'm more mad at myself than anyone else."

"Gabe, you mean?"

Kara tilted her head, nonplussed.

"See?" Mickey said, opening his palms upward and nodding. "I'm not just a buncha muscle. I see stuff. I can be sensitive." He raised his eyebrows in a hilarious attempt at loftiness. "If you cut me, do I not...uh..."

"Bleed, Mickey," Kara said, laughing. "But I don't think you're quoting it right."

"Yeah, whatever," he said, pointing at her. "I heard that somewhere, and I get it, sort of."

"Okay, Mr. Sensitive. What makes you think I'm upset about Gabe?"

He shook his head and placed his hands on the top of the

desk. "I ain't saying anything unless you tell me he's the one you're upset about."

Now Kara looked around. The last thing she wanted was Tiffany sneaking up and eavesdropping.

"Yeah, okay," she said. "I was kind of a jerk with him yesterday, and I feel horrible about it."

"How big a jerk?"

Kara sighed. "This is private, okay, Mickey?"

He raised his eyebrows. "How much gossip have you ever heard from me?"

That was true. And a neighborhood gym was almost as active a gossip mill as the local hairdresser's.

"All right," Kara said. "I was short-tempered with him because I was feeling insecure. And I sort of acted as though he were keeping stuff from me about..." She looked around once more. "...about Tiffany."

"Oh! So you and Gabe are an official item now?" he asked.

Kara frowned at him. "Are you being mean to me?"

Mickey put up a hand. "No, no! I'm serious. Those just sound like things dating people fight about."

Kara nodded. "Exactly. That's how big a jerk I was to him. My friend."

He squinted his eyes, curiosity in the shake of his head. "Why would you worry about him and Tiffany? I mean, she's fine and all, but there's nothing going on up here, you know?" And rather than tap his head, as Kara expected, he tapped his heart. "I would think she'd be the least of your worries when it comes to Gabe and other women."

"Well, she's just so—" Kara stopped, once Mickey's meaning sank in. "What do you mean? Is someone else after him?"

Mickey chuckled. "Kara, where have you been? Half my female clients are after the guy. And I suspect a couple of my male ones, to tell you the truth. My training schedule has been great since Gabe started coming, I'm telling ya."

Two young mothers walked in with their toddlers, greeting Kara and Mickey.

"Hi," Kara said, handing them clean towels. They headed back toward the nursery, and Kara returned her attention to Mickey.

"But I never see anyone, you know, throwing themselves at him the way Tiffany does."

He cocked his head back. "Oh, yeah. Well I set 'em straight right away. Soon as they ask me about him or even start looking at him all moony."

"Set them straight?"

He raised one shoulder. "About you two."

Kara's eyes widened. "But, Mickey, you can't be telling people Gabe and I are a couple. We're not."

"Hey, don't worry about it. I just tell them he's interested in one of the women who works here. Never mention your name."

In an effort at redeeming herself, she said, "But, Mickey, that's not really fair to Gabe. He'd probably be peeved if he found out you were interfering—"

"Gabe's the one who told me to do it."

Kara's stomach fluttered so suddenly she stood upright from the rush. "He...he did?"

Mickey gave Kara a big, proud grin. "Now, aren't you glad you talked to ol' Mickey?"

Kara smiled reluctantly. "Well, I have to admit I feel a little more confident now. Thanks, Mickey."

He cuffed her gently under the chin. "Anytime, sport. And don't worry about your being a jerk with him. He's got thick skin."

As he walked away Kara suddenly remembered something from the Florida trip. She turned and walked as quickly as possible to catch Mickey before he entered the men's locker room.

"Mickey!"

He turned and faced her. "Yep. What's up?"

She spoke very quietly and pulled him away from some clients.

"Is there any chance that Tiffany ever heard you telling those women what you just told me?"

"That Gabe's interested in you?"

"No, no," Kara said, "that's not what you've been telling people, right? You've just been saying he's interested in—"

"One of the women who works here, yeah."

"So, could Tiffany have heard you say that to someone before?" Kara asked. "Like before we all went to Florida?"

Mickey looked upward and stroked his nonexistent beard. Then he nodded at Kara. "Sure she could have. She's probably the worst eavesdropper here, don't you think?"

Kara smiled at him. "Thanks again." She walked back to the front desk, a new bounce in her step. Even though she had brewed up a storm with her recent attack on Gabe, other areas were starting to clear up.

She remembered that evening at Addie's house. When Kara and Ren had interrupted Tiffany using her syringe. Tiffany had bragged that she had it on "good authority" that Gabe was interested in her. If she had eavesdropped on Mickey, of course she would have assumed she was the woman he meant.

Another puzzle piece had been put into place, and the picture was looking so much better than Kara previously realized.

Now, if she would just get out of the way and stop poking holes through the pretty picture, maybe the Lord would bless her despite herself.

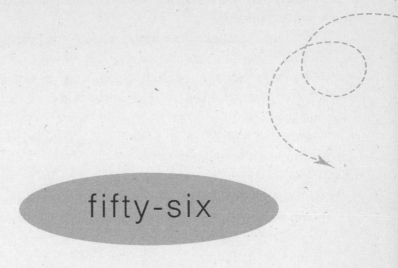

fifty-six

Kara ignored the advice she usually gave to clients and worked out at the gym late that night. And just as late workouts tend to do, her routine got her all revved up. She struggled to relax once she got home.

She had stayed at the gym and exercised because, to be honest, she had a fleeting wish that Gabe might end up coming in to lift weights after working at the deli all day. He planned his grand opening for the upcoming weekend, so Kara knew he'd be especially busy, but she held out hope until nearly closing time.

She was also not particularly eager to spend the evening alone. She had never been one to get lonely at home the way Ren complained of doing. Kara actually enjoyed solitude. But tonight she couldn't stop thinking about Gabe and hoping that Mickey had been right about his having a thick skin.

She could call him and apologize again, but she felt certain that she still needed to back off and give him time.

So she called her mother instead. Sighing, she picked up a slice of the pizza-with-everything she bought on the way home and got comfortable on the couch.

"Hey, Mom," Kara said when Mo answered. "Am I catching you in the middle of anything?"

"Not at all, sweetie. I just started reading a novel for my book club. Haven't gotten hooked on it yet. You back in the swing of things since getting home?"

"Yeah, pretty much. I worked late tonight, though, so I'm eating pizza right now. I'll try not to be noisy."

"I thought you had cut back on working at night."

Mo had encouraged Kara to avoid having to come home late at night, and Kara had adapted her work schedule, partly to ease her mother's worrying mind.

"Well, I actually didn't work that late, but I stayed and lifted weights."

Mo sighed. "Mercy, I'd think the last thing you'd want to do after working all day at a gym would be to actually work out yourself!"

Kara chuckled. "I have to do it sometime. What kind of advertisement would I be if I'm all flabby myself?"

"Yeah. You flabby."

"Mom, how long did you know Dad before you two started dating?"

"Oh." Mo was clearly taken off guard. "Does this have anything to do with being flabby?"

Kara laughed. "I don't think so! I'm just curious."

She could almost hear the smile in Mo's voice. "You're changing your mind about Gabe, then?"

"Well, I'm certainly leaning in that direction. But that won't mean much if he and I aren't in agreement."

"He called here, you know."

"What? Gabe called there? When?"

"Let me think...it was two nights ago. Or, no. Maybe it was just last night."

He probably called them before Kara let loose on him. But maybe it was after they quarreled, which would actually make her feel a bit more hopeful. If he called them even after she lost her temper with him, then he hadn't been too horribly fazed by it. Unless...

"What did he sound like? What did he say?"

"Oh, you know, just thanks for having me, it was nice to meet you, that sort of thing."

Well, he could have said that in lieu of saying a more dramatic "Farewell forever."

"Mom, did he sound...sad?"

"Oh, Kara, I don't think he called because he missed us particularly. I think he was just being polite."

"No, Mom. I mean, could you tell if he might have been a little sad underneath the polite talk?"

Kara could hear Mo tsk before she spoke again. "For goodness' sake, honey, what are you trying to find out? What's going on?"

Kara had just taken a bite of pizza, and the entire slab of cheese slid off the crust and slapped up against her chin. She yelped at the heat and frantically wrestled with the cheese as the mass of ingredients fell all over the coffee table. While she raced a ring of black olive to the table's edge, she tried to say, "Just a minute!" But she sounded as though she were talking around a mouthful of socks.

"What?"

By the time Kara caught the olive and two rogue mini-balls of sausage and freed herself from the cheese, she was hunched over the coffee table like a Neanderthal. Not for the first time, it occurred to her that she was still best suited to living alone. "Hang on, Mom," she mumbled into the phone.

"Ah," Mo said. "The pizza." Her voice was prim when she said, "I'll wait."

Kara wiped her chin and swallowed what little bit of crust had actually made it into her mouth. "Sorry, Mom. Lost my cheese."

"See, that's why I use a knife and fork when I eat pizza."

Kara shook her head. "That's like using a spoon to eat your popcorn, Mom. It's just not normal."

"Okay, forget normal. We were talking about Gabe."

Kara couldn't help but laugh at that one. "Yeah, Gabe." Then her tone became more subdued. "I kind of had a fight with him yesterday."

"Oh, honey, I'm sorry to hear that. Serious?"

"I'm not sure yet. That's why I wanted to know how he sounded to you. I haven't talked with him since, and I don't know if he talked with you before or after we fought."

"Well, he sounded fine with me, but he talked longer with your dad than he did with me. Dad's asleep right now, though. Can it wait until tomorrow?"

"Oh, yeah. You know Mom, Dad doesn't even have to call. I doubt Gabe would have bared his soul with either of you anyway, even if he were feeling down."

"Hmm, I don't know, honey. Dad and I were both pretty impressed with how frank he seemed to be when you were down here. He showed a lot of humility and confidence, all at the same time, just by what he was willing to talk about with us."

Kara smiled at that description. Gabe's openness was one of her favorite qualities too. Then she remembered her own behavior when they argued. "Ugh. That's exactly the opposite of how I acted with him yesterday."

She heard Mo sigh. "Well, I'm afraid none of us shows our best side when we fight."

"But Gabe didn't get ugly. Just me. I get more embarrassed every time I think of it."

"So, honey, just make it right. You can be pretty frank, yourself, when you want to be."

Kara smiled. She picked at another piece of pizza.

"You know, your dad and I had our first fight before we even started dating."

"No kidding?"

"No kidding. It seemed very serious at the time, but I can't remember what it was about. I do remember that it helped me get over my...

shyness, I guess you could say. I was always a little awkward around your father before that. I was so afraid I'd make a bad impression."

Kara didn't have time to review all the goofy things she'd done recently before Mo spoke again.

"But after I acted like an idiot when we fought that first time—and I do remember that much, at least. I was a complete ninny. After that fight, though, your dad was still interested anyway. So I stopped worrying so much. I relaxed."

Kara smiled. "And you stopped being awkward?"

"Oh, well. I'm still a bit clumsy. Don't tell me you've never noticed that. It's not just my driving that needs work."

"But you're not uncomfortable around Dad anymore."

"Oh, goodness, no. How could anyone stay uncomfortable around your father?"

"And...how soon did you two start dating each other?"

Mo laughed. "Sweetie, I roped your dad into taking me to the movies before he knew what hit him. I was one of a group of girls at church, and I just corralled him into going with us. Little did he know we were on our first date."

"Huh," Kara said, actually shocked. "You hussy, you."

"I suppose so! But, like I said, he was already interested. He just needed a little...guidance. And then we dated a solid year before we got engaged."

"I guess everyone takes the approach that works best for them."

Mo's chuckle died down a little. "Well, everyone takes a different approach, that's true. But I can't say everyone takes the one that works best for them. I think we'd have a lot less divorce in the world—in the church—if people gave that a little more thought."

Kara said nothing.

"I'm glad you and Gabe gave it thought, Kara, and chose to get to know each other before dating. I think that was a good fit for you. Whatever you decide."

Whatever you decide. That sounded less than hopeful to Kara. But after she and Morine hung up, she thought about it.

She knew she wanted to date Gabe now. And she wasn't sure what he wanted.

But if marriage was in God's plan for Kara, then the bottom line was to seek a marriage that would last, not a gorgeous boyfriend. Not a Hottie McLicious, as Mary called Jeremy. And certainly not someone who would take off running, like Greg had on Ren the moment conflict arose.

Kara hoped God would bless her with a husband with whom she was comfortable, like her mom and dad. With whom she had pleasure, like Leslie and her husband.

She suddenly felt peace when she realized that, if Gabe was uneasy about dating her, they probably weren't meant to date.

She and Ren had prayed that she would accept God's will.

"Whaddya know?" Kara said aloud. She just had.

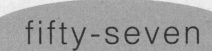

fifty-seven

I can't tell you how much I missed you lovely birds," Jeremy said as he walked past the Ashburn Town Center shops with Ren and Kara a few days later. He ran his hand through his soft, sandy hair, which promptly fell back onto his forehead.

Kara laughed. "I'm sure you pined away for us twenty-four/seven the whole time we were away, didn't you?"

"And not a moment less," he said. His T-shirt had come loose in the back, and he tucked it back into his jeans. In his more casual clothing, Jeremy looked like a college boy. "Seriously, I don't know when I laugh more than when I'm with you two."

They had just finished a meal at the local Thai restaurant and were now walking down the street to the multiplex, the women on either side of Jeremy.

"What movie are we going to see, anyway?" Kara asked.

"We're playing it by ear," Ren said. She pulled a pack of gum out of her purse and handed pieces to Kara and Jeremy. "Let's just see what we're in time for."

"And if our sole choice is that sci-fi flick with the shapely blonde, you two are game?" Jeremy asked.

Kara smiled. "Anything for you, Jeremy."

"There, you see? I simply don't hear that often enough."

"Poor baby," Ren said. She looked around him to talk to Kara. "He's gone a full week without a single bit of flirtation sent in his direction."

"A full week?" Kara said, acting aghast. "I thought you looked deprived. But weren't you going to be tutoring that young substitute while we were away?"

He sighed. "Yes, well, unfortunately, I actually did tutor her. She used me like her personal valet, practically. But I thought it best to wait until she finished her stint there at the school before asking her out. Propriety and all that, you know."

"And then the music teacher stole her right out from under Jeremy's adorable, trusting nose," Ren said, her voice sad, but with a slight twinkle in her eye.

Kara put her arm around Jeremy and gave him a big squeeze. "That snake. Well, next time—"

"Too right, next time. Next time I go for inappropriate right at the ready."

"I don't buy that for a second, Jeremy," Ren said. "You have your principles, just like the rest of us."

"I wouldn't go so far as that. I wouldn't say I've got Kara's principles, refusing to even date a bloke before the honeymoon."

Kara cracked up. "Be nice, now. At the rate I'm going, I might just turn out to be the first woman in history who's a jilted bride before the first date."

She caught Ren staring at her, a look of amused calculation on her face.

"What?" Kara asked. "What's cooking in that mind of yours?"

Ren smiled. "I was just thinking." She made wide, innocent eyes and tilted her head as she spoke. "That dinner was really wonderful and all, but I could really use a nice latte and a chocolate pastry of some kind. And I just remembered that Lorna's bookstore is right around the corner. Remember hippie-chick Lorna?" She looked at Jeremy. "Lorna has fantastic homemade chocolate chip cookies and heavenly coffee at her bookstore."

Kara grinned. "You mean the bookstore down the street from Gabe's deli?"

"Oh!" Ren said. "Is that where it is?"

Jeremy looked at Ren and shook his head. "Is this the kind of scheming that women do about me, I wonder?"

Kara looped her arm through Jeremy's. "I certainly hope so."

He smiled at her. "Thank you, love. But does this mean no shapely blonde sci-fi movie for me tonight?"

On his other side, Ren looped her arm through his. "Like I said, let's play it by ear." She leaned forward and gave Kara a wink. "We'll see what we're in time for."

When they reached the bookstore, however, Ren walked right past.

Jeremy slowed. "I thought we were stopping here for coffee."

"Um, right," Kara said. She glanced at Ren. "Right. We were going to get coffee and dessert."

"Oh, pooh," Ren said. "There's time for that later. He might go home while we're in there stuffing our faces." She raised an eyebrow at Jeremy. "Honestly, Jeremy, haven't you had enough to eat?"

Kara started laughing.

"But..." Jeremy said.

Ren took him by the arm again and guided him along.

"You've got me craving coffee and sweets now, you know," he said, pretending disappointment.

"First things first," Kara said. She was fully caught up in Ren's playfulness, even though she felt a slight tremor of fear that Gabe might actually be at the deli.

But as they neared the shop, it was clear that only minimal lighting was turned on. They peered through the windows and saw no sign of Gabe or anyone else.

"You know what?" Jeremy said. He stepped back and looked at the front of the deli. "I thought he had a Grand Opening Coming banner across the front window before. Or Grand Opening Soon. Some such thing."

Kara stepped back with him and a heaviness formed in her stomach. "I think you're right, Jeremy. He had that up before we left for Florida."

"Well, you said his opening was Saturday, right?" Ren said. "Maybe he has a plain old Grand Opening sign to put up. That's only two days from now."

"Nope. Saturday's grand opening was canceled."

All three of them turned around at the woman's voice. Kara recognized Lorna immediately, even though her long gray hair was down around her shoulders tonight. She wore a sleeveless, tie-dyed T-shirt with Bob Marley on the front over a multilayered purple gypsy skirt. And there was that patchouli smell again, mixed with a faint whiff of body odor.

Ren said, "You're Lorna, right? From the bookstore?"

Lorna smiled. "I am!" She reached up to pull her hair back, as if she were going to make a ponytail, and then she dropped it down her back.

Kara tried not to cringe when she saw that Lorna didn't shave under her arms.

"Are you customers of mine?"

Ren nodded and opened her mouth to speak, but Kara broke in. "I'm sorry, but did you say Gabe wasn't going to open the deli Saturday?"

"Nope. I mean, yes, I did say that. He's not opening. He went to Florida."

"Oh," Kara said, smiling, "we already knew about that. Actually, he went with us."

Lorna looked at Kara as if she might be crazy. "And yet here you are."

"Well, we all came back," Ren said. "Gabe too."

"Okay, folks. All I can tell you is that he asked me and some of the other shop owners to keep an eye on his place for the next day or so."

"Ah, so he went back to Florida, is what you're saying," Jeremy said.

Lorna beamed at him. "Well, don't you have a wonderful accent? Say something else."

"Eh..." Jeremy looked concerned that Lorna might actually be interested in him.

"I'm sorry, Lorna," Kara said, drawing Lorna's attention away from Jeremy. "So you don't know why Gabe suddenly left again?"

"Sorry, no." Lorna shrugged. "Didn't even know it was sudden or again. Now you've got me intrigued." And she belted out her one-note laugh. "Ha!"

Jeremy drew back, startled.

"Anyway, gotta go, kids. Stay cool." And even after she had her back to them, she flashed them the peace sign with a lazy lift of her hand.

Jeremy sighed. "I suppose this means I'm not getting any coffee or cake, eh?"

Kara didn't respond. She was watching Lorna still, but her thoughts were elsewhere. "You guys didn't get the impression that he was leaving for good, did you?"

Ren shook her head. "No. I can't imagine why he would do that." She looked at Kara. "You mean, because of you two having that fight?"

"Blimey," Jeremy said. "If he turns tail that easily, I say you're well rid of him and should take up with a real man. Like me, for example." He gave her a silly grin.

"He didn't turn tail, and don't you go...you know, impugning his manliness." She gave his shoulder a little punch, and he grabbed at it.

"Ouch. You have sharp little knuckles."

Both women laughed.

"Yes, you are quite the man, Jeremy," Ren said.

Kara folded her arms. "I guess that is a stupid thought, that Gabe would dash off to Florida just because of me."

"It's strange for him to leave again like that, though," Ren said, "without saying anything to any of us. Especially you."

Kara lifted a shoulder. "Well, he and I weren't exactly talking. I just hope everyone's okay in his family."

"You could call them, you know," Jeremy said.

Kara instantly checked her watch. "Not tonight. Maybe tomorrow. It's too late right now."

Jeremy lifted his eyebrows. "But not too late for the movie, eh?"

Ren sighed. "Kara, let's get this boy to his movie or we'll never hear the end of it."

Kara smiled, and they all started walking back toward the theater.

"Just try not to be disappointed if we're too late for your sci-fi blonde, Jeremy," Ren said.

Jeremy said something in return, but Kara wasn't listening. She was busy thinking of Gabe. And trying to ignore some disappointment of her own.

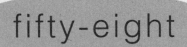

fifty-eight

Kara!" Rachelle burst into tears the moment Kara identified herself on the phone the next day. "I prayed for help, and you called!"

"Rachelle, what's wrong?" Kara's heart raced so suddenly that she stood from her chair without any awareness of the movement. "What's the matter?"

Rachelle spoke quickly and with such whimpering that Kara was unable to understand anything but the words "he" and "leaving."

"Wait, Rachelle," Kara said, speaking as calmly as possible. "Stop for a minute and take a few deep breaths."

While Rachelle apparently attempted to do just that, Kara paced in her living room and let her imagination go wild. She pictured Gabe in a canoe on the Amazon River with fellow missionaries, seeking greater meaning in life than slicing salami and dealing with an erratic, body-conscious wacko.

Between hiccup-like fluctuations in her voice, Rachelle said,

"I...always thought...I could count on him. But he... he's..." and the wailing resumed.

Kara sighed. She wanted to hug Rachelle and then throttle her. "Rachelle. Sweetie. Are you talking about Gabe?"

Rachelle abruptly stopped and then sniffled a few times. "Gabe? Of course not. I'm talking about Jake."

Kara sighed and whispered, without thinking, "Ah, good."

"Huh?" Rachelle said. "Kara. Did...did you just say good?"

"No! I mean, yes. I'm sorry, Rachelle. I didn't mean this was good news. I'm just worried about Gabe. But tell me what happened with Jake. Did you two fight?"

Rachelle sniffed, and then Kara heard her blow her nose. "No. We didn't fight. If only. Then I could just apologize and everything would be all fixed."

The corners of Kara's mouth barely curled up when she reflected on the simplicity of Rachelle's teen love. When a simple "I'm sorry" could erase everything, no casualties left behind.

"He's going away!" Rachelle said, a trace of anger in her voice. "To college! He's leaving me and going to college. He didn't even tell me!"

"He didn't tell you? Well, why did he tell you now?"

"He just found out for sure. He got the letter today."

"Oh," Kara said. "Well, that was pretty quick to tell you, don't you think?"

"No!" Rachelle shot back, and Kara yanked the phone away from her ear for a second. "He should have told me he applied. I mean, I would have applied if I knew he might go. Now it's too late for me. I'll be stuck here working at one of Mom and Dad's delis. My whole life is ruined. I missed my big chance at college and love and...everything."

Now Kara did smile, but with fondness and not a little nostalgia. She sat back down on the couch. "Oh, Rachelle. Please believe me. I know you're devastated right now, but you haven't missed any of those chances. I promise you."

Rachelle's voice was petulant. "Yes, I have."

"Listen," Kara said. "I'm one of those who didn't go to college straight after graduation from high school for a number of reasons. I didn't know what I wanted to do, and I was wrapped up in a boyfriend I didn't want to leave. Just like what you're going through. But I did end up going eventually, and the fact that I waited two years didn't keep me from having a wonderful college experience."

"Two years? But you were so much older than everyone else."

Kara laughed. "No, I wasn't. Anyway, if you're worried about that, go ahead and get some applications together now and do community college while you're working for your parents."

"But what about Jake? What am I supposed to do about him?"

Kara sighed. "I'm afraid you're supposed to miss him, sweetie. And maybe see him on breaks." She didn't bother to mention the probability of their growing apart and moving in separate directions. The poor girl didn't need that news today as well.

Rachelle whimpered again. "I wish you were here, Kara."

"Oh, Rachelle, so do I." Kara's eyes teared up, and she was surprised at how much like a little sister Rachelle had become. "I'm so glad to hear you prayed."

"Mm-hmm. I did pray. And then you called." She sniffed. "Oh, but you called here for a reason, didn't you?"

"I called for Gabe, actually. But I was glad to hear your voice."

"Why?" Rachelle asked.

"Why was I glad?"

"Why did Gabe ask you to call?"

"He didn't. I just wanted to talk with him."

"So why did you call here?" Rachelle asked. She sounded completely confused.

"Because...isn't he there?"

Rachelle actually chuckled, despite her situation. "Man, he only stayed here a couple of days after he took you to your parents' place, Kara. He drove home a week ago." She suddenly gasped. "You haven't seen him since he left?"

"Oh, yeah, I saw him. Several days ago. Monday. He got home safely," Kara said, now thoroughly flummoxed. "But last night—"

She stopped to make sure she had heard Lorna correctly. Yes, Lorna had definitely said Gabe was going to Florida. But, then again, he had lived there all his life. He could have gone down to see plenty of people other than his family. This could even be tied in to his opening day at the deli.

"What's going on, Kara? You're scaring me a little."

"No, don't be scared, Rachelle. I'm sure Gabe's fine. Just do me a favor and tell him I called if he shows up there, okay?"

"I'm going to call his cell phone."

"Good idea. I'll do the same."

For just a moment after they hung up, Kara considered that Gabe had suddenly decided to visit her parents. To ask for their blessing on his dating their daughter. She caught her breath at the idea. So chivalrous.

After all, they lived in Florida too.

Then she remembered her last sorry exchange with him, not to mention the fact that he was always so frank about his feelings. There were many ways to describe him, but Man of Mystery wasn't one of them. He would have discussed with Kara the idea of talking with her parents and the argument they had at the car dealership before dashing off to Morine and Stan's.

Kara frowned and flipped open her phone to call him. She had worked very hard at giving him his space. And now he'd not only failed to call her, but he'd even disappeared from sight. She was still open to not dating, but this was taking it just a little too far.

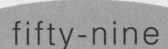

fifty-nine

The following morning Kara drove into the parking lot in front of the gym. And there he was. Leaning against one of the columns outside, his long legs crossed at the ankle. He was in black jeans and a clean white T-shirt, a little snug around the biceps. The morning sun had just crept over the building's rooftop, and it hit him like a spotlight. All he needed was a theme song.

"Yowza," she whispered. She hadn't seen him for, what, five days? And she had forgotten how stunning he was.

He obviously hadn't seen her yet.

She parked the car and removed the keys before she realized she had just said "yowza" again. If her memory served her correctly, that was the same stupid word she said when she first met him.

"Oh, no, Kara," she said aloud, stopping to peek in the rearview mirror and touch up her lip gloss. "You are not going to be the giddy klutz with Gabe anymore. You know him now. You're friends. And

God is in control!" She was so emphatic, she was pointing in the air to emphasize her points with herself.

She finished her gloss and her speech, and then turned to open the car door.

Gabe was standing right there, watching her, as amused as she'd ever seen him.

As soon as she opened the door, he said, "Are you in trouble with yourself again?"

She groaned so loudly she was almost yelling. "I give up!" She got out of the car and grabbed her gym bag. "There's something about you, Gabe. When I'm around you, I do not function normally." She slammed the car door. "It's who I am. Let's just accept that, okay?"

He laughed. "Your reaction to stuff like this is the best part, Kara. I love the way you—" He stopped himself. "Well, I just don't want you to think there's anything you should change."

She could not believe how wonderful he looked, so she didn't know what else to do but start walking toward the gym.

As he did at the car dealership, he kept pace with her without a trace of effort.

"I...I need to apologize to you, Gabe," she said. But then she stopped abruptly the moment they stepped onto the sidewalk. She turned to face him. "And where were you, anyway?"

He opened his mouth to speak, but she interrupted him.

"No. No, I didn't mean that." She glanced down, trying to gather her thoughts. She scratched at her forehead. "I meant to say that I was horrible to you at the car place. And that was all me, that whole mess." She looked back up at him. "None of that was your fault. And why in the world didn't you return my call yesterday?"

"Oh, did—"

"Never mind," she said. "That's not what I wanted to...see, I lost it with you the other day just because I was embarrassed, okay? Because I was so afraid you were going to reject me, although I realize it wouldn't really have been rejection if you had said you still didn't want to date, but still, that's what I was freaking out about." She flailed her arms in an imitation of how she had behaved at the dealership.

He laughed and said, "But I—"

"And then to go all that time without any contact, and then you're suddenly gone and...and hippie-chick Lorna with her armpits tells me about Florida and then you're not in Florida, and then you don't return my call so I start to worry that maybe you got mugged or something, you know, at the airport or something—" She stopped to catch her breath. She sighed and looked at Gabe, who had stopped trying to speak. "So, anyway, I'm sorry."

His eyes crinkled at the corners.

Then she made a little fist and gently punched him on the chest. It felt so intimate a gesture she almost started crying. She was just so glad to see him. And so mad at him for all the emotions she had just spewed all over the sidewalk. She looked down and actually wondered what she had just said to him.

He simply said, "Kara."

She looked up at him and he was about to put his hand on her arm. But an annoying scream of glee interrupted them.

"*There* you are, you cad, you!" Tiffany said, bouncing up—several parts of her—to Gabe. "Were you waiting for me to get here? Oh, but my word, you've been a naughty boy!" She pushed her lips forward in an exaggerated pout. "Were you hiding from me, Gabe? Were you?"

The gym door opened, and Mickey leaned out. "Yo, Kara. Your nine o'clock is on the phone. Can you take it or should I tell him—"

"No, no," Kara said. "I'll...I'll take it, Mickey, thanks." She glanced at Gabe and went inside.

The phone call was brief, but it felt like hours while Kara watched Tiffany through the front doors, posturing like the star of an MTV video, touching Gabe as often as possible. It looked as though he wasn't getting any more words in with Tiffany than he had with Kara.

Kara sighed. Poor Gabe.

When she hung up the phone, Gabe and Tiffany were still out there, but it looked as though he was actually getting a chance to speak. Kara didn't want to just stand there watching. She was afraid she'd start trying to read lips.

So she went back to the locker room to put away her things. She didn't plan on being back there long. Her client was due soon, and she wanted time to hear whatever Gabe had come to tell her.

She went back to use the bathroom, but before she emerged, she was riveted by a sudden storm of banging and swearing that erupted in the changing area. The voice was unmistakable. Tiffany had charged back there, opened and slammed several locker doors, and rattled off every profanity Kara had ever heard. And a few she never had. Amid all the swearing were some actual phrases.

"Thinks he's God's gift!"

"Took *me* for a ride, that's for sure!"

"Lying, cheating..."

"Doesn't know who he's dealing with!"

When the noise died down, Kara came out to an empty locker room. She walked out and saw Tiffany heading swiftly toward the front door.

"I'm taking my break!" Tiffany yelled at Mickey, who stood at the front desk.

"Didn't you just get here?"

Like a banshee woman, Tiffany turned on him and nearly screamed, "I'm *taking* my *break!*" She tried to slam the front door, but it had a slow-close gizmo attached, so she wrestled with it for a moment before giving up and stomping away.

Kara reached Mickey by then and heard him mutter, "Don't be drinking no coffee, girl, that's all I can say."

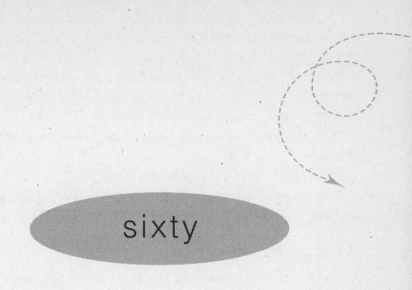

sixty

Kara saw Gabe sitting on the bench outside. Tiffany rushed past him as if he had suddenly become invisible. He turned, looked through the glass, and met eyes with Kara.

He smiled and stood up as if he were going to come into the gym, but she headed for the door.

"I'll just be outside, Mickey."

Mickey glanced up from the front desk, saw Gabe, and gave Kara a thumbs-up. "Got it."

As soon as she was out the door, she said, "I'll bet you'd like a chance to talk without a woman spazzing out on you, wouldn't you?"

He laughed. "You know, I heard this Christian speaker once. He said women need to say something like twenty thousand words a day." He glanced at his watch. "I just didn't expect to hear all of them before eight thirty in the morning."

"From two of us," Kara said, laughing. "But I'll try to be quiet and give you a chance to talk." She grimaced. "I'm afraid I have a client coming soon, though."

He shook his head. "That's okay. I knew I was taking my chances just dropping by. And it's not like I have a speech or anything."

Kara nodded. Not a word.

"But," he said, "there are some things I want to talk with you about."

"You want to sit?" Kara pointed at the bench.

They sat, and Gabe immediately said, "I'm sorry about not calling you back, Kara. I didn't know you called. I lost my cell phone."

Kara looked down and shook her head, chuckling.

He smiled. "Be nice, now."

"Gabe, I should probably tell you that I also called you when you were driving to your parents' place. You know, after you left my mom and dad's to go back home to Miami."

"Oh? Hmm. I hadn't yet lost my phone then. But I'm sure there wasn't a message from you."

"No, there wouldn't have been because you picked up."

"Did I?" Gabe frowned in confusion. "But we didn't talk?"

"Well, you talked. But I...um...it was obvious that you thought I was..."

He suddenly opened his eyes in realization. "Tiffany. I thought you were Tiffany." He put his hand against his forehead. "You were the hang up." He looked at Kara, his eyes sad.

"I'm so sorry, Kara."

Kara shook her head. "No, really, it wasn't a big deal after I thought about it. You certainly didn't sound happy to hear from her, anyway."

He chuckled ruefully. "No. Not happy at all. That's actually part of the reason I lost my phone. I turned it off so she couldn't reach me anymore. And then I left it somewhere and couldn't even call the number to find it again since it was turned off."

"Well, maybe you've put an end to that particular problem.

Tiffany, I mean. She seemed pretty ticked off at you just now."

He nodded. "Well, I probably should have called you anyway after we had that argument at the car place. But there were a lot of things I wanted to think about, and I needed to think about them without... any input from you."

"Okay."

"When—"

"Oh!" she said. "I'm sorry to interrupt, but I just remembered that Rachelle said she was going to call your cell phone too. I think I might have gotten her worried about you. Maybe you should—"

He put his hand on her arm. "I saw Rachelle yesterday afternoon. There's no problem there."

"Ah. Good."

Yesterday afternoon? He had been busy!

"So, anyway," Gabe said, "when we were driving to the car dealership, and you mentioned that lady from the plane—"

"Leslie."

"Right. When you mentioned her and her husband, I was...well, I just wasn't at all tuned in to what you were working up to. I mean, I was thinking about finding a parking space at the dealership or stats on Toyotas. Something like that."

Kara smiled.

"So I was just talking right off the top of my head. I'm not even sure what I said."

"You said you thought they started dating each other too soon because they had only known each other as long as we've known each other."

He looked at her. "Really? Is that what I said?" He frowned. "What a bonehead."

Kara tilted her head. "Well, to be fair, that's not what you said word for word. I just think that was the gist of it."

"Well—"

"And also to be fair," Kara said, "that was my first reaction to what Leslie told me too. And then I had time to think about it before I said anything to you."

"Right. And since then I've had a chance to think about it too. I'll admit I was angry right back at you for some of the things you said at the car place. But I think our mistake hasn't been in saying too much to each other."

"What do you mean?"

"I think we're both trying so hard to dodge romance that we're afraid to discuss what we learn about each other." He looked her in the eye. "What we like about each other."

Kara smiled. He was right. She had shied away from discussing with Gabe most of her positive thoughts about him, and he must have done the same thing. In trying to avoid flirting, they had also avoided simple nurturing. "I can't believe we're both so bad at just being friends."

Gabe said, "I think it just doesn't come naturally when there's an attraction. It's a real effort to do it well." He chuckled. "I even got my no-dating book out and scanned through it again. You know, we didn't exactly follow this guy's advice."

Kara raised her eyebrows. "Tell me about it."

"But we both tried. And our approach to building whatever our relationship turns out to be? It's still a lot healthier than most approaches. You know, the worldly, let's-throw-our-hearts-out-there-and-see-what-sticks attitude."

"Yes." She tried not to say anything else. But she'd heard that "sticking" term applied to cooking spaghetti noodles and throwing them up against the wall. She fought the awful image of actual hearts being thrown up against a wall. This was definitely worse than looking for a parking space while the other was baring her soul. She looked Gabe in the eyes to regain focus.

"Okay," he said, "what did I just say wrong?"

She sat up. "Huh? Nothing. Why?"

"Your lip was curling just now. Like something stunk. Was it me?"

She started laughing. "Oh, Gabe. I'm so sorry. You don't stink.

You always smell great."

He smiled. "Actually, I meant, did I say something that stunk. But I'm glad to know I don't personally stink."

She shook her head. "Ugh. I'm thinking so literally this morning." She made her eyelids heavy and jutted her jaw out, like a scholarly snob. "I'm usually so much deeper than this, you know."

When she stopped mugging she saw him studying her. She immediately thought of how unattractive she probably just looked, making that face at him.

He had a slight twinkle in his eyes. "I really love how often I laugh when you're around."

That made her smile. Not necessarily romantic—after all, Jeremy had just said something similar to Ren and her the other evening— but Kara put a lot of store in laughter too.

"And I enjoyed that trip to Florida so much," he said. "Especially the time I got to spend with you. I mean, really, Kara. Not just because I'm attracted to you, you know?"

"Me too."

"Plus, I'm hopeful that maybe we could try getting involved in one of the ministry opportunities at church. I think it would be another great way to spend time together and grow in Christ too."

"I do the nursery work right now," Kara said.

"Yeah, I remember that," Gabe said. "And I'll do that with you, if you're up for it. Maybe that's the ministry we should do together. Do they let guys do nursery?"

Kara laughed. "Let them? I think they've actually tried holding children hostage to get their fathers to help. Most guys are diaper-phobic."

Gabe cocked his head. "Well, I can't say it's my medium of choice, either. But if you enjoy serving there, I'd like to give it a shot. I love kids and babies." He shrugged. "How bad can it be, changing diapers for ninety minutes?"

"You'll certainly find out!" Kara said with a chuckle.

"So, you like the idea? Of our spending more time together?"

"Sure! I'm thrilled you want to do that. How else are we ever going to, you know, build our friendship? We'll never figure out if we should date if we just pass each other in the night. Or the day, whatever."

He opened his mouth, but waited a second or two before saying, "Oh. But, Kara, I already know how I feel about the dating."

Her stomach flipped. So this wasn't just about doing church work together. She sent a quick thank-you prayer up to God.

"I already figured out that I don't want to date you."

What?

"You...you don't? Not ever?" She wanted to get off this roller coaster. But this time, when the little voice told her to keep calm, she listened.

Gabe turned so he could face her more squarely on the bench. He looked down at her hands and gently took them into his own. "See, I thought we had both decided against that."

She sighed. He was right. But by taking her hands in his, he was confusing her. Anyone looking at them would think they were a couple, sitting out here, holding hands.

"That's why I, well, I hope I didn't overstep in doing this, but I went back down to Florida this week to talk with your parents."

She gasped. He was a Man of Mystery after all! Except she had kind of thought maybe he did that. But then she thought he didn't! So if not a Man of Mystery, at least he was a Man of Confusion. Was that a good thing?

"You're not speaking. But your eyes are...kinda freaky right now, to tell you the truth. Are you okay?"

She looked up at him. "But, Gabe, I called my mother about us. After you and I fought. I know my mother. She would have told me you were there, even if you made her promise not to."

He chuckled. "That's exactly what your dad said when I called him. I called before I flew down. Gave him an idea of what I wanted to discuss. He told me not to tell Morine I was coming down or she'd be on the phone to you before my call had even disconnected."

Kara laughed. "There's a man who knows his wife."

"But after I went down she promised to wait until you called her, after we talked. I think she's in actual pain, holding the information in, so maybe you could call her after I leave."

She squeezed his hands. How could she ever let him leave?

"And then I went to see my family and talked with them. They were ecstatic. Rachelle stopped crying about Jake and started crying about you. They're all so happy."

"Even your mother after the pineapple thing?"

"I'm telling you, Kara, my mom likes to laugh as much as anyone I know. She'll be sharing that story at our—"

He stopped in the midst of his enthusiasm and suddenly looked embarrassed. "Well, that brings me to...you. I didn't really tell you what I went to discuss with our families. I'm sorry that you're the last to hear this, but all of this is kind of old-fashioned, you know? I wanted to honor our parents."

"So tell me, already."

He laughed. "Okay. Here it is." He renewed his hold on her hands. "I'm not proposing marriage, Kara. Not yet. There are still things we need to learn about each other. I think there will always be things to learn about each other. But I'd like to court you. I know that right now I'm still operating while under the influence of infatuation, sort of."

That made her smile.

"But what I'm feeling sure does feel like love."

Kara's eyes teared up.

"I want to commit myself to you, Kara. Not as a date or a boy-friend, but, hopefully, as your future husband. And I'm asking you to commit yourself to me too. I want us to spend the next...I don't know how long. However long we think we need. But I want us to consider each other frankly. And to try to win each other's heart."

Kara looked down at their hands. She was surprised when she started to speak and found she barely could. "I'd probably just go on ahead and give you my heart right now. But I think it's stuck in my throat at the moment." A tear fell from her eyes and landed on

Gabe's hand.

He put his fingertips under Kara's chin and lifted her face to meet his. Several dark curls hung down on his forehead. His eyes were the warmest brown they'd ever been, and she'd never seen them quite so full of emotion. His clean-shaven skin was the creamy color of caramel.

Kara noticed, not for the first time, how full his lips were, especially when he looked serious.

Her mind raced. They hadn't discussed the whole kissing thing. Some people waited until their wedding day. Some allowed kissing but made sure they had chaperones around to help them go no further. Should they discuss—

And in that second he gently kissed her and shut her mind right up. Yes. They would definitely need a chaperone. His lips were soft and warm and vaguely...sweet.

She might never need chocolate again.

They heard a casual cough and turned to look at a middle-aged man approaching the gym. He looked embarrassed to have interrupted their kiss.

"Hi, Kara," he said. "Sorry."

Kara flew back down to earth and said, "Not at all, Oscar! You're right on time." She waved him closer and looked at Gabe.

"Gabe, this is one of my favorite clients, Oscar Mendez. Mendez, right, Oscar?"

Oscar nodded, smiling so humbly Kara wanted to give him a hug. Instead she put her hand on Gabe's back. How should she introduce him?

"And Oscar, this is Gabe Paolino. He's...he's..."

Gabe smiled and gave her a wink.

She suddenly grinned. "He's the guy I'm not dating."

about the author

Trish Perry is an award-winning writer and editor of *Ink and the Spirit,* a quarterly newsletter of the Capital Christian Writers organization in the Washington DC, area. She has published numerous short stories, essays, devotionals, and poetry in Christian and general market media, and she is a member of the American Christian Fiction Writers group.

Says Trish:

"I live in Northern Virginia with my ever-patient husband and brilliantly funny son. I have a gorgeous grown daughter who eloped with the perfect son-in-law and eventually blessed me with an amazing grandson. We also have three lovable, goofy dogs and two feral cats who think they're our pets and force us to feed them."

If you would like to contact Trish, you may do so by mail at:

Trish Perry
c/o Harvest House Publishers
990 Owen Loop North
Eugene, OR 97402

Or via her website at:
www.trishperrybooks.com

Other Great Chick-Lit Books
by Harvest House Publishers

Hope Lyda

Hip to Be Square

A funny thing happens to Mari Hamilton on the way to a life makeover—a stopover in her past shows her it was in her old life that God was doing a new and incredibly hip thing.

Altar Call

In this sequel to *Hip to Be Square*, Mari and friends face their emotions about tying the knot and discover that life is less about finding Mr. Right and more about doing the right thing.

Mindy Starns Clark

The Trouble with Tulip

Jo Tulip is a smart chick about everything except her own love life. Her best friend, Danny, solves mysteries with her even as he tries to subtly woo her behind the facade of friendship.

Blind Dates Can Be Murder

When Jo's blind date is killed in the middle of their evening, she has two mysteries to solve: Who was this man really, and what on earth is going on with her own love life?

Siri L. Mitchell

Kissing Adrien

When dependable, responsible Claire goes to Paris to tend to family business, she encounters the flirtatious Frenchman, Adrien. Will his spontaneity drive her away, or will it help restore the joy of her faith?

The Cubicle Next Door

When self-proclaimed computer geek Jackie Harrison develops feelings for her popular and social cubicle neighbor, Joe Gallagher, she uses her online journal to express herself. But will she ever risk sharing her heart offline?

For a complete listing of Harvest House Books, check out our website at www.harvesthousepublishers.com